© Alan Adler

---

*About the Author*

---

ROBIN MAXWELL is the bestselling author of *The Secret Diary of Anne Boleyn*, *The Queen's Bastard*, and *Virgin: Prelude to the Throne*. She lives in California.

*The*
# WILD
# IRISH

*A Novel of Elizabeth I and the Pirate O'Malley*

ROBIN MAXWELL

Perennial

*An Imprint of* HarperCollins*Publishers*

A hardcover edition of this book was published in 2003 by William Morrow, an imprint of HarperCollins Publishers.

FIRST PERENNIAL EDITION PUBLISHED 2004.

*Designed by Stephanie Huntwork*

The Library of Congress has catalogued the hardcover edition as follows:

Maxwell, Robin.
The wild Irish : a novel / Robin Maxwell.— 1st ed.
p. cm.
ISBN 0-06-009142-8
1. Elizabeth I, Queen of England, 1533–1603—Fiction. 2. Great Britain—History—Elizabeth,1558–1603—Fiction. 3. O'Malley, Grace, 1530?–1603?—Fiction. 4. Ireland—History—1558–1603—Fiction. 5. Women revolutionaries—Fiction. 6. Women—Ireland—Fiction. 7. Women pirates—Fiction. 8. Queens—Fiction. I. Title.

PS3563.A9254W555    2003
813'.54—dc21            2003042184

ISBN 0-06-009143-6 (pbk.)

09 10 11 ❖/RRD 10 9

1593

# 1

THE SUN WAS WARM on her face and she wondered, *Where were the mists?* London was perpetually shrouded in fog, was gray and dreary. And it stank. Or so her father'd said. Owen O'Malley had sailed into London once and only once in his life, but for his two wide-eyed children, the art of his conjuring had forever after painted the city a dank and fetid hole. Yet today Grace O'Malley was blinded by sunlight. The bow of Murrough ne Doe's galley sliced the Thames like a seamstress's scissors through a length of glittering cloth—a river of diamonds, it seemed.

Perhaps, thought Grace, Elizabeth would be wearing diamonds when they met. The Queen of England—what would she look like? In her portraits the woman had a strange look about her. Cold. Brittle. Sharp beak nose. And the hard gaze of a man. No, 'twould not be diamonds, Grace corrected herself. 'Twould be *pearls.* The first Elizabeth, it was said, swathed herself in pearls, both black and white, some as tiny as a bead, some large as a goose's egg, the rare black ones her favorite.

A din rose from the clutter of docks and warehouses on the river's north shore. The long, narrow waterfront properties were abutted seamlessly together, ships large and small clamoring for their place at the jetties and water stairs. Brawny shoremen grunted oaths as they labored, loading and unloading vessels, hefting plain and exotic cargoes back to high, timbered warehouses. Carts full of wares rumbled away down cobbled streets behind. The loudest ruckus came from the wharf receiving a shipload of wetfish whose odors—pungent and familiar—filled her nose. Fishermen were the rowdiest sailors, she knew, more so than merchantmen. Pirates even. She glimpsed seamen hurrying to finish their chores. They'd be keen to be done, to leave the ships they'd crewed for weeks or months and swagger down the planks in boisterous bands for a night of brawling and whoring in the world's mightiest city.

Stretched out beyond the waterfront was the endless sprawl of London's squat and storied houses, hundreds of streets. Church spires by the dozens pierced the sky, more in one place, thought Grace, than she'd even seen in Spain. Deep in the city rose the tallest of all the steeples, surely the famous cathedral of St. Paul's. And up ahead was London Bridge, still too far in the distance to see the heads of traitors rotting on their pikes.

Commercial landings now gave way to fine residences, each as large as a small castle, broad lawns sweeping down to the river's edge. Those were the homes of the great lords, she knew, some of whom had been wreaking havoc in Ireland. The sight tightened a knot in her gut. She must stifle her hatred. Remember her purpose. But here she was, sixty-three years of age. Her maiden voyage into London Town and she was a *passenger* on a ship not her own. Sure her colors flew below those of Murrough ne Doe O'Flaherty, but it was humiliating all the same. Infuriating.

Well, she had come to remedy that. She would pay a wee call on the queen, at Greenwich, and see about the disturbances. Grace wondered if she was as tall and bony and yellow clackered as they said she was, if the alum and eggshell face paint she wore cracked grotesquely at the corners of her mouth and eyes. If she'd loathe the woman on sight, her enemy for more than thirty years.

She would know soon enough, thought Grace, gripping the rail with her strong, sun-browned fingers. Soon enough indeed.

# 2

THE IRISH GALLEY brazenly flying her two rebel flags had, but a moment before, sailed beyond sight of the mullioned window at Essex House. Robert Devereaux, second earl of that name, that house, had come to gaze at the river with an eye to calming his frayed nerves. He'd found that the sight of ships and wherries and barges on the wide, moving ribbon of water slowed a racing heart, measured his ragged breaths, even occasionally lifted the dark veil that had, periodically, fallen since childhood like a shroud on his soul. Out there, the sun glinting off the Thames, life appeared simple, mundane, whilst behind him in his study was a roomful of Queen Elizabeth's courtiers—friends, relatives, admirers (schemers one and all)—and in their company was every complication of which a man could dream.

*Twenty-four, and I am already a great lord of England,* thought Essex. He'd recently astonished even himself, being granted a seat at the table of the Privy Council. He was Master of the Horse, a Knight of the Garter, and Elizabeth's undisputed favorite. *Yet I am poor,* he thought bitterly, *the poorest earl in the kingdom.* This, like his title, was a legacy from his father, Walter, first Earl of Essex. He bemoaned that fact every day of his life and cursed his father, altogether conscious of the sin, but cursed him nonetheless. At age seventeen, with Walter Devereaux dead and disgraced in Ireland, and his mother despised by the queen, Robert had to come to Court a penniless lad. Had he owned an ounce less of character and cunning, he often reminded himself, he'd have been swallowed alive by the beast that was Elizabeth's Court. Instead he had risen more quickly—nay, shot like a star across the heavens—than even his benefactor, the Earl of Leicester, had envisaged he might. Yet it had been tooth and claw all the way to this moment, Essex knew, and whilst the Privy Councilship was assured, his military exploits already the stuff of legend, and his popularity with courtiers, beautiful waiting ladies, and the public equally vaulted, much was nevertheless at stake. His very livelihood! He could remain poor and irritatingly bound in Elizabeth's debt, he knew, eking out endless loans from the most tightfisted monarch who'd ever lived, or he could, with the stroke of a quill, become a man of status, a man of means.

It seemed a small thing, really. All he needed was her granting to him the Farm of Sweet Wines. The sugar-laden wines imported from the islands of Greece—the malmseys and muscatels, romeneys and bastards—brought twice the levy of other wines, and he had been sniffing round this particular favor since the death, six years before, of its last holder, Robert's own stepfather, the queen's beloved Robin Dudley, Earl of Leicester.

Essex needed the grant desperately, for his current financial embarrassment was acute. He had inherited nothing but debt from his father, and there was no way he could squeeze another penny from his various tenants. But with administration of this Farm, even after paying the Crown its part of the customs levied, the profits he pocketed would provide him with a handsome and steady income for the whole of the long-term grant. More important, it would mean security for raising larger sums of money on credit, crucial for his standing at Court. He would finally be able to afford to redeem his debts to the queen, would no longer be beholden to her.

*But how could he wheedle the prize from her?*

And was this, in fact, the best use of his time and energies? There were the Bacon brothers to consider, most important Francis. If he could convince Elizabeth to grant his protégé the post of Attorney General, it would benefit Robert immeasurably. But, Essex reminded himself, Francis Bacon had disgraced himself in his first ever Parliament earlier this year by obstructing the passage of an increased-subsidy bill. One did not, Essex knew, and had wrongly assumed Francis knew as well, argue publicly *against* putting more money in the queen's treasury, especially to take the side of mere gentlemen, whose finances would be stretched to pay the taxes.

But the deed had been done. Francis had been disgraced . . . but temporarily, Essex was sure. His own influence with Elizabeth, sweet talk and intimate laughter, would soften her. The post would eventually be Bacon's.

The gabble of voices behind him exploded into laughter and Essex, planting a smile on his face, turned to join his retainers in good cheer. He'd come to think of the second-floor longhall of Essex House, now his study, as a great hive buzzing with golden bees—the Queen's Bees—beautiful, forward young men, all of a certain generation. His razor-tongued mother, Lettice, referred to the place as a "nest," the implication unspoken but nevertheless understood that she described something more akin to a home for vipers than a family of birds.

She was wrong, of course. There was, for example, nothing remotely deadly about Anthony Bacon, thought Essex as his gaze found the tubby, sweet-faced young man, squinting nearsightedly into a large ledger. Though he deftly coordinated a brilliant ring of continental spies, Anthony was far too soft and sickly to be thought dangerous. Essex had rarely known the queen to be so anxious to meet a man as she was Anthony Bacon. It was clear she meant to reward his good works and astonishing network of contacts with a plum position at Court. But each of the many meetings Essex had so carefully arranged between the two had been canceled as a result of Anthony's ill health. If it was not a gout so severe he could hardly hold a quill, it was the stone that laid him low. No, Anthony was no viper. Of the four secretaries he managed—*juggled* might be a more apt description—only one, Henry Cuffe, could be said to claim any ambition at all.

Certainly Anthony's brother, Francis, boasted a rare and incisive mind. He wrote brilliantly, his extraordinary essays having caused more than a small stir at Court and abroad. He was adept at using others for his own advancement, and recently Essex was the one being used. But this was a quality to be respected and, besides, he was using Francis Bacon equally.

Where *was* the man? thought Essex. Francis should have been back from Court hours ago.

Essex's eyes fell on Henry Wriothesley, the Earl of Southampton. This graceful and gorgeous young man stood with his arm draped about his latest "find," London's most talked-about poet and playwright. He could see that between his patron and himself, Will Shakespeare held a sheet of parchment that was the subject of their scrutiny—and perhaps their laughter. Southampton had, at twenty, already earned a rightful reputation for profligacy, his warmth and enthusiasm matched only by his petulance and hot temper. Now *here* was a man worthy of Lettice's suspicions. In station and title more Essex's equal than any of the others, and with family and social ties binding them tightly, Southampton was the closest thing Essex had to a friend.

"What, may I ask, is so humorous?" Essex demanded.

"Why, Master Shakespeare has been reading your verse," replied Southampton, managing to keep a straight face.

"What!"

"The sonnet to your latest mistress. 'Beneath the Smile.' " Southampton began to read from the parchment and Essex felt his face flush pink, horrified by the poet's scrutiny of his amateur attempts.

*Worthy Lady, think me a man of imperfections, but one that*
*For your love endeavors to be good*
*And rather mend my faults than cover them . . .*

Essex snatched the parchment from Southampton's fingers, forcing a smile he hoped was not too sour. "My private thoughts, gentlemen," he said, skewering Southampton with his gaze. "Not to be broadcast to all the world."

"We may be great, my lord," quipped Southampton, "but we are scarcely the world." He turned and gazed with open desire at the young dramatist. "You think the poem good, don't you, Will?"

"I do," said Shakespeare, holding Essex, rather than Southampton, in his clear, steady gaze. "Your images are bold, and you've wisely chosen to eschew the nauseating flowers most amateurs delight in."

Essex was grateful for the compliment but teased, "What *else* would you say of it, Will? A too harsh criticism of the queen's 'most beloved' might land you in Irish exile with another poor poet."

Everyone laughed at the expense of Edmund Spenser, once the court's most famous versifier, now disgraced for his criticism of William Cecil, Lord Burleigh. In his satirical "Mother Hubbard's Tale," Spenser had likened Elizabeth's oldest and most trusted adviser to a chicken thief. Before he knew what had happened, Spenser had been banished, along with the English army, into the quagmire that was Ireland. Little had been heard from him since.

"Master Shakespeare is too clever to anger the queen." Anthony Bacon had risen from his bench and approached the group. He held out to Essex a freshly powdered parchment filled with Henry Cuffe's unmistakable scrawl.

"This is . . . ?" Essex inquired.

"A list of all Her Majesty's subjects recently sighted at King Philip's Court, my lord. Papists, all of them. Their purpose, it appears, is to make mischief on the queen's armies garrisoned in Ireland. And there is rumor of a Spanish invasion to be launched on Guernsey and Jersey. Oh, and the latest report on Philip's lunatic son, Don Carlos."

"Very good," said Essex, beaming at Anthony. His smile was genuine, for this was the sort of intelligence that Elizabeth most craved these days.

The heavy wooden door of the study opened and Francis Bacon blew in, the air of a black storm hanging round him.

"How now, Francis?" Essex called out, careful not to exude more good cheer than the obviously gloomy man could countenance.

Francis Bacon laid down his ledger and bulging document case, sighing deeply. "Beware the Gnome," he intoned morosely and took the bench recently vacated by his brother.

"What has he done this time?" demanded Essex. "The Gnome" was Lord Burleigh's son, Robert Cecil—the queen's secretary—a swarthy little hunchback who seemed determined, at every turn, to make their lives a misery.

"He cornered me in the Presence Chamber this afternoon."

"In itself a revolting vision," said Southampton.

He, Essex, and Anthony came to surround Francis, all exuding sym-

pathy. Will Shakespeare, not of this charmed inner circle, hung back quietly, but all ears.

"Patronizing little prick," Bacon went on. "He began by compliment-
ing my most recent essay, then inquired in that irritating whine if I didn't
think I would be happier with the lesser post of Solicitor General than
with that of Attorney General."

"He didn't!" cried Essex.

"Bastard," Southampton muttered.

"What did you tell him, brother?" Anthony Bacon demanded.

"To stuff a stout pig knuckle up his twisted little arse," replied Francis, beginning to regain his good humor, now back among his friends.

"Seriously, Francis," interjected Essex. "How did you respond? Are
he and his father still insisting on Edward Coke for the position?"

"Of course. 'A man of experience and levelheadedness,' " he said, in
a nasal whine, imitating Robert Cecil.

"But he made no mention of your parliamentary debacle?"

"No need, my lord. As the Gnome spoke he kept his beady eyes
always on the queen, as if to say, 'She is still angry with you and will be
angrier still if you persist in your suit for this office.' "

"Damn him!" cried Essex.

Southampton offered, "If one could die of smugness, he'd be worms'
meat."

"Was Burleigh there as well?" asked Anthony.

"Thankfully not," Francis replied. "I could not have borne father and
son at once."

There was silence then amongst the coterie of gentlemen, all lost in
the same thoughts, the same memories. "Burleigh's Boys" they called
themselves privately. For each and every one had shared the distinction
of growing up a ward of that great lord. After the deaths of their respective fathers, they had fallen under the guardianship of the elder Cecil,
and though they had been adequately and appropriately guided through
their minorities by him, they had been shown only the most minimal
kindness and consideration, whilst the skinny, hunchbacked son, Robert,
received all.

After his father's funeral, Essex—age nine and more sensitive a child
than was healthy—had left his home in western Wales to live at

Burleigh's great palace, Theobalds. He'd taken pity on the man's small, pale, deformed son and heir, had taken pains to entertain him, wrench a few laughs from the overserious child. He'd even on occasion remained behind to play with him whilst everyone else rode after the hounds to hunt or hawk.

But Robert Cecil had, with a soul as sadly twisted as his back, always despised young Essex, loathed his fine opalescent skin, the curly ginger hair, strong, straight spine. Once he'd even fabricated a story of some cruelty perpetrated on himself, a hapless victim of Essex's wicked prank. Before the year was out, Essex found himself shipped off to Cambridge. The education, whilst premature for a ten-year-old, had been appreciated, indeed embraced, by the precocious boy. Philosophy, mathematics, civil law, theology, astronomy, Greek and Hebrew, dialectic. He had earned his Master of Arts degree by age fourteen.

But Essex had never forgotten Robert Cecil's treachery, nor forgiven the blatant nepotism Burleigh had displayed in forwarding his son's career at everyone else's expense. The elder Cecil had seen to it that the Gnome had smoothly slipped into his role as secretary to the queen, as though changing partners during a gavotte without missing a step. Father and son together were a powerful force with which to be reckoned, for Elizabeth's trust in the pair was absolute, and it was imprudent to position oneself on the opposite side of an argument with them.

Such was the case of the Attorney Generalship—*Bacon* versus *Coke*. But in this case, all in this room knew, Francis Bacon had more than a fighting chance, as his champion was the Earl of Essex. Elizabeth's love for Essex was a weapon as mighty as her respect for the Cecil team at its most persuasive.

"I shall see to it," Essex announced suddenly, strapping on his sword.

"Now?" asked Francis.

"There is no better time than now. The queen misses my company, I have heard from several ladies." Essex smiled disarmingly and he knew they saw clearly why he was Elizabeth's favorite courtier. Despite his outrageous disobediences. Despite the childish tantrums. What they could not know, he thought, was that he would use this meeting with Her Majesty to forward more than Francis Bacon's cause. To be perfectly honest, the Farm of Sweet Wines was uppermost in his mind. Without a small fortune at his disposal, despite his gifts of charm and wit and beauty, he would soon tumble from his place of prominence at Court. Even a brilliant ally in the Attorney General's office would be of no use to him then.

He must see the queen.

ESSEX HAD NOT expected to meet his mother on his way out, and as he was busy concocting entertainments of the mind for Elizabeth's pleasure, he found himself startled to come face-to-face with Lettice Devereaux, Lady Blount, at the foot of the great staircase, still in her traveling clothes.

"Mother, I thought you were in the country."

"I *was* in the country, and now I am here in my city house. I sent you word that I was coming to see my grandchild." Her voice bristled with annoyance, and Essex cursed himself for his forgetfulness. Lettice, still physically luscious at forty, was a cunt of a woman when displeasured.

Essex kissed both cheeks with an heroic show of enthusiasm. "I'm glad to see you, Mother."

"No, you are not. You and your nestmates prefer me as far from London as possible."

Essex decided he was in no mood to placate her. "You're right. It's impossible to keep Elizabeth even-tempered when she knows you're flouncing about the city in your gilded carriage trying to out-queen her."

*"Flouncing!"* She reached out suddenly and gave her son's ear a vicious twist. "You were a rude child and you've become a rude young man."

He sighed. "Mother, must we fight?"

The door opened and Lettice's latest husband, Christopher Blount, entered. Only five years older than his stepson, Blount seemed haggard and had a sour look about him. But this was not surprising, for he had suffered seven hours of a jouncing carriage ride, as well as his wife's foul humor. Truth be told, Christopher's sour countenance had lately hardened into a perpetual expression of disgust, the result of a mere three years as Lettice's spouse . . . or more to the point, her most recent cuckolder. She was famous for many reasons, but most of all her infidelities.

When Essex had been a young boy, his father, Walter Devereaux, had become the cuckold of the Earl of Leicester, and after Devereaux died and his mother had married Leicester, she'd cuckolded *him* with Blount. Essex wondered if the wan, irritated face of his current stepfather was at least partially a result of his cuckolding by Lettice's newest amour.

"Hello, Christopher, and good-bye." It had taken only a few moments, but Essex was now incapable of remaining in his mother's presence. "I'm off," he announced, not bothering to hide his relief at going.

"Robert!" Essex's hand was already on the door latch when his wife's voice stopped him. He sighed and turned back to see Frances coming toward the group at the door, carrying their infant son. Lately, just the sight of his kindhearted and dreadfully dull wife caused an upwelling of confused emotions in his chest, for she moved him so little. Even his firstborn child elicited only the weakest surge of affection. These feelings he knew to be entirely unnatural, and it worried him, agitated his soul. What kind of man was he, so unmoved by his own family?

"Frances, you've caught me on my way out."

"To Court?"

"Yes, my love," he said, reaching out to caress the babe, Robert, named after himself. Essex was at least careful to keep up the pretense of familial affection.

"Send my love to the queen," Frances said with true sincerity. Their relationship was as long as his wife was old, as her father, Lord Walsingham, had for so many years served Elizabeth in the closest and most vital capacity—spymaster. Frances's first marriage to Elizabeth's godson, Philip Sidney, had strengthened the bond to such a degree that when she had secretly married Essex after Sidney's tragic death, the queen had forgiven the indiscretion in record time. Others—Leicester, Raleigh—had spent time under house arrest or in the Tower of London for contracting marriage without the queen's permission. Essex had always believed it was Elizabeth's love for Frances that had lightened their punishment to a mere slap on the wrist.

"I'll give her your kindest regards," said Essex and again made for the door. Lettice's hand was laid over his before he could open the latch.

"Dear son." Her voice had changed. It was warm and silken, like her skin, and he felt gentleness exuding from her, as sweet as it was false.

"Yes, Mother," he said, groaning inwardly. He knew he'd not have to wait long to learn what it was she wanted from him.

"You will speak to my cousin the queen once again about our meeting." It was more a command than a request.

This was the last subject Essex wished to broach with Elizabeth this day. Any day. All previous attempts at reconciling the queen with the woman who had secretly married the one man she had ever truly loved had ended in disaster. Had Lettice been one iota less arrogant, ostentatious, or heart-stoppingly beautiful, perhaps Elizabeth would have forgiven her, allowed her back at Court. But his mother, in all the years of her marriage to Leicester, had refused to be cowed by her royal cousin. She was, after all, a grandniece of the queen's own mother, Anne Boleyn. Lettice was proud to a fault, and whilst still Lady Leicester, she had flaunted that title, her husband's wealth and status, driving Elizabeth to furious distraction. Now married to a mere boy, a *nobody*, Lettice knew her position to be vulnerable, possibly dangerous. And she had recently begun seeking a rapprochement with the queen. Of course she would use her son's exalted position to forward her cause.

"I cannot promise I'll speak to her today, Mother," said Essex. He felt, rather than saw, Frances stiffen at his response. Once he had left, she would bear the brunt of Lettice's outrage at her son's insolence.

"Robert." His mother's voice was threatening and her grip on his hand tightened, but with his other hand he pried off the vicelike fingers.

"I am going now," he said in a cold, clipped voice that brooked no argument. He turned to Frances. "I may return home tonight, or I may stay in my apartments at Court."

She nodded and smiled weakly. "Wave bye-bye to your papa," she said, flapping little Robert's hand. Essex felt sick leaving his wife and son with the dragon, but his urge to escape was greater still.

It took all of his restraint to close the door quietly behind him and squelch a whoop of joy. Once outside in the sunlight, the prospect of an evening in Elizabeth's glittering Court ahead, Robert Devereaux, Earl of Essex, found his mood had brightened considerably.

E SSEX LOVED the brief water transit from his home upriver to
Greenwich castle, and the early September gloom that had quite suddenly fallen over the Thames did nothing to dampen his mood. He
enjoyed the bustle, the noise, even the stink of it, for he saw the river as
the lifeblood of London. Riches were ferried into the city on these
waters, as well as the most famous and infamous personages, and the
most vital intelligence from abroad. All great enterprise originated here.
Each time Essex came out on his mother's gilded barge, memories sailed
across his vision like the tall-masted ships towering above him.

He remembered his first entrance into the city as a boy, awe of the
place bulging his innocent's eyes. He thought of the day Leicester had
taken him, a nervous seventeen-year-old, to be presented to the queen.
His aging stepfather had personally overseen Robert's dressing and pol-
ishing for the event, and whilst on this very barge had proffered last-
minute tutoring to guarantee, he hoped, Elizabeth's acceptance. He
recalled the glitter and breathless excitement of his first evening water
party, seated at the queen's right hand, the river reflecting the exploding
fireworks overhead. Essex saw again the night he had secretly spirited
himself out of London on the *Swiftsure,* hiding from the queen his sudden departure, and his rendezvous with her fleet, which was headed for
an attack on Lisbon. Elizabeth had previously demanded that her new
favorite attend her at Court, expressly forbidding him to join Francis
Drake's raiding party of King Philip's second Armada lying at anchor in
Lisbon Harbor. Risking royal displeasure, Essex had, with clandestine
precision, outfitted the *Swiftsure* at his own expense, and with blatant disregard of her orders, had joined the expedition already at sea. Some
thought him merely foolhardy, others outrageous, but his brave—if theatrical—exploits in Portugal had profited him enough fame to outweigh
the queen's displeasure. His reputation as a national hero had sprung
from that journey, and a popularity so broad that the long, square,
"shovel-shaped" beard he'd returned wearing had quickly become all
the rage in London, with nobles and common men alike copying the
style. And the journey had begun *here,* on the River Thames.

In the space of his musings, the barge had reached the Greenwich quay. As he disembarked Essex began again the obsessive argument with himself of whether to discuss, first, the subject of Francis Bacon, or the Farm of Sweet Wines, and therefore barely registered the hubbub that surrounded the almost barbaric-looking galley docked beside him. The Dockmaster was engaged in a heated exchange with the ship's captain, but Essex dismissed it. Shiploads full of exotics and extravagances had been arriving for weeks now, in preparation for the queen's sixtieth-birthday celebration, a round of festivities that promised to eclipse all those that had come before it, and he took no notice of several guards trotting from the tower gate up the elevation toward the galley.

Greenwich was a great, redbricked hodgepodge of a castle, whose long main wing with its row of high, transited windows overlooked the river. Essex moved along the brick path to the south gate, accepting greetings from gentlemen of the Court—young and old, high peers and eager hopefuls. Their demeanor was deferential, even, he thought with an inward smile, reverential. He, of course, returned the salutations with a warm grace that never failed to delight the recipient. Essex's pace was leisurely, with an eye to prolonging the pleasure of adulation, but today there was further reason to take his time. He was playing a game with himself, wondering where he would find the queen. He prided himself on knowing her well, guessing her mood. He'd even memorized her schedule. Now as she grew older it became more regimented, both daily and weekly.

It was late afternoon, and Elizabeth would have done with her dozens of audiences, he reasoned. She would be finished with the endless pile of paperwork that she'd attended to, sitting straight backed at her desk as the secretaries Walsingham and Cecil laid the documents before her. He could picture them waiting patiently as she marked them with her studied and flourished signature, to be set carefully with a vellum roller and the finest perfumed powder from France. She would already have taken her exercise, perhaps a brisk walk upon the castle's battlement—she had ridden out with him yesterday—and would have completed her daily translations and double translations of Greek classics, her favorite hobby, she claimed. Today was Monday, and there was very little planned for the evening. A light meal taken in her rooms. Perhaps some music, but no dancing. Perhaps a night of gambling. Essex hoped this was the case, as the pleasure of dice and cards always cheered Elizabeth . . . made her more receptive, even to his "incessant nagging," as she'd come to call his more and more frequent requests for favors.

So, he reasoned, if it were not to be a formal evening, her late-afternoon toilette would be abbreviated, perhaps she might even forego changing her gown. If this were the case, where might the queen be just now? A fitting with her seamstress was possible, or a meeting with her Master of Revels in preparation for her birthday celebration.

*No! None of those places.* Essex was suddenly sure he knew her whereabouts. All at once three of Elizabeth's ladies burst from around a corner into the wide corridor, gorgeous in their varicolored silks, fluttering and chattering like a trio of tropical birds. He breathed easier to see that Katherine Bridges was not among them. His latest mistress was entirely delightful and, a married woman, never demanding, but Essex was at this moment seething with single-minded purpose and wished for no distractions. He nodded with graceful exaggeration to the ladies, fixing each of them in that moment with a private, hungry glance. It was prudent, he had discovered, to keep the women of the Court in a state of mild but constant desire for him. Favors of every sort were far easier to extract that way.

Without bothering to confirm his guess at the queen's present location, he turned into the corridor of the castle's north wing; Essex strode past the now deserted Privy Council Chamber, nodding to the two guards, both of whom sported the squared-off beards, standing at attention at the heavy wooden doors. He took great but secret pleasure from the fact that the place was now one of his official destinations. The Privy Council table was the very heart of government, and he was at home there. Indeed, the other Privy councilors, all older and, they believed, wiser, were forced to begrudgingly admit that Essex was a faithful and hardworking cohort. No one, in fact, spent more time at Council business. No one demonstrated more raw enthusiasm for the job. He was young and wild and too well loved by the queen for his own good, but the older men were, in the end, forced to agree that he was a brilliant logician, a clever tactician, and regularly spouted unique solutions to previously insoluble problems.

A final turn down a short hall found Essex at a doorway undistinguished other than by the two armed soldiers who guarded it. At sight of the men, he silently congratulated himself, recognizing them as Elizabeth's personal guard of this hour, who protected whichever room in which the queen was present. He greeted them, warmed by their obvious admiration for him. They were common men, brave soldiers who had seen battle, and they respected him. The public, he knew, perceived him, despite his title and standing with the queen, as a man of the people. He liked that, liked that he was welcome in the company of low- or highborn men.

When Essex entered, the guards uncrossed their halberds and opened the door.

As ever, the sight of Elizabeth amazed him, paralyzed him. Bathed in orange afternoon light, she stood for her portrait wearing a low-bodiced, brocaded gown, draped round in a robe the color of fire. Her eyes were fixed on the young Flemish artist, and though she had not turned when the door opened, Essex was sure she knew it was *he* who had entered. Quietly he shut the door behind him and, moving behind Marcus Gheerhaerts, settled himself on a bench, the better to gaze at the queen and the nearly completed portrait.

There was a fabulous quality to the painting, undoubtedly the most sumptuous and beautifully wrought that he had ever seen. In ways, it recreated Elizabeth in shocking, lifelike reality, yet it imagined much. It sang with allegory, Gheerhaerts having planted dreamlike, mythical elements at every turn, allowing one to stare endlessly at the portrait and continue discovering its mysterious details.

Despite the pale gray that shadowed Elizabeth's temples and cheeks, the artist had chosen to depict the queen's angular features with a lush roundness, a fullness of the lips and breasts, the soft, sloe-eyed gaze of a lover. 'Twas as though the painter had chosen to see the woman at her life's ripest moment. The way, thought Essex, that Leicester had described Elizabeth in her thirties, when they still shared a bed.

The gown's high, rounded ruffs were such fine gauze as to be transparent, only noticeable by their jeweled borders, and the tips of the proud, feathered headdress that evoked Diana, goddess of the hunt, were lost beyond the top of the canvas. Her wig, hung with huge, teardrop-shaped pearls, was the color of fresh carrots, its long, curled tendrils hanging down along her bosom. Pearls hung as ear bobs, ropes of fat pearls encircled her neck as well as a necklace dangling in the cleft of her pale raised breasts. On her puffed left sleeve, a jeweled snake symbolizing fidelity was made all of pearls and twisted into a love knot, whilst the serpent grasped in its mouth a red ruby heart.

Clearly Gheerhaerts had reworked the fire-colored cloak draped round Elizabeth's left shoulder and right hip since Essex had seen it last, for now it was dotted—most extraordinarily, he thought—with eyes, ears, and mouths! This young Netherlander, thought Essex, must indeed have studied the queen's life in some detail before beginning his portrait. How else would he have known to symbolize in his rendition of her the three most important men in her life? From the earliest days of her reign, Elizabeth had literally called Leicester "My Eyes." Walsingham, her master of espionage, was "My Ears" abroad. Old Burleigh, bottomless well of wise counsel that he was, who most often spoke the words the queen herself was thinking, would, had she given him a pet name, surely have been "My Mouth."

But by far the most disturbing new object in the painting was a long, arched tube of some vaguely transparent material, perhaps frosted glass, that Elizabeth grasped with the thumb and four fingers of her right hand. Whilst posing she had been instructed to hold the doweled back of a tall chair, and since Essex's last viewing—through strange turns of the artist's mind—the dowel had transmogrified into this surprising element. Parts of her dress could be glimpsed through the tube, very peculiarly, and it seemed to dissolve into her cloak at the level of her groin, disappearing to become part of the yellow-orange fabric. But now, on closer observation of the arched tube, Essex could see along its front curve a rounded ridge. It was most astonishing. For at the very place where Elizabeth grasped it lightly with her long delicate fingers, the object most resembled in size and shape a man's erect member.

Surely the queen had viewed the portrait's progress. She must have observed the object and the erotic nature of its appearance. Had it disturbed her—as it now did Essex—she would certainly have had it painted out. Why did it unsettle him so? he wondered.

In that moment Elizabeth, looking past the artist, met Essex's gaze. Nothing in the calm repose of her features changed except the deep brown, almost black eyes, which bid him warm welcome into her world. She was pleased to see him. But in that moment of connecting their souls,

Essex realized the nature of his discomfort at the painting's raw sexuality. He began to blush like a schoolboy, turned from Elizabeth's gaze, and walked across the room pretending to see something of interest out the mullioned windows.

"Careful, my lord Essex," Gheerhaerts warned, "you block the last of my precious daylight."

"Sorry." Essex moved again, refusing to acknowledge Elizabeth's amused expression.

"And you, Majesty," the painter commanded, "please do not smile."

Essex willed himself to a state of calm, but all at once he was lost, four years in the past, remembering.

1589. Leicester was not long in his grave, but he had died on the heels of England's stupendous victory over the Spanish Armada, and so whilst all celebrated, Elizabeth grieved. The queen had been forced by circumstance to publicly rejoice in her navy's triumph, but so much of her soul had died with Robin Dudley, her suffering so private and terrible, that it was only with the greatest of effort that she managed every day to place one foot before the other and continue to rule.

Essex, only recently installed as Elizabeth's newest favorite, was— aside from herself—perhaps the only individual in England with any reason to mourn the widely despised Earl of Leicester.

Leicester was the one man who had taken great pains with the young Earl of Essex's grooming and advancement at court. Sensitive and observant, Essex had emulated Leicester's best qualities—a cutting wit and a fine intelligence, riding impeccably, excelling in the martial arts, dancing superbly. And, Leicester had pointed out, his stepson had been blessed with the physical traits that all her life the queen had found irresistible in a man. He was tall—taller than she— broad shouldered, with thick red wavy hair and beard. Both of the queen's true loves—Thomas Seymour and Leicester—had shared those very qualities with the first man Elizabeth had ever adored— her father, Henry VIII. Even at eighteen, Leicester had insisted, his protégé had the bearing of a king—a man his queen could admire, could advance. Could love.

There had never been a conscious plan to seduce Elizabeth. After

Leicester's death Essex was, however, the one courtier whose company the queen constantly craved. Though they never spoke of it, she understood that the young man sincerely missed his stepfather, and his sympathy for her loss was genuine. They'd spent more and more time together, riding, dancing, gambling. It was not long before she began to call him Robin, which at first he believed had been a mere slip of the tongue, but later realized had been a conscious, if uncharacteristically sentimental, decision. He had, surprisingly, found her physically attractive at fifty-five and always exciting, but never discovered how much of her allure was genuinely erotic and how much was owed to her status as the most powerful woman in the world.

He engaged her in spirited debates on the finer points of Greek literature, enjoyed long, loud arguments over a word or phrase whose translation was questionable. She adored gambling and he matched her, bet for bet. She knew he played his best at dice and cards, and she beat him roughly half the time. He had learned how to make her laugh and begun to crave hearing the bawdy bellowing from such an otherwise dignified personage. Their evenings together began extending all through the nights, he not leaving her rooms until the sun had begun to rise.

He was nevertheless unprepared when, as he was helping her down from the saddle after a hard ride, Elizabeth had slid effortlessly into his arms and returned, with as much fervor as it had been delivered, a kiss he had not consciously intended to bestow. He never knew who had been the more surprised of the two, for the queen knew better than anyone that she was quite old enough to be his mother, indeed his grandmother. But that night she had led him more than willingly into her bed and he, suffering from a blinding enchantment of the moment, had followed.

Hardly a virgin, he'd endeavored to dazzle the queen with his manly prowess and he was sure—from the abandon with which she touched him and moved, and how in the end she had cried out ecstatically—that Elizabeth had been fulfilled in her womanly pleasures. Afterward, when they lay side by side, she had held his still erect manhood in her delicate white fingers and wondered at the tirelessness of youthful passion.

Then she had risen quite suddenly from the great Bed of State, pulling her robe around her. Essex had watched as she'd moved to the silver-framed looking glass and commenced staring at her own reflection. He had spoken very little in their tryst, and when he'd found enough voice to call her name, she raised her first finger to him as if to silence him, as if she were too heavily engaged in a discovery of great import to be bothered. So he had lain quietly, watching her.

Shortly, he felt the air changing in the room, growing cold where moments before it had glowed with red heat. He became alarmed as her self-observation in the glass continued on and on. With dawning horror he realized she must be seeing the web of fine wrinkles, the pockmarked cheeks and forehead where the face paint had been kissed away by the boy still lying in her bed. Then he saw Elizabeth stiffen, saw her raise herself up to her full height, and never meeting his eyes said, in the gentlest voice he had ever heard her use, that he should go. She was very pleased with him, she was careful to say, but when she'd tried to continue, her voice had cracked and thereafter she had stood motionless, still staring into the looking glass.

He'd risen and quickly dressed himself. When he moved toward her, she lifted her finger once again to stop him from approaching, but he would not be stopped. He had been her lover this night, not a boy she could hold back with a gesture or even a queenly command. He took her shoulders and turned her full to face him and saw tears of sheer misery shimmering in her eyes.

"I am yours, Elizabeth, always yours," he said simply, then kissed her. He had prayed in that moment that she might melt into his arms, cling to him again, forgive herself her age and ugliness so that she could let herself love him as she had Robin Dudley. But she did not soften, did not speak. Only silently bade him go.

Thereafter she had heaped honors on Essex, favored him above all her other men. She showered him with affection, openly caressing and embracing him. She made him many rich gifts and continued even to call him her "Robin." All the Court knew of their tryst and she had not disabused them of her change of heart. As far as her ladies and gentlemen were concerned, she and Essex were, in the truest sense, still lovers. But never once after that night did she allow him into her bed.

The depth of his hurt had surprised him. He'd not realized the precise nature of his affection until her rejection of him, and he was faced with the truth: Elizabeth was not a trophy. He took no pride in the accomplishment of bedding the Queen of England. He had loved her as a woman. Worshiped her body. Joined his mind and spirit with hers. He had never felt so deeply for anyone. Ever.

She had refused to allow him to leave Court, even to privately lick his wounds. He had desperately needed time to think, to ponder his heartbreak. His grief was therefore protracted, his understanding delayed.

It came to him one afternoon when his mother had summoned him to attend her on a matter of finance. They'd sat side by side poring over the household ledger. Lettice had been haranguing him for several minutes regarding some gambling debts, though he knew her recent bitterness was in large measure caused by his love affair with the queen, one that recalled her second husband's obsession with the same woman. As her tirade had continued, he refused to meet her eye. Now as he turned to face her the sound of his mother's voice faded and her lips moved in silence. The strangeness of the event rattled him, but he was suddenly aware that he was seeing Lettice clearly for the first time.

She was a bitch and a whore, and she had never loved him. Had never even seen him. She'd neither rejoiced in his brilliance nor accepted his shortcomings.

Elizabeth had.

He was forced to turn quickly before the tears overflowed his eyes and his mother think him hurt by her ranting. Risking her fury he excused himself, claiming one of his sick headaches, and locked himself in his rooms.

He lay motionless on his bed. His thoughts were jumbled, memories flooding his mind. A severe childhood fever, cared for by his nurse, Lettice never once coming to his bedside . . . his father raging before the fire at his cold, faithless wife . . . the queen's face softening as she silently read the small verse he'd written in her honor . . . at a New Year's feast, Elizabeth's long white fingers affectionately tickling his neck . . . those same fingers lightly grasping the hardness between his legs. Elizabeth . . .

He knew enough to realize that the rejection from her bed was a matter of personal vanity. She was too proud to ever again be seen in her imperfect nakedness by any man. But she loved him nevertheless. Would keep him near her, forward his career . . . forgive him his tantrums and indiscretions. He was, he realized in that moment, to be the last man to whom Elizabeth would ever give herself.

"Robin . . ."

Essex was wrenched from his reveries. He turned to see the queen standing behind him in her white, brocaded gown. Gheerhaerts had involved himself in cleaning his brushes, and the solid orange robe on which the artist had imagined embroidered eyes, ears, and mouths now hung in careful folds over the top of a tall screen.

"Majesty." Essex bowed low and, taking Elizabeth's hand, kissed it with delicate passion.

"You're very pale," she said. "Are you ill?"

"I could be if it would make you fawn over me this evening," he teased.

She smiled indulgently, a self-conscious, closed-mouth smile. Her ivory teeth had recently begun to turn brown. "What do you think of the portrait?" she said.

"I've already told you," he replied, loud enough for the artist to hear, "that I do not think Master Gheerhaerts is doing justice to your beauty."

The queen was used to indiscriminate flattery, knew most of it to be false, but demanded it all the same. It had become a ritualized form of greeting that was necessary before genuine conversation could begin.

"How are Frances and little Robert?"

"Excellent, Your Majesty. She sends you her love . . . as does my mother," he added, quite surprising himself, as he had not expected to raise the subject of Lettice this day.

"Is she still yearning for an audience?" Elizabeth asked, taking his arm and indicating that he should escort her from the room. With a tap on the door, it flew open and the two of them exited into the corridor.

"You know she is," said Essex.

"Then she shall have one."

He was bemused by Elizabeth's sudden acquiescence on so prickly a matter.

"Arrange it for next week."

"I'm most grateful, and so will my mother be." He felt his heart suddenly thumping in his chest. This was a great coup. Lettice would be overwhelmed. But he must carefully steer her from any ostentatious displays in either her dress or mode of transport to the meeting. It would not do for her to arrive for the long awaited occasion arrayed in one of her expensive French gowns, riding like royalty in a gilded carriage pulled by six plumed, white stallions. His mind raced. The queen's mood was more than affable today. Should he broach the Farm of Sweet Wines, or Bacon's appointment? Or should he perhaps consider mentioning neither of them? He pondered the question as they moved with stately grandeur down the long corridor. Every man who passed stopped and bowed. Ladies ceased their tittering and gossip and dropped into deep, solemn curtsies.

"So," said Essex, "shall we play at cards this evening? Or dice?"

"Neither," said the queen. "You already owe me far too much money. You, my lord, cannot afford to lose another shilling. In fact," she added, "I am wondering when I shall see my three thousand pounds repaid to me."

He had his opening!

"I was thinking just now, Your Majesty, that if I were granted the Farm of Sweet Wines, I could easily repay the debt. Within a year. Two at the most."

"The Farm of Sweet Wines?"

Elizabeth appeared surprised by the request, but he knew she was playing with him. Like the Mastership of the Horse, the Farm had been one of Leicester's grants—indeed his predecessor's principal source of income.

"That is a very rich gift you are suggesting I make you, my lord."

Her voice and mood were suddenly unreadable. Essex knew he was on dangerous ground.

"Perhaps if you made your queen a gift . . ." she began but didn't finish, as her attention was drawn to the figure now approaching them. "Ah, Robert." She extended her hand to be kissed by the graceless Robert Cecil.

Essex seethed quietly. The Gnome had destroyed his moment.

"Your Majesty. My lord Essex." Cecil's voice was urgent. "I've just learned that an enemy of England has had the temerity to sail upriver and dock at the castle quay."

"An enemy of England?" said Elizabeth. "Who?"

"The Irish rebel, Your Majesty. The woman . . . the pirate . . . Grace O'Malley. She is"—Cecil was flustered and could barely say the words—"demanding an audience."

Elizabeth began to move down the hallway flanked on either side by Essex and Cecil, in long strides with which the Gnome could hardly keep abreast. The queen seemed altogether undisturbed by the strange news. On the contrary, she seemed delighted.

"So," she said, " 'the Mother of the Irish Rebellion' wishes to answer our interrogatory in person."

"So it seems, Your Majesty," Cecil answered.

Essex was annoyed. Whilst he certainly knew who Grace O'Malley was, he had no knowledge of an "interrogatory," and neither Elizabeth nor the Gnome seemed inclined to apprise him of its mysterious contents.

Neither would he give them the pleasure of begging to be informed.

Elizabeth was silent as they followed her toward the Privy Council Chamber. Essex sensed that her mind was working at a most accelerated rate.

"Robert, bring me a copy of her answers," she snapped at Cecil.

"Yes, madam." Without another word the Gnome peeled away from them and disappeared back the way he had come.

Essex and Elizabeth reached the Privy Council Chamber and the guards flung open the double doors.

"Will you see her, Your Majesty, or have her arrested?" Essex finally asked. He was becoming more and more irritated. An "interrogatory." Her "answers."

Elizabeth did not deign to reply. He persisted. "Grace O'Malley has the distinction of having transported more shiploads of Scots mercenaries to Ireland to fight the English than anyone else in history."

"Sometimes the Scottish Gallowglass fight on *our* side," Elizabeth argued with infuriating calm.

"The woman is a traitor many times over, Your Majesty. A known cutthroat!"

"She is indeed. But our Philip Sidney thought enough of her to continue a long correspondence, from the time of their meeting in Ireland till his death. And her answers to my questionnaire have piqued my curiosity. Despite her reputation I believe she has something in her character to recommend her. I wish to see such a woman with my own two eyes. See what she is made of."

Elizabeth saw Essex's frustration growing, and obliged him. "She recently asked me for several favors."

"Favors? From a known rebel?"

"I replied with an interrogatory of eighteen items. She responded in early July."

"But—"

"You will have the Presence Chamber readied for an audience," Elizabeth interrupted, irritation growing in her voice. "And see if my Irish cousin, Tom Ormond, is about. I know he'll wish to be present."

Essex stood unmoving, entirely bemused. The queen's temper was rising.

"Robin, listen to me now," she said, fixing him with a look of grave intensity. "You have been so preoccupied with your military obsessions and your Bacons and your Farm of Sweet Wines that you have not been paying attention."

"Your Majesty, I object! I have been paying very close attention to your business *and* the business of state."

"Yes, you have. My *domestic* agenda. But what of my foreign policy? What of Ireland? You know nothing about the rebellion there. You shy away from the subject, as most men do, because the very thought of that savage country makes your blood run cold. When you do think of Ireland, you're reminded of all the Englishmen who've died there. Were ruined there. Your father, for one. Your brother-in-law, Perrot, for another. But you don't think about *my* Ireland. *My* problem.

"Did you know, Robin, that the last act of my mother's betrayer, Cromwell, was to talk my father into taking control of the Irish nobility?

His "Surrender and Regrant" policy was either the most brilliant idea he'd ever conceived, or the most boneheaded. Who knows, perhaps Thomas Cromwell was the first of Ireland's victims. He died by the ax not three years after the program's conception. My father paid it half-hearted attention. It was a distant problem in my brother's reign, and even in my sister Mary's.

"But distances have shrunk, my sweet man, ever since the Spaniards began their bloody conquest of the world, and Ireland is suddenly *at my back door!* Philip has dangerous papist allies there—confounded Irish aristocracy! There's one and only one amongst them—Tom Ormond—who knows the true meaning of loyalty. The lords of that unfortunate land blithely swear their fealty to my governors one day, then slaughter my troops the next. I send colonists there, soldiers and horses, and they die of disease or battle or go insane. The Irish are an unfathomable people," she said, looking away, then added, almost to herself, "I worry they'll be the death of me.

"My treasury is hemorrhaging money. If I continue raising taxes, my people will come to hate me. I cannot afford this war, Robin! And I cannot afford your ignoring it any longer. If you wish to be my most trusted adviser—and I know you do—then you will henceforth educate yourself on this matter, *interest* yourself in it, because it means very much to me, and will in the future mean even more."

"Yes, Majesty." Essex was humbled, knowing her altogether right, and grateful that she understood him so well. She tutored and directed him in the affairs of state, was so forgiving.

"Go along now," she said, as if he were a mere page and not a New Man of the Privy Council. "See to the audience. And pay attention in this lady's presence. She may be a traitor to England, but she has much to teach us both."

Essex exited as Robert Cecil returned bustling with importance. He had a rolled parchment tucked beneath his arm. As the doors closed behind him, Essex could see him spreading on the long table what must have been the pirate O'Malley's answers to Elizabeth's interrogatory. He chided himself for allowing the Gnome to best him on Elizabeth's most pressing foreign affairs. He'd kept abreast of the war in the Netherlands, of Scotland and France, and Spain's continuing crusade to convert to Catholicism every man, woman, and child who lived. But he had dismissed Ireland. The queen's attempts to colonize it, and the great rebellion it had spawned, had escaped him. But no longer. He would make it his business to understand that strange hellhole of a country.

And he would begin with Grace O'Malley.

# 3

THE GOWN WAS long out of fashion, Grace thought, staring at herself in the glass that hung on her tiny cabin wall. It was English in cut, a fine lady's dress. She'd plucked it from its owner's shipboard cupboard whilst the woman, cowering and bug-eyed with amazement, gaped at the female pirate brandishing a pistol and looting her room. Sweet Jesus, how long ago had that been? Ten years? Fifteen? 'Twas surprising that the garment was not chewed up by moths or mold—a pretty thing, the blue velvet, trimmed with green and with a low square-cut bodice that the English had favored for so many years.

'Twas equally surprising, thought Grace, turning to view herself from the side, that it fit her much the same as it did when she'd lifted it from the bug-eyed captain's wife. She was fit at sixty-three, the same as all Irish women who managed to survive to that ripe old age. If you weren't hardy, she thought, you were dead, and that was that. She'd taken more time with her hair today than she had in years, braiding the dark tresses, now streaked with silver, into long, thick plaits, and pinned them up in a style she had once admired on a Turkish girl.

*Shite! She looked ridiculous. What in the name of God was she doing in an English gown?* Grace grabbed her wool chieftain's cloak from its peg and threw the long, sleeveless garment over one shoulder. The *brat* was a soft sea green and well worn, but the brown fur that trimmed it was still thick and beautiful. And it was Irish, by God. Traditional. With a sudden inspiration she flung open the studded leather chest on the shelf above her narrow bed. The solid-gold brooch she removed from it filled her entire hand and was heavy as a rock. The design, she thought with satisfaction, was clearly Spanish. It shouted out its origins—King Philip's Treasure Fleet from the New World. Aye, thought Grace as she fastened the cape together at one shoulder, leaving her bodice partially exposed, let Elizabeth be reminded of the Spanish presence in Ireland. Let her squirm a bit.

She reached again into the chest and considered a pair of Egyptian gold ear bobs. There was something pagan about the style—to the stilted English eyes, she thought, even barbaric. She smiled as she put them on. Sure the meeting was an important one, but there was no reason she should not amuse herself at her enemy's expense. Now the image that peered back at Grace satisfied her. Perhaps she wasn't terrifying, as the reputation preceding her was bound to be, but she was striking, even distinguished.

This occasion, she thought, was long overdue. All the other great clan chiefs of Ireland knew the Queen of England personally. "Black Tom Butler"—known as the Earl of Ormond here—was treated as family, and spent as much time on English soil as Irish. Gerald Fitzgerald, God curse his blighted soul, the queen's so-called earl of Desmond, before his misbegotten Munster rebellion had spent seven years in the Tower of London, all the while his wife Elizabeth's confidante. And then there was The O'Neill. Raised in Sir Henry Sidney's English country house, Hugh O'Neill had surrendered to the queen and, after helping to put down the Desmond rebellion, had assumed the earldom of Tyrone. He'd treated with the English on many occasions, but had broken most of the treaties he had made. His loyalties, despite outward appearances, had always been very clearly with Ireland.

What would her father think to see her gotten up like the dog's dinner for this occasion? He would think it momentous to be sure, though he'd caution against any hint of groveling. After all, he'd never groveled to the queen's father. Whilst all the other chieftains had succumbed to King Henry's nonsense—surrendering their allegiance to England, giving up the old ways and the Brehon laws, to be given in return their very own lands back to them, and an English title that everyone knew was phony as the year was long—Grace's father had refused to budge. 'Twas a clear fake, this Surrender and Regrant program, for all knew full well how reviled were her countrymen. To the English they were savages. Scum. White monkeys. "The Wild Irish." The policy, Owen had lamented, had appealed to the worst in the clan chiefs' natures. Had wreaked more havoc with Ireland than any could remember. But Owen O'Malley had clung steadfastly to the old Gaelic ways and refused to add a title to his name.

Grace had herself, many years before, allowed her husband to submit to Henry Sidney, but it had been for expediency's sake. And she had never taken an English title. In fact, she thought with a small smile as she pushed open her cabin door, she'd not even taken her husbands' names after she'd married. Grace O'Malley she'd been born, and Grace O'Malley she would die.

She was ready to meet the queen, she thought as she climbed to the deck, already bathed in evening shadows. She had come with a purpose and meant to have her way, no matter what it took. Lives were at stake here, and she would accept nothing short of success.

# 4

THE AUDIENCE had been hastily thrown together, but the gathering in the Presence Chamber, decided Essex, was a distinguished one nonetheless. He'd rounded up the Earl of Ormond and sent frantic and no doubt mysterious messages to Southampton and Francis Bacon to attend him at Court immediately. They were just now taking their places with the other courtiers along one wall of the wood-paneled chamber, as Elizabeth's waiting ladies took theirs along the other.

Katherine Bridges was amongst the women, coyly attempting to catch his eye, but he only answered with a brief nod before turning back to the business at hand. It would be unseemly, he knew, to appear to be flirting with his mistress so soon after Elizabeth's admonition to seriousness.

The queen, seated on a small throne, was looking altogether severe, though Essex knew there was excitement seething beneath the chilly facade. Leaning down to whisper in her ear, his hunched back grotesquely exaggerated in this posture, Robert Cecil appeared a living gargoyle. How, wondered Essex, could she bear such a creature so close to her?

Then again, he realized, this was not the first time she had taken a fancy to a warped, disfigured man. The queen had been engaged for eight years to the French dauphin. The Duke of Alençon—she'd called him "my frog"—had been short, pockmarked, and misshapen, and although the long engagement had most certainly been for show, she had truly seemed fond of the little troll.

The tall double doors were pulled open, and with a trumpet fanfare that Elizabeth had expressly requested for her unusual guest, the rebel woman Grace O'Malley strode into the chamber.

Indeed, thought Essex, she was *striding*. He'd seen no other woman but Elizabeth use such a forceful gait, exude such a presence. Grace was tall—perhaps a hand taller than the queen—but whilst Elizabeth was straight and as thin as a rail, her visitor, he could see, was full-bodied, with rounded breasts topping the square-necked bodice. Despite her obvious strength there was a willowy quality about the woman, a grace-fulness, as though she were quite at home in her body, as an animal might be. Her face had once been darkly beautiful. He imagined her at twenty, at the height of her womanly charms, saw her with a cutlass clutched in her hand, fighting on the deck of her pirate's galley. Astonishing, thought Essex, a feminine sea captain!

"Quite the picture," whispered Francis Bacon as he moved up beside Essex. "I owe you a favor for this invitation, Robert." He was greedily devouring the richness of the scene with his eyes.

"I'll want your opinion when it's done. Come, stay close to me. I want to get nearer."

As the O'Malley woman approached, the queen suddenly rose from her throne. Soft gasps were heard round the chamber, as this action strayed mightily from protocol. The rebel was stopped in her tracks at the sight of Elizabeth, and the queen, her eyes planted squarely on her audience, took the two steps down and met her guest in the center of the dead-quiet room.

Elizabeth raised her hand to be kissed, indeed was forced to raise it as high as she would for a tall man. Without hesitation Grace took the queen's hand and touched the fingers gently with her lips. But she did not lower herself into the expected curtsy.

"Your Majesty," Essex heard the woman say in fluent Latin, "I would drop to my knees, but my joints would protest it."

Elizabeth cocked her head to one side, both with surprise that the audience was to be conducted in Latin, and the realization that, with her first sentence, Grace O'Malley had challenged her authority. All subjects, despite their age or infirmity, bowed or curtsied to the queen. No excuses were tolerated.

Elizabeth recovered her wits the next instant, choosing gracefully to ignore the slight. "We welcome you to England," she said. "Come, meet my men." One by one Elizabeth made her introductions. Only the Earl of Ormond knew Grace O'Malley—his countrywoman—and Essex heard her say to him with more than a hint of irony, "You seem altogether too at home in this place, Thomas."

When she approached them, Essex and Bacon—in unison—bowed low to the queen.

"The pair of you remind me of your stepfather and his brother," she said to Essex. "The earls of Leicester and Warwick were my beloved Fric and Frac." As they rose Elizabeth said in the Latin she knew both understood perfectly, "Meet Grace O'Malley, our loyal subject from the west of Ireland. Mistress O'Malley, my lord the Earl of Essex. . . . And a very clever lawyer named Francis Bacon."

"Your father was Walter Devereaux," Grace said to Essex, more a statement than a question, and stared searchingly into his eyes.

"He was," replied Essex, taken completely off guard. Both knew of his father's bloody deeds in Ireland. And it was strangely unsettling to be reminded of them by this forthright woman.

"Let us walk," Elizabeth suggested to her guest. Before turning away from them, the queen signaled Essex with her eyes that he should follow. As the two women walked and talked quietly, their heads tilted toward each other, Essex and Bacon quietly observed and listened.

" 'Tis extraordinary," Elizabeth began, "to have in our midst so famous a pirate."

"There is another pirate in the room more famous than myself," Grace replied. To the queen's questioning look she answered, "Yourself, Majesty."

Essex could feel Elizabeth pause at the impudence of the statement, but the queen did not miss a step.

Grace O'Malley continued. "You're a pirate by proxy, and every head of state in the world is well aware of it. Drake and Frobisher and Hawkins, everyone knows you finance their ventures. And everyone knows as well that they call their activities 'privateering,' but what it truly is, is pirating. What we do not know," she said with a sly smile, "is what part of their booty ends up in your treasury."

Elizabeth stopped so suddenly in her tracks that Essex and Bacon nearly collided with the two women.

"Have I spoken out of line?" Grace seemed not at all rattled by the queen's obvious discomfiture. "If I have, you have my apologies, madam. But these are well-known facts."

Essex watched as Elizabeth's expression softened suddenly, almost as if she had relaxed into a tub of hot water. Perhaps she had decided to take no offense at Grace O'Malley's frankness. Everything the woman had said so far, whilst impertinent, had been altogether true. Perhaps, he considered, the queen *liked* Grace O'Malley's audaciousness.

"I received your petition as well as your answers to my question-naire . . . ," said Elizabeth, and stopped before her throne.

Essex wondered if this action had been accidental. But of course it was not. Elizabeth left nothing to chance. She wished to symbolize her authority in this way, rather than using words or tone of voice.

". . . and I am considering your two requests," she continued evenly, then smiled. "The idea that the Crown should make arrangements for a pension for yourself—since you hold *us* responsible for the loss of your livelihood—is a curious one, but I have taken it under advisement. Regarding your second request—the removal of Governor Bingham from your home province of Connaught—this is a delicate situation, you understand."

"There is nothing delicate about Richard Bingham, Your Majesty. He's a cruel and murdering scoundrel, and he's more a liability to you in Ireland than a help."

"You should know that Governor Bingham has written to me regard-ing *you*."

"A complimentary letter, no doubt."

"He called you 'a notable traitoress' and thinks you very dangerous. To Ireland and to my own best interests."

"Oh, does he?"

Essex could feel Grace beginning to smolder. He wondered how long the woman could contain the fury boiling beneath the calm exterior.

"He has my son, Your Majesty, in his custody in Dublin Castle. Richard Bingham is threatening to hang my son Tibbot Burke on trumped-up charges. Did he write you that as well? Did he say his men murdered my gentle son Owen in cold blood, after he'd given your English troops the best of his hospitality, or that his persecution of my family will never stop until he sees us all in our graves? Did he say that!"

Essex found that his hand had unconsciously strayed to the hilt of his sword, his fear for the queen's safety growing with Grace O'Malley's outrage. But Elizabeth appeared altogether calm, even sympathetic to talk of Grace's sons, and Grace seemed uncaring that the timbre of her voice had risen far above that which was acceptable in speaking to the Queen of England.

"I've come here to ask a pardon for Tibbot Burke, Your Majesty." Grace now held Elizabeth's gaze with the same intensity as she'd recently held Essex's. "You must not let that pig of a man kill my son."

"Why do you suppose Richard Bingham is persecuting you and your family, Mistress O'Malley?"

"He's a woman hater, pure and simple. He most loathes a female with power, sees her as an unnatural creature, an abomination. He said so to my face. I'd wager that in his heart of hearts, your Governor Bingham despises *you* above all women."

Elizabeth, far from offended, nodded sagely, then with her eyes, requested Essex's arm to help her up the two steps to her throne. Once she was seated she gazed down mildly at Grace O'Malley.

"We shall consider your petitions with the utmost gravity."

"Thank you, Your Majesty. I am most grateful."

"Is that all then?" said Elizabeth.

"I beg your pardon?"

"Are you quite sure you have no other demands?"

"I would call them *requests*, Majesty, never dema—" Before she could stop herself, Grace O'Malley sneezed loudly, just managing to turn her face away from the queen.

Even so, Elizabeth reflexively sat back farther in her throne.

"Begging your pardon," said Grace, clearly attempting to stifle another sneeze.

Essex stepped forward instantly, holding out to her a fine linen and lace handkerchief.

"Thank you, Lord Essex," she said, and in the next moment blew her nose loudly and vigorously into it.

At once the room was awash with whispers. Of all Grace O'Malley's actions and words, this was the most outrageous. One never took such a personal liberty in the presence of the queen.

Elizabeth herself was altogether nonplussed, shocked into silence and further taken aback when, without her leave, Grace O'Malley turned from the royal presence, strode to the fire blazing in the hearth, and tossed the handkerchief in.

Dismayed gasps were heard from every corner, but the woman seemed entirely oblivious. She returned to her place before the queen as if nothing at all had happened.

"My good woman," said Elizabeth, regaining her voice, "that handkerchief was a *gift* from Lord Essex."

"Aye, and I soiled it with the contents of my nose, I'm afraid." Suddenly Grace was aware that her actions had been perceived as a blunder. "What would you have had me do, Your Majesty, put the filthy rag in my pocket?" She looked round at the assembled nobility with an incredulous expression and, unable to hide her amusement, added for all to hear, "It appears we Irish hold to a higher standard of cleanliness than do the English."

Essex blanched and Elizabeth sat as still as a post. The silence in the chamber was complete, all but the sound of the crackling fire and the rustle of the ladies' taffeta dresses. In the next moment, Essex thought, the queen would certainly put an end to this rude and preposterous performance.

Instead she laughed.

All eyes turned to Elizabeth, who was roaring like a Drury Lane whore.

Essex, who best understood the queen's bawdy humor, was the first to join in, but before long, as Elizabeth's guffaws showed no signs of abating, one after another of her courtiers, counselors, and ladies joined in the merriment, until the Presence Chamber resembled nothing less than the pit at the Globe Theatre during one of Mr. Shakespeare's comedies.

The Earl of Essex caught sight of Grace O'Malley. She too was laughing, but nothing, he saw quite clearly, could mask the fierceness of purpose that burned in the old woman's eyes.

NOT TWO HOURS later Essex found himself on a secret mission. He was mildly chagrined that the queen had made him a messenger boy. There were few people about, for the queen, after her audience with Grace O'Malley, had dismissed her court, announcing that there would be no entertainment this evening, none at all. The disappointed ladies and gentlemen had quickly dispersed, some of them no doubt headed for London's taverns and others to the Bankside brothels.

The path to Greenwich landing was entirely deserted and dark, save for the torches flickering at intervals along the way. But up ahead Grace O'Malley's vessel twinkled with welcoming light. Announcing himself to the sailor who guarded the plank, Essex was quickly given leave to board. He found Grace at the mess table below, sharing a companionable drink with several mates, and quickly requested a private word with her. He followed the woman down a passageway to her tiny cabin. Once the door had been shut behind them, she turned to face Essex.

"Well then, that was quick. When she said she'd take my petitions under advisement, I expected to wait for her answers. And wait. And wait."

"I haven't come with answers to your petition."

"What then?"

She had fixed Essex with that searching stare again, and he resisted the urge to look away.

"The queen wishes another audience. This one private."

Grace was unable to hide her surprise. "A private audience? When?"

"Now, Mistress O'Malley."

She considered the request for only a moment before she reached for her cloak.

"The queen wishes you to come in disguise," Essex added quickly. "The meeting is to be more than private. Secret, in fact."

"You look to be not much older than my son," she said, a softness coming into her voice.

"The one imprisoned?"

She nodded once. "You know, the queen is my junior by three years, almost exactly."

Essex waited for Grace O'Malley to make her point, and having known her but this short while, knew that indeed she would have a point to make.

"They say you were once her lover," said Grace.

*Ah, the point*, he thought, then said, "That is a private matter between the queen and myself . . . and rude of you to say."

"So it is," she replied.

He found he could not take his eyes off this woman.

"Do you plan to stay here while I change my clothes?" she asked with mild amusement.

"No!" He found himself flustered and, without another word, let himself out of Grace's cabin. Essex was suddenly suffocating in the close confines belowdecks and quickly climbed the stairs to topside. He gulped in the cool night air, trying to clear his head. This woman confused him, he realized, tipped him off balance. Comfortable as he was with the convoluted nature of Elizabeth's mind, he was finding Grace O'Malley a troubling enigma. She defied every law of femininity, at age sixty-three still an attractive specimen of her sex. She flaunted the protocol of Elizabeth's Court as well as the laws of England, yet the queen appeared delighted with her. *Worse*, thought Essex, *she was able to see into his soul*, much the way Elizabeth did. Yet she was a stranger to him. A rude foreigner from a savage land.

"Robert . . ."

He turned to see that Grace O'Malley had, astonishingly, transformed herself into a man, an Irish sea captain, he presumed. She wore breeches and hose and a short jacket. Her hair was tucked beneath a cap. Strangely, she looked at ease in the disguise, as if moving thus, between the sexes, came most naturally to her.

"May I call you Robert?"

"You may," he said, "if you allow me to call you Grace."

"Why not?" she said.

He realized that she liked him, and was curious as to why he was pleased by this. "Shall we go and see the queen?"

"If that is her pleasure."

"I would offer you my arm," he said, chagrined, "but you clearly have no need of it."

Grace smiled. "I can see why it is Elizabeth had to have you in her bed. The question is, why in the world didn't she keep you there?"

⬧⬧⬧

H E HAD DELIVERED Grace O'Malley to the queen moments before. They'd entered her bedchamber via the secret passageway that connected Elizabeth's apartments to his, the choice rooms that had, until his death, belonged to Robin Dudley. Essex always marveled at the "Virgin Queen's" brazenness in keeping her lover so close at hand. Now she wished himself to be near her, able to come and go from her private sanctuary at her command. Grace, in the guise of a man, had openly accompanied Essex to his rooms, and no one had been the wiser when she passed into Elizabeth's sumptuous bedchamber.

Somehow the queen had divested herself of every last one of her waiting ladies, guaranteeing the privacy of their meeting. She'd not bothered explaining her reasons for wanting to see Grace alone, only commanded Essex to stay in his rooms until he was called to take her out again the way she'd been brought in.

It had been a searing image—the two female titans standing face-to-face before a blazing hearth, Grace removing her cap to allow the dark waves of silver-streaked hair to fall about her shoulders, and Elizabeth, even regal in her dressing gown, offering her guest one of two comfortable chairs by the fire.

Oh, mused Essex, to be a fly upon that wall . . .

⬧⬧⬧

W HEN THE DOOR to the secret passage clicked shut, Elizabeth smiled pleasantly and in English, rather than Latin, said, "Will you share some spiced wine with me?" Then she lowered herself, straight backed, into one of the chairs before the fire.

Grace smiled to herself, strangely gratified that the queen had found her out and replied, in English tinged with a heavy brogue, "I will have some, yes."

"Where did you learn the language?" asked Elizabeth, suppressing a smile and pouring the warm wine into two heavy jewel-studded goblets.

Grace eyed the cups, recognizing how well they belonged in this insanely opulent room, its enormous Bed of State intricately carved with beasts and vines and flowers, every inch of wall and floor hung with rich Turkey carpets and tapestries shot with gold. The queen's dressing gown was spun silver and powder blue, and embroidered with a thousand tiny pearls.

"When he was fourteen my son Tibbot was taken hostage and held in the home of your man Bingham. Spent several years there. Learned the language. After I liberated him and brought him home, he taught it to me. I thought it wise," she added, "to know the language of my enemy."

*Damn my eyes!* thought Grace. She had promised herself to keep a civil tongue in her head. Well, what was the point, after all? Either the woman would grant her petitions or she would not. Grace raised her goblet. Its jewels sparkled in the firelight.

"To your health, Majesty."

"And yours, Mistress O'Malley," Elizabeth said, matching the gesture.

They both drank, then fell silent. Grace would let the woman speak first and explain why she'd brought her here, in these highly mysterious circumstances.

"I've had very little time to consider your petitions," the queen said finally, putting down her goblet, "and I am loath to make hasty decisions without a great deal more intelligence brought to bear on them. That is why I have invited you here this evening."

Grace regarded the queen with growing suspicion. "*I'm* to provide you with this intelligence?"

"Correct."

"I'm afraid I don't get your meanin', Your Majesty."

Elizabeth cleared her throat. "In your written petition to me and in your answers to my interrogatory, you touched briefly on several subjects—the general state of western Connaught, your two marriages and three children, and the customs surrounding provisions made by Irish husbands, after their deaths, for their widows."

"Aye. I took great pains with those answers."

"Indeed you did."

Elizabeth took up her cup again with long pale fingers that, Grace observed, had kept their youthful appearance much more than had the rest of the woman.

"I think perhaps you took *too much* care," Elizabeth added.

"What in the world does that mean?"

"You mentioned nothing of your career in pirating—how you came to such a profession—nor the reasons for your imprisonment at Bingham's hands, or Desmond's, nor your part in the rebellion in Ireland."

Grace stared incredulously at the queen. "You're askin' me to spill the contents of my soul to you, right here and now?" Her voice grew more sarcastic. "So's you can make an 'informed decision' about my son's release, my pension, and the fate of that lame little prick Richard Bingham?"

Elizabeth nodded, straight-faced.

"Pigs'll fly first, Your Majesty." Grace stood to go.

"Please . . . ," said Elizabeth.

The Queen of England, Grace realized, was begging her not to go. She stared down at her. Elizabeth was old and her teeth were going brown. And only Jesus knew how many wrinkles and pox marks were hidden beneath the white alum face paint. But the woman still had a fire in her eye, and inside her head was a steely mind. Despite a thousand contrary reasons, Grace was forced to admit she *liked* Elizabeth. This was irritating beyond measure, but that was the truth of it.

"Let's you and me do a bit of negotiatin'," said Grace.

"Like a fisherman and a fishmonger for a boatload of cod?"

"Somethin' like that. You tell me honestly why you want to hear my story. And none of this business about needin' more intelligence. You convince me *properly* of your reasons, and I'll spill my guts to you. After all, I'm Irish and I love hearin' myself talk as much as the next person."

Elizabeth suddenly looked sheepish, and with dismay Grace reckoned that she had overplayed her hand. But there was nothing to be done. Either the queen would reveal herself, or Grace would be shown the door, perhaps having sabotaged the happy outcome she had hoped to secure for her requests.

"I have in many respects led an extraordinarily sheltered life," Elizabeth began.

Grace attended the queen's words respectfully and lowered herself back into her chair. She was very still as Elizabeth collected her thoughts which, it was obvious, she had never expected to have extracted from her this evening.

"Whilst I have treated with the princes of every nation, with ambassadors and spies, engaged in commerce with all of the continent, financed privateering missions from the West Indies to the west coast of America, even conducted wars, I have never *once* left this island. My life, since infancy to the present moment, has been closely observed—scrutinized—and carefully arranged for me. The life of a princess and a queen, whilst pregnant with education and luxury and endless opportunity, is nevertheless a gilded prison. I am bound tightly by protocol. I have no privacy. Until the cessation of my monthly courses, my sheets were thoroughly examined by my waiting women and my physicians. When I chose not to marry, I created an uproar which to this day has left me no peace, and when I chose to love, I was besieged by my councilors who frothed at the mouth at my outrageousness. My lover was universally despised, vilely punished for the crime of receiving my love. For political reasons as much as personal, I chose spinsterhood, and my punishment has been a Council, a Parliament, and a people who are obsessed with the name of my successor. These are not complaints, but they are the facts of my existence. An existence . . . which can be no more different than your own.

"You desire the truth of my motives, Mistress O'Malley. The truth is, I am overbrimming with curiosity about a life such as yours. You are, like myself, like my mother before me, a woman with the soul of a man. This is rare. But what is rarer still is your wealth of experience in the wide world. You have traveled, I understand, as far as Africa. You have won the loyalty of many hundreds of men, captained fleets of ships, boarded enemy vessels on the high seas. You have fought hand to hand with men with guns and steel. And you claim two husbands and three children of your body. 'Tis a rich life," said Elizabeth, holding Grace's eye, "and I am hungry to know it in every detail."

"Well," Grace said finally, "that had the ring of truth about it. And a deal's a deal." She stood abruptly and moved to Elizabeth's bed, grabbing a large feather pillow, then returned and thrust it at the queen. "You might be needin' to stick that under your arse, and I'd best throw another log on the fire."

Elizabeth, bemused, did as she was told, pushing back amongst the cushions till she was comfortable. Grace was suddenly in charge of the evening, the queen a guest in her own apartments. Filling Elizabeth's cup and then her own, Grace began to speak.

FIRST YOU SHOULD know about Owen O'Malley. Know how I loved him. Adored him. I worshiped the boards he walked upon, my father, for had Owen not burned with that great fearsome soul, had he not loved me so peculiarly, I can promise you I'd not be sittin' here this night, eye to eye with the very Queen of England, she as hungry for my story as a starvin' man for a meal. Indeed, there'd naught be a story a'tall. Here is the truth, and no one would argue it: Owen O'Malley did nothing less than save his daughter from the hell of oblivion—the fate of a mere Irish wife—and delivered her to the wide ocean of freedom. For that I am grateful and eternally bound. For that I owe him my very life.

He was a large man, tall, and broad at the shoulders, handsome and dark. I do remember when his hair was still pure black and hung about his shoulders like a thick fur cape. A fringe of it crossed his wide forehead, here and there curlin' down below his deep brown eyes, eyes set far apart that flashed, or gleamed, or twinkled—dependin' on his mood. His hands were large and callused and he used them to tell a story, sometimes tuggin' at the full black beard that covered the whole of his prominent jaw. He had lungs like bellows, which he needed to shout his orders over the howlin' wind and crashin' of waves on deck. Aye, he had a wild appearance, and was so powerful that when he walked, the very ground would shake beneath his feet. 'Twas easy to see why they'd clapped him with all the monikers they did—"Black Oak," "The O'Malley," "High Chieftain of Connaught," "King of the Western Sea." He was all those things, and there was no one in the wide world like him.

You'd think from that description that the man was a brute, an animal.

But he was kind, as kind a man as I have ever known. That bellowing voice could be soft as a whisper when he put me on his knee and drew me in close to weave me a tale. The muscles in his arms, hard as iron, were as comfortable as any mother's embrace. And the thing of it was, Owen O'Malley loved me every bit as much as I loved him. This was very odd, a man lovin' his daughter to distraction. 'Twasn't done, you see. Fathers naturally loved their sons, and only after the boys had received their share of affection did the girls get any a'tall. But Owen never did anything the way he ought to have done, only the way he saw *fit*.

And I was the apple of his eye—thick black curls and bright dark eyes, round ruddy cheeks and, like him, a mighty pair of lungs that could wake the dead.

My mother always claimed 'twas on account of my resemblance to Owen's mother that he loved me so. Black-eyed Maria from Spain, who my grandfather, Dermot O'Malley stole away from the warm lazy hills of her father's Andalusian vineyard to come to western Ireland, where the wind howlin' down off of Scotland is so freezin' cold that even the cows cry.

Of course Owen was of the sea, by the sea, for the sea. 'Twas the mother of all life, he said, the only place that wisdom was revealed. The truth was more practical. The sea meant *freedom* to Owen O'Malley, a passport to foreign lands, exotic destinations, the warm sun of Spain in the dead of Irish winter. When I glimpse him now in my mind's eye, it's at the helm of the *Dorcas*, his favorite ship, the wind lashin' his face and hair, causin' his heavy cloak to cling on one side to the tall mast of his body, and flap like a broken sail on the other. He was a human wind vane, and I would always know the directions of the breeze just from the sight of him.

There were lessons I learned from Owen O'Malley—to treat kindly with your crews but brook no complainin', nor warfare within, for these men were clan and therefore family. "Without," he used to say, "are the enemies, the monsters, and we will lose everything if we fight between ourselves." Indeed, Owen's code extended to his family on land as well—to his castles, his booleys, the *septs*, and the whole of the O'Malley territories. Sure there were lapses. Crimes of passion. Crimes of drunkenness, thievery, and youthful rape. But the cattle raids that were the curse of the clans all over Ireland and caused the greatest death and misery were absent in his reign. For he had sworn covenants with the neighbors on every side of him—the O'Flahertys to the south in Connamara, the Lower Burkes to the north in Mayo, and the Thomases to our back—so my childhood was one of peace and tranquility.

Bless my father. Bless his soul for that.

My mother, well, my mother, God love her, she tried. Bein' married to a man as strange and stubborn as Owen O'Malley was one thing. But havin' me for a daughter on the top of it dearly tried her good nature. Margaret O'Malley never knew what to make of me. 'Twas a constant fight, my upbringing. Once I was out of nappies, Owen wanted me with him wherever he went—riding to the boundaries of his territories, hunting fallow deer. But most of all on his ships. His great compulsion was that I should come to love the sea as he did. And he was not disappointed. Perhaps it was the tender age at which I walked the boards, toddled them, really, but I never did fear the wide ocean nor the fearsome winds nor even the mountainous waves. They and my father's fleet were as natural a home to me as the green rolling hills of Murrisk or the bogs of Clare Island. My first and favorite memories were of Owen standin' me on a crate before the wheel to reach it, he urgin' me to "steer" the ship while of course he stood behind, eye on the horizon, his own huge hands holdin' her steady.

My poor mother. She argued with her husband and argued to no avail. Concerns that I'd grow up unfit for a good wife and mother fell on deaf ears. And all her attempts to teach me the womanly skills were ignored. That's not to say she taught me nothing. She was, even more than my father, a keeper of tradition, of everything Gaelic. If Owen forced me into learnin' at the monastery how to study Scripture, how to read and write in Latin—for that was the universal language of trade—my mother imbued in me the old ways, the ancient religion, worship of the goddesses of water and war.

We were a small family, just my mother and father, my brother, and me. You might think Donal Piopa would have coveted the affection my father lavished on me, but from the beginning he was a child unto himself. 'Twas strange how purely satisfied he was with his own life. He cared nothing for the sea, and while he gave my father all the respect due him, he never strived for the sea nor any livelihood it afforded. He took pleasure from the land and the great herds of cattle which, along with my father's maritime ventures, constituted our family's wealth. He saw to the beeves and the sheep and the small Irish horses, lovin' to ride across the rocky hills and marshes, keeping the boundaries of the Murrisk barony safe from intruders. And his character therefore developed fiercely, in the O'Malley tradition, though not as a seafaring man, but of the land. Later, in the rebellion, he became a great warrior, and that was why they called him "Piopa"—Donal of the pipes that the Irish played in battle.

My father was full of appreciation for my brother, that he never raised a stink about his favorite bein' his daughter and not his son, and for findin' his own way in life. I loved my brother too, and remember most fondly the times we'd ride out together in the summer, hunting with our great hounds, animals so mighty one could, by itself, take down and kill a full-racked fallow deer in the blink of an eye. Like everyone else, Donal thought me an odd child, but he rarely teased me and never abused me, and for that I was altogether grateful.

How do I describe the territories of the O'Malley clan? 'Twas water as much as land in the first place, the rivers and lakes amidst the inland fastnesses—rolling hills and bogs on the mainland, Crough Patrick where the sainted man himself ascended to its peak for his fast of forty days. And most important Clew Bay, wherein the family's slew of islands and sandy reefs lay. The largest, Clare Island, where the castle of my childhood summers stood guarding the inlet to the bay; the small isles without—Inishturk, with its great cliffs and wild boars that roamed the windswept highlands; Inishbofin, with its tight-necked harbor and castle too; Inishark, a mere rock in the ocean; and Cahir, the holy place where none but holy men lived in stone huts. And of course there was the wide Western Sea beyond, which the O'Malleys claimed a part of as their own. Whosoever should wander into those waters were wise to know that. Fishing fleets from England, France, the Low Countries, even Spain, paid my father well for the privilege of fishing there. And 'twas to him they came when they wanted their vessels piloted safely along those treacherous shores.

Galway was the closest town of any size or import, the heart of trade for Ireland, and in those days England too. But the city fathers of Galway were a spineless lot, scared of their own shadows, and built great walls round about them to protect the citizens from the likes of us. Their laws were made to keep us out—O'Malleys, O'Flahertys, Burkes—we all were kept from doin' our business there. The truth is, the city feared us, shat themselves with terror at the thought of their country neighbors. A sign that hung above the gate of Galway City told it all. "From the ferocious O'Flahertys, good Lord deliver us." Have you ever heard of anything so lame as that?

The sea was our home but the land sustained us too. In my youth the pastures were green and rich, supporting our vast herd, the farming tracts large in their bounty. There was never a man, woman, or child who wanted for food. There were great forests, dark and mysterious, where my brother Donal and I would go to scare ourselves, pretendin' the monsters and wicked fairies who lived there were out for our blood, and we'd battle them with our wooden swords, whose use I had learned from my father.

The O'Flahertys of Connamarra were our neighbors to the south, and our friends. The tie that bound them to the O'Malleys was the sea, for they were an old seagoing clan of great renown, great as the O'Malleys were—their fleet as mighty, their sailors as apt. And they had been so since ancient times. 'Twas written that the High King of Connaught never went out to sea or high sea without the fleets of the O'Flahertys and O'Malleys protectin' him.

Gilleduff O'Flaherty had been our father's friend since childhood, they playin' together in the same wood as we had, even sailing out together once—a journey to the Barbary Coast on my grandfather's vessel. It must've been memorable, for the two were thick as thieves from that time on. Brothers were never closer. 'Twas on that voyage, they liked to say, that they planned the marriage of their children to one another. Swore that if, when they married and sired a girl and a boy, they'd one day join the clans by ties of matrimony. And so while all the other clans in Ireland were raiding and murdering and pillaging their neighbors, our two families, who might have been enemies clawin' at each others' throats for the title of "Sea Kings," were sharing the wealth of it instead. They were two of the wisest men I ever knew.

The times I spent on my father's ships were nothing short of a miracle. What other little girl in Ireland—or the *world*, I used to think—was blessed with such excitement and adventure? Even the fishing expeditions in local waters were amazing. The rush in your chest the moment a fair wind took the sails, the ship speedin' across the waters. Sometimes you felt as thought you were in flight, racing with the sea birds. 'Twas magnificent, truly magnificent. And where else could you stand amongst so many big, strapping men at congenial work, smell the salt air, behold the workings of a fine ship, sails flapping, the noise of the tackles and winches hauling nets crammed with wriggling silver fish? The best part was, the sailors put me to work as soon as I was able. Taught me all the nautical knots, and my nimble little fingers were soon better than anybody else's at fixing a broken net or a snagged line. I came to love the smell of pitch and wet wood. Indeed, life onboard was a sight fresher than the air inside our castle rooms.

My mother never knew that the moment we put to sea and were out of her sight, I'd rig myself in boy's clothing—woolen breeches, a linen shirt, short jacket waterproofed with wax, my long hair braided and tied up close to my head and covered with a cap. Like all the men I went barefoot on the slippery deck. Truly, a ship was no place for a girl, so I would become for all intents and purposes a boy. Margaret, God bless her, would have died of mortification had she known.

Sometimes we'd head north for Scotland, and 'twas on those trips I first met the great Scots clans and their chieftains—the MacDonalds, the MacSweenys, and the MacDowells. These were the fierce men I'd later ferry across to Ireland to fight with us against the English. The Scots Gallowglass are hands down the best fighters in the world—perhaps because they're all a bit off their heads. But in later years they remembered little Grace, a tiny sailor standin' on deck by her da, so proud.

But nothin' compared to the long trips south to Portugal and Spain. Oh, the feel of the air and the water turnin' warm, the great chill of Ireland left behind, days of bright sun on the sea. There was somethin' delicious about such a day, my father takin' me aside for a lesson in pilotage. He'd haul out a big chest he kept in his cabinet and unroll a map of the coastlines from Ireland to Africa. Then he'd take me up on deck and we'd survey all within our sight. Much of the time we traveled not far from the shore, except a dash out of sight of land, across the Bay of Biscay. Owen would point to a hill or promontory, then stick his finger on the map and say, "There she is, and farther on down is the mouth of the such and so river, and here is a safe landfall." And I loved that, knowing what we were seeing with our eyes was actually a point on one of my father's maps. 'Twas nothin' really, but for a child it felt a small miracle. He had rutters too—maps of the sea floor—and these he made me study with great care. For there were rocks and shoals and shallows that, unaccounted for, could sink a ship. So by the age of twelve I knew the ocean below and its currents, as well as the myriad points along the coast. My favorite of the fabulous sea creatures were the gray whales, which we would spot when they rose themselves from the water to a considerable height, only to crash down again with such great weight and force that no matter how many times I saw the animals, I marveled at them.

Come the foul weather—and the foul weather would always come—there would be more lessons, these taught in a sterner voice, for these were lessons of life and death. I learned how to smell a storm on the way, the signs in the sky, on the wind, on the water. Even by the birds and fish. When the wind howled and waves were moving mountains, threatening us every moment with destruction, Owen would take me below and lash me to his bed so I'd not be tossed about and injured. Later, when I was older, he'd allow me topside, but lashed me to a fat mast, for he knew that if the sea ever claimed me in this way—if he were not also killed by the storm—he'd surely be killed by my mother.

My father at the wheel had the look of a Fury, black mop of hair clingin' wet to his skull, eyes blazing, spitting curses that he should be forced to do battle with his old friend the sea. I'd watch the brave sailors manning the decks, waves breakin' over 'em, time and time again. Owen's courage and the steady hand of Providence would always protect us, and it was in those terrible storms I lost all fear of the water and came to see it as my home. You could say I was bred to the sea, and though there were times in my life when I was kept from her, the saltwater was always there in my blood.

Like I said, 'twas my father who taught me to fight. He'd carved a couple of wooden swords—mine he'd made to fit my small hand. He was skilled as a swordsman, but the size of him, and the passion with which he wielded his blade made him a deadly force to reckon with. Not havin' Owen's size I at least inherited his passion and became an able fighter, surprising more than a few men who crossed their swords with mine.

When we'd dock in the foreign cities, I'd go down to my father's cabin, open the cupboard holding my belongings, and strip off the garb of a cabin boy. I'd give myself a good scrub, wash the salt from my hair till it shone black again, and put on a pretty gown, likely somethin' Spanish that my father'd bought me on the last trip, that I'd now grown into.

Owen'd take my hand and march me down the plank into town. He was so proud with me by his side. We'd go round to the homes of the factors who purchased his goods for selling at a higher price. These were great villas filled with gorgeous wares and oddities from every corner of the world. There were the long teeth of elephants that I marveled at, skins of African horses with black and white stripes, tapestries from the east, bolts of silk in fabulous colors I never knew existed. There were walls full of weapons of every shape and size, curved scimitars and short daggers with jeweled handles. As I wandered round, peeking at these treasures, I could hear my father striking his deals with the factors. He always got the best price for his goods, hides and tallow, cloth and fish. The more he made the more he'd have to spend on wine—that commodity for which he was best known—to import back to Ireland.

But lest you think my whole childhood was spent aboard his ships or in exotic lands—though I would have been quite content had that been the case—the better part of my time was spent in Connaught, in one of my father's castles near the sea, or in Clare Castle on an island of the same name.

Mind you, these were not castles as *you* know them, but four-square, storied keeps. They were built hundreds of years ago by O'Malley chieftains for strongholds against their enemies, and were truly impregnable. Nothin' but big gray stone boxes, you would think to see them. Tiny slits for windows—narrow as a skinny lad turned sideways—and only one door of the heaviest oak, girded with iron. The ground floor was a stable in winter, the second an armory, the third a storehouse and larder. 'Twas only on the topmost floor that the family lived, and in close quarters, to say the least. We were luckier than most, for Owen would bring back from his travels all manner of lovely things for my mother to outfit the place. Turkey carpets to warm the floor and cover the always damp stone walls. Draperies of heavy velvet, fine leather chests, and carven cupboards.

The winters in my father's castles were a struggle for me, and I braved the weather, except at its fiercest, to be out of doors. For the great stone towers, surely the best in western Ireland, and even the *bawns*—the stone courtyards around them—were like prisons to a girl who knew the freedom of the sea. Whenever she could get her hands on me, my mother plied me with instructions on proper womanhood. I'd run a house or many houses of my own when I was grown and married, she insisted, and needed to learn the making of butter and buttermilk and candles. How to spin and how to weave and how to doctor. I was interested in none of it, and I'd drive her mad with my inattention, or worse, my sloppy attempts at the given tasks. Invariably I would burn the oat-cake—a near impossibility for anyone with half a brain. My mind would wander out the window to the near neighbors in their thatched cottages of wood and stone, to fields where the cattle grazed, but mostly to the gulls flyin' past, remembering how on my father's ship we would race with the birds through the waves . . . and I would overchurn the butter and ruin it.

The only joy I had in land-bound winters was my education. I learned my Irish letters quickly from my mother who, bless her soul, defied tradition and kept me home, rather than fosterin me out at the age of seven like most children. She taught me numbers too. And I could read by the time I was six. But 'twas at the Abbey of Murrisk that I received my wider education—the Latin—which my father had insisted I should get. The monks there tutored me, and though they were kind and finally grew to love me, they thought it mad to teach a little girl the likes of the Roman language. What good would it do me? they often asked my father. To tell the truth, Owen never offered much in the way of an answer, for it was *his* abbey, built by *his* ancestors, and the monks were there by his leave, under his protection. So they did as they were told and taught me Latin and tried their hardest to instill their religion in me. Their frustration on this last account was boundless, for my father was not a religious man in the Catholic sense, and my mother was an unapologetic pagan.

I thought a lot about Jesus Christ. Thought he was a great man who died a terrible death for our sins, but I kept in the deepest regions of my heart a love of the old goddesses of nature, and the warrior goddesses who were, to me, more heroic and exciting than Jesus was any day.

The summers were a sight better, for we moved—the lot of us—outdoors to my father's booleys. These were makeshift structures, long and narrow, and thatched with rushes, built new each year and set in the midst of our upland pastures amongst our herds. Aye, we lived with our animals, somethin' the English could never fathom. But it was a marvelous thing, livin' so close to the land with the very beasts that were so great a source of our wealth. 'Twas very green and the weather soft, and the booley house smelled of fresh rushes. The women would spin and weave. And sometimes we'd hunt with our hounds, or hawk with our falcons.

There were more serious days, when the Brehon judges would come round on their circuit of Connaught to hear the civil suits, and cases of crimes committed in my father's territories. 'Twas our ancient Gaelic law that they practiced—the very one that the English and the Christian Church so abhorred and wished to destroy. They could never understand the leniency with which we punished our thieves and murderers. The English like to flog a man to ribbons, cut off his hands, his head, rip out his very bowels for such offenses. And the Spanish Inquisition with its insane tortures and burnin' people alive—quite unfathomable. Under native Irish law we demanded a payment of compensation that was equal to the crime, and paid to the family by the criminal—punishment enough. Or he lost his civil rights, became what we called an outlaw. That was much more sensible, we thought, than common vengeance.

And the Church's views on marriage were nothin' short of ridiculous. It had to be celebrated in public, and the marriage was *permanent*, for mercy's sake. We preferred to do things more clandestinelike, for marriage, after all, is a personal affair. And after a year, if the man was not up to his wife's standards, she could boot him out the door. Say, "I divorce you!" and he was gone, just like that. Canon law did agree with native law in one respect. It said that a woman could own property. Nice, you say. Sure, so the woman could leave her property to the Church! Hypocrisy, pure and simple. And the feckin' clergy—they made whores of all women who would lay with a man she lusted after. What sense is there in that?

Most congenial, the booleying life, though never as exciting as the sea.

Sure you'll be wondering, with all these cheerful stories, about the pirating, the profession of which I am a justly notorious member. Indeed, I learned it from Owen O'Malley, who was himself a pirate of great renown. I have a memory of him, on a day when a shipful of Turkish pirates had tried their best to overcome us. There'd been a moment of confusion when nobody knew who was boarding who, or on what boat the battle would be waged. Then I caught sight of my father, somethin' I will never in my whole life forget. He was standin' high on the rail, his sword outstretched, his black hair whippin' in the wind. He was raving like a Fury, roaring a thousand oaths, and his men, borne up by his passion, with their cutlasses, pistols and swords, overswarmed that Turkish ship with their own cries and curses that curdled my very blood. He was a true pirate, Owen O'Malley was, though he plied the trade more of necessity than love, for he loathed the loss of his clansmen to violent death. But that was the price that his freedom demanded, and that was the price he paid. He *was* an opportunist though, exploited the finer opportunities when they went sailin' past his nose. He never could resist seizing a ship for a fair prize.

There were loads of vessels in the local waters of course, comin' from everywhere to trade in Galway City or on their way to Scotland, and the ones that paid him proper tribute he left alone. The others were fair game—a French sloop laden with wine and brandy, a Netherlands carrack with a load of Flanders linen. The other of his favorite marks were the English "privateers." He found the whole notion laughable, really—merchants, or merchant adventurer families, who wished to profit from seafaring, not simply goin' about their business like men, makin' their way however they could and be done with it. No, they had to be thought *gentlemen*, honorable gentlemen. So they'd get a paper signed by their monarch—their "letter of marque," which, for Jesus' sake, gave them the title of privateer and *permission* to steal another man's cargo. Worse, they had to hand over a portion of their hard-won booty to the king. Equally daft was your English League of Cinque Ports. Was it not established to protect the English Channel from pirates? It was. But in no time a'tall it had degenerated itself into a right league of cutthroats who protected their own ships and attacked everybody else! The whole thing was so mindbogglingly stupid to Owen O'Malley that he took the greatest delight in relievin' the English of their cargoes every chance he got.

His fleet was large, and dependin' on the hand of Providence in any given year, consisted of between twelve and twenty ships of every variety. Some had been in the family for generations, custom-built for us, others taken as prizes. So there were carracks and cogs and roundships thanks to the English and Dutch and French. These, with their huge hulls, we used for huge cargoes. But the Venetian galleys—now these were *fighting* ships—long and sleek and low, and they boasted both sails and oars. That was the key, the oars. A nimble galley could dance a jig round a cog or a carrack, all the while keepin' safe from her broadside cannon, and firin' at will.

So the galley was my father's ship of choice for pirating. It goes without sayin' that we were expert sailors and kept the lateen sails in perfect condition, but the beating heart of the galley were the oarsmen. All clan and no slaves, they were the toughest men I ever had the pleasure to know. Arms like oak limbs and big, handsome chests that you couldn't take your eyes from. Thirty rows of sweeps, six men deep on an oar. 'Twas the greatest livin' machine on earth, the galley was.

And my father was the greatest pirate.

One summer I remember best, I was twelve, no longer a girl, not yet a woman. My mother was in a state, naggin' me to put on my Spanish gowns and act like a proper woman of my station, but of course I refused.

This particular year Gilleduff O'Flaherty and his family came to our booley for a visit. 'Twas strange and wonderful, the two sea kings so out of their element on land, comin' together like two jolly giants, great bear hugs and backslaps, good-natured curses and laughter all at once. But there was talk of our two families bein' joined in matrimony—me to that truculent rascal Donal O'Flaherty. I whispered to my mother that if I were forced to marry the snot-nosed little thug, I'd do as Brigid of Kildare had done when pressed to marry—thrust her finger into her eye, pullin' it from the socket till it dangled from her cheek. Marriage, I thought. Me, a married woman. Impossible! And wife of a chieftain at that, for the truth was, my intended was *tanaist* of the O'Flaherty clan. This meant that—as tradition dictated—when the current O'Flaherty chieftain died an election would be held by the *septs* for the title. It so happened that Donal's father, Gilleduff, was not the high chieftain, but Gilleduff's brother, "Donal Crone" O'Flaherty, was. So the election of young Donal, while in this case expected, was never a foregone conclusion. We Irish were alone, of all countries, in this way of choosing our leaders. Everywhere else in the world 'tis a firstborn son who's heir to the title—in England, your primogeniture—and no questions asked. But *tanaistry* was how the Irish chiefs were made, and it had always served us well.

Aside from wishin' the ground would open up and swallow me whole to save me from Donal O'Flaherty, I remember a fierce debate that my father and Gilleduff had one afternoon sittin' over the roast at the long booley table. They were talkin' of King Henry the Eighth's "Surrender and Regrant" program, a topic of unrivaled possibility for disagreement—a rare bounty for two men who'd give their right arms for a good argument.

"Most of the other chieftains in Connaught have succumbed already," said Gilleduff, and Henry calls himself 'King of Ireland.'"

"King Henry is a buffoon," Owen snapped. "He could've been a great man, comin' as he did from good Welsh stock, but he's so addled with women he has no time for important things."

"The way I see it," Gilleduff said, "is that England—no matter how bloody or ignorant its king—will conquer Ireland in the end, for one reason and one reason alone."

"And what is that?" demanded my father.

"Centralized government. Loyalty from all—or most—of the great lords of the land to one ruler. What have we got here? A hundred chieftains who think of themselves as the 'High King' of a valley, four hills, and a lake. And every one of 'em, 'cept you and me, are murderin' and thievin' and pillagin' one another year after bloody year. We've weakened ourselves so miserably, it's no wonder that when the chiefs are offered the English titles, they take 'em."

"Well, *you* don't mean to surrender, do you?" my father said, glaring.

"It's only a name," argued Gilleduff, trying to provoke my father to passion.

"So why submit? I know this as sure as I'm sittin' here across the roast from you. They're tryin' to bury our law and eradicate our language. And once they take your name, they'll take your freedom too."

"No one's goin' anywhere with my freedom. And don't worry yourself, Owen. If I do accept myself a fine English title, I promise I won't insist that *you* call me by it."

"That's very kind of you, you feckin' idiot."

Gilleduff laughed and punched my father in the shoulder. Owen laughed too. I myself was too young to know how right my father had been, or how the English army would one day, in the not so distant future, somehow make it across those impenetrable forests and bogs of Ireland, and smash our sea defenses, all in the name of murderin' the old Gaelic order, our very way of life. But it was a warm summer night, and we were booleyin', and the bard was settling down by the fire to begin his telling of histories and generations back through the mists of time. And we soon forgot about the English and their titles and their fears of the "Wild Irish" out beyond the Pale.

By my fourteenth year, despite my attempts to forestall it, I was showin' all the signs of womanhood. My head of thick black hair was my one concession to femininity. Even I had to admit it was gorgeous. But never, I believed, did a child loathe the prospect of adult life as much as myself. My mother, on the other hand, could not contain her glee, for my impending maturity meant that my unrepentant wildness and irresponsibility were soon to be history.

Then one afternoon in March my father returned home from inspecting his fleet and announced he'd be sailin' with three ships for Cadiz in a week's time. My mother and I were simultaneously rooted to the spot like a couple of elms, and struck just as dumb. Her mind was clearly racing as fast in one direction as mine was in the other, and we both stood starin' at my father with such silent ferocity he concocted some lame excuse, and got the hell out of there.

Then the screamin' began.

I would accompany my father to Spain over her dead body. *I would throw myself off the peak of Crough Patrick if I couldn't go.* I was a young woman preparin' myself for marriage and childbearing and had no business on a stinking ship with a hundred horny sailors sniffin' round me. *She was a foul-tempered, wild-arsed bitch who knew nothin' about nothin'.*

She struck me for that, of course, and I deserved it. Such language, she announced haughtily, was the best argument for my not goin'. Where else would I have learned such crude oaths besides on my father's ships?

I rushed away in tears, with her screamin' after me that I was not the only one who would feel her wrath. This was all my father's fault, and he would reap the whirlwind of her displeasure the next time he showed his hairy face to her.

I ran, my face streamin' with tears, down to the beach past the men caulking their curraghs and mending their sails. When I could go no farther, I fell to my knees and wept inconsolably. Had I sailed my last voyage with Owen? Was that blessed freedom I had always known from this time on only a memory? I cursed my mother. I cursed her goddesses and I cursed Jesus, all to pretty much the same degree, which was substantial. And I even thought for a brief moment of carryin' out my threat about leapin' off Crough Patrick. For what would my life be without the sea? Then I thought to myself, *Christ, I'm a freak of nature, a woman who hopes never to marry or bear a pack of squallin' brats. All I want is to sail round the world with my father and a crew of brawny Irishmen.*

But my fate was sealed. Even my father was set on my marryin' Donal O'Flaherty. The truth was, a young woman of marriageable age had no business workin' and livin' amongst all those manly sailors. Then all of a sudden it hit me: *I'd not go to Cadiz as a girl. I'd go as a lad.*

I ran back to a beach shack that held the fleet's various tools and ropes and netting and extra sails, then quick pulled out my knife and cut a long, thin strip of canvas from one of the ragged old sails. Unlacing my bodice and chemise I pushed them down so I was standin' there stark naked from the waist up, then began wrapping the cloth round and round my breasts, pushin' 'em flat, bindin' 'em tight as I could manage and still be able to breathe. That done, I grabbed a shank of my mane and, gripping the knife in my hand, *chopped it off,* down to within an inch of my skull. I took another handful and hacked that off too. Back, front, and sides— I cut 'til I was shorn altogether. I saw some clothing somebody had left hangin' on a peg and donned it. Finally pulling a wool cap over my head I left the shack and started down the beach, finding to my delight that none of my father's men workin' there recognized me as I passed. I lurked near the keep 'til Owen returned home and went in. Climbin' the stone stairs like a condemned man on his way to execution, I managed to pull myself up to my full height, stick out my chest—what was left of it—and stride into the room.

Margaret and Owen stared at me openmouthed, first as if I were an intruder, then an apparition, perhaps the ghost of some long-dead relative drowned in a shipwreck.

"Grace?" 'Twas my father speakin', actually a whisper was more like it. He recognized me first, as he'd seen me dressed as a boy before.

"What's goin' on here?" my mother said in a highly suspicious tone. Her eyes were fixed on my head. Clearly there should've been lumps and bumps where my thick mop was stuffed under the cap, but it was layin' awfully close to the skull.

"Grace. What have you done?" Owen said, very quiet like.

"I'm goin' with you, Da, to Cadiz. One last time. Mam said a young woman didn't belong on your ship." I reached up and pulled off the cap. My mother gasped, even though she knew in her heart what was comin'.

Suddenly, and to my complete surprise, my father snorted quite loudly, a sure attempt at stiflin' a laugh. My mother turned and glared at him venomously, but that was all he needed. He began to roar laughing. Doubled over he was, tears runnin' down his face and into his beard. He wouldn't stop, or couldn't, and his laughter was so rollicking that my mother started too. 'Twas me, shocked that I hadn't been killed by the pair of 'em for my outrageousness, who laughed last. They both hugged me, and my mother cried, and I cried, and finally when my brother Donal came home and found us in this condition, and me with my chopped hair, he nearly shat himself. In honor of the occasion, he gave me a new name, "Granuaile," which is Gaelic for "Grace the Bald." And the funny thing is, it's stuck with me all my life.

So in the end I traveled with my father to Spain one last time. 'Twas a grand journey, the memory of which I'll always treasure. Owen was so gentle with me, makin' sure the crew's teasing about my hair was kept to a minimum, and that I had my privacy on the days I bled. Though I looked more that voyage like a boy than I ever had, my father treated me more like a woman. God, he was a dear man. When the sailin' was smooth, we'd stand together gazing out over the horizon and he'd talk to me about the things I would need to know in this life, once I was far from his house and protection. The way of the world was extremely harsh, he said, even for a woman of my standing. He told me what made for a good man, a good husband, the virtues of honesty and kindness first and fore-most. There were other things as well, easy laughter being one of 'em. And he said the one thing a man could under no circumstances do with-out was respect for himself, for such a lack would poison his life, and every other person's around him. He wasn't sure what kind of husband Donal O'Flaherty would make me, for the boy had a temper on him that was troubling, but Donal's father, Gilleduff, was a rock, and would be a good friend to me should I need one.

Finally we sailed into Cadiz. Oh, 'twas the grandest city of southern Spain. Most of the town was built on an island just off the coast and it, together with a portion of the mainland, enclosed a fabulous harbor. This was always filled with great ships from every part of the world, for Cadiz was the gateway to the Mediterranean Sea, the Barbary Coast, and to the east, the land of the Turks. The city itself, with a great fortress at the head of the bay, was astonishing in its variety. There were markets filled with exotic goods, and faces in the crowds the likes of which I'd never seen. Turks, and Blackamoors—some who were slaves and others who were masters—Indian traders and Mongols, even Chinamen. And there were, of course, the Spaniards and Italians, French and German, so every language in the world was spoken there, like the Tower of Babel, it sometimes seemed.

Of course I was desperate to go ashore with him, but I had the prob-lem of my hair, and though he'd offered to buy me a proper lady's wig I said no thank you—the thought of wearin' somebody else's cut hair gave me the willies. So he brought me a suit of clothes fit for a young grandee—a suit of blue satin, silk stockings, and fine blue-leather shoes. Gloves and a feathered hat finished the picture. When I presented myself thus to my father, he smiled, stifling his laughter, for he knew I'd be mor-tified if he laughed. Instead he strapped to my waist a sword that clanked heavily at my side when I walked, and together we climbed down to the dinghy and let ourselves be rowed across to the city.

On Cadiz Island Owen took me to see the fort at the mouth of the harbor and said 'twas a splendid ediface, one of the strongest he'd ever seen. He took especial note of the artillery—*huge* cannon facing out into the harbor, set into the walls which, he claimed, were twenty feet thick. He coveted those guns. A direct hit from one of 'em would blow a ship to Hell and back. 'Twas lucky for the enemies, he said, that the Spanish were such notoriously terrible shots.

We strolled the streets and plazas of the city for the rest of the afternoon and night. He, to my great dismay, bought me fine Egyptian sheets for my wedding chest. Finally, after supper at the city's best inn, we made our way back toward the dock where our three ships lay at anchor.

We had no warning of our attackers, for they jumped from the shadows on either side of us. 'Twas fortunate there'd been only two of them. Surely they'd meant to rob us in the dark alleyway, and they must've been desperate in the extreme to attack a man the size of my father, even if he were accompanied only by a slender young "lad" like myself.

The moment they were on us I felt a rush in my blood and a strange taste of metal in my mouth. My hand found my sword and I drew it as easy as an intake of breath. My father had done the same, and without a word spoken we took our stance—back to back—as he had taught me to fight. There was no time to think, for the robbers were armed with swords as well, and as I said, desperate. The man I was fighting was terrible to behold—filthy, with a fresh scar across half his face, still red, stitched badly and oozing pus. He fought without grace but powerfully, his slashing wild. But my training had been better than his, and besides, I had my father's encouragement being shouted in my ear. Owen was fightin' for his life as well, but with enough confidence in his own victory to urge me on. "Slash to the neck!" he cried. "Keep his eye!" Metal met metal time and again. "Hang on!" he shouted. "I'll have this bastard dead in a moment!" And let me tell you, 'twas not a moment too soon, for the man I opposed, though not as agile or skilled as I, was certainly stronger, and this was takin' its toll. His crashing blade had pushed me to one knee, and I was forced to fend off his blows from below. Then it happened. His hideous face was sneerin' down at me one second, and the next . . . 'twas *gone*, replaced by a fountain of spurting blood. My father, having vanquished his own attacker, had swiveled round and with one

sweep of his sword, had deprived mine of his head. Strangely, the man
did not fall immediately, the body shocked to be suddenly headless. So
Owen gave him a wee shove. He toppled like a felled tree. My father
quick pulled me into his arms. He was trembling and he held me so tight
I thought I'd be crushed. "Da," said I, "I'm all right, really. You can let
go of me." He did this and then raced away, leavin' those two dead carcasses in the alley.

I can tell you, it was quite a scene on the ship that night, my father
tellin' the men the story of our fight to the death, with great relish and
not a little exaggeration. He was as proud as any father of a son. For
myself I was one half proud, the other half sickened to have witnessed
such a gruesome sight not three feet in front of me. But the men were
delighted. Their little Grace—a fit fightin' partner for the great Black
Oak O'Malley. One of 'em even wrote a song about it, and though 'tis
long forgot, I think 'twas that story told over and over again for years,
every time embellished a little more—till it was *me* who'd whacked off
the robber's head—that proved me in those sailors' eyes. It brought me a
measure of esteem from them, and more important, my own self-respect.

The voyage back from Spain was part bitter—for I knew 'twould be
my last—but sweet as well, for the love that moved between my father
and me was as strong as a river tide. On the day Ireland first came within
our sight, we stood gazin' at the shore side by side. He said, "You know,
Grace, I've been meanin' to say that if Donal O'Flaherty ever lays a
hand on you, I'll kill him. But what with your performance in Cadiz, it
seems the lad's got a fair share more to fear from you than the likes of
me. I think," he continued somewhat wistfully, "that had you been born
a boy, you would've made a great noise in the world. A very great noise
indeed." He pulled me to him, wrappin' us both in his great cloak, as he
had since I was a little girl, and I cried then, for the loss of my freedom,
and bondage to the narrow life I knew was to be mine. There was not a
thing he could do to change that, for I *had* to marry. I *had* to bear children. There was simply no place for a woman at sea. So he just held me
and we watched as the coast of Ireland and my future came nearer to
embrace me.

'Twas inevitable . . . and a very sad day indeed.

So it was that I married Donal O'Flaherty. I had turned sixteen, and despite my attempts to forestall the inevitable, I'd become a woman in every way, and therefore bowed to my fate. The losses were many, first and foremost my freedoms—to travel, to assume the guise of a boy and live a boy's life at sea. Worst of all I ached for my father's company, his stories, his easy wisdom, the feel of his strong arms around me, the sight of his broad, handsome face. But it was that which he had taught me growin' up that saved me from total despair. Self-pity and complainin' had always been forbidden around Owen, and he would've been ashamed of me had I given in to brooding. The old habits of staunchness and resolve were more ingrained than I knew. So in the end I made the best of my new life and counted my blessings, which were substantial.

First of all the marriage was a welcome joining of the O'Malleys with the O'Flahertys, strengthening the friendship that had long existed. Owen and Gilleduff, closer than some brothers since childhood, were now in-laws and looked forward to their inevitable shared grandchildren. And the O'Flaherty territories were nothin' short of gorgeous. South of the O'Malley lands were, of course, the coastline and several islands. And inland, besides the rivers and loughs, forests, bogs, and rolling green hills, were the Twelve Bens, western Ireland's most magnificent mountain peaks. The O'Flahertys had built many fine strongholds, and upon his marriage Donal was given two, Bunowen and Ballinahinch. So overnight Grace O'Malley gained herself a young husband and became the mistress of two castles.

We first took up residence in Bunowen, near Slyne Head, a great keep hidden from the shore by a narrow tidal inlet that merged with the Bunowen River. The only access to the place was by a small boat across the inlet, so it felt altogether safe and secure. 'Twas a new castle—only a hundred and fifty years old—so it hadn't the mold of a thousand years clingin' to its rock walls, which made housekeeping less of a chore. There was a bawn to the north of it in which I planted a medicine garden and kept the fowl. A pretty hill called Doon was to the west of it, with the ruins of an old fort at the top. A parish church stood at Doon's foot, boasting an ancient well in memory of the "Seven Daughters"—though *whose* daughters they were had been long forgot. So together with the cottages of the Bunowen O'Flahertys that nestled round the keep, there was the feel of a small village of which Donal and I were the heart. 'Twas in some ways strange and in others altogether familiar.

I prettied up the top floor of the tower where Donal and I lived, with cushions I'd stitched—badly, for I wasn't much with the needle—but they were lovely despite me, made as they were from gaudy silks and brocades from the East. I asked Da for a gift of two elephant teeth, which I arched over the connubial bed. I should say a word about the marriage bed. In those early days it was well used, for despite Donal's obvious faults, which were to manifest themselves quite stubbornly in our years together, he was a fine bedmate. What he lacked in finesse he made up for in enthusiasm. He was a tireless young buck and sincerely craved my body, appreciatin' especially the abundant parts of me—my bosom and my arse. He frequently paid compliment to my face, which he found pretty, though all such comments were reserved for the moments when we were most intimately engaged. The other times I might as well have had the look of a monkey, for all the attention I got. But in those days I thought such behavior all a woman could expect from a husband, and in that way I was content. I myself loved makin' love. 'Twas the most I could feel the divers senses of my body. Out at sea, the work in my muscles, the stretch of my joints as I climbed the rigging, the thrill in my chest of the great ride across the waves, the explosions of our cannon in a firefight—all such sensations had been lost to me. But movin' with Donal in our bed I learned other uses for my muscles, discovered the great *internal* rush, and explosions of another kind altogether. Indeed it made the early days of our marriage bearable, and grew a fondness between us that was sufficient, though 'twas never quite love.

I could not, for the life of me, get used to the household chores, those which my mother had tried relentlessly to instill in me, and was constantly derided by Donal's nosy sister, Finula, who was quite a bit older than her brother and had been like a mother to Donal after his mam died. She was all sharp edges and points—features, body, disposition, and tone. Hard to get along with, and of course, nothin' was good enough for Donal. She was married to David Burke—chieftain of our neighbors, the Mayo Burkes—whose Gaelic title—to confuse things—was "The MacWilliam." Finula thought herself very grand indeed.

Of course the greatest blessing was the children. In truth I believed

I'd loathe motherhood, for what vestiges of freedom I still possessed would be extinguished. 'Twas a good thing my first was a girl—Margaret, after my mother—for she was as sweet as a flower, fair haired and gentle, and so easy to love. I'd thought that as she grew I'd give her some of the freedoms of a boy that I had had, but she proved as soft as an Irish summer, the most feminine of girls with no desires outside her sex.

Margaret's brother Owen was a sight too gentle for a boy, so said Donal, who'd been expectin' a small version of his warlike self. To me Owen was a lovely child who had a natural way with animals of the forest as well as the herd. This was his saving grace in the eyes of his father, for at least if Owen was not a warrior he could have a useful life in husbandry.

My third child, Murrough, was everything Donal could've wished for—a strident little brat from the moment he came squallin' into the world. He was barely out of nappies before his father made him his first wooden sword, and he terrorized his brother and sister and even tried it on me, though it was a short-lived attempt. One day he'd come pokin' at my bottom, quite vicious, with his wee sword. I wheeled round sudden like, picked him up by his shoulders, held him at eye level, and shrieked abuse at him. Well, I must've appeared a right Medusa, for the poor child shat himself where he hung. But it was the last time he meddled with his mother, I can tell you that.

Of course my fourth child was Donal himself. Jesus, he was a wild thing. Even now, when I think of him I cringe. We hadn't been long married when he earned the name that was to stay with him the rest of his life—Donal an Chogaidh, meanin' "Donal of the Battles." Very apt, that name, for every day there was a new fight to be fought. If it didn't come his way, he'd go out and find one. Failin' that, he'd invent one. It didn't matter the size of the altercation. He'd be just as happy with a dogfight as a skirmish at the border, so long as somebody else's blood was spilled and it got his own to boilin'. Excitement to Donal was every bit as important as the air he breathed.

Of course the drunkenness didn't help things much. All men like to drink, but in Donal's case it poisoned his soul. The meanest temper and the basest instincts welled up in the man and spilled out of him when he was deep in his cups, and I could see he lacked the self-respect that my father always told me was so necessary for a peaceful life.

One summer when we were booleyin', our turn came to host a gathering of the clan. 'Twas a great excitement for the children, who loved to see their cousins from all over the O'Flaherty territories, and endless opportunities for mischief. We'd set up our booley that year near a magnificent forest that teemed with red and fallow deer, and nothin' was more anticipated than the hunts in the wood.

As hostess of the gathering, sure I had my responsibilities, but I was not about to miss the hunt, not for the world. I'd done a bit of plannin' beforehand and bribed a number of the O'Flaherty women who I knew to be the best cooks and bakers and cheesemakers, to tend the fires and prepare the feast while I was off with the men. So I rode away that morning through the well-worn paths of the wood surrounded by members of my new family, altogether happy to be alive. But what I saw up ahead of me quickly dampened my spirits.

My son, Murrough, eight years old, was up ridin' there amongst his cousins, and like a perfect monster was knockin' 'em, one after the other, off the trail and into the thicket. One poor little O'Flaherty landed in a briar patch. I rode abreast of my son, and before he knew what had happened, I'd reached out and plucked him completely off his horse and onto mine. I pulled him down to the ground and grabbed him by the shoulders, shakin' him hard.

"What in Jesus' name do you think you're doin'!" I cried. "Those are your cousins you knocked into the bushes, your kin!"

"They were ahead of me," he replied, as if I were stupid.

Then Donal arrived on horseback to see what the commotion was. I told him of our son's appalling behavior.

"And so?" said Donal in much the same tone that Murrough had answered with. "That is what children do, Grace. 'Twas how we played when we were young."

"No," I said. "We were not mean-spirited like this child is. From what I've seen, our son enjoys givin' pain to others."

"Well, he'll be an ideal warrior when he grows up then," replied Donal, settin' the boy back up on his horse and slappin' its rump so that it took off with Murrough, glad to be free of his mother's clutches.

"You're teachin' our son some very dangerous lessons, Grace," said Donal with an evil eye on me. "His older brother is already hopelessly weak."

"Owen is not weak!" I cried. "He's simply good and kind."

"Good and kind will get Owen killed, you mark my words. Now I'll not waste another minute arguin' with you, you silly woman."

My mouth fell open when he said that, and I swear I would've snatched him bald right there had not a group of O'Flahertys come galloping up behind us. I didn't dare humiliate Donal in front of his kin, and anyhow they hollered at us, "What are you doin' off your horses? There's a pair of full-racked bucks up ahead, just beggin' to be taken down!"

Donal glared at me as if I'd made a special effort to ruin his day, leapt back on his horse, and disappeared into the wood. I'd suddenly lost my taste for the hunt and rode back to the booley in a state of dejection. When the hunt was finished and everybody came riding merrily home with both bucks and a couple of does as well, we started seating the family at the long trestle table, set for the feast. But I was shocked to see that Gilleduff O'Flaherty had been seated all the way at the far end of the table while his son, with great fanfare, was placing Donal Crone and his wife, Ellen, right in front of the roast. The two seats opposite them were empty, reserved for Donal and myself.

I knew that Donal considered his uncle the "guest of honor" for the day. Gilleduff's brother, Donal Crone O'Flaherty, was the clan's high chieftain and my Donal worshiped him, honored him excessively and always kissed his arse. I quick went up behind him and pulled my Donal aside.

"What's your father doin' at the low end of the table?" I demanded. "Why is he not near the roast with his brother?"

"Because his brother is The O'Flaherty," replied Donal with an ugly sneer, "and Gilleduff is not."

"But he's your *father* and deserves to be honored." The truth was, Gilleduff, as Owen had predicted, had become a rock in my new life, a great shoulder to lean on, especially when Donal's truculence or drunkenness became too much for one person to bear.

"The chieftain of a clan and his wife are afforded the honors, Grace," he went on. "And when *I'm* The O'Flaherty, 'twill be me sittin' before the roast, and you next to me, and I doubt you'll be complainin' about it either. Now take your place at the table and shut your mouth."

Well, I was beside myself. I was not about to host a feast that would so dishonor my father-in-law, who by now I loved very dearly. So, quiet like, I came up behind Gilleduff—who was too proud a man to make a fuss—and whispered that there'd been a mistake with the seating, and that the empty place next to his son, across the roast from his brother, was meant for him. Smiling and gracious I showed him to his place, and ignoring the murderous looks from Donal, walked away, takin' Gilleduff's empty seat at the far end of the trestle.

That night in bed Donal put his hands round my neck and said, as he began to squeeze, that if I ever embarrassed him in public like that again he'd kill me. His fingers were cuttin' off the air, and I fought against panic risin' up in me. Then I got angry and did the only thing I knew would stop him. I grabbed his balls and squeezed them with a bit more force than he was usin' on my neck. He squealed like a stuck pig and fell out of bed with a great crash. I leaned down and whispered to his writhing self that if he ever so much as looked at me sideways, he'd spend the rest of his life as a eunuch. What was a eunuch? he asked hoarsely, clutchin' himself. "A gelding," I replied, and he moaned, knowing that if nothin' else, I was good for my word. I lay back smiling and thought about Owen O'Malley and how proud he'd be of me just then. And then I fell into a peaceful sleep.

I suppose it was the year that Gilleduff O'Flaherty wintered his fleet in Bunowen Inlet that my course in this world began to change. Here at my doorstop were ships and sailors and all that went hand in hand with a seafarin' life, that which was as natural to me as breathing. My father-in-law had a stone cottage overlookin' the inlet built for himself, and to my delight, began to visit Bunowen Keep with some regularity. He loved his grandchildren—even the terror-monger Murrough—and plied them, much as my own father had done, with adventurous tales from the sea. And Gilleduff—gettin' to know me better, grew to love me as well.

'Twasn't long before I was drawn down to the water where the boats were anchored. Some were beached to be worked on—caulking and refinishing, new masts and oars carved and fitted. 'Twas a joyful place for me to wander about, what with friendly seamen weaving their nets and sewing their sails, their lively arguments about foreign ports and heinous Barbary pirates and fabulous plunder. They soon learned I was more than a little familiar with it all, and that I took no offense at the colorful language and crude stories of their favorite Lisbon whores.

I made it my business to stock their medicine chests with herbs from my garden—comfrey, foxglove, and barberry. And plenty of molasses and limes, these mixed together and shot up the sailors' poor pricks in a long syringe for the poxes they'd catch in foreign ports. I replaced all the eating utensils in all the ships' galleys, and at my behest, the Bunowen women wove new sleepin' hammocks for every man in the fleet. Whatever comforts I could provide I did, and before long I'd become a welcome figure among the men.

The fact was not lost on Gilleduff and so, come spring, when the fleet went out to fish, he begged me to join them. Oh Jesus, the thought of that day still brings tears to my eyes. I doubt whether Gilleduff knew what a gift he was givin' me. I hadn't, in so many years, felt the spray of saltwater on my face, heard the song of the sails and the winches, seen the brawny sailors heavin' ho, the green waves all round me. I thought I might die of pleasure. Then Gilleduff came to me and whispered, "Take the wheel, Grace. Go on now." He didn't have to ask me twice.

'Twas pure heaven that day, and a clear light shone on my future. This was my calling, I knew it, despite my sex, despite motherhood. I'd been bred to the sea and the sea was my destiny. It was no good denyin' it. Bless Gilleduff O'Flaherty's sweet soul. He saw where I was headed and by his grace gave me the means to that road. He'd watched me at the helm that day, questioned me gently but thoroughly on navigation and weather and the handlin' of a boat, all of which, I guess, satisfied him of my competency.

The next time a Spanish ship came to our local waters, he sent me to pilot her safely through. The Spaniards were outraged of course, but it was *me* at the helm or bein' grounded on the shoals. And so I became a regular fixture on Gilleduff's boats.

There was but one fly in the ointment here. 'Twas a parrot named Molly, a green bird from Hell. Gilleduff had won the thing in a card game in Coruña, and after thirty years the two were inseparable. He kept it perched in his cabin at sea, and while at home just near the foot of his bed. Sometimes in fair weather he'd sit the bird on his shoulder and take it up on deck. You could see she enjoyed it, very proud to be perched near Gilleduff's head, and close to his red beard, which she preened 'tween the two parts of her hooked bill. They were intimate, the two of 'em—unnaturally so, I thought. Gilleduff would chew up a mouthful of food and the parrot would eat the mush out of his mouth. They'd lie together in his bed, and one day the bird he'd known as Paco laid an egg on his chest, which gave him a clue to the parrot's true sex, and so he'd renamed her Molly.

She could speak, which was eerie, and though she had many words and phrases, sounds and songs, her favorite word was "Duff," her beloved's name, which she muttered under her breath over and over again. The evil bird had no use for any of the crew, but me she detested altogether. Perhaps 'twas female jealousy, but whatever the reason, Molly would lunge at me if I got too close, and several times I sustained a painful bite. I used to ask Gilleduff why he put up with such appalling behavior from a parrot, and he always replied that Molly didn't think of herself as a bird, as if that was answer enough.

Later that summer Gilleduff took his fleet to his favorite fishing grounds, and to my great surprise and greater delight, he gave me charge of my *own* ship, a small carrack with only one sail and a crew of forty. Let me tell you, the moment those men climbed aboard and clapped eyes on their new captain—as well as they knew me from hangin' about them all winter—'twas like the air was sucked from the world. Dead silence. Nobody moved. 'Twas mutiny, bloodless and unspoken, but mutiny all the same. I knew that nobody but me could turn the tide, make them accept the command of a woman. So with hands on my hips I stuck out my chest and lifted my chin the way I'd seen Owen O'Malley do when he spoke to his crews in difficult times. I was quakin' inside but determined that these men should never know it.

"Give me this day," said I. "This one day. Demand of me what you would of a man. No more. No less. Watch me. Judge me. If I fail in your eyes, I don't deserve to be here. But if, in a fair test, I win your good faith, then you must let me stay." I looked them square in the eye and asked sincerely, "Is that too much to ask?"

They were quiet for a moment more, but then I heard a few mumbled "nos." Somebody cracked a joke about a captain with bosoms, and when everybody laughed I knew 'twould be all right—at least for the day, this one blessed day.

To tell you the truth, I cannot now remember the small points of that mornin' and afternoon, except that once we were out to sea it was smooth sailing. 'Twas strange, even to my ears, to hear commands called in the voice of a woman, but my voice was powerful enough, and the commands were sure. The sea gods to whom I'd prayed the night before must have heard me, for we took a mighty haul of herring, fillin' our holds after only half a day.

At Bunowen Harbor I took the last dinghy back to shore. The men were all waitin' there in a somber group. One of 'em stepped into the water, lifted me out, and carried me to dry land. He put me down in the middle of 'em and they just stared at me, straight-faced, for the longest time. I stared back at them, knowin' my future was in their judgment of me. Then I felt a hand on my shoulder. A pat on my back. Someone ruffled my hair, and then they began to laugh good-natured like. All at once I could see the answer in their eyes, as well as shock at their decision. I tried not to weep but it was impossible to hold back the tears. Of course they teased me for that, but it was all right, for they had accepted me as their captain, and from that day forward I was home again, where I belonged. On the beautiful Western Sea.

By now my little Margaret was of a marriageable age and had her sights set on a fine young man—one Richard Burke—*another* Richard Burke, not Finula's son—who had earned the name "Devil's Hook" for his fierceness. But unlike my Donal, his aggressions always seemed well placed and not a matter of general wildness. To my great delight they wed, and Devil's Hook became as fond of me as I was of him. My beautiful girl was well taken care of in her husband's house, and I was content.

Gentle Owen, though still a lad, had finished with his studies and was spendin' all his time with our herds. You could see he'd grow up to be a wonderful wise man, if not a leader of men. But that was fine, for his younger brother Murrough, who'd shunned schooling no matter how much I theatened him, was showin' all the signs of a chieftain in the making. Donal had taken him under his wing—which was alarming in itself—but the inescapable truth was that Murrough was his father's son in every way, and as young as he was, was already seen as the O'Flaherty *tanaist*—after Donal, that is.

Then came that awful night in May. 'Twas late and I was sleepin' when, with a terrible racket, Donal arrived home, cursing and crying. I quick lit the lamp and when the light fell on him I wished I hadn't. Donal stood there as wild-eyed as I'd ever seen him, and covered with gore. 'Twas soon apparent it wasn't his own blood, so I pressed him to know what had happened. But aside from his hideous appearance, he was raving drunk and I could wrench only a few coherent words from him— somethin' about a cattle raid on a Burke village.

"Why on earth would you do such violence to the Burkes?" I demanded. "They're our friends and neighbors. For Jesus' sake, our daughter and your sister are married to Burkes." But he wouldn't answer, or couldn't, so I peeled off the blood-soaked clothes, cleaned him as best as I could, and watched him fall into a stuperous, snoring sleep.

'Twas all very ominous and unsettling, so much so that I never slept again for the rest of the night. I was still awake when a messenger came from Donal's uncle, Donal Crone, that we needed to quick come to his castle at Moycollen. There'd been a murder. The dead man was David Burke's son Tall Walter, and he was worse than murdered. He was horribly butchered, and could we please come now?

My head was spinning. What was Walter Burke doing at Donal Crone's castle, and who on earth would have cause to kill him?

With terrible foreboding I shook Donal awake and told him the news. "Oh," he said, "Finula will be torn apart."

"And David," I added. "Walter was his natural son."

"Aye, David too."

Of course it entered my mind that Donal had come home covered in blood on the very night Walter Burke had been murdered, but though Donal was violent by nature, he had no cause in the world to murder his sister's stepson.

We dressed and rode to Moycollen, neither of us speaking, and by the time we arrived a dozen Burkes and even more of the O'Flahertys had gathered. Never was there a more somber occasion, and tensions were already mounting. 'Twas gruesome as well, for as we walked through the bawn, an old woman was leaving, carrying with her two pails of bloody water, that which had been used, no doubt, to clean the corpse of Tall Walter Burke.

One mystery was solved immediately upon our arrival, for I learned that David Burke, Finula, and David's two eldest sons had been there at Donal Crone's castle to visit Finula's kin when the murder had happened. A Brehon judge had been sent for to preside over the inquest, and so that the proceedings would be altogether fair and impartial, he was of neither the O'Flahertys nor the Burkes, but an O'Connor. As the day wore on, more and more of the families arrived, and all convened in the great stone gathering room built next to the keep.

'Twas like walkin' through a dream that day, a terrible dream. Sure there had been violence all round me growin' up, but nothin' like this had happened so close to our family. Worse, it was found that Walter had been ambushed from behind, for there were two deep wounds in his back. This meant that the murderer—or murderers—aside from the heinous act itself, were cowardly bastards as well.

But of all the events of that black day, none was worse to me than the arrival of Gilleduff O'Flaherty. I'd not seen my father-in-law for several months, as he'd been away trading in Spain. One look at his ashen face told me the man was dying. I'd seen that color in the skin before, and always on a person with the wasting disease. Gilleduff's eyes were sunk in their sockets and shone far too brightly, as though all that was left of his life force was shootin' out from his eyes. I hugged him and found that under his bulky cloak he was indeed thin. Oh, it took every bit of strength I had not to show him I knew. But at the first opportunity I fled the confines of Donal Crone's gathering room. I walked out to the river and sat, just watchin' as the tide receded, and thought how *life* was receding from Gilleduff O'Flaherty's poor body. It occurred to me then that he'd known his condition for some time, and that bringin' me into the fold with the fleet when he did was deliberate. 'Twas hard to believe he was meanin' to pass on his livelihood to me, a woman. Well, I cried then, more tears than I had shed in all of my days. Gilleduff's kindness and understanding of myself had made my existence whole again. And now the man was dying. I wondered what, under heaven, I could do to repay him, but it just didn't come to me. 'Twas gettin' late and I knew I'd be missed in the gathering room. So I started back.

Just before I reached Moycollen Village I spotted two figures standin' together behind a cottage. Comin' a bit closer I could see it was Donal and Finula. They were downwind and too far away for me to hear their words, but any fool could see they were arguin'. I was keen to know what the two of them had to argue about just now, but I could get no closer without bein' spotted myself. So I proceeded on to the castle, where the Brehon judge had just arrived.

The inquest began soon after, with all that was known about the dreadful affair brought to light. The woman who'd found Walter's body told how she'd stumbled over it in the dark. How she'd fallen and found herself covered in gore. She'd run for her husband, who'd brought a lamp, and they'd seen the god-awful sight. The judge asked her questions, in particular the time she'd found him, and whether the blood was warm or cold. Whether the body'd begun to stiffen. The judge then questioned Donal Crone to learn the state of the household the night of the murder. Who was about? Had there been any strangers in the village in the days preceeding? What was the reason for the Burkes' visit? Who was sleepin' with whom and where, and had anyone heard a commotion?

While all of this was goin' on, I watched Finula out the corner of my eye. She was sittin' there, surrounded by her family—husband David, and stepson John on one side, her father Gilleduff, on the other. She kept wipin' under her eyes at her cheeks and snifflin', but I could see that her eyes were *dry*. She was playactin' her grief, I was sure of it. And then the Brehon judge called Walter's brother John to testify. Here was a man with a clear motive, next in line, as he was, for the MacWilliamship, after Tall Walter Burke. The judge wanted to know whether John had been in bed all through the night. Might he have been wanderin' round the castle or grounds? Might he have seen or heard somethin' amiss?

Had I not been so carefully regarding Finula I would have missed the change in the angle of her eyes. She was gazing at my husband, sitting beside me. And turning ever so slightly, I could see he was gazing right back at her!

'Twas like a swift kick in the belly, seein' that look pass between 'em. 'Twas collusion, pure and simple. Shortly thereafter Finula excused herself and left the gathering room. I slipped out quiet like and followed her. She was headin' for the keep, I figured, to relieve herself. She took the long climb to the top, and like I suspected, she entered the privy chamber off Donal Crone's living quarters. A small room, it jutted out a bit from the main wall and had a ledge with two holes cut in it for doin' your business. The tide far below would wash it away.

I followed her up the stairs and marched into the wee chamber just as she was pullin' up her gown and settlin' herself over the hole. She looked up at me, her face the perfect picture of annoyance.

"Can you not give me a little privacy, Grace? 'Tis a terrible time for me after all. I've just lost a son."

"Not a son, Finula," said I, moving farther into the privy, crowdin' her a bit. "A *step*son."

"I brought him up from a boy and I loved him just as much as I love my Richard."

"Really?"

"What are you sayin', Grace?" Finula's eyes were two slits in her face.

"With Tall Walter out of the way, your Richard would be one step closer to the MacWilliamship. Only one more brother to dispose of."

She came at me then, all fangs and claws, but she hadn't counted on my strength, which was, from my work on the boats, far superior to her own. I slammed my sister-in-law up against the wall and pinned her there by her shoulders. She fixed me with the most withering look, one with which I'd seen her demolish many a strong man. But it had no effect on me.

"How could a woman take down a man the size of Tall Walter?" she hissed at me.

"You've got no blood on your *own* hands, Finula, and we both know why. Donal O'Flaherty came home last night covered in Walter Burke's gore. My question is, how in Jesus' name did you get him to do such a terrible thing? And why? What was in it for Donal?"

Finula refused to answer me, just kept up the withering gaze. I could feel her squirmin' beneath my hands, but I wouldn't let her go. "You'll tell me," I finally said, "or I'll bash your head up against this stone wall till it's nothin' but pulp." I gave her shoulders a wee jolt then, so she'd know I was able to carry out my threat.

Then her eyes went cold and dead, and the sight of 'em chilled me through and through. I almost wished in that moment that I'd not forced the truth from her, for clearly that was what I was about to hear—and it could not be less than horrifying.

"You think you're so smart, Grace O'Malley," she said. "Well, the truth is, you know nothing. You think your husband is a fearsome warrior, that your son Murrough takes after his da. You're wrong. Donal is *my slave* and always has been. He killed his mam in childbirth and never had a mother besides myself. When he was small he was a weakling, scared pissless, with no spirit of fight in him whatsoever. Our father was always away at sea, and so it fell to me to care for the poor child. I was there for his every need. Changed his shite-filled nappies, dried his tears, held him when he was scared—and he was scared of everything. Finally I grew disgusted with him. What would become of such a boy? Surely with such a nature he'd be passed over for *tanaist* to the O'Flaherty clan. And a girl like myself was much more highly thought of with a strong brother at her side. This child would only bring shame to the family.

"So I took Donal in hand. I hired Sean, the toughest young O'Flaherty I could find, to help me. Donal's little body needed hardening, so Sean would take him on long runs up and down the hills, climbin' trees, leapin' across streams. Donal'd come home exhausted, in tears, his skinny legs cramped and aching. But there was no stoppin'. I found him a teacher of the sword who was a great believer in harsh treatment makin' a man strong. So Donal suffered, was beaten mercilessly by his tutor until he began to do things right. It took years, but finally Donal began to come around. He had learned to fight, indeed, he had learned to *love* fighting. And his teacher was the first to feel Donal's wrath. 'Twas meant to be a practice, as they'd done so many times before, but on this particular occasion the man received so great a wound to his throat—an accident, Donal claimed—that he was drained of all his blood and died in agony without a word. Of course by then Donal didn't need a teacher.

He reveled in violence, and his reputation for fierceness began to grow. Before long he was named *tanaist* to the O'Flaherty title. I was well contented. I'd done my job, and my reward was a good marriage."

"Fine," I said, "so you're the one who made him into a monster, but what possessed him to kill Walter Burke?"

"He wasn't keen to do it at first. But I pressed him. Because of me, I said, he would one day be elected The O'Flaherty. All I wanted was *my* blood as a clan chief as well—my son, Richard. Donal owed me that. I swore to him that once Richard became the Burke MacWilliam, and with Donal chief of the O'Flaherty clan, they'd be allies like no others, that together they could repel the English from their borders forever. Still he refused me. Oh, don't look at me that way. You're no angel, Grace O'Malley."

"Just finish the story, Finula," said I with continuing threat.

"Well, I could see there was no movin' Donal on my present course, so I threatened him. I said if he didn't do my bidding, I would tell the world what a weak child he'd been, afraid of his own shadow. How it *really* was that he'd come to his present condition. How it had taken a young girl to make a man of Donal O'Flaherty. The stories would spread, I told him—as stories do in Ireland—and everyone would know and laugh behind his back, and he would die of shame. All I was askin' was a small favor, me—his sister—the one person in the world he owed his very life to. That was how he agreed to the murder, but I swear I had no idea he would make such a mess of the man. He told me today he'd drunk a good bit beforehand, and almost didn't do it a'tall. But he hid in the shadows, thinkin' of the shame I'd bring down on his head, and he grew wild with fury. By the time Walter passed in front of him, he'd gone a bit mad, or so he said. He claims no memory of the deed itself, which is a good thing, I suppose."

I have to say I was struck speechless by Finula's confession. What can one say to such a cold-blooded fiend? I was wracked with equal measures of horror and pity, and knew no way to make the world right again. All at once I realized Finula was tryin' to pull from my grip. I let her go and she quick settled on the hole to relieve herself. She seemed completely at ease, as though she'd just given me a new recipe for oatcake and not the details of an outrageous assassination.

I suppose I was starin' at her with a dumbfounded look, for she said, "What do you want now?" I didn't answer, still speechless. "Oh no," she said. "You don't really think you'll repeat what I've just told you. Think again, woman. That Brehon judge will impose the steepest of penalties, and on whom? I ask you. Donal could be named an outlaw, and banished. Where would that leave you and the children? Or if he levies fines against Donal, it'll ruin him, and you. I'm a woman. I have next to nothing in the way of possessions myself. They'll fine our father instead, take away Gilleduff's boats. Make the O'Flahertys pay the Burkes for their loss. So in the end, David, my husband, will be the richer, and you the poorer." Finula rose like a queen from her throne. I had still not uttered a word, nor did I move to lay another hand on her. With a final look of disdain, she turned her back and left the privy.

I stayed for a bit longer to calm myself, order my disordered mind. I walked very slow down the stone stairs and back to the gathering room where I found the judge consulting with David Burke and Finula, while all else sat in respectful silence. Clearly the inquest had proved nothing. I gazed at Donal, who was slouched in his seat, and looked at Gilleduff O'Flaherty, tall and proud, doin' his best to hide his pain. Me speaking the shameful truth about his son would probably kill him faster than the wasting disease, and Finula was right. The fines they would levy would be too heavy for Donal to pay alone. They would take Gilleduff's ships—how many I did not know. Could I open my mouth and do it to him? Could I do it to my own family?

The Brehon judge sent David and Finula back to their seats. He had taken his long staff in hand and was moving to the center of the chamber to make his pronouncements, which, of course, would be inconclusive. He'd struck the staff on the floor three times and had opened his mouth to speak when I stepped forward. I could see Donal sit up straight in his seat, and feel Finula's brimstone eyes burnin' a hole in my back. "I have somethin' to say," I began. "Evidence to bring to this inquest. I wish to be heard."

And so it was that I accused my own husband and sister-in-law of the murder of Tall Walter Burke. There was outrage, to be sure, and Finula tried to weasel out of her part in it. But Donal, miserable for what he'd done, tearfully confessed in the end. For the crime, we were made to pay

a full half of our herd to David and Finula Burke. Donal was spared out-
lawry, by virtue of his sincere confession. Gilleduff, whose two wicked
children had conspired so appallingly, was forced to sell six of his ships
to pay David Burke for the loss of a son who was *tanaist*. But after the
inquest, when everyone had left the hall, my father-in-law, great man
that he was, took me aside and pulled me close to him.

"That was a brave thing you did, Grace. And I thank you for it."

"How can you thank me?" I said. "You're poorer six galleys than you
were yesterday."

"And I also know that my grandchildren have at least one honorable
parent. And besides, it's not me that's poorer six galleys. It's you."

Gilleduff died within the year, and he left the whole of his fleet to me,
Grace O'Malley, a woman. When all was said and done, Donal and I survived with no real trouble with half our wealth taken, but it did gall me,
as Finula said it would, that all the fines paid the Burkes made her richer
in the end. She was shameless, and so the truth about her part in the
crime, comin' out as it did, affected her not in the least. The Fates took
her side as well, and her other stepson John Burke died of a pox. Richard,
her blood, was named *tanaist* to the MacWilliamship, after his father, and
more will be said of him, but later. Strange as it may seem, the murderer
Donal O'Flaherty was not relieved of his title of *tanaist* which, I suppose, says more about the Irish and their Brehon law than I can do in a
thousand words.

I could scarce believe I had a fleet of my own and crews of men loyal
to myself. Sometimes I would lie awake, torn by strange thoughts—that
I was in truth a madwoman merely dreamin' this life. That I'd wake to
find myself an Irish wife and a household drudge. But the joyful existence had kept on for too long to be a dream. I came to see that I'd been
blessed since earliest childhood with a rare existence, protected by angels
in the flesh—my father, and my father-in-law after him. So I thanked
Jesus and all the goddesses of old who I knew must have had a hand in
such a fate.

In gratitude for my blessings, I showed great kindness to my men.
Like my father I was strict but fair, and brooked no complainin'. My
sailors had the best I could afford—daily comforts and decent victuals.
Ships were clean as they could reasonably be, trapped out with spare sails

and anchors and masts. Drunkenness onboard was forbidden, though gambling—for it was my weakness too—was always encouraged.

As I'd inherited the fleet, so too had I inherited that tiny green terror. It nearly killed that parrot that Gilleduff was gone, and she glared at me so fiercely it was clear she thought that *I'd* done away with him. I left a wide berth round her when I came into my cabin, that which had been her beloved owner's before me. But the place was small, and several times she leapt at me, and once or twice sank her beak into the flesh of my arm. It took all my gumption not to murder her, but the truth was, I felt sorry for Molly. She'd lost the love of her life, and sat for hours puffed in a ball of green fluff, muttering, "Duff, Duff, Duff, Duff." Months after his death she sulked so inordinately, refusin' to eat, that she grew very skinny, her long breastbone stickin' out like a knife blade, and I thought she might herself croak. Much as I despised the bird, I owed my life to Gilleduff O'Flaherty, who'd put her in my charge. So I babied the little demon, holdin' out tidbits of food I knew she liked. Of course she took every opportunity to chomp down on my poor fingers, but before long she deigned to take the food, holdin' it in her strange clawed foot, nibblin' at it very delicate like. Soon she grew fat again, but she never showed me any signs of gratitude, and we existed side by side very warily indeed.

Me and my crews fished when the fishing was good, but I preferred traveling to foreign ports. First time out on my own I called on all my father's Spanish and Portuguese factors who, when told a woman merchant was at their door, refused to see me. When I sent the servant back to tell their master 'twas little Grace O'Malley grown up, with wares as fine as they could buy from any man, they saw me—most of them did—and once recovered from their shock, did business with me. At first they tried to cheat me, thinkin' I'd be too shy to drive a hard bargain, but they found out soon enough their mistake.

For my onshore jaunts to Lisbon and Cadiz I had, at first, surrounded myself with a party of sailors, for safety's sake. We'd visit the market squares and plazas, take in festivals. These were very frequent events, as the Spanish would find any reason a'tall to take to the streets with processions and public feasting. But it soon became clear that the men all longed to be gone to the whores and their drunken revels, and who was I to stop them, for they had earned it. So one by one I'd give them leave to leave me to my own devices.

Once alone, I found I liked it. At the inns I caused a stir—a lone woman, well dressed and unveiled, dark Spanish looks, perhaps no longer young but pretty enough. And keen to gamble, with money in her pocket. Men who didn't know me thought me a strange kind of *puta*, but if they approached with the wrong idea, I'd educate them with a few cutting words or, if needed, a quick unsheathing of a blade, held to the chin.

In those days, I had dreams of sailin' into the Mediterranean Sea. The problem was my men, who had no intention whatsoever of pursuin' such an adventure. Those were strange waters, and Irishmen hated the Moors and those fierce Turkish pirates. A face-to-face battle once in a while was all right by them, and the booty was good. But being trapped in an inland sea surrounded by their enemies was a truly hateful thought. 'Twas bad enough I'd taken them down the African coast of Guinea. We'd only gone once, to trade for sugar, dates, almonds, and molasses, which fetched a high price in the north. I'd won a Portuguese rutter in a game of dice. Of course the Portuguese and French were the only ones who knew those waters, and I was most curious for the sight of Africa. But the coast of Guinea was a hell like we'd never known—dangerous surf, an appalling climate with prostratin' heat, and strange maladies that nearly killed the lot of us. Only Molly thrived, for the heat and moisture in the air were much like that of the New World jungle of her birth. Even the beautiful fruits and wavin' palms and thoughts of their pockets lined with gold were no incentive for the crew to return. So my quest to see the whole of the great creature whose long teeth I had hangin' above my bed would simply have to wait.

Back in O'Flaherty territory, things had changed. Donal insisted we move upriver from Bunowen to the island fortress at Lough Corribe. The reason was the Joyces, a neighboring clan who had taken the mind that *they* owned the fortress and the lake, which was pure nonsense. It'd been the O'Flahertys' since time began. Perhaps some Joyces had taken exception to Donal, and this was their way of being a bone in his throat. Whatever the reasons, the besiegement was constant and was worse than annoying. The Corribe Island folk were peaceful, unused to the constant attacks, and more than a dozen had been killed. For the most part the

Joyces came up empty-handed, as Corribe was a mighty fortress built on an island in the center of the lake, and therefore hard to successfully besiege—though it didn't stop them tryin'. The raids had raised Donal's ire to an altogether new level, if you can believe that. He fought so fierce and tenacious against them he was given a new name—"the Cock"— and the fortress itself came to be known as Cock's Castle.

By now all the children were grown and my life was mine again. Donal I tolerated as a husband, though since Walter Burke's murder I pitied him his weakness as a man. His appetite for warfare never failed to amaze me, but the fight for Cock's Castle I found legitimate. Perhaps 'twas the unfairness of the Joyces' claim. In any event, I fought by his side to defend it.

But there were other changes afoot, these of much greater consequence than the ownership of a fortress on a lake. The English were beginning to make their presence felt in Connaught, and it would alter the life of every Irish man, woman, and child alive.

I'd gone to visit Owen O'Malley, whose company I craved more, and not less, as the years went on. Sure he was aging, but the man was a bull, as tall and strong and handsome as ever. My mother had passed away, sudden like the year before, and we had all mourned her, though it was Da's life left with the greatest rift.

He and I decided to sail together for old times' sake on one of his ships. 'Twould be a short trip to Scotland for the purpose of transporting Gallowglass soldiers to The O'Neill, who at that time was called Shane, a mighty northern chieftain, perhaps the most feared in all of Ireland at the time. He was fightin' a local fight and he depended upon the Scots mercenaries we brought him for his victories. 'Twas a fine journey north on the *Dorcas* with the wind at our backs. The crew were a high-spirited lot, tickled to have the infamous female pirate aboard their ship. As if they knew 'twas a special day, whales breached all round us, and my heart leapt every time they did, as it had done when I was a little girl.

Da, still The O'Malley, was privy to the latest news, which was serious indeed. By this time Henry the Eighth was dead and his two eldest children as well. You had come to the throne, pursuin' your father's Surrender and Regrant program with vigor. The English Lord Deputy of Ireland, Henry Sidney, had begun takin' a keen interest in the west—the lands beyond the Dublin Pale. He'd summoned to him the west's most powerful chieftains—the Earl of Clanrickard, and David Burke, The MacWilliam, and they had both answered his call. Clanrickard had long ago made his submission to the Crown, but no MacWilliam had ever yet surrendered, and all the other western chieftains waited for word of the outcome of that meeting.

The point, as far as Lord Sidney was concerned, was Shane O'Neill. Sidney was loath for Clanrickard or David Burke to collaborate with so powerful a northern chief, for if Shane gave back his loyalty to them and the three united, all of western Ireland might be lost. Henry Sidney was a clever man and managed with who knows what promises to extract not only support *against* The O'Neill from both chiefs, but the first submission ever from a MacWilliam. While Da knew David Burke had most likely sworn his loyalty to England for expediency's sake, it meant that Owen O'Malley, of all the western clan chiefs who'd not surrendered, now stood alone.

"As if we haven't enough worries," said Da, starin' back at the misty coastline of northwest Ireland, "Murrough ne Doe O'Flaherty is on a rampage. He's attacked the Earl of Thomond's territories and won some ground there, and just last month he trounced Clanrickard outside Galway City."

"What's he hope to accomplish?" I asked, perplexed. "Murrough ne Doe's a minor chief with very little land, and even less power."

"Well, he's makin' a name for himself. Perhaps he means to become a great chieftain."

"Brehon law won't allow it," I argued.

Owen's face was grim. "Brehon law . . . ," he said but never finished. I knew he was thinkin' the old laws, the Gaelic way of life, were under attack and might be lost.

"Da—" I began.

"I won't surrender, Grace." The tone of his voice was dire. "I will never submit to the English Crown. I'll die first, I swear I will."

The hand I placed on his arm found him trembling, for he was the last of a breed of proud men, and he could clearly see the future of Ireland loomin' ahead. It sickened him, but he was old, and all his allies were dead or had forfeited the Gaelic order to the English, believin' it the only way to preserve an ounce of power in the ever changing world. Then Owen looked at me, stared deep in my eyes, and I could tell he saw my own future there as clearly as he saw Ireland's.

Not two months later I was home with Donal at Cock's Castle when Donal Crone O'Flaherty came bangin' on our door. He was in a state all right, red-faced and furious, with veins bulging in his forehead. "The feckin' Queen of England has decided that Murrough ne Doe is too dangerous to ignore and too fierce to overcome."

"What does she know anyhow?" said Donal. "He's a lesser chief and totally insignificant."

"That's what you'd think, but *no*. Lord Deputy Sidney has asked for Murrough ne Doe's submission, and he's given it quite willingly."

"But what does a submission from someone like that mean?" said I.

"That's what I'm tryin' to tell you. The English have thrown down Gaelic law, *deposed* me—the legitimate chief—and named Murrough ne Doe The O'Flaherty!"

"They have no authority to do that!" I cried.

"Well, they've done it. And Murrough is prancin' about with his new title like he properly earned it."

I caught sight of Donal out the corner of my eye. He was pacing before the fire and it was clear by his black expression that he understood the implications of such an act. For if Donal Crone was no longer The O'Flaherty, then my husband was no longer *tanaist* to that title.

The world we knew had suddenly, unalterably changed.

"We'll fight this!" Donal cried. "To the death!"

"Indeed we will," Donal Crone agreed. "And God damn the English!"

I was with them, of course, and I offered the support of my fleet for their battles. They would need the Scots Gallowglass to bolster their troops, and supplies and arms delivered. Yet I remembered the look in my father's eyes, and saw his fears for the future suddenly realized. How, with a mere stroke of the quill, the Queen of England had overruled a thousand years of Gaelic law, and how from this day forward a monarch—not our own—would stand with one foot planted squarely on the beating heart of Ireland.

David Burke, The MacWilliam, shortly thereafter renounced his submission and rebelled against the Crown, with Donal Crone and Donal O'Flaherty fighting by his side. But the English troops were strong and brilliantly armed, and David Burke—defeated—was forced for a *second* time to submit to Sidney. Within the year, he died. 'Twas shame that killed him, I'm sure of it. Like my father, he'd been born into a world where a chieftain knew the boundaries of his lands, and within those bounds he ruled undisputed. Shorn of his dignity, David Burke could simply not live. Finula lost a husband and Richard Burke a father. Richard, too young yet for high chieftain, stepped aside and Shane Oliverus Burke donned the MacWilliam mantle.

Soon after came a darker time, turmoil the likes of which I had not yet known. It started on a gorgeous autumn day, brisk, with silvery clouds crossin' the sky like God's own flotilla. Donal and I had taken to the wooded hillsides to the east of Lough Corribe to hunt together. We were happy, the two of us, like children again, laughing at nothing as we rode through the greenwood. I had raced ahead of Donal, throwin' great clods of turf up behind me, chuckling to myself that he'd be filthy at the end of the day—how he best liked to be—but I'd send him to the bath-house and perhaps I'd go with him to soak. And if his temper stayed sweet, perhaps we'd forget for the moment our battles and woes. We might even make love, the way we had done in our youth.

It struck me, sudden like, that Donal was farther behind than I'd reckoned, and here I'd thought we were racing. So I turned my mount around, ready with a mouthful of tart abuse for him, and rode back a ways through the wood. There was his horse up ahead, and there was Donal slumped over its neck. My eyes fixed on the thin shaft stickin' out the back of him, and my heart lurched in fear. I rode quickly to him, knowin' any moment an arrow might find me as well, but I had to bring him home. The arrow that had felled him had found its mark at the base of his head and torn through his throat. The horse was covered in Donal's blood, and I hoped he had died quickly. But there was no time for wonderin'. I grabbed the reins and rode as fast as the horses would take us and not lose Donal from the saddle. I thanked Jesus there was a lone boatman at the edge of the lake who helped with Donal's body, but as we rowed away to the castle, I looked back and saw a sight I would not soon forget.

There were the Joyces, half a hundred of 'em, gloatin' over their kill. And behind them, spread out along the ridge of the hill, was *a whole English regiment*. I tell you, it chilled the blood in my veins to see them on O'Flaherty land—invaders with no business for bein' there a'tall. So the Joyces, bloody cowards that they were, had joined forces with the Crown to murder Donal, and now were ridin' down from the ridge to the lakeside to besiege Cock's Castle as well.

Of course there was no time to mourn Donal, only to prepare for battle. Like I said, those who lived on the island in the tiny village within the bawn were weary to the bone from the Joyces' attacks. And if that wasn't bad enough, their brave "Cock," who'd always led them to victory, was dead. Sure *I* was alive and willing to serve in his place. My reputation meant something, and I'd fought at Donal's side in previous attacks. But as a leader I was adept on the sea, a fine captain and pirate, but what did I know of fighting a siege on land? I saw the doubt in the people's eyes, and in my weaker moments even I despaired of my ignorance. But loathing self-pity as I did, I pushed aside such thoughts and very brazen like, strode out among them to speak.

"Aye, 'tis the godless Joyces who come again to do us mischief. But what soft-bellied cowards they've become! They dare not fight us alone but have brought the English to do their work! If those soldiers think our resolve will crumble at the mere sight of 'em, that we'll weep in terror and surrender this castle, then it's a sure thing those soldiers have never done battle with the O'Flaherty clan!"

I must have been convincing, for the islanders cheered me, their eyes gleaming, their expressions full of trust. They awaited my orders.

"First," said I, "we must assume a siege is ahead, and perhaps a long one. So gather all the food and wine you've got put by in your homes, and laying chickens and milking cows, and bring them to the keep. This evening we'll meet in the armory and take stock of artillery. If any of you men fought in David Burke's rebellion, come forward now, for you'll tell me all you know of English strategies. We'll survive this, I know it. Donal O'Flaherty may be dead, but he's watchin' us all, and if we fail to fight as bravely as he has for this castle, I promise you, his angry ghost will haunt you in this life as well as the next!"

Well, I was right about the siege bein' long. While they camped in comfort on Corribe's shore, the Joyces and the English kept us prisoners for a month on our own island, till we began to starve. Of course a starving enemy is a weak enemy, and once they believed our condition dire, the attack began. They came in dozens of small boats, carrying their guns, small cannon, and siege ladders. 'Twas hard to watch them cross the watery breach between us, we with much of our courage dissolved away with the flesh off our bones. Children cried as the men and women took their posts on the ramparts. So helpless a feeling it was, waiting and watching as they gathered outside the walls. I'd never wished so much for Donal O'Flaherty's company in all my life, but there was no use moanin' about it.

Then it began. First we suffered their fire from arquebuses and cannon, which was no more than cover for their more dangerous work—the setting of explosives in our fortifications. We could hear their digging under our walls and knew that a breach in the stone would mean the end of us.

"Listen up!" I cried. "A dozen of you, stay at your posts on the ramparts and keep them busy with your fire. Everyone else—children too—come with me!" I led the people wordlessly up the stairs of the keep and onto the castle's roof. The sun shinin' on our backs, the sounds of battle below us, we ripped off the lead that covered it, and pile by pile hauled it below. Great fires were built using wood torn off the sides of our sheds and houses. There in vats we melted the metal down, carrying it careful like up to the ramparts. The first explosions rocked the walls, and a man called out that the siege ladders had been flung up to their places, soldiers beginning to climb. 'Twas now or never, I knew, so I shouted the order, prayin' with all my heart that it was the *right* order.

At my word the men in the ramparts tipped the cauldrons over the turrets, and down upon the heads of our enemies broke waves of molten metal. Oh, the shrieks and moans were marvelous to hear! Dozens of ladders filled with men fell backward, soldiers and clansmen burned and broken below.

It was chaos altogether. The firing stopped and all attempts at breaching the walls and tunneling beneath were finished. There were dead and injured to be rowed ashore, wounds to be licked, recriminations to be levied, one commander to the next. Who were these O'Flahertys? the

English would be sayin'. Who do they think they are? You Joyces swore they'd not fight with their leader dead.

In Cock's Castle we allowed ourselves a wee celebration for our victory, and somebody said the place should be renamed. 'Twas "Hen's Castle" now, for the Cock's female had led them all out of harm's way. But there was no sign of the enemy quitting their camp on the mainland side, and we were forced to face the dire thought of starving to death on Corribe Island. It occurred to us that no relief had come from the O'Flahertys outside who, strange as it seemed, might be unaware of our plight. How could we get word to them that we were trapped on this island, surrounded by enemies?

"I seem to remember," came a feeble voice from the back, "a secret tunnel from the isle to the mainland."

All eyes clapped on old Porrag O'Flaherty, who was blind and very frail in his limbs. He had lived on the island since boyhood, the castle's steward for many years.

"I know nothing of a tunnel," said I. "Can you tell us where to find it, Porrag?"

"That's another matter entirely," he replied, and though others had a vague recollection of such a tunnel, try as they might, no one could remember more than Porrag, and the brief hope of salvation began to dim.

"Ma'am." I heard a tiny voice from behind the crowd of villagers.

"Who's that speaking?" I called.

"'Tith I." A small figure appeared then, a boy about eight named William, with two front teeth missing from his head.

"What do you know about a tunnel, William? Come now, we haven't much time."

"There'th a playth that I play thomtimth . . ."

His mother's eyes went wide with understanding. "The times that I cannot find you?" she said to him. "When it seems you've fallen off the face of the earth?"

"Aye," he whispered, eyes downcast. "For I've gone *into* the earth."

Thank Jesus for that toothless little boy, for he led us to a shed off the back of Daniel O'Flaherty's cottage, and there in the floor was an old trapdoor—the tunnel of which Porrag had spoken, and though dark, with crumblin' walls seeping water, altogether intact.

Two of our fleet-footed young men were chosen to go and they disappeared into the bowels of the earth.

We waited and watched for days, and cringed as the troops amassed anew. By now hundreds of Joyces had come from afar and swelled their ranks. The boats were loaded again and attack was imminent. All was lost, it seemed, and we in Hen's Castle prepared for our fight to the death.

That's when we heard it—a shrieking cry comin' o'er the hill, and out of the blue, a huge array of fire-tipped arrows rained down upon the boats on the shore, setting them afire. 'Twas the blessed O'Flahertys in their number, a great seething mass of 'em, sweeping down on the enemy camp, all unaware. So, what with the ambush—the troops and the Joyces trapped between the O'Flahertys and the water's edge—'twas a great rout, and a victory disputed by no one. The siege on Hen's Castle was lifted, and the enemies—both Irish and English—soundly defeated.

With Donal dead, I tried to collect my "thirds." In Ireland a clan chief's widow is granted one third of all her husband's possessions. Brehon law was on my side, but Donal Crone was not. Still furious at his deposing by the English, he was looking out for any chance to bring another to grief. And his fury fell on my head. Who did I think I was, he demanded, to claim Gilleduff O'Flaherty's whole fleet as my own? Never mind it'd been bequeathed to me very legal like. I was wealthy on that account, he said, and had no right to Donal's thirds as well. Not to mention my husband was poorer by half, what with my bringing to light his part in Walter Burke's slaying.

I took the case before the Brehon judges, who listened quite respectfully, but Donal Crone came bargin' in very loud and made his case against me. I was a *woman*, he cried—as though that was a great surprise—who had no right to be carrying on such a manly enterprise. My name, he said, should be struck from the annals of Irish history, and unless I took the proper role of a woman, I should be given no more honor nor sustenance in O'Flaherty territories from that day forward.

My sons Owen and Murrough were present of course. Young men by now, they'd been granted their share of their father's inheritance, but wielded no power to help me win mine. My sweet child Owen would have, if he could, but I always thought that Murrough, in secret, agreed with Donal Crone. In the end the judges denied my thirds and I was forced to leave the O'Flaherty lands.

Thank Jesus I had the fleet and several hundred men so loyal to me that they'd go where I took them, and where I took them was back to my father's kingdom and the waters of Clew Bay.

My new life was about to change once again. 'Twas a dark, windy morning in September, not altogether auspicious for a pilgrimage on St. Brigid's Day to the Holy Well on Cahir Island. But my men, just back from a storm-racked voyage to Spain, wished to give thanks for their safe return home. So we took to the curraghs and rowed round the island to the beach nearest the well. There were many small boats already there, their wind-whipped pilgrims hiking in a long line up to the holy site. We'd all just gathered on the shore when Ryan O'Malley's curragh slid onto the sand, but rather than a family of somber folk ready to climb in pious silence up the hill, they were all atwitter. It seemed a foreign ship had foundered on the rocks of Achill Island.

Well, that made a quick end of piety and thanksgiving. My men were foamin' at the mouth to search for survivors, but even more keen for the plunder, if there was some to be had. They all fell to their knees on the sand, crossin' themselves in the general direction of the Holy Well, and took to the boats so quick they nearly left me behind.

By the time we reached Achill, a proper storm was blowing. We could see the local villagers on shore, themselves hopin' to pick survivors out of the crashing surf or, if God was willing, salvage.

There was wreckage afloat in the waves where we were—very dangerous—and what with the choppy seas and howling gale, 'twas all we could do in our small boats to keep from drownin' ourselves. But there was no one alive out there. How could there be? We gave up hope for finding any poor soul or the smallest booty, and besides, the storm was wicked. Fearin' for our lives we chose to go ashore to Achill Island rather than row home to Clare in that blow.

Let me tell you, the breakers we rode in were fifteen foot high, breakin' hard on the shore. My heart was in my throat as we sailed through the air and crashed down on that beach. Thank Jesus none of our boats was lost but only slightly damaged, and we all said St. Brigid must've heard our wee prayers to her, even though we'd not made it up to the Holy Well.

All the villagers had staggered home empty-handed, but we remained on that beach thankin' God for our lives. Darkness was upon us and the men were arguing whether to camp the night there under our boats or go seek shelter in the village.

Then I saw it. 'Twas a pale creature movin' in the sand just at the place the breakers were crashin' down. A cry was ripped from my throat as a giant wave descended on it. That scream scared the piss out of my men, who'd not seen what I'd seen and thought I myself was bein' killed. Unable to speak I rushed to the water's edge, but in the receding wave there was no sign of that poor creature, which might, I now thought, have been a figment of my imagination. My men pulled me back out of harm's way as another giant breaker smashed onto the beach. But this one deposited, for all of us to see, the thing I had glimpsed before.

'Twas a man, altogether naked, the work of the waves havin' torn every shred of clothing from his form. We quick pulled him back from the surf, this moaning survivor with a good crack to the head, limbs broken in several places, and close to death.

We carried him to the village, knowing his life depended on heat and comfort. An elderly Achill widow took him in, with me as his nurse, while all my men took shelter in her barn. As he lay on the old woman's bed very still, even as we set his broken bones, I was struck with the strangest emotions for that sorely wounded stranger, a painful longing and terrible grief that he might die. I could see by the lines of his sunburnt torso that he must be a sailor, and by the pale color of his skin and hair a Norseman. I could not ask him his name, for though alive, he was altogether dead to the world, and considering his injuries, that was a blessing.

I stayed on Achill Island for a month or more, a nurse to this man. By his good luck and mine, the old widow, Agnes Murphy, had nursed her own husband for years before he'd died, and welcomed the company and another chance to use her skills.

The sailor was slowly comin' back to us, unintelligible as his words might be, but then on the fourth day an ague took hold of him and he was gone again, closer to God, it seemed to us, than before. Oh it was terrible to see the agonies he suffered, trembling chills, burning fevers, and the occasional sharp cries of pain, as though he'd been run through with a blade.

Through my ministrations I grew to know his body, every inch of it. His skin was pale where it was not bronzed by the sun, and his hair, similarly touched, so fair as to be white. He was tall and long limbed and his face was beautiful—jaw, cheeks, and nose made all of angles, but lips soft and full like two tiny pillows. I could barely take my eyes from those lips and found, to my own surprise and amusement, that I longed very much to kiss them.

Agnes and I had sealed a silent pact—each for our own reasons—that we would not, under any circumstances, let him die. I slept on a pallet near his bed to be close at hand at night. We searched her overgrown garden for healing herbs, and she'd send me on journeys into the Achill hills to find patches of wild-growing medicines, and down to the rocky coast for certain seaweeds. Side by side we'd grind these into poultices and ointments, brew them into teas, ferment them into tinctures. And we kept him clean as a newborn babe, rubbing his skin with oil to keep it supple. Never was a man so well doctored as our nameless stranger.

Agnes teased me mercilessly, for she saw very clear what I felt, but I think she was just as relieved as I when nearly two weeks from the day of his rescue the poor man opened his eyes and saw us for the first time. Well, I'm ashamed to say I burst into tears like a stupid girl. The look on his face was pure confusion, but you could easily see why. First he's on a ship with his mates battling a storm off the coast of Ireland. The next thing he knows he's flat on his back in a room he's never seen, with an ancient lady starin' down at him, and a strange woman next to her bawlin' her eyes out.

His name was Eric Thorson, and he was a Frieslander. This was all we could learn that first day, for he was weak as a kitten. In the days following, the facts of Eric's life were slow in coming, for he spoke no Irish and his Latin was rusty. He conveyed that he'd not been the captain, but his ship's first mate. That the waters were new to them and that his captain had failed to heed the warning he'd heard of the treacherous west coast of Ireland.

He was as sad a man as I'd ever seen, for his brothers had all been aboard that ship, and many of his friends, and now they were all at the bottom of the sea. So as he regained his strength and the use of his limbs, Eric was pained in his mind as well as body. But the beauty of it was, even when sick, he was noble, and even when suffering, mild.

He had a pair of screaming blue eyes that I found, to my great delight, following me round the cottage as I did my work. When I would lay my hands on him—which was whenever I had an excuse—a smile would play about those luxurious lips, and it was all I could do to keep myself from leaning down and planting my own on his.

Finally Agnes and I deemed his bones properly knitted, and he fit to rise from the bed and take a few steps. We took our places, one on either side, and brought him to his feet. He stifled a groan and fought the inevitable dizziness from a month in bed. But there was a shock in it for the widow and I as well, for though we knew he was tall, we had not expected the man to tower over us like a church steeple. We walked him round the small cottage and he asked to get a breath of fresh air, which we obliged.

'Twas a cold and blustery day and the sea beyond the hills was all gray chop. There was pain in his eyes as he gazed at the water, a graveyard for his friends and kin. I felt his arm tighten about me for a brief moment, as though he were clutchin' all he had left in the world. Then he asked to go in again, but not to his bed, for he wished to sit at the table like a man, and not the helpless child he'd been for so long.

He'd grown very thin, Eric had, and his muscles were weak, but once he'd taken his place at Agnes's table all that changed. The man's appetite was prodigious and he quickly emptied her larder, but I paid the widow handsomely for our keep, and she cooked us many fine meals. Soon he was strapping as he had been, and the daily walks we'd take on hills and shores brought the life back into him.

'Twas funny how easy we were with each other, though our languages differed completely. He taught me bits of his and I taught him bits of mine, and together we retrieved the Latin he had learned as a boy. Of course there was a fair amount of gesturing with our hands. But it was, after all, in the language of the sea and of sailing that we spoke the easiest, for it was clearly the language of our hearts, and there was great joy in this. Like myself, he'd been born and bred to the life, and nothin' under heaven made him happier than a great journey across the water. He'd been to places I'd never been—the New World for one—and he'd seen the famous Maelstrom of Lofoten, a great natural wonder of the world. He marveled that I was a captain with a fleet of my own and was humbled by it, for that was never to be his fate.

When he did speak of leaving, I realized how sorely my own heart ached.

"Must you leave a'tall?" I finally said one day. "Stay here." 'Twas a shy whisper.

"Here?" he said, confused.

"No, not *here*, on Achill. Come home with me to Clare Island . . . and sail with me, Eric, wherever I go."

Well, he smiled then. I suppose I haven't mentioned his smile before, with teeth very white and straight, or his great, boomin' laugh that I loved so much. The truth was, I loved Eric, loved him like I'd loved no other man, though he'd never yet laid a hand on me that way.

"You're smiling," I said. "Can I take that for a yes?"

"*Ja!*" he cried, and grabbed me, pickin' me up in his arms and swingin' me round and round.

'Twas the start of Heaven on earth for me. All the worries and woes of life just faded away and the sun shone even when it didn't, if you know what I mean. So Eric came home with me to live, and we married—a very private affair—just him and me on the high cliffs of Inishturk Island, the westernmost place in all of Ireland, and overlooking the sea, which we knew would be our second home. Owen O'Malley heartily approved, for he saw my happiness, and wished for that above all things. He joked with Eric, callin' him a Viking invader, but he made a handsome gift to him of three ships of his own. Eric very nearly wept at that, for he'd never in all his life expected to captain his own ship, much less a small fleet. Even Molly liked him. After our return to Achill, the parrot took one look at my new husband and promptly fell in love with him. It was Gilleduff O'Flaherty all over again.

Eric wanted most to return to the New World, that which his ancestors found five hundred years before the Spanish had done. 'Twas not the southern coasts and islands from which the treasure fleet sent gold by the ton to Spain, but the *northern* coast come down from Greenland. It was a place, he said, of flat, rocky coastline, and farther south of lush forests where roamed savages fierce enough to chase away the Vikings themselves. Where halibut and codfish swam in such abundance that at low tide in the great pools round the rocks they could pluck them by the thousands. Where berries and corn and wheat and fruits and even grapes did grow, and 'twas after the grapes they named the place, callin' it Vinland.

But Eric knew of my dream of the Mediterranean, Aegean, and the Nile, and teased me, saying we'd go there first, for I'd give him no rest till I'd seen the elephant teeth lodged in the heads of the living beasts who'd grown them. So 'twas decided that we would not wait—that life was short enough as it was—and we would go on a kind of marriage trip, a voyage for pleasure, which was all but unheard of.

In those years you could not conceive of the Mediterranean without thinking of Suleyman the Magnificent. Growing up, Owen had told tales of that mighty blue sea and the Ottoman sultan who owned it. Sure the Holy League claimed it and tried to keep their trade routes alive, but its members—the Pope, the doges of Venice, and that fat-lipped Hapsburg emperor, Charles—were just kidding themselves. No league—holy or otherwise—could contain the power of Suleyman. Even the fearsome Barbary pirates swooping up from the northern coast of Africa were nothing compared to Suleyman's Turkish Terror Fleet and its captain, Barbarossa.

All places exotic were there on the shores of that sea. Places of consequence—Morocco, Barcelona, Rome, Venice, Cairo, Athens, Crete. The Holy Land, for Jesus' sake. I'd learned of them from the Latin books I'd read under the beady eye of the Clare Island friars. The Greek myths, their gods and monsters. The Cyclops! Isis with her poor husband chopped up in fourteen pieces and scattered round the world. Daughters jumping full grown from the foreheads of their fathers. I always liked that one—Athena and Zeus—and used to tease Owen that I'd leapt straight out of *his* head, and not my mother's womb a'tall.

I'd been told of the beauty of the Mediterranean, a sea of islands, of the indescribable blue, and the bleached white of the hillside homes. Of the vast and teeming markets and bazaars, hubs of trade, and the Great Silk Road. I was frothin' at the mouth to go. 'Twas another thing, though, to crew a ship for such an adventure. As I said, the Barbary Coast was nowhere that my men wished to explore. I was forced to bribe them with double wages paid in advance, a minimum of work, guarantees that our vessel would be armed to the teeth, and the promise of a long on-shore leave in Egypt, where the whores, I swore, were more beautiful than any others in the world.

The Maritime Alps, just north of Nice, took our breath away, and Rome . . . Well, in Rome you'd rather not breathe a'tall. Sure the painted cathedrals boggled the mind, and the old Roman ruins brought to memory the great civilization risen to such lofty heights, only to be flattened by Barbarian invasions. But Venice, now that was another story altogether. It shouldn't surprise you that I would love that city, it being part and parcel of the sea, and still the greatest trading center of the world. A place, unlike anywhere else, where trade is religion itself, and the merchants its high priests and noblemen.

One festival night, we stumbled on a gondolier, altogether drunk and wasted on the dock near his boat. Eric grinned at me like a little boy and, bending down to the oarsman, tucked a coin in his pocket and whispered that we'd be "borrowin'" his vessel for a wee while. He took the oar and poled out into the Venice Lagoon till the whole city was a vista before us. All the torches were aglow and windows lit from within. I'd never seen a sight so lovely as that, Venice in the moonlight. Then at the stroke of midnight the church bells began to peel and to our amazement the sky was all of a sudden lit like the day with fireworks. 'Twas magic, pure and simple, and I fell happily into Eric's arms and lay back on the fur bed he'd made on the gondola's deck. Let me tell you, the fire in the sky was nothin' compared to that which burned on the floor of that boat. Oh, 'twas the sweetest night of my whole life. I loved that man to distraction and he loved me the same. What more could a woman want?

I haven't the time to regale you with the whole of the Mediterranean voyage. We tried to visit the Greek isles, only to find them swarming with Turks, and thought better of it. The Holy Land was similarly occupied, and there were rumors of fighting, so we did not go there either. Egypt was no different, under the hand of Suleyman for fifty years, but I was not to be deterred in my quest for the huge beasts with the giant teeth, called elephants. I do admit I was most curious about the River

Nile, and Cairo, and the great monuments I'd heard about since I was a child.

We arranged to travel upriver on a covered barge and floated very lazy up that wide river, green on each side, but beyond the narrow strip a burnin' desert like Hell on earth. And then came the day when I saw them—the elephants—on the banks of the river. A whole tribe of 'em. Imagine a creature as big as a house! Their legs were like tree trunks, yet they moved with a certain grace, even on land and in the water where they bathed, and in the mud where they wallowed. I thought with surprise as I watched them lumberin' about that they feel *joy*, these beasts. And seein' them touching their young with those long, fabulous trunks, *tenderness*. Had I ever touched my children with more delicate sweetness?

'Twas only then I saw their teeth, called tusks, and I remembered them hangin' over my bed, and I felt a sharp stab of pity. The thought of so magnificent a creature lyin' dead, with maggots crawlin' round in the place his great teeth had been ripped out of his head was suddenly terrible. I turned away with tears stinging my eyes, and Eric saw this and questioned me. I said 'twas an insect in my eye and nothin' to worry about. Kind and sweet as he was I knew he'd think me mad for such sentiments. Elephants were game, like all other of God's wild creatures, there for man's use and pleasure. I never did tell him the truth.

Well, I'd seen what I'd come to see, so we turned and floated back downriver in a sweet daze. We were deep into tomb country and could see that fully half the business done on the river was that of tomb raiding. Barges were piled high with the spoils of piracy—Egyptian style. Beautiful gilt statues, painted furniture, urns and chests. But most of all, mummies. Sure I knew of these strange corpses. They fetched high prices in Europe's markets, for ground up into powder and mixed into potions they were known to cause miraculous cures, from plague to ague. I even bought a few of the monstrosities, makin' sure they were put into boxes so none of my crew would be the wiser of their contents.

I can scarce describe the happy chaos of our minds as we boarded the ship in the port of Cairo. We were like two ticks, gorged with memories, the grit of the desert sand still in our mouths, the smell of dung fires and cinnamon wafting in from the city. The crew was the same, dazed with delight. Indeed, the whores had been lovely, black-eyed creatures with honeyed skin and thick, oiled hair and the scent of the east about them. The crew returned drunk with experience, and laden down with exotic wares for which they'd dickered in fantastical markets. Gorgeous Turkey rugs, crocks of rich spices for their mammies, lengths of colored silks for their wives and sweethearts, carved stone deities the merchants swore were three thousand years old. There'd been brawls for those who loved brawling, though we did not lose a single man. And some, bitten by the same bug of curiosity as Eric and me, had taken off for parts unknown, on camel back with caravans into the brutal desert, others exploring the great stone pyramids. Still others, befriended by generous families, lived among the Egyptians in their river villages.

All in all 'twas a brilliant success. Even the parrot Molly, abandoned for weeks by her beloved, refrained from her usual rude behavior on our return—just cooed and cuddled and prattled endlessly, trotting out every word and mumbled phrase she'd ever known, even the little used "Duff, Duff, Duff, Duff . . ."

The world was changin' so fast it made your head spin. We'd been gone but five months, and on our return to Ireland I found my father had aged five years. His body was thin and frail, though his mind was as sharp as a blade. There was no complainin' of aches in his joints or pain from his old wounds, but they were there in Owen's eyes when he moved, and the cold and damp seeped into every cranny of his drafty stone keep. I grew alarmed when I found he'd not visited his fleet in more than a fortnight, but was reluctant to question him of it for he was, if nothin' else, a proud man and loath to show his weakness.

I conjured up a lame excuse to visit, sure to fool no one—somethin' about caulking a boat—and took a basket of his favorite foods I'd had my cook fix for him. I found Owen alone on the top floor of the Belclare Keep, starin' out his western window at the sea. He made room for me on his bench and we sat gazing out his window. He showed me what he'd been watching when I came in—a great galleon far out to sea, a huge vessel used by Spain for its Treasure Fleet. He wondered what it was doin' in these waters, if maybe King Philip was hiring the Scots for mercenaries in his Netherlands war. "That is one bloody battlefield," said Owen, looking quite dejected. "I fear it's the destiny of Ireland as well."

"It won't happen here," I said.

"Oh, darlin' girl, right now you're in love and the world is beautiful. Part of you is still floating down the Nile on a barge. Your ships come home from the fishing grounds half filled and you don't even care. You've no trips planned for the autumn, and you brought nothin' back from your voyage for profit but a few shriveled-up old carcasses."

"I sold those mummies in Baltimore for a fine profit, I'll have you know."

"Grace, your mind is elsewhere, and I promise you, you cannot afford it. Not now. You've got to keep your eyes open. Eric is a grand husband, but he means nothin' to the clans. He brings you no strength or standing in the eyes of your allies. And with the English encroaching on Connaught, and the chieftains falling one after another—"

"They submit, but they don't mean it," I argued.

"But more and more they're becoming two-faced, or maybe it's just confused. Some are weary of native disputes century after century. They've lost their faith in the Brehon ways of succession, of territorial rights, and then they see the orderly English governance. They're taken in by promises—'You can keep your land. You can keep your power. Just fight your friends and neighbors when we tell you to.' But then the Jans rebel against the chiefs, claiming they want no change in the old ways. But in truth, the rebels want power for *themselves*. After submission, a chieftain might be forced to fight his English patrons to keep his Jan happy, supposin' it easier to gain a pardon from the Crown at a later date. And it many times is. Jesus, what a mess it's become!"

"It has indeed," I agreed, spreading out a small feast on the trestle table. I was feelin' guilty that I needed such a lecture from my father at my age. That I—a silly, love-struck girl—would risk the ruin of the great empire my father and his fathers before him had built with their sweat and blood. "It's time I came home from my marriage trip," I said, though I couldn't meet his eye. I moved to his bed and began straightening his bedclothes. "And it's time you came home to live near me."

He was altogether silent and I knew my words had hit him like a fist in the face. In truth I'd expected outrage and argument, so the silence was unnerving. And it seemed to go on forever. I suddenly wondered how many fur rugs I could pile, how many cushions I could rearrange in this terrible silence. Finally I steeled myself and turned back to him. He'd taken his place at the table and was eating a slice of cold roast. He looked up at me from beneath his graying fringe.

"I heard you, Grace. It's a fine offer." He broke an oatcake in half and chewed on it. "I'll think about it."

Well, in the end he came to Clare Island, without a fuss, for it was the best way to keep his dignity intact. We built him a snug cottage inside the courtyard, and I found a widow named Barbara—not too old and not too ugly—to keep his house and cook for him. She was honored. 'Twas the great man Black Oak O'Malley after all.

His fleet was moved to the waters off Clare Island where mine and Eric's were anchored, but less and less did Owen climb down the rock stairs to the beach. Finally he gave his ships over to me, sayin' 'twas better to gift them now while he was alive, so there'd be no argument after he was dead. With Owen, grace and honor had served him as a younger man, and so they now served him as an old man. Lookin' at Da puttering round his house and garden, acceptin' the unacceptable, treatin' so kindly with Barbara, made me weep with gratitude. It made me think of what a terror Donal O'Flaherty would have become had he grown old. Eric, I knew, would age with the grace that Owen had.

Soon after this we were called by the Crown's Lord Deputy, Henry Sidney, to a meeting of all the clan chiefs of Connaught. There was an uproar to begin with, as only two of these chiefs—Clanrickard and Thomond—were used to being summoned by anyone. But there was news to be had of Gerald Fitzgerald, Earl of Desmond, the Lord of Munster. He was the greatest landowner in southern Ireland. And there were rumblings of a rebellion there, which we were keen to learn about, no matter what the source.

Owen, still The O'Malley but having never submitted, refused to go. He was curious nonetheless and wished for me to go as his "ears." I did reflect on the honor of this—his trust in me, his belief I would hold my own with the great chiefs of Ireland. Eric went with me and though, as my father had said, he held no sway with the clans, he was a sea captain in his own right, with a fleet as hireable as my own for the chiefs' many purposes. Besides, I was proud to have him at my side, and wouldn't have thought of leavin' him behind.

We convened in the great hall at Castlebarry and Lord Deputy Sidney greeted me with more than a little interest, no doubt noting Owen O'Malley's absence, but recognizing the name Grace O'Malley, which by now had certainly come to the Crown's attention for my exploits on land and sea. Then, very dignified—for Sidney was a good man despite being English—he began his report. He told us that in yet another episode of that age-old feud between the Desmonds and the Ormonds, Gerald of Desmond had been shot in the hip and taken prisoner by Tom of Ormond, who delivered him into English hands. Gerald had been tried in London as a traitor to the Crown to whom he'd, for so many years, sworn his allegiance, and now sat prisoner in the Tower of London.

Such news was shocking enough, but when Sidney told us that as punishment for his treason—which, between you and me, was his failure to pay a penny's rent on his properties—Gerald had been forced to forfeit all of his land, and that *half of Ireland* had been given over to an Englishman by the name of Peter Carew, you can imagine the uproar.

The "First Munster Plantation" 'twas to be called, and already Englishmen and their wives and children had moved there. And though 'twas not said aloud, we all knew that the Irish, across the length and breadth of the land, were being evicted from their homes, family seats of a thousand years.

What can I say? We were all outraged. Much as we despised the Earl of Desmond, we could clearly see what his capitulation meant to us all. The English blight that had once been contained by Dublin, and the Pale around it, was quickly spreading all across Ireland. 'Twas the beginning of the end. I knew that, as sure as I knew my own name.

Clanrickard and Thomond advised the chieftains capitulation, swearing that the only way to survive was by siding with the English. Some grudgingly agreed, but others roared with indignation. There was some name-calling, red, angry faces pushed into other red, angry faces, even some pushing and shoving. 'Twas the sorriest of sights—the great chiefs of western Ireland reduced to a flock of squabbling chickens. With so much fury about us, nothing of any worth was decided, and the meeting slowly fell apart.

Eric and I were takin' our leave, very quiet like—our hearts were so sore—when John MacMahon, the chieftain's son, barreled up to us, his face livid.

"Where's your feckin' father!" he shouted in my face. The MacMahons were a large clan, but roundly disliked for their general ignorance and unnecessary acts of violence.

Of course Eric grabbed him and shoved him away, but he kept comin' back at us, unheedful of the danger he was putting himself in.

"I want to know where Owen O'Malley is! Why he thinks he can send a woman and a foreigner in his place. Does he think he's so much better than us?"

At that, Eric, with his huge mitts, grabbed MacMahon by the throat, liftin' him clear off the ground. At once the man began to choke, his eyes bulging from his head. And then my beloved, in his broken Irish, but quite understandable, said, "He does not think he's better than you, you low turd. He *is* better than you by a hundred leagues!"

"Eric, put him down," I said. Well, he did, rather hard, on the stone, so much so we heard a loud crack, probably MacMahon's tailbone breaking. But by then some other men had come out and seen it, so together with the pain was humiliation, not even at the hands of an Irishman, but a Swede.

When we got home we made our dire report to Owen. He listened, very somber, nodding his head at all the news of Desmond and Ormond, the Englishman Peter Carew and the First Munster Plantation—all of it as though he'd heard it before. Nothin' surprised him. 'Twas just as he'd prophesied.

He had advice for both of us. To me he said, "I know you to be mighty, Grace, but to most in the world you're still a mere woman. But female or male you will need alliances to survive. You must look to our old friends—the Burkes, the O'Flahertys, even Murrough ne Doe. They may swear loyalty to the Crown, but *they won't fight you*. Count on that. The best thing you can do is to keep your fleet strong. Always sail at least two or three ships together for strength. You cannot afford to lose control of our coastal waters, or your freedom to trade with Spain. Keep your fleet intact and you can keep your independence long after all the others have fallen the queen's victims. The sea is your salvation, Grace, you take my word on that. And Eric." He turned to my husband. "I'm most grateful at how well you watch my daughter's back, but you need to be watchin' your own as well. The MacMahons are a hateful clan, and they'll give you no end of grief for that drubbing you gave John in public. Watch yourself, son. We don't want Grace a widow twice over."

Oh, that Eric had taken that advice to heart. How strange that after all these years I choke on the words. I wish . . . I wish my memory failed me in this story. But no such luck. I remember it like it was yesterday.

Eric and some of his sailors had gone to Achill Island to hunt red deer. He would visit with Agnes too, he said, bring her the pretty brocaded shawl we'd bought her in Venice, eat some of her fine cooking. We'd parted with a touch of acrimony, as I wished him to stay and tend to repairs on our fleet. But he was keen to hunt that day, said repairs could wait, and I would be happy when he returned with fresh venison and several soft skins. I kissed him good-bye, but out of pique withheld the full measure of my passion. Oh, how I regret that withholding!

He did not return that night, but I thought nothin' of it. The hunting must be good, I reckoned. But the next day passed, and the night, and the next day after that. I began to feel a tightness in my chest, and I knew in my heart that something was wrong. I found myself starin' out at the headlands, watching for signal fires to be lit for some news of danger. Funny, when I first saw the beacons, lights stretching up the coast and ending at Achill Island, I was not surprised, for I'd been expecting something dreadful. Knew it was coming. Knew that Eric was dead.

I pulled a crew together and sailed the *Dorcas* to Achill Island. Went straight to Agnes's cottage, which was lit very bright. What was left of Eric's hunting party were standin' about outside with the most doleful expressions. No one said a word, but as I passed between them they each laid a hand on my shoulder or my head. I stopped short of the threshold, unable to enter, unwilling to see what lay beyond. It occurred to me that I could turn away, refuse to look on the face of death, but then Agnes came to the door. Her eyes were wet but she wore the sweetest expression—not at all what I'd expected—and holdin' out her hand, led me inside.

There he was, stretched out on the same bed in which we'd nursed him. Strange, there was no strife in that scene, for Agnes had cleaned him and laid him out with perfect dignity. Those long limbs were so still, his face in such comfortable repose. The brocaded shawl we'd brought her was neatly laid across his forehead and over the pillow on either side. I moved closer and in the firelight saw the square chin, those beautiful lips, pale and waxy. I lifted the shawl very slow and just enough to see his poor skull, crushed like a melon.

I did not cry that night. I did go out and speak with the men, who told me what had happened. 'Twas the MacMahons, of course, who'd lain in wait to ambush their party. It had been a general rout, with others slain as well, but the purpose had been clear from the first. A group of four, led by John MacMahon, surrounded Eric. He'd fought bravely, but he'd been outnumbered after all. He'd never had a chance.

Owen worried of course, but he had no good advice for me, nothing that would really ease my pain. All he could do was have Barbara feed me, and I did eat. Miserable as I was, I did not want to die—I knew that—for there was something of great import left for me to do.

After weeks with little sleep, just starin' at the fire or out to sea, I was half a madwoman, half a ghost. I can only imagine what I looked like. Then word came—almost unbelievable—that a dozen or more of the Ballycroy MacMahons had dared to go on pilgrimage to the holy isle of Cahir. I remember feelin' strange then, rememberin' our own island pilgrimage as the very place I'd first heard news of the ship that had foundered with Eric aboard. And I thought how odd that he should be saved on Achill Island, and die on Achill Island. All at once my mind, previously whirlin', or dead numb, was clear and filled with purpose.

I gathered thirty of my most trusted men and we rowed in to Cahir. When we arrived the MacMahons were still engaged in their religious duties, but we found their boats and hacked them to pieces. Then we climbed the pilgrim's peak, found the sons of whores on their knees in prayer and slaughtered them, every one. John MacMahon had not been among them, so we took ourselves off—before word could precede us— to Doona Castle, the MacMahon family seat in Blacksod Bay.

'Twas night, and they were not expectin' us. Indeed, the stronghold gates were open in expectation of the pilgrims' return. What a rude shock they got instead—Mad Grace O'Malley, her heart seethin' with black revenge. We were kinder at Doona Castle, killing only their chieftain, Patrick, and puttin' the rest of 'em out of their homes at sword-point. I found it a pretty place on a good harbor, so claimed it in the name of O'Malley. I could never live myself in the place, so I gave it as a gift to what loyal men would take their families there.

But the true point of our assault—John MacMahon—had fled, escapin' into the night. It took several weeks more before news of his whereabouts found me. The murdering scum had taken refuge in a small church on a small island in Clew Bay. There a holy hermit lived alone, and he'd given sanctuary to MacMahon.

We surrounded the church and at first besieged it, hoping to force John out. But my patience ran thin long before he and the holy hermit starved, and so on a Sunday mornin', very bright, with the sun gleamin' off the water, we stormed the church.

The old hermit, silent in his vows for many years past, was so appalled he cried out, "Fie to you all! This is sanctuary, *sanctuary*!" We just ignored him, searching in every nook and cranny for MacMahon, but he was nowhere to be found. I was tearin' my hair at the thought of his escape till I saw an unlikely pile of plaster on the floor below a painting of the Virgin. We quick removed the portrait, finding a hole in the wall and a long tunnel that John MacMahon had dug through the rocks.

My man Brian climbed in and called back the direction the tunnel was headed—'twas a steep rock cliff on the southeast side of the island, towering over the sea itself. I ordered some men to stay with the hermit, for we didn't trust him, and the rest of us headed to our boats.

We rounded the island just in time to see MacMahon climbin' a rope down from the tunnel, against the rock face, hoping to drop into the dinghy moored below. Just then Brian emerged from the tunnel hole and, seeing his prey beneath him clingin' to the rope, began to shake it fiercely.

John screamed curses up to Brian, who kept up the shaking. He could see us coming by now and was very desperate indeed. Still high off the water he let go of the rope, and with more luck than should have been allowed him, fell into his waiting boat. I heard him cry out in pain and hoped he'd cracked his tailbone again, but he picked up the oars and began to row toward a place where a stiff current was known to run, one that could quickly bear him away and into the open sea where, after all, anything could happen.

But without a word from me, my men at the oars rowed like the Devil himself was after them, and soon we'd caught up with the dinghy. We grappled it and pulled it to us. John MacMahon was unarmed, and knowing there was no escape, put up no struggle a'tall. He just stared at me, defying me with his eyes to kill a defenseless man.

I wondered what to do as we rowed him back to the beach of the hermit's island, scraped ashore, and piled out of the boat. As they pushed him down on the sand, he tried to speak, but I told him to shut his mouth, I was thinking.

Indeed, I thought of the Brehon law that would set this murderer free for a goodly sum paid to me. I thought of my father, and of honor and of pride. I thought of right and justice and what was fair. I thought of tradition. Then I thought of Eric, lyin' there dead, and those sweet lips I'd never in my life kiss again.

I don't remember grabbing Brian's sword, but sudden like it was there in my hands, and with a cry from the pit of my miserable soul, I took John MacMahon's life with one swift blow.

Well, I was glad he was dead, he and his devilish kin, but I felt no better for it. Whoever it was said "revenge is sweet" was a fool, for there's no sweetness in a shattered heart, nor a soul searchin' in vain for its true mate.

⬖⬗⬖⬗⬖

AS IF WAKING from a dream, she'd begun hearing her own voice, her pained words ringing in her ears. To her horror Grace felt wetness on her cheeks and quickly brushed the tears away. Then she caught sight of Elizabeth, the once rigid figure now slumped in her chair, forehead clasped in her long white fingers. The painted cheeks were streaked with black rivulets, eyes still brimming with tears, and the mouth a jagged, quivering gash across her agonized face.

Though she sat before the queen, Grace knew she was as good as invisible, for Elizabeth's gaze was turned inward. *No*, thought Grace, *backward*. Backward in time. 'Twould be best to leave her, spare the woman the humiliation of a stranger seeing the great woman in such a condition.

Grace rose, and finding her cap began to tuck her hair beneath it.

"Mistress O'Malley," came Elizabeth's feeble voice.

The piteous sound of it pierced like a dart through a tough hide. "Why don't you call me Grace, Your Majesty?" She found her tone had gentled.

"Then you must call me Bess. Please, don't leave just now."

Grace removed the hat and returned to the chairs by the fire, which had, through neglect, burned down to a pile of embers. She sat, gazing across at the queen, with her ruined face so utterly assailable.

"I am truly sorry for your loss," said Elizabeth.

Suddenly Grace understood. "I'm sorry for yours as well."

Elizabeth fought to control her quivering mouth. "My Robin . . . ," she began but could go no further, as the tears began to flow again.

"Perhaps it's best to think on somethin' else just now."

"No." Elizabeth blotted her cheeks with a handkerchief. "He will be gone five years this month. I've not spoken of him to anyone since his death."

"Nobody?"

"They all hated him. Rejoiced at his passing." She paused to dab at her eyes. "He was a beautiful man, dear God, so beautiful. You should have seen him on the back of a horse. He wished for nothing more than to marry me. I came very close, once, to marriage with Robin Dudley. But I was convinced otherwise."

"And who did you let convince you?"

Elizabeth's gaze turned backward again. "My mother," she whispered.

"Anne Boleyn? But I thought—"

"They hated him," said Elizabeth, her interruption pointed, "because I loved him best. Trusted him entirely. He was the one, the only one who understood my heart, whom I allowed to love me as a man loves a woman. He knew every soft, secret part of me. From the time we were children, he made me laugh. Cried with me. We shared our losses, shared our love of England. And he endured all that was harsh in me, cold, mannish, ugly. All of my rejections . . . and forgave me every one.

"They knew nothing of his unflinching loyalty, his generosity to me when there was no hope of my succession, when I was nothing but the bastard daughter of a headless whore. I had no money, could barely pay my tiny household their salaries, so he sold his properties and gave me the profits. How does one ever forget such an act of kindness?"

Elizabeth absentmindedly worried the fine red hairs beneath the painted line of her eyebrow. "He died of a fever shortly after our victory against Philip's Armada. I'd given him commission of the land forces in all of England. I trusted no one more with the protection of this country. Still, they were amazed by how desperately I mourned him. Believed I should be rejoicing in my great victory over Spain. They could not see that my heart had been crushed"—now Elizabeth turned her gaze on Grace—"like yours had been when Eric died. And like you I had no choice but to go on. England's mantle lay heavy on my shoulders, as the O'Malley clan's lay on yours." Elizabeth straightened herself in the chair, regaining her regal posture. "We are very close in age, are we not, Grace?"

"I'm older than you by three years."

"We're well past our prime."

"Aye, but I hear you ride every day. Still take your exercise regular like."

"Deprived of it I would surely die."

Grace grew silent, unaccountably aware of the strange intimacy grown up between the queen and herself. "I haven't finished my story, you know."

"Indeed you haven't. But it's almost morning. Will you come back this evening and continue?"

"You're a strange character, Bess."

Elizabeth's eyebrows arched in amusement. "And you are a very brazen woman to say so."

"Well, I figure I've hooked you, like Scheherazade and the sultan. You won't have my head till I've finished my tale."

Nodding in silent acknowledgment Elizabeth rose stiffly from the chair and moved to the curtained door of the secret passage. "I'll call my lord Essex and have him return you to your ship."

"He's a fine-lookin' man, your lord Essex. But now I understand."

"What is it you understand?"

Grace had again tucked her hair under the cap and stood before Elizabeth's silver-framed looking glass, checking her disguise. "Why he no longer shares your bed. Sure he's beautiful and dashing and a hero to England, but he's no Robin Dudley."

The women exchanged a knowing smile.

"I do have hopes for him as politician, a councilor, a diplomat."

"Not a soldier?"

Elizabeth was thoughtful. "He is too rash for a soldier. Sometimes I think he is too rash . . . for a man."

Grace and Elizabeth laughed.

"But that's how we like them, our men," said Grace. "Rash. Bold. Outrageous. We wouldn't want them any other way, would we now?"

⊰⊱⊰⊱

ESSEX, ABOVE HIS COVERS, was stretched out abed, boots off and eyes closed when Elizabeth entered through the adjoining passage. The candle had not yet burnt out. She sat beside him for some time, watching the slow, regular breathing, the broad chest as it rose and fell, the eyes twitching under the lids.

He wondered if she believed his pretense of sleep or had guessed that he'd spent the entire night lying in the darkened passageway with his ear to the slightly opened door, hidden behind the curtain. He'd almost laughed aloud when Grace O'Malley had compared herself to Scheherazade. The woman was far better educated than he'd realized, and altogether fearless in taking liberties with the queen. At that moment he'd quickly and quietly risen, tiptoeing in stockinged feet back to his room and his bed, whilst Grace and Elizabeth said their good-byes. It had been long enough to calm himself and assume the appearance of deep sleep.

"Robin," she said, shaking him gently. "Robin, wake up."

He opened his eyes quickly, as though startled, then seeing her face smiled a warm sleepy smile. "What time is it?"

"Almost dawn. If you hurry you can return Mistress O'Malley to her vessel before first light."

"Were you happy with your interview?" he inquired, sitting up to pull on his boots.

"I'll require you to bring her to me this evening at the same time," was Elizabeth's only reply.

He'd come round the bed and now knelt at her feet where she sat. Like a small boy he laid his head on her knee and she—a fond mother—dandled his hair.

"You're very noncommittal," he insisted with a touch of petulance.

"And you are very nosy." Her tone was mild. "I did enjoy my interview."

Essex looked up at the queen's face. She was far away. Without disturbing her reverie he stood and moved to the passageway door. *What a strange pairing*, he thought, wondering what tales of adventure lay ahead, on the morrow.

⬥⬥⬥⬥⬥

AWAKE THE WHOLE night long, Essex was weary, but too much remained to be done for him to sleep the day away. He'd returned Grace O'Malley to her ship just as the Greenwich quay guards were dousing the torches, she as reluctant to speak as Elizabeth had been. But he now understood as much about this woman as the queen did, and her story boggled the mind. Somehow, thought Essex, he must get some rest before this evening, for the tale would no doubt continue to enthrall, and it would be folly to fall asleep in the midst of it.

He visited Will Meek, the apothecary, and paid him for a mixture of lavender, fennel, and foxglove, for wakefulness. Then sought out Francis Bacon in the castle library, where he was a faithful visitor. Indeed, he was found poring over a dusty book of law, his spectacles drooping down almost to the tip of his nose.

"Francis."

"Essex! Where have you been? I thought you'd stayed the night in your rooms, but they were locked and you did not answer even my loudest pounding."

"I slipped away with Katherine," he lied, hoping Bacon had not spoken to his mistress.

"Ah," said his friend, satisfied with the answer. "You know I think I've discovered a precedent for interpretation of land transfers between unrelated parties." He pushed his spectacles back up on the bridge of his nose and skewered a passage in the law book with his finger. "If one or more—"

"Francis, I need to discuss the Farm of Sweet Wines with you."

"It seems to me that the one you must speak to is the queen."

"She is immovable," Essex grumbled.

"This is indeed hard to fathom," said Bacon, looking up. His law book forgotten, he plunged enthusiastically into the subject of his patron's dilemma. "Elizabeth loves you dearly. No one entertains or delights her more. She's granted you a place on the Privy Council and Mastership of the Horse, and forgives you your most blatant outrages. Why she denies you the one thing that would guarantee your wealth at no cost to herself seems so ungenerous."

The earl's eyes narrowed. "Ungenerous," he whispered. He was remembering something Elizabeth had said to Grace O'Malley about Leicester. *He had been generous, unflinchingly generous.* Yes, that was it! "I must make the queen a gift," Essex announced.

"Gifts are always appreciated."

"A *large* gift."

"You're very poor, my dear boy, but I needn't remind you of that. Every property you own is mortgaged to the hilt, and what cash you owned was paid to outfit the *Swiftsure* for your dramatic adventure in Portugal."

"Not every property."

"Make *sense*, Robert!"

"Not every property I own is mortgaged. There is Keyston, in Huntingdonshire."

"But what rents you can squeeze from your tenants there will never in a hundred years make you rich enough to buy the queen a large gift."

"No, Francis. I mean to gift the queen Keyston itself."

"What!"

" 'Tis a fine house and a lovely estate. 'Twould be a generous gift." Essex was thrumming with excitement.

"A generous bribe is more like it. And if you're counting on the queen gifting you the Farm of Sweet Wines in return for Keyston, the odds are *overlong*, Robert."

"They might be, for a man who does not know the queen's mind as I do."

"Still, 'tis a dangerous gamble."

Essex, afire, planted his hands on either side of Bacon's law book and leaned down face-to-face with him. "What am I, Francis, if not a gambling man? I mean to do this, and I mean to succeed. Now will you help me draw up the papers, or must I seek another lawyer?"

Bacon slammed shut the law book, sending up a fine cloud of dust. "Your wish is my command, my lord." He stood and put his arm around Essex's shoulder. "So come away. We have work to do."

EVEN IF ELIZABETH did not in the end grant him the Farm of Sweet Wines, thought Essex as he jumped down to the deck of the Irish galley, the expression on her face at the offer of Keyston had been payment enough. He'd made a pretty speech to go with it, very humble, saying he would willingly give her all the land that he owned with hopes that this "one poor manor" might answer the sum that he owed her.

Her face had softened and the steely glint that had never left her eyes since Leicester's death turned to a playful sparkle. Her fingers covered her mouth, its rusty smile she could not entirely hide.

"My lord Essex," she'd replied with the sweet lilt of a girl being courted, "you know very well the value of that property far exceeds the debt you owe me."

"No, Your Majesty," Essex had replied, "nothing in the world I could gift you could ever repay the deep account accrued by your faithful love of myself." He remembered that when he'd spoken these words— despite the deviousness with which they'd been planned—he'd found himself strangely moved by the utter truth of them. He owed the queen his very life, all hope of his fortunes and future. And he did love her, more deeply than any woman alive. Now everything, for better or worse, had been laid in the Fates' hands, but he found himself dizzy with unaccountable joy.

Grace O'Malley was waiting on deck, fully disguised, with a stout, bushy-bearded Irishman. "Meet my cousin Murrough ne Doe O'Flaherty." She spoke in Latin. "He's the captain of this ship and my host for this voyage."

Essex was, for the briefest moment, taken aback. Here was Grace O'Malley being ferried to England by the hated usurper of her husband's chieftaincy. He quickly regained his wits, bowing graciously to the man, receiving a curt nod back, and suddenly Essex was trembling with anticipation. He was hungry for more of this woman's stirring account. How, he wondered, had she gone from widow twice over and captain of a modest local fleet to "Mother of All the Rebellions in Ireland"? And how had she come to be a guest aboard her old enemy's ship? Had she lost her fleet? And who was this son of hers in Bingham's custody? Certainly not Owen, nor Murrough O'Flaherty. Had she born a son to Eric?

The blood in his veins was tingling. He'd not, after all, have need of Will Meek's potion for staying awake this night. All he would need for that, thought Essex, were Grace O'Malley's words.

# 5

I SUPPOSE there's no way to tell the rest of my story without mention of the three Irish earls."

"By that," said Elizabeth, settling back into her chair, "I take you to mean Ormond, Desmond, and Tyrone."

"You take me correctly. Your cousin Tom of Ormond I feel the least for, neither love nor hatred. He was brought up a Protestant, and was English in all but his place of birth. You have between you the ties of blood, which are very strong, so it doesn't surprise me that Tom was loyal to you from the start. I imagine he'll be so till the day he dies. Now Tyrone—Hugh O'Neill—I've known since he was a child."

"As have I," Elizabeth said. "He was raised in the London home of Henry and Mary Sidney."

"Aye, Henry Sidney. He was the best of your Irish governors."

"And his wife was my dear friend—Robin Dudley's sister."

"Is that so? I'd not made that connection."

Elizabeth, suddenly wistful, gazed into the fire. "Their boy Philip was my godson."

"I'm sorry for your loss. He died too young, but war has a way of claimin' the young."

"It was your loss as well, was it not?"

"Indeed. Philip Sidney wrote me the loveliest letters for several years before his death. Sometimes verse . . . I've always been fond of younger men. But you understand that, don't you, Bess?"

The two women cackled like a pair of conspirators.

"I heard the tale of Essex's grand gesture in the Netherlands war," said Grace, "takin' up Philip Sidney's sword as his own after the poor man's death."

"He took up his widow as well," Elizabeth added.

"He married her, did he?"

The queen nodded.

"Does he love her?"

"I think not. And if I'm not mistaken, he never did."

"Men are strange creatures. Even the best of 'em. Well, like I was sayin', your Earl of Tyrone—who'll always be "The O'Neill" to me— has a real affinity for the English. Perhaps 'twas his upbringing in the Sidney household that did it. But the O'Neills and the O'Malleys go way back. Owen and them were trading partners. And of course he ferried the Scots Gallowglass to North Ireland for all The O'Neill's local battles."

"And *you* brought them, more recently, for their rebellions against the English," Elizabeth added, managing to keep her tone even and mild. "The hiring of Scots mercenaries was made a capital offense before I came to the throne."

"Well, pardon me for sayin' so, but the Gallowglass are too brilliant as fighters and far too entrenched to be stopped by a mere English law. And let's be honest, Bess. *You* hired the Gallowglass whenever England needed their help. As for Hugh O'Neill," said Grace, "he's a stout-hearted Irishman, very brave, and I love him dearly."

"But is he England's friend . . . or foe?"

"Like most of his countrymen, he takes both sides of the fight as they suit him. But Hugh O'Neill plays his hand very close to the chest, so I haven't a clue as to your answer. And you know very well that if I did, I wouldn't tell you anyhow."

Elizabeth grimaced at the mild chastisement.

"It's Gerald Fitzgerald, your Earl of Desmond, I wish had never been born." Grace's expression grew severe. "He was a blight on the Irish landscape, a traitor to humankind. Gerald was a man lacking any principle a'tall. Duplicitous in the extreme, with the moral fiber of a groat."

Elizabeth fixed Grace with her eyes. "Let us be honest, Grace. You most despised Desmond on personal grounds. He had you imprisoned. Very nearly hanged."

"All right. I hated him for that as well. But the truth is, no one of us in Ireland ever rained down so much death and destruction on our own countrymen and women as Desmond did in the three short years of his rebellion."

Grace grew silent, for she was soaring—a winged creature—back through the shadow of years, searching for the precise moment in time on which to alight and begin the telling of her story again. Suddenly it was found, but judging by the wretchedness of her expression, there was no joy in the discovery.

OWEN O'MALLEY lived to a ripe old age, but as he was of hardy stock, his body survived intact long after his mind had gone. He was never, even at the end, a querulous old fart like so many who live beyond their useful years. 'Twas just his memory that faded, like a piece of colored silk, crumpled and left in the sun too long. At first it was unendurable to watch, but later I could see that he was in no pain himself. I told him nothing of the events in Connaught—the same ones that he'd once told me would come to pass. What good would it have done? He was livin' in the past, a much better place, and one I sometimes wished I could go to as well. But that was impossible of course. There was only the present and future, and those looked very strange indeed.

I was a widow again, this time with no thirds to inherit. My father was near death and my children were grown and fending for themselves and their families. True, I owned the biggest fleet in western Ireland, counted three thousand loyal followers and a large herd, which made me a rich woman. But Ireland was like a great war map in those days, with clans and English gathered in their places. Pawns and soldiers, fleets and Gallowglass. Queens and lords and Palesmen just waitin' to march and maraud across the land. All with ambition. All with blood in their eyes.

I was alone, a woman with no alliances, responsible for all the families that followed me. I had to do something, so I looked around for a husband.

I didn't have to look far. My father's words had never left me—"Stay close to the O'Flahertys and the Burkes," he'd said. "They'll never fight you." I was loath to go back to the O'Flahertys, and in truth the Burkes were stronger. The MacWilliam, Shane Oliverus Burke, had himself a wife already, so I looked to the obvious, the *tanaist* of that title. 'Twas Richard Burke, a true shit of a man with very little to recommend him. He was coarse, uneducated, and a foul-tempered drunk. His grown children—three sons and a daughter—were bastards and had little to do with him. Worse, his mother was my old sister-in-law, Finula O'Flaherty Burke, who was slaverin' at the thought of her son finally becoming The MacWilliam. And of course she hated me with a passion.

But he was strong, by virtue of a great horde of men who followed and fought for him. And wealthy, with a vast herd of cattle, and several rich mines from which he earned the moniker "Iron Richard." The name made him sound much mightier than he was, for in truth his mind was mediocre and his will quite malleable. Perhaps that's why I chose to marry him. I knew Richard Burke would never rule me.

To everyone else it appeared a fine match. Together our wealth was enormous. My fleet, our herds, our lands, our castles, our followers. We were a force to be reckoned with, though in the privacy of his keep at Rockfleet, we were somewhat less formidable. He found me attractive, even at my age of thirty-six, and was not averse to havin' his way with me. Truly I hated it, but nights in the connubial bed were my duty as a wife, so I bore his pawing hands and stinking breath, and sought the bathhouse almost every day.

I was at home at Rockfleet Keep. 'Twas on an inlet of the northeast coast of Clew Bay, and on a clear day I could even see Clare Island. My fleet had a good harbor there, and the castle was a mighty stronghold, four stories high. At the top, where we lived, there was a beautiful large window facing west, and from there I could see every ship comin' into the inlet, and from the ramparts every ship within fifty miles.

The truth was, I saw very little of Richard for, like Donal, he was most often out in his territories fightin' some battle or another, less with the neighboring clans and more with the English. Few of my O'Flaherty sailors and their families had yet uprooted themselves to live in the Burkes' territories, near the fleet. I traveled very little and felt most abandoned. My father and Barbara had come to live in a cottage nearby, but the move nearly killed him, and he grew weaker by the day. Even the old memories had flown from his mind, dark and echoing like a ship's empty hold.

That first year at Rockfleet I grew very sad and morbid. All I could do was count my losses. Eric. My home on Clare Island. The freedom of my voyaging. I sulked and brooded and stayed to myself—'twas not like me a'tall, and I knew that my father'd be ashamed if he saw how self-pitying I'd become. But even that thought brought me back to Owen's condition, which was so unkind an ending for so brilliant a life.

One day in July Barbara came running in to say I should come now if I wished to see my father before he passed. Inside his house he was lyin' there—that once huge and powerful body now thin and wasted by time. He was handsome still, with his long thick hair spread out round his head like a silver halo. His eyes were open and I do not know if he saw me, but I thought not. His hand was warm when I took it up to hold, and though 'twas a feeble grip, I like to believe he held mine back.

Day turned to night. Candles were lit and Barbara plied me with warm wine. He did not go gently, my father, standin' on the battle-ground of life and death. I began to pray, though I don't remember to whom I prayed—to Jesus, the old gods and goddesses, to my mother, to Eric, to anyone a'tall who would take poor Owen out of his misery.

And then he was still, and it shocked me how quick the life and the color drained from his face. And I couldn't believe he was gone. I couldn't believe my father was dead. I knew not what to do. I just sat quiet and still like stone while Barbara, calm and knowing, took up a brush and brushed his hair.

Word went out all over Connaught and beyond, and soon people were streamin' in to pay their respects. I was wrenched from my sorry state to bring the gathering together and make my father a funeral worthy of him.

It had to be on the sea, of course. I'd realized that, once I'd come to my senses. So every ship in the fleet was needin' a crew. Those I pulled together from the seamen who'd come from O'Malley and O'Flaherty lands. I was glad to see them, and they me. There was much embracing and laughter and remembrance of Owen. And there were tears shed as well, theirs and mine. Finally, thank Jesus, mine.

The great flotilla—the *Dorcas* at its head—took sail to the west-southwest. 'Twas a fair wind that took us out over the shinin' waves on a gorgeous day my father would have loved. As we rounded Clare Island, I called the order to drop anchor. All was silent 'cept the slappin' of the waves on the hull and the screamin' of the gulls above us. My husband Richard had even taken time from his skirmishes, bringing with him the pipes that were played on the field of battle, and his best bagpipe player as well. He might have been a ratbag, Richard, but he did respect my father, and the tune his piper played as Owen splashed down to his final rest brought tears to every eye.

Owen's death and the great gathering at his funeral was the medicine I needed to heal my wounded heart. I mourned my losses and put them behind me, realizing I was still alive, still the mistress of a great fleet of ships. The sea was callin' me again and my men were ready to follow wherever I'd lead. Richard, I decided, could be left behind to fight our battles on land.

The English were coming to Connaught, that was for sure. Walter, the first Earl of Essex, had already slaughtered hundreds of Irish men, women, and children on Rathlin Island—our very own St. Bartholomew's Day massacre—and the Mayo Burkes were arming themselves, ready to explode in rebellion.

So I escaped with six of my best ships and crews and began a year-long voyage to fish and trade and pirate. I had no idea of the future and no regrets for the past. Once on the water with my fleet and crews, I regained my good humor and all the appreciation I'd had for the sea as a young girl. I would eagerly scan the white-flecked waves for a glimpse of a breaching whale, find myself lulled by the watch pilot singing his humdrum chant to the steersman, feel unaccountable joy in the lighting of the night lantern atop the high poop.

In my mind, my men and I coasted the shores of Africa's bulge and I watched through the spyglass to find the stone pillars that Diego Cão had erected as signposts on his six-thousand-mile voyage south. Or like Bartholomeu Dias, find the Cape of Good Hope by chance, after a thirteen-day gale. If I was lucky I might persuade the crews to do what Vasco da Gama had done—leave the reassuring coastline, and allowing the southeast trades to belly his sails, and guided only by the stars and his instruments, head into the heart of the mid-Atlantic, finally to bear east round the Cape and north to India, land of spice and silk. I was comin' to believe that these were not impossible dreams. That we could go adventuring as no other Irish before us had gone.

We'd not been at sea a month when I found myself rushing to the rail to heave my guts out. I was pregnant, and that was a rude shock, I can tell you. Sure I'd been sharin' a bed with Richard Burke, but I thought I was far past childbearing age, a grandmother and all. The crew were delighted, for it gave them fuel for their teasing, and the larger my belly, the sharper their jibes. "No need for a milk cow aboard!" they'd cry. "We'll use Grace for an anchor!"

I, on the other hand, was most unhappy. For Jesus' sake, I'd just regained my freedom, and had no desire for a whimpering child at my breast, especially Richard's child. If the little creature proved anything like his father, I was bound to loathe it entirely. There was no chance of sailin' to India now, for I would not put the babe in danger, and wished it to be born in Ireland.

But the journey, more modest than my grandiose dreams, was more than pleasant. I found a new factor in Lisbon who was wild for my tanned hides and gave me a good price. We made prizes of several vessels—French, English, Flemish, even a Venetian galley, and our holds were soon piled high with rich booty.

Then, halfway up the coast from Cadiz, just south of Lisbon, we were beset by such a sudden and violent hurricane of wind that before we could brace ourselves, the seas had raised mountainous high. As they broke, the white spray comin' off them looked like nothin' so much as *snow* on their moving slopes. Sight of the other ships in the fleet was lost, all except a glimpse here and there between the waves. Our decks were awash, so we pumped and bailed, hoping the squall would go as quick as it had come. But still the winds mounted, screaming somethin' terrible, and men began to pray for themselves and their cousins in the other boats, and so did I—to Jesus and the goddesses of Ireland and the great gods of the sea.

Then, as a strange answer to our prayers, we were struck by a monster wave that in the space of a breath swept over the deck entirely and set us all a-swimming. When we came to our senses, we saw it had raked us so violent like that it'd snapped the mainmast and bowsprit, and washed them overboard, bower anchors and several forward cannon with them.

Someone called from below that a gaping hole had opened in the side of the ship, and the sea was pouring in. I rushed below to see the disaster with my own eyes. The water was icy and waist deep, and me with my swollen belly waded slow and clumsy to the trouble. Several men tied by their waists with long ropes, and fighting the sea beating over 'em through the open hole, with hammers and canvas were nailing the cloth over it. Others were manning the pumps. They were doin' their best, and no need for orders, so I shouted my prayers for success into the roaring chaos and started back to the deck.

In truth I thought we were lost, that the Fates had decided that on this day, in this ocean, I and the O'Malley fleet, and Richard Burke's unborn child, would meet their end. But of course I was wrong. The winds died very sudden like and it fell calm, as though our prayers had taken a wee while to reach the ears of the gods, but once heard were deemed worthy. Looking down they thought, "Well, somethin' better be done quick or we'll lose those O'Malleys and O'Flahertys, and it's not their time to go just yet."

The snowy mountains of water vanished and now I could see my fleet. All five of the other ships had survived, though well battered they were, trying to limp toward the *Dorcas* as best they could with missing oars and masts and rudders and ripped sails. Lucky that most of 'em were galleys, so at least we were not altogether bereft of propulsion.

My cabin was half destroyed, but I'd learned from Owen that the things one valued most should be stored in the highest place, and so my maps and rutters and instruments were saved, and even the blue dress that I'd stowed in a chest on a high shelf.

The fleet had rowed within shouting distance of the *Dorcas*, and we called to one another our losses. Twelve men had been killed. Our stores of provisions and water were all but destroyed, most by seawater, but some by rats. 'Twas found that the little devils had gnawed off the tops of the jars of biscuit and bread, eaten them, and with no way of escaping, had died in the jars. The hen coops with all their birds had been swept off the decks of all but one of our boats, and the poor remaining fowl were bedraggled and half dead. What with the damage to the ships themselves, we'd been much disabled by the storm, and the coast of Portugal was nowhere in sight.

When, six days later, the mate called from the crow's nest that he'd spotted land we all fell down on our knees and gave thanks to Jesus for savin' us, though they added a blessing for me, their captain, who had also had a hand in their salvation. It took near two months in Vigo to careen the ships, repair, and provision them, and by the time we were ready to sail, I was burstin' the seams with Richard Burke's baby. We made haste for home so the child could be born there, but that was not the way 'twas to be.

We were two days out of port, hugging the coast of northern Spain, in the Bay of Biscay, when I was brought to bed. Lucky for me, Seamus O'Flaherty had found love in Vigo—a young prostitute named Margarita, with raven hair and violet eyes. He'd stolen her from her brothel and brought her aboard the *Dorcas* the night before we'd sailed, and I'd kept her in the cabin with me, there bein' no place with Seamus in his quarters with the other men. She proved a lovely girl and, happy for me, a midwife of sorts. She said she'd delivered three whores' children and they'd all lived.

She was good to her word, Margarita was, for I surely would have died and the child too, had it not been for her skilled hands. The boy chose, like I had done before him, to be born feetfirst, his little arms outstretched like Christ on his cross. These would have torn me apart entirely had the girl not reached inside and pulled the wee limbs down. When young Theobald Burke—"Tibbot" for short—let out his first wail with lungs like a blacksmith's bellows, I heard a great cry go up from outside my cabin door and knew the crew'd been there all the time, perfectly quiet, waitin' for the good news.

Then the strangest thing happened. Margarita placed the clean and swaddled babe to my breast and all at once I felt a rush of joy like a great wave overtakin' me. I'd not felt such a thing at the births of my other babes. I looked on Tibbot's face, red and wrinkled like a little monkey, and I fell in love—just like that. That he was Richard Burke's son no longer mattered, nor that I hadn't wanted him a'tall, nor that he'd nearly killed me on the way out. There was somethin' unexplainable in my heart, which was just about bursting. Within hours Molly the parrot was cooing sweetly, and so it was I heard the softness that had come into my *own* voice.

There was celebratin' on the deck that night, and from the sound of it, most of the crew were in as drunken a pickle as can be imagined. I'd sent Margarita topside for a night with Seamus, and I fell asleep with my boy snuggled to my heart.

I awoke, to my horror, to the sound of commotion on deck, and no celebration, this. There were shouts, a woman's scream, running feet, and last the sound of sword on sword. We'd been boarded, that was for sure—and for the first time in my life I lay paralyzed, torn apart at the middle, with a helpless babe in my arms and a crew above me, best that I could tell, in a drunken stupor.

Just then the door flew open and I beheld my mate, face white as Flanders linen, and half his arm gone from his body. "Turks!" he cried, and fell in a dead heap.

Well, what could I do? I crawled out of my bunk with Tibbot, who was screamin' blue murder. I quick wrapped him in a blanket and made for the galley, stowing him in a drawer with pots and pans, worried that the first place the Turks would plunder would be the captain's cabin. I cursed God then for havin' to leave my child like that—perhaps to go to my death, and he, if captured, to his own. Or worse, a life of slavery. A terrible pain in my lower parts sliced through me, but there was no time for it. Grabbin' a sword I made my way down the hall and up the steps to the deck.

Thank Jesus it was light—just after dawn—and I could see the mayhem goin' on, the air filled with grunts and shrieks, the sharp clanking of metal on metal. My crew was gettin' the worst of it, those damned Barbary pirates—all strangers to drunkenness—completely sober, while the Irish were fighting leaderless without me, and hungover in the extreme. I had to do somethin', and I had to do it fast.

Standing still unnoticed in the doorway I searched, desperate in the chaos, for their captain. With Mohommetans, he was always the most richly dressed, with a tall, feathered turban on his head. I spotted the turban first and the back of his fine silk tunic—he was fighting on the deck with two of my men, wielding his sword with terrible fierceness. I stepped out into the mornin' with no thought in my head but to rally my crew and save the ship. I strode across the gore-slick boards, fights on every side of me, cryin' out for the Heavens to hear, "Your captain's on deck, and with God is behind you!"

At the sound of a woman's voice shouting above the mêlée, that captain turned and looked at me. He was a thin, hawk-nosed creature, not overlarge, but quick and wiry. He stared in disbelief at the wild-haired female in her shift, but he saw the sword in my hand and with a cry to Allah came flyin' at me. 'Twas only my equal speed in turning away that left his blade stuck hard in the mast. I lunged in that moment of opportunity, but he ducked low and quick lunged back at me with a smallsword. I could see him shocked and cursing that I was a woman—a *female infidel*—meetin' him thrust for thrust.

Thus we fought, my advantage a full sword and an upsurge of a mother's protective passion. His, prodigious skill and a man's greater strength. 'Twould have been fine had he not swiveled, retrieving his sword from the mast. Now he was doubly armed, and as I fell back under his assault I struck my head on the lintel of the door above the stairs going below. I tumbled down the steps, cryin' out as my ribs cracked, the breath knocked out of me. I'd lost my sword and 'twas all I could do to crawl to my cabin, hopin' to make it there before that pirate captain followed me in. The door was still open from my hasty exit, and as I crossed the threshold on my hands and knees I heard his footsteps clompin' down the stairs. A gun was stored in a cabinet 'neath my bed, and I caught a glimpse of Molly, her head cocked sidewise as she eyed my frenzied attempts at opening the warped drawer.

I heard a laugh then, for the damn turbaned Turk was standing in the doorway lookin' down at the pathetic sight that was me—a crazed woman, naked under a bloodied shift, just cryin' out to be raped. He dropped his longsword and, keeping the short one in hand, undid his breeches, at the same time movin' across the threshold and into my cabin.

Well, that was when it happened. That small green demon from Hell exploded off her perch, all beak and claw and flapping wing. She went straight for the face, Molly did. He never knew what hit him, but his shrieks were wonderful to hear, and by the time he'd regained sense enough to wrench the parrot off his face, she'd taken out his eye. She was busy biting the hands that held her, and I knew the pirate's shock was wearin' off, so I quick wrenched open the cabinet and grabbed the blunderbuss. I heard Molly screech once before I turned and fired point-blank, blowing a great gaping hole in the Turk's chest. Well, the recoil from that hammered my poor belly somethin' fierce, and then the dead Turk fell hard and heavy on top of me. I blacked out from the pain and, dead to the world, never came to till the next day.

I awoke to the feel of Tibbot gnawin' at my nipple, and when I opened my eyes, I found myself cleaned up and snug in my bunk. The first thing I saw was Molly's empty perch. It all came back to me and the sight wrenched a sob from my throat. I'd like to tell you why that parrot saved my life, for I thought she hated me. And in truth I'd not been alto-gether fond of her. But she was a hero nonetheless and was buried at sea with honors like the rest of our mates. Twenty-two of us were lost and we mourned them, but all agreed 'twas a blessing that Seamus O'Fla-herty had been one of the dead, for his sweet Margarita had been taken by the Barbary pirates, and now faced a terrible fate. Sad and sobered and shorn of our profits and treasures, the fleet sailed home.

The Ireland I found there was one I had never known, torn apart by rebellion and famine and plague. And the English had come in their numbers. Soldiers and settlers swarmed like locusts over the land—peo-ple who despised us, believed us to be wicked and filthy and godless. They began, with great enthusiasm, stealing that which had been ours for a thousand years.

I'd like nothing more than to place the blame—all of it—on En-gland's back, but that would be unfair, for 'twas the Irish chiefs them-selves, petty and squabbling and disorderly, who gave our enemies so great an opportunity. They had hated Gerald, the Earl of Desmond, cov-eted his enormous wealth and lands in Munster, and cheered his fall and imprisonment. But this allowed for Carew's armies and plantations to take hold in the south, made the blighted Englishman bold.

Peter Carew was a horse's arse, ignorant and mindlessly cruel. His first mistake was filling his army's ranks with *bonaughts,* the lowest of the low of Irish society. *Bonaughts* are mercenaries and so will fight even against their own, but these men were worse. Scum, outcasts of their clans, drifters, entirely uncontrollable under anyone's command. Carew's second blunder was to fight your Earl of Ormond's brothers, Edward and Edmund. And for what? A few raids onto Carew's "new lands." Cattle raiding is as old as Ireland, and nothin' to be taken personal like. Instead he punished them, invaded Ormond territories. Allowed his *bonaughts* to burn Killkenny, Black Tom's ancestral home, one of Ireland's most prosperous towns. They despoiled the church, broke into the castle, and publicly raped Edward's poor wife. But Carew wouldn't be stopped. He captured Edmund too and ravaged through the countryside murdering men, women, and children.

But some good came of it. The midland clans were united in their outrage—even the Mayo Burkes, who hated the Ormonds—and we fought back. For the first time in history, Irish lords and chieftains banded together against a common foe, and we destroyed the First Munster Plantation before the Crown could send reinforcements.

The English didn't know what'd hit 'em. They'd been trained to fight in spirals and squares on open ground, solid ground. But we were warriors of another sort altogether—the kings of ambush. In bogs and quagmires, forests and glens, wieldin' our battle axes, darts, spears, and broad blades, even crossbows, we were fearsome indeed. Like somethin' out of another time, like the Norsemen invading. The rebels would often just vanish abruptly from a fight, into the hills and fastnesses, leaving the English to scratch their heads in confusion. Then, when 'twas least expected, Carew's men would find themselves covered on either side by felled trees woven into mighty barricades, behind which lurked the rebels, who came down upon them with war cries that curdled the blood.

The abduction of Edward and Edmund Butler was a great humiliation for their brother Black Tom, and Carew was pressured to release them. Of course once freed they turned and attacked his troops with all their fury, but it was nothin' compared with the might of Ireland's first true great military leader.

His name was James Fitzmaurice Fitzgerald, a Munsterman, and the Earl of Desmond's cousin. But as Gerald Fitzgerald was still languishing in the Tower of London, Fitzmaurice seized upon the need for leadership amongst the Irish and rallied the chiefs round him, proclaiming himself "the Captain of the Desmonds." 'Twas amazing, the loyalty he provoked from all the divers clans, including Clanrickard, and even some Protestant kinsmen of Ormond. In the fever of resistance, some of the lords even gave back their fancy English titles.

But James Fitzmaurice was more than a fighter. Oh yes. He was a shrewd politician. Like most men, he hated his lordly cousin, the Earl of Desmond, but it didn't stop his announcing to the English that the reclaiming of Gerald's rights and lands was the same thing as restoring "native rule," as well as the Gaelic chiefs' hereditary rights and lands. 'Twas a brilliant ploy, but he was not finished. No, not in the least.

James Fitzmaurice saw clearly what strength in unity could be found *in the name of God*. Now the Irish were not what you'd call religious, but Fitzmaurice openly denounced your English Act of Conformity that made Catholics into Protestants, whether they liked it or not. And he denounced *you* as well. The Queen of England, he proclaimed, was a heretic, a bastard and an antichrist. His attempts to restore the Church of Rome to Ireland earned him the ear of the Pope and King Philip of Spain. Philip even sent his man Mendoza to treat with Fitzmaurice. I don't have to tell you what fear that provoked in English hearts, and what joy in the Irish.

We were buoyed with righteousness in our cause, and where Carew had scourged the native countryside 'tween Cork and Kinsale, now Fitzmaurice's armies swept through and savaged the Crown's settlements in the same places. English colonists were killed or driven naked from their walled towns and plantations and into the waiting arms of the very Irish whose homes had been stolen from them. Theirs was not a pretty end.

Fitzmaurice's army—infantry, horse, and kern—fighters in their steel skullcaps and mail shirts, wielding their ancient weapons, took back all that Carew had stolen from us.

I wish to Jesus I could say that's where it ended, but in truth that was just the beginning. Henry Sidney was called in to "pacify" Ireland, to open the overland routes 'tween Cork and Limerick, and Limerick and

Dublin. But he was short of men, like so many of the first English armies, so he made up for his lack with savageness. That good gentleman took the lands and castles of the rebel chiefs—ravaged them, slaughtering cattle, burning fields—so that they, in defending their homes, were forced, one by one, to abandon their leader, James Fitzmaurice. Sidney left in his wake many a hanging tree with the bodies of every able-bodied Irishman who'd not been killed in battle, dangling there as carrion for crows.

The poor countryside, scoured and scorched by Carew, had the same done to it by Fitzmaurice, then finally by Sidney. Beautiful Munster was destroyed altogether, and the first of many famines was upon us.

But like I said, 'twas only the beginning.

Sir John Perrot, who some said was the bastard child of Henry the Eighth—for he certainly looked like him, hugely fat, red bearded and redheaded—came next. He was your earl of Essex's brother-in-law. His idea of restoring order was brutal subjugation, cessation of all native custom and law. Men were forbidden to dress as Irish tradition set forth, but only in the English style as, he said, our woolen mantles left room to hide weapons in their folds. Women could not wear their rolled head-dresses or open smocks with great sleeves, but instead were to wear "decent attire" with hats and laced-up dresses. Perrot said the Irish could not travel about, or even speak the Gaelic tongue. And any man found to be wearing his long forelocks over his face was punished, for it was claimed the thick hair hanging down over his features obscured identity. Even rhymers and bards were outlawed, message carriers too. 'Twas feared they would carry the stories and memories of our people to rally them.

Perrot banned the Brehon laws, "blood money" in particular—the payment for murder—instead to be punished, like the English, with death. He tried very hard, the rotund English governor, but in the end nothing changed. It only got worse. Men and women dressed as they pleased, wore their forelocks and rolled headdresses, spoke Irish, and brought the bards to sing at their suppers. And the Desmond rebellion raged on, moving farther and farther into the west.

Fitzmaurice was still on the loose and southern Ireland lay in ruins.

John Perrot was mad with frustration. His troops were pitiful and ragged, deserting by the hundreds every day, and the Munster Plantation was lost. He realized finally that the Desmond rebellion could not be won in the way the Crown had always waged war, and decided he would fight "the Irish way." Jesus knows what went on in the mind of the man for him to challenge James Fitzmaurice to combat, one-to-one on horse-back, to the death. Winner take all.

I'm sure his cohorts believed the "Irish sickness" had infected Perrot. And perhaps it had. He showed up at the hilltop at the appointed hour attired in native Irish garb, armed only with a broadsword, the poor Irish pony sagging under his immense weight. A heavy rain began to fall, and his army behind him watched and waited for Fitzmaurice to come. And waited. And waited. But the only one who came was a messenger from Fitzmaurice, with a note that said the Captain of the Desmonds would not be comin' a'tall. It said if he killed Perrot, the queen would simply send another deputy in his place, but if Perrot killed *him*, no one could replace him, the rebellion's only leader.

That was true enough, but Perrot—soaking in his saffron cape and scarlet breeches—rode from the field in disgrace and humiliation, his troops laughin' behind their hands. It's true that later, starvation conquered Fitzmaurice, and he fled to France. But Perrot had been changed forever. Ruined, the English would say. He was not the first nor would he be the last.

That was when you freed Gerald, the Earl of Desmond, from captivity and sent him back to Ireland. I suppose you thought he was loyal to the Crown and would hold the south together for you. And the people of Munster, those poor wretches who slunk out from their burned hovels and scorched fields, they believed he would lead them in resistance against the English. Nobody knew then that the only one who'd receive any help from Desmond was Desmond himself.

Well, he made a good show of it at first. On his journey south from Dublin, he'd thrown off his English garb and donned the garments of a great Irish chieftain, and astride his white horse he gathered round him an army of many hundreds of warriors. It took no time a'tall to reclaim his lands from the English. It took even less for the Crown, no doubt shocked by his betrayal, to offer a pardon, the return of his earldom, and all his revenues, in exchange for submission, of course.

Thus began the deadly dance that became the *second* Desmond rebellion, one that cost Ireland countless lives and land, and me my freedom.

Jesus, it pains me to tell the rest of the story. I'd seen the deaths of my loved ones, but those were natural, in the scheme of things, even the murders. But the slow death of the old ways—that was unbearable to watch. The Crown invaded the waters off the western coast with their merchantmen, which we plundered, and their troop ships, with which we did battle. I'd not fought the English since Cock's Castle, and never on the sea. But now my men and I fought with a fury for our home waters, and we won every battle, sinking your ships or taking the best for our fleet.

The English admirals grew incensed that the "mere Irish"—and a woman captain at that—could inflict so much damage on their proud navy. So much did they want revenge on me that one March when Richard was away fighting and little Tibbot was still a toddler, they sent a whole flotilla and six hundred soldiers to trap me at Rockfleet Castle.

For three weeks we were besieged, your troops on land preventing my seamen and me from boarding our ships, anchored in Rockfleet Harbor. But Richard, thank Christ, returned with his ranks and a force of Gallowglass, all of whom I'd brought over in my boats, and who'd never have made their season's wages without me. They broke the siege and allowed us passage out of the keep, and down to the inlet and the fleet. That turned the tide entirely, and we flew from the harbor like a swarm of angry bees, driving off the English, who ran scared, hearing the sound of our fearsome shrieks across the waves. They were madder than a sack of wet cats, and they vowed to destroy Grace O'Malley and capture her fleet once and for all.

If there was one joy at this time, 'twas my son who, in honor of his maritime birth was named Tibbot ne Long—"Tibbot of the Boats." But I suppose he could just as well have earned the moniker for his love of the sea and of ships, which—like my own—showed itself early in life. He was a beautiful child who resembled Owen O'Malley more so than Richard Burke, with a wide forehead and brown sparkling eyes. Tibbot would nag me in all his waking hours, could he please go down to the water? He loved it when the brawny sailors picked him up like a sack of oats and plunked him onto the seat of the dinghy to be rowed out to our ship.

And watching my Tibbot, all wide-eyed, learning the ropes from the seamen, hearing the tall tales of monsters and shipwrecks, was like turnin' back time. 'Twas me again, a little girl with nimble fingers at the knots, weaving nets, sewing sails, climbing the rigging like a dressed monkey. I would steal a look at Tibbot only to find him, face into the wind, eagerly scanning the water for sight of a breaching whale, shouting with laughter as we crashed through the waves.

But for all the love I bore that child, I could see too a trait—a troubling one. I sometimes thought he'd been wrongly named. Should have been "Tibbot of the Winds," for he was so changeable. Aboard my ships he was cheerful, loud and full of fun. Nothing hurt the boy, jibes rolled off him like water. He was sweet and kind and helpful, always there with an unasked-for cup of cool water for a thirsty man. And yet when Tibbot went off with his father to hunt or to war, he became his father's son altogether. A ruthlessness—always submerged in my presence—came boilin' to the surface. He was cunning and brutish and already demanded his small measure of power over the clan. Worse, he wore a cloak of anger, though I never thought it his own, but borrowed from his father. It troubled me, this trait in Tibbot. But what could I do? I tried once to speak to Richard of it, but he saw no problem with his son's two-facedness. Tibbot, he claimed, was in good company, for all the chieftains in Ireland were speaking from both sides of their mouths.

The times Richard came home from his wars he was always in a low rage. War and mayhem and mutual deceit—what chieftain was submitting to what deputy, which atrocities the Crown was perpetratin' on the Irish, and how long the truce had lasted. And worse, the English were coming, like afternoon ants to the roast. There were the gravest tidings. The Burkes' MacWilliam, Shane Oliverus, had submitted to Henry Sidney—sore news for Richard. English interference with the rights of the Burke clan elections meant Richard, *tanaist* to the title, had less hope of the MacWilliamship when Shane Oliverus died. As if there could be worse news, The O'Malley—my father's successor, Melaghlin O'Malley—had submitted as well. I felt a hand squeeze my heart at the news, glad that Owen in his watery grave would never know it.

But the truth of it was, my husband would have been hateful and angry in any event. He was just like that. Richard was not a big man, but he took up a lot of space in a room. And he smoldered like a buried root after a fire, ready to burst forth in flame when you least expected it. It was tiresome bein' married to a man like that, and our only salvation was livin' apart.

Though it seemed impossible that things could get more confused in Connaught, they did. At one time or another, every clan was fighting another, or raising rebellions against the Crown. The Earl of Desmond was crossing from Munster north into Mayo—the Burkes' lands—plundering and murdering his own countrymen in the name of the queen one moment, defending his "native rights" the next. Then Shane Oliverus Burke, The MacWilliam, in a moment of weakness or perhaps just expediency, went to war against the sons of Clanrickard and their Gallowglass, all longtime friends and kinsmen through marriage. Henry Sidney rewarded Shane with a castle taken from his own cousin, which of course provoked a family feud.

'Twas a terrible time. Clans rebelled. Rebels were pardoned. And those pardoned submitted to the Crown, only to rebel once again.

I watched and I waited, keepin' informed by a string of messengers and spies. Like I said, Shane Oliverus's submission had weakened Richard's chances for election to the MacWilliamship in the old way. And of course the old way was dying a death all around us. But I'd not suffered this miserable marriage for nothing. Richard *would* become The MacWilliam, come hell or high water. 'Twas time to act, swift and decisive. And it was up to me, for my husband knew nothing of politics, only of battle.

I was out with my troops in the field when I learned Lord Deputy Sidney was coming to Galway to hear submissions. I quick sent my runner to Richard, who was then battling with some of Desmond's men, and told him to meet me at Rockfleet, at once. That his future was at stake. He returned, grumbling. What kind of man was he that came to the call of a woman? But once he saw the look in my eye—hard and sharp as his broadsword blade—he quieted.

"We're goin' to Galway City. Today," I said.

"And why are we goin' there?"

"To see Henry Sidney and submit."

"Submit! Unrequested?"

"Submit. Surrender. Kiss arse," I said. "Call it what you like."

"You said you'd never surrender."

"I won't, but *you* will. Now go to the bathhouse and have a wash. You smell like a goat."

Of course I explained it to him later. He was not a complete idiot. He knew, like I did, that good relations with the Crown of England would only help our cause, and refusal to submit would no doubt harm us. 'Twas better, I told him, to submit now of his own accord, from a place of strength, than later from a place of weakness. The English had proved they held the power to rescind and grant the most ancient of titles, as they had with The O'Flaherty, takin' it from Donal Crone and givin' it to Murrough ne Doe. And I thought if Henry Sidney found "Iron" Richard Burke a worthy and cooperative chieftain, perhaps he would help in securing the MacWilliamship for him once his time came. Sure it rankled—to my very bones. But I saw the future for what it was, and I thought that the gamble—risky as it was—would pay off handsomely in the end.

So we went to Galway City, me in my blue velvet dress, lookin' like a fine English lady, and Richard, clean and fragrant for the first time in years. 'Twas a great gathering indeed, a proper ball with music and dancing and a feast, with many courses brought on platters by servants. Dozens of chieftains had come, some with their wives all done up in the Irish style, their finest saffron gowns, and golden ear bobs and bracelets, twisted bands in their hair. Mine was the only English gown, and I must admit I flaunted myself quite proudly, like a Spanish peacock.

I was bold making the submission for Richard in Latin, quite eloquent like, if I do say so myself. I swore his loyalty, and offered the services of my fleet. Three galleys and two hundred fighting men—though in truth we had many more. But what sense was there in tipping my hand? Richard was silent the whole time, for he'd never learnt Latin, and besides was tongue-tied in the presence of his enemy. I surprised myself by the ease with which I moved amongst them. 'Twas a game to be played, and in truth it excited me.

The happy surprise of the day was Deputy Sidney's son, Sir Philip, who'd accompanied his father to Ireland and Galway. I remember the first sight of him, so slender and pale. He looked like the poet he was, with a face that spoke of emotions, fathomless emotions, and I loved him at once, a strange affection somewhere between that of a woman for a man and a mother for her son.

I suppose I had never encountered a mind such as Philip Sidney's. We argued Homer and Plato and Livy, and I remember sitting there, my rough-skinned hands laid against the soft blue velvet of my lap, thinking that here I was, Grace O'Malley, carryin' on a fine conversation with one of England's greatest men, and how had I come to this? He spoke with love of his queen—his godmother, Elizabeth—and what a brilliant woman you were. He hated with a passion the Duke of Alençon, to whom you were then engaged, and hoped you would send aid to the Netherlands—a substantial army—to fight against Philip of Spain. 'Twas a war in which he hoped to serve, he told me, and I said I could never imagine so tender a heart as his in battle. He laughed at that, saying a poet and a soldier were not so very different, for they both plumbed the depths of love and hate, life and death, and spoke in the language of the heart.

We even talked of religion, and the dreadful curse of fighting in God's name. The thought of the St. Bartholomew's Day massacre, which he had witnessed, brought tears to both our eyes, and he took my hand then, as if holdin' it would comfort us equally. Jesus, he was a dear man.

Lord Deputy Sidney, perhaps on Philip's urging, paid me more than my due of attention at that gathering, and requested that the next day I take them and a delegation of English on my ship for a trip round Galway Bay. Of course I obliged them, but there I found myself, on a gray, blustery morning, hosting my enemies on a tour of the harbor's defenses. What was the world coming to?

Sir Henry had me pointing out the seawall with its mounted cannon, the castle at the mouth of the bay, and the largest ships anchored there, and what was their tonnage? And who did they belong to? He seemed to be enjoyin' it so much that he had me sail them up the coast and down as well. We were out for the better part of the day, and to my delight I had a chance to speak at length with Philip once again. We tied up at the Galway dock and the English party were taking their leave, very cheerful and good-natured. I found Sir Henry with his son, lingering on the poop, and went up to them with a smile.

"You enjoyed the day?" said I.

"Very much indeed," the Lord Deputy replied. "You are a brilliant captain, Mistress O'Malley, and a fine hostess."

"Thank you for the kind words, Sir Henry, but I wouldn't exactly call me a hostess."

"A host then?" he said, laughing at his own jest.

"No," said I. "Not that either, for at least in Ireland a host does not ask for payment from his guests."

"Payment?" Lord Sidney was perplexed and then his face grew red. Philip stifled a chuckle at my impertinence. "Payment. Of course! Of course you shall be paid for your services today. What do you require?"

" 'Twas a whole day of my time, and wages for my crew, of course," I answered as though calculatin'. "A gold crown should cover it."

"Will you see to it that Mistress O'Malley is paid, Philip?"

"Of course, Father," he said, repressing his smile.

And then with cordial good-byes they departed.

In truth I hadn't needed the money. But I wished to know the true measure of the man. He had seemed respectful enough the evening before, but appearances can be deceiving, especially with the English. But he'd passed my wee test, and much to my surprise his son, when he brought me my payment in gold, requested that we correspond in the coming years. He'd enjoyed our conversation so much, he said, and wished our friendship to endure.

Well, of course I said yes, and we did begin to write to each other, but this—in addition to Richard's surrendering to the Crown—left me torn, like holdin' both sides of the rope in a May Day tug-o-war. Finally I saw how the chieftains felt bewildered and confused, and were mourning the loss of a clear light to guide their way in the dark night descending on Ireland.

'Twasn't long after that the Earl of Desmond drew us all into his dreadful web. So desperate was the man to prove his loyalty to the Crown—a loyalty that was rightly doubted—that he pitted Irish against Irish, and with more savagery than we'd seen from any Englishman. He'd pillaged his way through the Munster countryside and, after a great slaughter of men, women, and children, had burnt the great town of Naas to the ground.

I had taken a hundred of my men—sailors turned soldiers—to defend the Burkes' southern border, where we'd heard that Desmond's fighters had invaded. Well, it was all too obvious where his troops had been. They'd laid waste to the pastures, killin' the cattle—for it was too far to drive them back to Munster—and dumped their bloated carcasses into lakes and rivers and wells to poison them. They torched the forest, and that broke my heart, seeing the black skeletons of ancient trees, and the burnt bodies of the red and fallow deer we'd hunted there. But worst of all were the villages.

Jesus, the cruelty! Cattle raids and skirmishing were one thing. 'Twas men against men, but here were grandmothers slain, infants with their brains bashed out. And the survivors, starving now, with skin hangin' off their bones like the livin' dead.

I met a young child—a girl, perhaps six. She was all but naked when she stood out from the ruin of what had once been a cottage. I think she'd heard my voice, a woman's voice, one not screamin' in terror or pain, but calm and calling out orders to her men. She just stared at me, dirt and tears and snot obscuring what had once been a beautiful little face. I climbed down from my horse and went to her, down on my knees, and without a word she put her arms around me and wept. Oh it tore my heart, for I knew she was alone, an orphan, and from the dreadful smell of the place, the bodies of her kin were not yet buried. I had my men inter them while I took her to the stream and washed her face, which was indeed as lovely as a spring flower. Her name was Alice.

"Can you tell me what happened, Alice? How many came? From what direction? And in what direction did they go?"

"I cannot say," she replied. "They came in the night. I was asleep with my mam." Alice began to weep again.

"All right. No need to remember. Here, don't cry, sweet girl."

"But they fell on her. All of them, and they killed her! And the babe inside her too!"

"Oh, Alice."

I held her again and she whispered hoarsely in my ear.

"She begged them. My mam said please don't harm me, for the

unborn child will die. They laughed and pulled down their breeches, one by one, and then . . . and then . . ."

*How could they?* I thought. *Irishmen. Neighbors from the next county. Desmond's Munstermen who raped and killed a woman pleading her belly.* Unconscionable! What on earth could Gerald be thinking? I had to know.

I'd not sailed the Shannon for many years. 'Twas the finest river of the west, wide and rimmed with dense forests on its shores, Limerick sprawled along its banks fifty miles inland from the coast. Fifteen miles before the city was the fork of the Deel River, and the island castle of Askeaton. I'd not visited there since I was a child, having gone with my father to treat with Gerald Fitzgerald's father, the thirteenth Earl of Desmond.

I remember that time well, for the earl had just incurred the wrath of Henry the Eighth. Your father had most generously offered that the earl's young son Gerald come to England to be reared with Henry's own son, Prince Edward, for a boon companion. A fine offer for an Irish lad, even one so highborn. But the earl refused it out of hand, claiming that the boy could learn all he needed of courtly life and state affairs in Ireland. Gerald's mother had suffered terrors that the fearsome Henry—a man not averse to whacking his own wives' heads off—would not more easily revenge an Irishman's insult, noble or not.

So I'd met Gerald, eight years old to my eleven. He was small and skinny and dark, with eyes too big for his head, but pretty all the same. He rode well, but there was bad blood 'tween father and son, as Gerald was spoilt, and a paltry swordsman to boot.

Now as we rowed the *Dorcas* down the Deel, I remembered the countryside round the castle. The flaithlands were as lovely and wild as anyplace in Ireland. Gorgeous rolling hills and green bogs, forests of mighty pines running with red deer, and rich plowlands woven with deep, swift streams. There were few roads, and with Askeaton even farther from Cork than from Limerick—both English-held towns—'twas secluded enough, and all the refuge the Earl of Desmond needed from the Crown.

The island castle came into view, huge and square with great round towers in each corner, except for the south, which was square and high and fit for defense. We were met by several boats full of Gerald's soldiers who demanded our business and insisted I come with two attendants only, for this unannounced audience with the great Earl of Desmond.

I chose my two best men, David MacSheey and Cormac Downe, and we were rowed to the castle quay, shown in through the gate to the huge courtyard with its gathering and dining halls within, blooming gardens and fish ponds, where two men were netting a good-size trout for their master's supper. We found the courtyard crowded and abuzz, and I waited with my men and Gerald's retainers, his tenants, bards, and musicians, while my presence was being announced to the Earl and Lady Desmond. 'Twas the closest thing to a royal "court" in Ireland, except perhaps Tom of Ormond's home in Leinster. But the Ormond court would be English and genteel and altogether Protestant next to this raucous melee. 'Twas Gaelic and Catholic and felt ancient, like times gone by.

When the page came from Gerald, callin' me in—me who'd just arrived, with other petitioners loitering about, some having waited a week for an audience—an outraged cry went up from them. I turned on my charm, claimin' 'twas no slight to them, for I was the only woman amongst them, and ladies went first. They booed and hissed all the same, but I was gratified that Desmond had shown respect in granting me a speedy audience. It crossed my mind that Eleanor, his wife, had a hand in it, for she was one of the few Irish women of our day who had a backbone in her body, and stood up to her husband.

Indeed, she reclined on a silk couch by his side at a long, otherwise empty table in a dining hall strewn with fresh rushes and hung with gold-shot tapestries. Eleanor had a face more sweet and mild than her temper, which was not harsh as much as staunch. She'd have been a fine man, I always thought, though she would have been improved by a touch of humor, which was altogether missing, as far as I could tell.

Gerald, the Earl of Desmond, was dark and brooding in his features and even more in his mind. I might have been too had I spent the last seven years in English captivity. He'd never quite recovered from the hip shattered by Tom Ormond's musket ball, and his pale face—the sharp slash of his mouth—was twisted in a mask of perpetual pain. 'Twas strange to see the grimace turn to a smile at the sight of me, and I saw all at once the quality that some women found so appealing. He seemed frail, as if he needed lookin' after. Some women liked that, though I was not one of 'em.

"Well, Grace O'Malley," he said, not bothering to rise. "Come sit on my other side."

Eleanor rose and embraced me as I went round behind the table and took a seat. I smiled as I sat, thinking how Desmond was flanked by two mighty women who together, if they'd wished, could make mincemeat out of the man.

"To what do we owe this pleasure?" he said, not altogether sincere.

"Well, I've missed you, Gerald. Horribly," said I with a light tone. I was not ready just yet to batter him with my scorn, nor my demands for fair treatment toward his countrymen. Of course he knew what was comin', but he played along.

"And I've missed you, Grace. Haven't I, Eleanor?"

She smiled indulgently.

"I was just saying the other day how I wished Grace O'Malley would pay a call on her old friend, finally out of prison and home in familiar countryside."

"Did they treat you ill, the English?"

"No. They seem to enjoy my company. Seven years was not enough. Now they require visits to Dublin, which I deny them, and constant communication, which I deny them. Unwavering loyalty, which I promise them. And copious proof of that loyalty, which I duly provide them. Shite! Betrayed by the Queen of England, I was! A caged animal for seven years, desperate to stay Irish in England, and now desperate to seem English in Ireland. What an existence!"

"You seem comfortable enough, Gerald," I said "And peaceful. I see no English troops garrisoned nearby, or coming to batter down your walls."

"For now they trust me. Tomorrow, who knows?" His countenance darkened and he drummed his fingers on the table.

"We've means to pacify them, sweetheart," Eleanor said to Gerald, smoothing his oiled hair. "Don't worry yourself."

All at once I felt the gall risin' in me. Here they sat in Askeaton's luxury—the king and queen of a Gaelic court—complainin' of their ills, while Desmond's captains were savaging the countryside.

"Well, Gerald," said I, the tartness come into my voice, "I wouldn't worry myself about the English, as much as goin' to flaming Hell when I died."

"Get fucked!" he said, his eyes narrowing to slits. There was no need to explain my curse. "Who do you think you are, marching in here to insult me in my own home?"

"I know who I am. It's *you* who are confused, allowin' your troops to commit atrocities against your own people."

"Only the ones who gave succor to Carew's Englishmen," he excused himself. "Those who supported Fitzmaurice, I left alone."

"But, Gerald, those poor people had no choice! They were tryin' to survive, that's all. You can kill a man, but you don't need to nail him hand and foot to his door frame. And for Jesus' sake, you don't have to kill pregnant women and the babes movin' inside 'em. *Irish* women. That's a disgrace, and unchristian as well."

"Let me tell you something, Grace O'Malley." He was leaning over me, though I refused to fall back. All signs of the pale cripple were gone, a cold-eyed snake in its place. "I was born Irish and I was born Catholic, but more important, I was born *noble*—son of the Earl of Desmond. That's an English title passed down from father to son by primogeniture, not Gaelic *tanaistry*. So before I am a Christian, before I am an Irishman, I am a *lord*, and a very great lord indeed. Lord of half of Ireland. It's mine, and the people are mine to do with as I see fit. If they're loyal, I'll give them succor and protection. If they smooth the way for my enemies, then God help them!"

"That's a revolting philosophy, Gerald, but there's a sick logic to it. But how do you defend your atrocities on Burkes' lands? And O'Flahertys? They had nothin' to do with Fitzmaurice."

He looked like he might throttle me. I saw Eleanor's hand grasp his arm.

"I don't have to defend myself to you or to anyone else. I do what I please!"

"Well, I'm telling you, Gerald Fitzgerald, great feckin' Earl of Desmond, you keep out of my territories and my sons' territories or you'll wish you were never born!"

"Get out!"

"Gladly."

I stood and pushed back my couch so violent like I knocked it over, and marched from the room. When I got to the courtyard, there was no sign of Daniel or Cormack, which perturbed me further. But my fury had blinded me, made me stupid, and 'twasn't till Desmond's men were upon me that I understood his treachery. And then it was too late. To the great delight of those gathered in the courtyard, I was dragged away and down into the dungeon of Askeaton.

Before they threw me in a gloomy cell, I caught sight of my men. Both dead, run through and lyin' crumpled like garbage in a heap. God damn Desmond's eyes! I could only wonder what had happened to my ship, anchored nearby. If my men, without me, had defended it. If they'd got away or fallen victim to a cruel ambush. For though I thought poorly of Gerald, I'd not expected such low contempt for a fellow chieftain.

'Twas days before he deigned to see me, first makin' sure I was chained hand and foot to the wall like a common criminal. He stood in the doorway, and by Jesus, 'twas a good thing I was shackled, for I would have torn out his eyes if I could've.

"What of my ship, and my men? The ones you failed to murder in cold blood."

"You'll be happy to know they survived our attack. Most of them. They turned tail and ran for it, though, leaving their beloved captain my prisoner."

"Exactly what I would've wished them to do," said I. "But why *am* I your prisoner, Gerald? What is it you plan to do with me? Certainly not kill me, for if that was the case I'd be a cold corpse by now."

Desmond paced about the tiny cell—limped more like. Lopsided on his feet he was, his bad leg much shorter than the good. And he smiled that grimacing smile he'd given when I'd first come, very pleased with himself now, like a man who's just raided five hundred head of cattle from his neighbor.

"It's like this, Grace. The English are having a hard time trusting my intentions. They've already fought with me my three-day rebellion and pardoned me for it. Certain of Elizabeth's men are whispering fine things in her ear about me. Others—mostly the men who've been to Ireland—are whispering their suspicions. What they need—all of them—is proof of my loyalty to the Crown." He came close to me then and looked me up and down, like a man does a woman, and I almost spit in his eye. "I thought I'd give them *you*," he said.

"Oh, you did?"

"You're a real prize, Grace O'Malley. According to the English, you're a 'great spoiler, chief commander of thieves and murderers at sea.'"

"So I'm to be a pledge of your loyalty."

"Precisely."

He reached out, and leering, cupped my breast in his hand. I strove to be calm and not struggle against my chains, for it'd make me look helpless and weak.

"You're a maggot, not a man," I said, and held his eyes very steady and cold.

"And you're a prisoner at a maggot's mercy," he said and pulled away, receiving no pleasure at the feel of me.

But I wasn't his prisoner long. Soon, still in chains and very filthy from my accommodations, I was carted off by boat for Limerick and the English prison there. Eleanor stood at the quayside, watchin' me go. Her eyes were hard to read, and I couldn't see if 'twas shame in her eyes for her part in this, or satisfaction. Gerald was an arse, but she stood behind her man in all he did, and would do until the day he died. Perhaps, I thought, my capture had been her idea.

The journey of fifteen miles upriver from Askeaton was perhaps the worst of my life, for as I reveled in the clean air and sunlight, the feel of the water lapping beneath me, the wind kissing my cheeks, I knew how short was my reprieve from dismal darkness.

Limerick was a miserable, soggy town with thick mists rising off the Shannon River and blocking out the sun's warmth, even in summer. If I thought Desmond's dungeon was foul, I was soon to know much worse. Her Majesty's gaol was the pit of Hell itself. Where before if I suffered, I suffered alone—which suited me—now I shared a small cell with two other women. Mildred, a whore; and Janet, a once fine English lady laid low by debts and now gone insane.

Jesus, we were a wretched trio. Watery gruel was our only food, and filthy vermin crawled about in the one straw mattress the three of us shared.

All I had was time and I thought endlessly of my children. Of Margaret, and Devil's Hook, who was as good as my own. Of Owen and Murrough, wondering if they'd tried for my release. And what of Richard Burke? Why had my husband failed to rescue me? Sent a hostage in my place?

One day, three months into captivity, two guards came—one a woman—and took me out. Mildred muttered, "Poor bitch," thinkin' they'd come to hang me, and Janet, who never paid me a bit of attention, began to wail, a high, keening sound that followed me out and down the long dark hall. On either side were thick wood doors. Faces peered out of the grates, and misery as I had never known.

I was brought to a bathing room, was bathed and combed and dressed in clean but humble clothing—an English gown and a hat that I pulled off, to my jailors' great consternation. They took me up some wide steps to a floor with proper windows, and into a small stone chamber meant for visiting. There was even a stool that my guards bade me sit on, but I wished to stand to meet whoever was come to see me.

'Twas no less than the President of Munster, Lord William Drury. He was large and florid and looked unhealthy, in the way Englishmen who come to Ireland do. He spoke in Latin, knowing no Irish. I doubt if ever there was an English governor of Ireland who knew its language.

"I see you're being well looked after," he said, regarding my clean dress and fresh-washed hair. I never disabused him of his foolishness, knowing it a waste of my time.

"How long will you keep me here?" I asked him.

"That is unknown," said Drury. He was lookin' at me, really staring, as though to understand how a woman like myself—very normal—could be the notorious pirate that I was.

"What right and reason have you to keep me here a prisoner for an indeterminate time, with no leave to communicate with my kin?"

"The right ensues from your sovereign, the Queen of England, and her laws. And the reason? Your exploits of course. Your plundering of our faithful servant, the Earl of Desmond's lands—"

"*My* plundering of *his* lands?"

"—and piracy on the sea, all following your so-called submission to Henry Sidney."

"My husband's submission," I corrected him. "I accompanied Richard to Galway."

"Lord Deputy Sidney wrote the queen describing the scene, as your husband accompanying *you*. 'A most famous feminine sea captain,' he called you, 'and more than Mrs. Mate with Iron Richard Burke.' "

I stifled a smile at that, thinking how furious Richard would be if he heard such a thing.

"Therefore," Drury said, " 'tis *you* who have betrayed the Crown and will pay the price."

"And what is the price?" I asked. I knew the cost of treason was a rope around the neck. My heart was suddenly pounding, but I tried to show no fear.

Drury's watery eyes regarded me more softly than his harsh words betrayed. "There is no word yet. You will remain here in Limerick Gaol until a decision has been reached."

The guards came in to get me, were leading me out, but I stopped at the door and turning back to Drury said, "Better watch Lord Desmond."

"Why? He is a faithful servant."

I snorted loudly.

"He delivered *you* to us. That was good and dutiful behavior."

I noticed a spark in Drury's eyes. Kindness, I thought.

"Mark me," I said. "You watch the Earl of Desmond. The closer the better." Drury regarded me warily. "You won't be sorry," I added and let myself be led away.

Within the month I received my first letter from Richard. Drury had seen to it, bless his English heart. The missive told how, together with Owen and Devil's Hook and a goodly force of men, Richard had indeed stormed Askeaton Castle to save me, laid siege to it for a week. But it had been futile. They'd been outnumbered, and besides, as they'd found, I'd already been moved to Limerick. They'd been lucky to escape with their lives.

Soon I had heard from all my children, save Murrough, who seemed not to care if I lived or died. Tibbot wrote me from the home where he was fostering. Highborn Irish children were meant to be sent away for their rearing in other men's households. They built vital alliances with their foster families, much like marriages did. My son loved his foster father, Edmund MacTibbot, as much as he did his natural one, though the boy claimed to miss the sea and my boats and the times we spent together on the water. I cried when I read in his scratchy scrawl that he, my youngest, had begged his father to join the assault on Askeaton. Richard had refused, Tibbot too young for battle.

Being my father's daughter I'm not one for complainin', but my year in Limerick prison was holy Hell. I could stand the dark and the damp, the stench, and the slop they called victuals. The rats and the roaches, the lice and the bedbugs were tolerable. I could even bear the hopelessness of my cellmates who, with no family or friends to sustain them, knew they would die there, more miserable than dogs. What nearly killed me, drove me insane, was confinement itself.

*Freedom.* It had been mine, unquestioned, my whole life. I'd gone where I pleased, done what I pleased, said what I pleased to whomever I pleased. Nothing I'd ever dreamt of was beyond my reach, even the shores of India. And now, four stone walls and a family of wretched strangers were my whole world. I steeled my mind against the pain of my losses.

INSTEAD I DWELLED on the Earl of Desmond, his betrayal of me and of Ireland. I wallowed in hate and anger. Dreamed of revenge. I wrote letters to Richard, long and detailed, of plans for assaults on Gerald—letters I knew he'd never receive. I outfitted ships with rows of cannon, imagined thousands of Burkes and O'Flahertys descending on Askeaton. I designed grim weapons of siege. Dreamed of Desmond on his knees, no more than a skeleton, begging for mercy.

The man had stolen my freedom, and there was no mercy to be had from me.

My salvation came not one day too soon. On a frozen morning in November, a whole company of guards came to remove me and two more Irish rebels from Limerick Gaol. President Drury had requested my presence in Dublin—or so the captain of the guard told me—though the prison there was to be my new home. I remember little of the overland haul, for I was half dead with misery and cold, and unwilling to hope for a happy end to the journey. The two rebels in transport with me did nothing to quell my fears, for they spoke of the horrors of Dublin Prison. There was no rack there for torture, they said, but men's feet were roasted in their boots over hot coals instead. And Dublin was the hanging ground for all of Ireland. They told how the English living there missed the sight of executions, which were numerous in their homeland, and how condemned rebels were brought in from all parts of Ireland to feed their appetites.

But once in Dublin and the prison, I found some reason for hope. I'd been given a cell of my own. 'Twas no dungeon either. A proper room it was, with a small window overlooking the prison yard, a bed, a bench, and a table. There was even a brazier, though the jailors—all English—were stingy with coal, and I nearly froze that winter, chilblains afflicting my hands.

I wondered to what or to whom I owed these improved conditions, and I soon found out. 'Twas President Drury who, not long after my arrival, came for a visit to my room. Earlier that day the guard, a surly Englishman, had brought a good load of coal for the fire. Grumbling, he'd even lit it for me, and I knew something was afoot.

Drury looked sicker than he'd been in Limerick, flushed with fever and a constant wheeze in his lungs. 'Twas quite alarming, as I believed the poor man was my only salvation. "Have you all that you need, Mistress O'Malley?" he asked, quite sincere.

"All but my freedom."

"Do you wonder why you're here?" he said, warming his hands at the brazier.

"To be hung at the queen's pleasure?"

He was taken aback by my directness, and then looked meek. "Well, perhaps in the future that may be your fate. But your present improvement in circumstance," he continued almost brightly, "is due to intervention by your champion at the English court."

"My champion?"

"Philip Sidney."

"Blessed man!"

"He wrote to the queen herself. Sang your praises. His word may not be enough to save you from a traitor's death, but at least from misery in Limerick Gaol."

Drury's red face grew suddenly pale and he lowered himself onto my bench. "Forgive me," he said in a weak voice.

"What's makin' you so ill?"

"This godforsaken country," he said with no apology. "For years I served Her Majesty bravely in Scotland—forced the surrender of Edinburgh Castle—and this is the reward I get. Appointment as Lord Justice in a land of savages."

"I think you're exaggeratin'."

"I was in Limerick to see an execution." His eyes glazed over, remembering. "The man was beheaded, his body drawn and quartered . . ."

"A savage *English* custom," I reminded him.

". . . and a woman ran forward and took up the head, and sucked the blood from it, crying that the earth was not worthy to drink it! I've spent most of my personal fortune to sustain this administration, for the queen will not support it with her own. When she sends troops they are paltry—altogether inadequate—made up of convicts and scoundrels, with arms and provisions for an army half its size. She is haunted by Ireland, yet chooses most often to ignore it. She despises spending her money on what she calls 'that unhappy island,' and procrastinates most blatantly when dealing with Irish problems. Yet perversely, she sends the finest of her men—soldiers and administrators—to deal with it, and all of them who do not die here return shattered and ill." Drury raked his fingers through his thinning hair. "I've lost my health and reputation in this desolate land." His mouth quivered. "My wife has threatened that if I do not take her back to London, she will leave me."

"Why would you stay, in that case?"

"I'm a loyal servant of the queen," he replied, as if I'd asked why he continued to breathe. "Outside of her court and her favor . . . there is nothing of value in England. Nothing."

"And how is my dear friend the Earl of Desmond?"

"Living quietly at Askeaton."

"Peacefully?"

"Yes."

"The queen's loyal servant?"

"She and her Privy Council have never forgotten his deliverance of yourself into English custody."

"I was *that* important?"

He nodded silently, with a sly smile. I believed then that the man liked me, and I thought I'd push my luck.

"Would you give me means to write, and permission to send as well as receive letters?"

"To whom would you write?"

"My husband and children."

"And you would promise me not to plot your escape?"

"You have my word," I told him.

"Lord Sidney had it."

" 'Twas my *husband's* word."

"Now I'll have yours."

I held his eyes. He *did* like me. Wished fervently to believe me. I nodded my promise. He stood and moved to the door.

"One more thing," I said. He turned back. "You'll give me fair warnin' if I'm to be executed."

"I will."

I wondered at Drury's promise, as one week apart the two Irish rebels who'd come with me from Limerick were hanged like dogs and sundried in front of my eyes. The first time, they'd shackled the prisoners— all of us—and took us out to the yard for a blessed breath of air, we believed. Then a company of English guards marched out to a drumbeat, in stiff formation, followed by the doomed man. Suddenly we knew 'twas no "breath of fresh air" but a group torture, forcin' us to behold the grisly spectacle, fuel for our nightmares. Well, the Irishman bein' led to the gibbit behaved himself with the greatest bravery, even when his captors denied him a priest, givin' him the choice of a Protestant clergyman . . . or nothing, which is by some ways of thinking a choice between Heaven and burnin' eternally in the pits of Hell. He refused them the satisfaction of hearing their heretic prayers, and we in the yard all prayed after him, silent and fervent and hopin' our prayers would speed him in the right direction. Still, it was hard, for the poor bastard swung and kicked for a long time, and finally shat himself when he let go of his miserable life. They forced us to stand for the longest time, watchin' his dead body swing, purple tongue bulgin' from his mouth, until the first crow soared down in a spiral, landed on his shoulder, and plucked out his eye.

Jesus, it was cruel, and it shook me to the core. Was I next? Could I trust Drury to tell me the truth?

My only true joy were the letters I received from my family, and knowledge they were receivin' mine as well. The hours I'd sit at my table writing were the best of my day. I would study the letters from Tibbot, more and more often with bits of Latin thrown in, and I'd silently bless old MacTibbot for forwarding my son's education. But I'd write to Tibbot sternly, with corrections, and admonitions to study even harder. Richard's letters, in Gaelic, were the crude epistles of a man with an indifferent education. They were nevertheless filled with news of Connaught and the invasion by Drury's most recent field commander there, Nicholas Maltby. All the chieftains there were playin' the game of alliance to the Crown—one day loyal, the next at attack—and Maltby was a right scourge to the countryside.

I'd been right about Drury. He liked his famous female captive and found in me a sympathetic ear. He would come to my cell and we'd talk, sometimes for hours, of the strange times we lived in. His health seemed worse with every visit, a man of my own age who looked a hundred. He was careful to keep from his enemy—me—all intelligence that, divulged, could hurt the royal cause, but I gathered much from his tales of personal woe. He continued to beg the Crown for help in liftin' the financial burden of Ireland off his poor shoulders. He wished, he said, to taste the queen's bounty, and in fact Lord William Cecil obliged him with four thousand pounds. But it was soon spent, and before long he was worried again for his frail constitution, and the fate of his wife should he die, all his money wasted in this desolate land. Worse, for all his trouble, he was sure that certain men of power in London were plotting his replacement.

For my part I whispered in his ear about the Earl of Desmond, who still swore his loyal obedience to the Crown. I painted him as he was—

A TRAITOR!" Elizabeth finished for Grace, sitting forward in her chair. Grace could see her eyes flashing with anger.

"He was that, all right," she agreed. "The thing about Gerald, he was a traitor to England and Ireland both." Elizabeth's countenance grew hard remembering, and Grace continued. "When Desmond's cousin Fitzmaurice returned to Munster he landed at Fort del Oro with the English Jesuit Father Sanders, and nine hundred troops from the Holy Father . . ."

"That was the real beginning . . . my worst fears realized." Elizabeth's body had grown straight and rigid.

"Aye. I suppose they would have been. For Sanders brought *religion* to the war. Very powerful, that."

"And threats that Philip of Spain would follow with *his* armies, my direst nightmare," said Elizabeth, looking pale. "Spanish troops massing just across the Irish Channel from England."

"Well, your English forces—puny as they were—made quick work of those nine hundred Italians at the Fort. I heard about it in Dublin Prison. I'd been whispering madly in William Drury's ear about Desmond. But he'd not listened. Drury wished desperately to believe in Gerald's loyalty. That he and his four thousand Munstermen would refuse to join his cousin Fitzmaurice to fight the English, but rise up to fight *for* the English. I told him he was dreamin' if he thought Desmond would do such a thing. But then, to complicate things further still, Gerald's brother, John, became involved, raising *his* army against the Crown. Now all the Desmonds were squabbling amongst themselves for power to lead the rebellion."

"And then one day," Elizabeth began, "the Earl of Desmond's four-thousand-man army—that which we'd counted upon to defend Munster—simply vanished."

"It would have seemed that way to you. Of course the Irish knew where they'd gone—over to John of Desmond—and we knew 'twas only a matter of time till Gerald showed his true colors—that he was loyal to no one but himself. But I have to thank the Earl of Desmond for his treachery to the Crown, for it proved *my* case against him. Lord

Drury saw it as my willingness to help the English cause. To him 'twas a show of my loyalty. He set me free, God bless his heart."

Elizabeth eased back in her chair again, though a haunted expression lingered on her face as Grace began her story again.

***

'TIS IRONIC THAT Fitzmaurice was killed not by the English, but by an Irishman, and a Burke at that. Only one part of the Burke clan was Protestant, and it was James Fitzmaurice's bad fortune that in the course of his rebellion he should run into one of the few Irishmen truly loyal to the Crown. Fitzmaurice was mortally wounded by a local Burke, but managed to get away with his men. He knew he was dyin' and ordered them to behead him and hide his head, knowin' the English would use that part of him for a trophy. His orders were followed all right, and his torso hidden in a tree. Indeed, the English found the body and carted it off to Limerick, where they hung it beside the cathedral to rot away to nothing.

That was how the Earl of Desmond inherited a full-on uprising, thousands of Irish rebels, a Jesuit priest, and the Pope's blessing to fight a holy war against England. Aye, the Desmond rebellion—the second one—was more brutal even than the first. It raged on for three years and took the lives of half a *million* Irish, destroying what had been a most beautiful land.

But back in Connaught I had troubles of my own.

Well, of course I was thrilled to be goin' home, to have my freedom again. But the Connaught I returned to was under siege, indeed the whole of Ireland was besieged, crawlin' with English who saw us all as the world's most detestable creatures. And my own life, that had changed as well. It was, in the coming years, to be dominated by three men—a teenaged son who needed protectin', an English governor who thought me an abomination of womanhood, and a feckin' idiot for a husband.

I arrived at Burrishoole in a fierce winter storm at the turn of the new year of 1580 to find nobody home. 'Twas dark and gloomy in the keep and not the welcome I'd dreamt of after nearly two years in prison. But soon I heard that Richard was coming, and my children—all except Tibbot.

My son Owen was first to arrive, alone, for his wife, Katherine, daughter of old Edmund Burke, had almost died two months before, givin' birth to their first child. Murrough, who came next, had not a good word for anyone. His brother, he insisted, planting his filthy boots on my table, had gone fat and soft. He was ashamed to count Owen as his kin. For me, his own mother, there was nary a word of sentiment and only a gruff embrace. Murrough had never married and it didn't surprise me, always content as he was with the Galway whores. 'Twas said that he'd sired several bastards, but they'd been girls, and he hadn't bothered to claim them as his own.

I was greatly alarmed by Margaret's arrival with Devil's Hook, for the girl was too far gone with pregnancy to've been traveling in such weather. But I was most gratified to seem them both, for they loved each other the way a man and wife should do, and the drafty old keep grew warm by virtue of their presence alone.

Then Richard came home and the laughter stopped. After riding two days he was wild and mud soaked and smelled disgusting, but the news he bore was worse than either his appearance or his odor.

"From where have you come?" I said.

"Limerick."

"And what was in Limerick?"

"A war council."

My heart sank. I knew it was coming, but still . . .

"Who did you meet with there?" Hook wanted to know.

"Certain chieftains," Richard replied. His mood was growing black and I was growing worried.

"Which chieftains would they have been?" I said.

"Shane Oliverus Burke."

"Who, besides The MacWilliam?"

"Some O'Malleys. Some O'Flahertys. A few Clangibbons."

He looked like he might brain me if I didn't cease my questioning. But I would not stop. "Who *else* was there, Richard?"

"Gerald and his Doctor Sanders the Jesuit, all right! The Earl of bloody Desmond called us and we went, the lot of us, to see what he would say!"

All the men leaned closer.

"What did he say, Father?" Murrough was near frothin' at the mouth with excitement.

"He asked us to raise Mayo in support of himself, and Sanders invoked the name of the Holy Father." Richard glared at me. "I said yes."

"You said *yes*?" I shouted.

"And everyone else did too, except The MacWilliam."

"You agreed to fight on the side of the Earl of Desmond, who put your wife in his dungeon and handed her over to the English?" I stood with Richard toe to toe, fury rising off me like a stoked fire. But he was shameless and held his ground.

"I did," he said, "for I don't like the English comin' into my territories."

"Well, neither do I, Richard, but throwin' your lot in with the one Irish lord the Crown has finally proclaimed a *traitor* will bring the wrath of the English down on our heads. This is reckless and harebrained in the extreme!"

"It's not harebrained, Grace."

"Let me ask you this," I said, tryin' to remain calm. "Do you still desire the MacWilliamship?"

"You know I do."

"Have you forgotten *who* granted that title to Shane Oliverus?"

"The English."

"That's right. And what reason do you suppose they would have for grantin' the title to a man who's thrown in with their worst enemy?"

"I don't need the English grantin' me The MacWilliamship. I'll just fight for it."

"I'll fight with you, Father!" Murrough cried, puffed up with stupid pride.

"The two of you, Jesus!"

"Look, Grace." Richard was gentler now. Perhaps he saw how betrayed I felt by his actions. "Western Connaught is remote," he said. "The English have never occupied her. They never will."

What could I say to such boneheadness?

As promised, Shane Oliverus Burke honored his pledge and fought on England's side. Richard, meanwhile, backed by the fiercest *sept* of Gallowglass in Ireland, and all the others, went out to do his brainless battle. Of course the English invaded Connaught with a force the likes of which we'd never known. They marched against Richard, Captain Maltby at their head. My husband, to his horror, could not, even with his Gallowglass, keep the field against the Crown's army, and was driven out of his own land, forced to flee to the islands in Clew Bay. 'Twas humiliation to be sure, but worse—much worse—Maltby occupied Burrishoole, took the abbey for his headquarters. And for the first time in our history, a force of English soldiers were garrisoned in Connaught.

I'd had no time to gather my fleet after my return from prison, but it was just as well, for if I'd joined Richard's battle, I'd not have been able to help him as I did. As it was, I waited till he'd been chased to Inishturk Island, he takin' refuge there on the windswept hills. I reckoned him too far away to do more damage to himself. Then I put on my blue dress and went to see Maltby at Burrishoole Abbey.

My heart broke to see the village swarmin' with the Crown's soldiers. They were busy building their fortress and barracks, razing the forests nearby for wood. They leered at the girls and I feared for their safety. They even eyed me—a woman of fifty—and I saw that they'd rip my blue dress off and rape me too, given the chance.

Captain Maltby was respectful enough. He hardly made me wait a'tall for an audience.

"William Drury's famous prisoner," Maltby said as a greeting. He sat behind the abbot's desk, and I wondered briefly where the priest and his brothers had gone, now with their church overrun by heretics.

"Lord Justice Drury is a fine man," I said. "For an Englishman."

Maltby laughed. "He always said you lived up to your reputation." He regarded me closely. "He said you could be trusted."

"Unlike my husband."

"He is a problem," Maltby agreed.

I went round the abbot's desk and sat myself on the edge of it, right next to Captain Maltby. I could see his surprise. He'd never known a woman so forward.

"Iron Richard Burke wants your pardon," I said. "Allow him to return and he will submit, pledge his loyalty to the queen."

"Do you speak for him?"

"I do."

"Does he know he'll be surrendering to me?"

"He will."

"And how do I know he'll honor his pledge?"

"You have my word."

"I see." He was gobsmacked by my impudence, but I wasn't done yet.

"I know that Her Majesty has no desire to spend a fortune waging war in as distant a province as Connaught. And she knows Richard Burke is strong. She'd rather have him as an ally than a foe. Am I right?"

"You are."

"Then be smart," I said, leanin' down with my face in his face, "and when it comes time, name my husband The MacWilliam. It's a sad and terrible thing that a Gaelic title as old and sacred as that should be bestowed on a *tanaist* by an Englishman. But that's the way it is. You give Richard Burke the MacWilliamship, and I promise you peace in Connaught. Tell that to your queen."

Well, he did, and when the time came—Shane Oliverus had died— Captain Maltby knighted Richard and appointed him The MacWilliam. There were conditions of course—the most severe being the banishment of the Gallowglass he'd employed in the uprising. Richard was forced to eject those Scotsmen, loyal to our families for so long, and eject them without pay, which was as much a worry as a joy. They were a fierce lot who could hold a grudge, but worse, when we needed them again, would they come?

Of course the title was not won without some bloodshed. It was Ireland after all. And Shane Oliverus's brother, Richard Oliverus, thought the MacWilliamship belonged to *him*. Maltby had appointed him sheriff instead, and that had been seen as an insult. Some men were slain on both sides, but things settled down and Richard's reign was, as I'd promised Maltby, peaceful on the whole.

We removed ourselves from Burrishoole and the awful sight of garrisoned troops in our village and, moving inland, took up residence on the green shores of Lough Mask. I loathed deserting the seaside and postponing the reassembling of my fleet, but I thought it prudent.

Richard needed distance from the English, and an assembled fleet just under their noses would have been an enticing target. I decided to bide my time and enjoy what peace was allowed us.

I visited Tibbot as often as I was able, and he was a great joy to me. He had moved homes and was fostered then with Myles MacEvilly—a great warrior in his own right—and his two boys, at Kinturk Castle. Tibbot's voice had barely broken and the first of his whiskers were sprouting on his pimply chin. But all my son could think of was fighting. I explained that for the moment the Burkes were *not at war* and he should revel in the peaceful times. I would have lured him back to the life of the sea, where his better side had always shown itself, but for the moment we were landlubbers, and I had no choice to offer him.

Though Tibbot was not so rude, nor stupid to say so, I knew he thought I'd gone soft. That I'd given in to the English, and made his father do the same. I tried to explain the benefits of peace but he could not hear me. He was too enamored of the arts of war, and as I watched him practicing swordplay with Myles MacEvilly and his sons I saw what had happened. That "trait" of Tibbot's, the one I'd seen in him early on—his changeability—had shown itself again. His loyalties shifted with the wind, and in his mind he was the son of the great warrior chief MacEvilly, ready to do battle with the English at any time.

I wrote to Philip Sidney with my thanks for his part in my release, and he wrote me back with bits of verse, and news of Spain's conquests in the Netherlands. More than ever he wished to distinguish himself in war, and I wondered at the folly of it.

Why did all men crave war? Sure in my years of pirating I'd spilled blood and relished a good plunder, but battles that killed hundreds or thousands and left the land ravaged round it . . . to wish for that I could not fathom. Philip Sidney said 'twas my sex. That even a woman as fierce as myself was still a woman. That the feminine gender at its core abhorred the atrocities, those without which men could not feel manly and distinguish themselves in the world. I thought there was a ring of truth to this, for never was there a gentler man than Philip Sidney, and he wished to march off to the killing fields as fervently as the next.

I should have known that Richard Burke could never keep the peace.

After three years the lust for bloodshed rose in him like sap in an oak. He knew I'd kill him if he broke his pledge to the Crown, so he did the next best thing. He rode off with a small band of men and raided a neighboring village, stealing two hundred head of cattle for the thrill of it. I was disgusted and refused to listen to his loudmouthed retelling of the adventure. I avoided him, for I knew if I spoke my mind I'd be nothin' but a nagging wife, and was damned if I'd stoop that low.

What I did not know was that he'd been wounded in the raid—shot in the side with an arrow. He'd wrenched it out of himself and stanched the flow as best he could, then ridden home flushed with victory and feeling no pain. 'Twasn't till a week later, when I smelled the putrefaction, that he showed me the wound. I told you he was a stupid man, and this was the final proof of it.

As it was, all my medicines and poultices were useless against Richard's poisoned blood. He burned with a terrible ague and his limbs grew black and purple, oozing with open sores. He grew pale and his lips shriveled, baring his gums—he looked like a gruesome corpse. Then he died, blessedly, and put himself out of his misery.

His mother, Finula, went mad with grief, wailing and tearing her hair. Her precious son, The MacWilliam, was dead. "Oh, how could God be so cruel?" she cried. I wanted to scream, "How could the man be so ignorant? Who leaves a wound in the gut untended for a week?" I was furious and had no pity for Richard Burke. He'd struggled his whole life for the greatest title in Connaught and won it. He had a son and a peaceful kingdom. And he threw it all away for a single night of cattle raiding. His epitaph said it all: "Here lies a plundering, warlike, and rebellious man."

The worst of it, of course, was that with Richard dead, the protection of the MacWilliamship was taken from Tibbot and me. The boy could one day try for the title, but I had nothing of Richard's unless I was prepared to fight for it. I'd learned the hard way how chieftains' widows—despite the law of thirds—were treated, and I'd not allow the same to happen as it did after Donal O'Flaherty's death.

I waited for no one to grant or deprive me of my widow's due, and simply laid claim to it. Gathering together all my followers, and with a thousand head of cows and mares, became a dweller in Richard's small castle, Carrickhowley, near Burrishoole. Tibbot, by then sixteen and man enough to live on his own, took up residence in Burrishoole Keep. The troops garrisoned in the village were at the time without a forceful leader—for Maltby had gone on to other battles—and we simply ignored them. Then I began to assemble my fleet again in Clew Bay, with great hopes of the future with my son by my side. But of course that was not to be. For it was then came the devil himself into Connaught.

And his name was Richard Bingham.

<figure>◇◇◇◇</figure>

WHAT IS IT?" Elizabeth sat forward in her chair.

Grace appeared stricken, overcome. She'd fallen silent, this woman whose seamless story had rolled like the endless procession of waves onto shore. She blinked back tears and her mouth twisted and pinched as she stifled her fury.

"He murdered Owen, my firstborn son."

"Richard Bingham?"

"In cold blood. 'Twas far more heinous than the clan murders of Donal O'Flaherty or Eric, or even Tall Walter Burke, whose killer lay in wait for him. My son was bound hand and foot when the English soldiers—on Bingham's orders—fell on him with knives and stabbed him twelves times, to death. Owen, who'd refused to fight them, who'd shown them nothing but hospitality." Grace stared into Elizabeth's eyes. "Did you not know Richard Bingham had my Owen murdered?"

"I did not. I knew that he'd once taken you into custody, that he'd deprived you of your livelihood. That he sometimes dealt harshly with the people of western Ireland."

"Sometimes dealt harshly!" cried Grace. "He was the 'Flail of Connaught,' a heartless bastard, and now he holds my son, my youngest boy, Tibbot, in his custody. He's threatened to hang him!" Grace bolted from her chair and, picking up the poker, thrust it angrily at the burning logs.

"Tell me," said Elizabeth in a most gentle voice. "How did it come to this?"

Grace wheeled to face the queen. "How it came to this is that *you* sent a demon with an army of demons into my homeland and gave them a free hand!"

Elizabeth's features grew rigid, and a rush of blood flushed the skin of her pale, faintly pockmarked face. No one spoke to the queen in this way.

"Forgive me, Your Majesty." Grace was seething and the apology stilted, far more necessary than sincere. The women held each other's eyes in a long, terrible silence. Finally Elizabeth spoke.

"Please go on. Finish your story."

Grace returned to her chair but sat leaning forward, forearms on her knees. Her words were calmly spoken, but beneath they simmered with outrage.

THE LOCAL CHIEFTAINS were all so tired of fighting their petty fights that they wearily signed your "Composition of Connaught." They were told 'twas merely a survey of the province, a means to fairly levy taxes on the people, and give them relief from the *cess*—the quartering of English troops on their lands at their expense. Jesus only knows if the chieftains meant to observe the indentures they'd signed, but it proved to be their ruination, pure and simple. It opened the door for the Crown's colonists and soldiers to steal what was ours, had been ours for a thousand years.

Worse, by signin' the Composition, the chiefs relinquished once and forever the old ways and the Brehon law—all that made them a Gaelic people. When Irish *tanaistry* was forfeited for English inheritance law, everything changed. No longer ruler to the wider clan, a chieftain ruled only his immediate *sept*. The reward, they were told, for adhering to primogeniture was that their sons—unquestioned—would inherit their titles and estates. No more fighting for election to chieftaincy. No more murdering of male kin in striving for the title. Of course this looked favorable, especially to the minor chiefs—of which there were many—for now without an overlord, they thought themselves very great indeed, and their sons were assured of their titles after them.

But it only looked good for a while. Foreigners laid claim to Irish family lands, and were granted them under the new laws. Properties owned by clans for endless generations were lost. And the few chiefs who'd not signed were all of a sudden at war with the ones who had.

Nothing was sacred. Betrayal became a way of life. The English put an actual price on the Irish rebels—"head money" it was called. Informers informed on their families and friends. Men arrived at the English garrisons carrying over their shoulders sackfuls of their brothers' heads. Village, field, and forest were put to the torch. Cattle died by the thousands. Famine was widespread, and weakened bodies succumbed to plague. And marching over the ruined landscape were English soldiers, brutalizing us all. The bloodshed was terrible, but it paled before the unraveling of the ancient Irish tapestry. Aye, that was the worst of it.

The man you sent into our midst to enforce the blasted Composition was Richard Bingham. He loathed the Irish. "If Hell were opened," he was heard to say, "and all the evil spirits roamed abroad, they would never be worse than these Connaught rogues—rather, *dogs*, and worse than dogs. For the Irish race is degenerate and debases all humanity."

Melaughlin, The O'Malley, signed the Composition, and so did most of the Connaught chieftains. But I did not sign, nor did my sons Owen and Murrough, and in this resistance—fighting for *tanaistry* and the old ways—were sown the seeds of our own misfortune and death.

Do you know why Bingham hated me so? 'Twas on two accounts, really. Number one—in our first encounter I defeated him. And number two—I witnessed his utter humiliation. Richard Bingham would have you believe I was an abomination of womanhood. That God, who rarely erred, had done so in creatin' me. Realizing his mistake the Lord had cast me down, and I'd been rescued by Satan himself, and whosoever destroyed me was in service to God Almighty.

I'll tell you the story of Bingham's defeat at Castle Hag at the hands of Grace O'Malley's rebels, for no one else will—certainly not him. 'Twas a rout pure and simple. We shredded his English troops like a lion's claw through China silk.

What you know as the Burkes' Rebellion first came to a head over that blighted title—the MacWilliamship—like the bursting open of a poisonous boil. When my Richard died, old Edmund Burke—eighty years if he was a day—decided his time had finally come. He was *tanaist* for the Burke clan's chieftaincy, and no English bastard could tell him otherwise.

Richard Bingham had been busy. He'd held his first "session" for the carrying out of the Composition of Connaught at the Castle Donamona. All the chief families of the province had been called, and those who had signed came to do business with their new English overlord. Little did they know that by day's end seventy of 'em would be in Mayo swinging from the end of a rope.

I suppose they thought, bein' chieftains and all, that they'd be fined and maybe flogged for their "offenses" against the Crown. But they were gathered in a line, two abreast, and marched from the great hall outside to the inner courtyard. Much to their surprise gallows had been built. Seventy in all. The men were hung with no fanfare, and those who'd been spared were turned out of Donamona like common beggars, the castle doors bolted behind them.

So that was how 'twas to be. Some chiefs folded, relinquished their power and dignity. Others, like Edmund Burke, at eighty with nothin' to lose, fought back. Edmund's wife was Morag, a tough old bird who'd decided they'd waited long enough for the highest Burke title. Bingham had named Richard Oliverus to the MacWilliamship, but by the old laws Edmund was *tanaist*, and he would have it or he would die trying.

In defiance he raided Richard Oliverus's lands and stole his cattle. Bingham objected—these were the queen's herds now, and Edmund's resistance must be met with force. The old man and his wife, gathering their most faithful around them, fortified Castle Hag, which stood on an island in Lough Mask, and took refuge in it. They sent their fastest messengers north and waited for help to arrive. The only one who made it before the English attacked was Devil's Hook and his fiercest fighting men. I was away in Galway trading and only heard of the siege at Lough Mask a week later.

I had listened in horror to the stories from Donamona. Nothing could stop the destruction I knew was the future of Ireland, but I could fight all the same. How could you wake and face yourself each morning if you didn't at least try?

I went to my son Owen and told him that. Edmund Burke was his wife's own father, but he would not fight. He chose peace instead. Said 'twas Jesus' way, to love his enemy no matter what. What can you say to that? Of course Murrough was deaf to my call, but all the same I'd gathered a mighty force without my boys, and we moved like silent wolves across familiar bogs and glens toward the shores of Lough Mask. We were less than a day away when one of my roving spies came runnin' to me. He'd been abroad in the pasturelands to the east of Lough Mask and told of a great column of English reinforcements marching toward the lake. We hurried our pace, now with no time to lose.

Castle Hag stood proud in the center of the island. We could hear the pop, pop, pop of gunfire from the battlements and towers. And there with his troops in fifty boats, halfway out to the castle, was Captain Richard Bingham—I'd not yet met the man—but I heard him shouting his shrill orders over the placid water.

By stealth we overcame the troops he'd left behind and captured the shoreside camp. Unlike other English troops Bingham's men were clothed in uniforms, a pretty robin's-egg blue. Some of my men donned the ones pulled from the bodies of the dead, and we made a great performance of manning the cannon as Crown soldiers. No one in the boats on the lake was any the wiser. With great care I took a small patrol—two carts filled with arms and other supplies—and made my way round to the mooring on the south coast of Lough Mask, down behind the castle. 'Twas altogether unguarded by the English—they'd not known it was there. I filled the two dinghies I found at the dock with the stolen ordnance, and rowed to the backside of Castle Hag.

We were greeted with the greatest joy and relief by Edmund and Morag and my son-in-law, Hook, and I quickly told them my plan. We'd have to move fast, escape the island altogether, for help from the northern clans would not arrive in time, and English reinforcements were close at hand. I had carried in a pile of English uniforms and everyone donned them.

Night was fallin' and Bingham's attack by boat was finished for the day. We heard his orders called, and watched as his flotilla retreated back toward the shore. Little did they know that manning their guns were Irish rebels, and as the first cannon roared out across the water at them, they fell back in horror and confusion. We in the castle moved fast. We took to our boats and rowed out *behind* the English, peppering them with fire from the rear. We watched as a ball struck a boat, punching a huge hole in her. She sank at once, dunking in the lake her squadron of men.

Few had been taught to swim and now, aside from the booming cannon and the high whine of small artillery, came shrieks of anguish, men pleadin' to be saved from a watery death.

But Bingham had no mind to rescue his drowning men, absorbed as he was in the frontal assault. I caught sight of Captain Bingham in the lightning of an explosion. He had the pinched face of a weasel and his beard was cut too neatly for a man. His eyes were wild with fear, for in that moment he knew that his enemy was not just onshore but there on the water in boats, in Crown uniforms, picking them off like sitting ducks. He shouted frantic like, and though 'twas in English, which I had not yet learned, I knew he was crying a warning to his men. But it was too late. Hook, in his boat, was an excellent shot and one after another, English soldiers toppled from the dinghies into the lake.

And then with a great roar a cannonball ripped through the side of Bingham's boat, takin' the leg clean off a soldier. It mightn't have sunk the boat, but the men, in a panic, all scrambled to the other side and it capsized. There was Bingham in the drink, hangin' for dear life onto his boat, screeching in terror to be saved. "I'm Captain Bingham!" he cried, "Captain Bingham!" over and over again. We rowed as close as we could to shoot more of them, and I was taking aim at Bingham himself when the sky was again lit by cannon fire, and somebody called my name.

I saw him turn at the sound, and in the quickly fading light he caught his first glimpse of the infamous Grace O'Malley. Pirate. Rebel. Now dressed in an English coat, dry and dignified while he flailed about in the cold water of Lough Mask, dodging bullets and beggin' his men to save him. In that moment I became his enemy. No, more than that. I became the symbol of all he hated and feared. In our first battle in full sight of his troops, I got the best of Richard Bingham. He would never live that down. Then he ducked behind his boat and I lost my shot.

I knew in my heart of hearts that he would come after me. He'd been publicly shamed by a woman, and that he could not countenance. But I never fathomed the true depth of the hatred—that he'd vowed to destroy me entirely. Take everything of value from my life. Killing me was too easy for Bingham, for I'd not suffered sufficiently. In the end I'd be forced to watch as he ripped apart my family, with each child's fate a different torture.

I'd returned to Rockfleet, for I'd never felt more secure than in that keep, my ships afloat in that harbor. One day my scout came to me with news—a huge company of English soldiers was marchin' in from the east with a herd of cattle in tow, no doubt raided from my lands. And from what he could see, they held fifteen prisoners as well.

I knew 'twas Bingham, but what was he up to? Certainly not battle, accompanied as he was by all that cattle. I shook out my long braid so my graying hair resembled a wild mane, wrapped my chieftain's cloak around me, and went out to meet him. Even mounted on his horse I could see he was a tiny bit of a man. There were no deformities, but he was certainly shorter than myself. I remember groaning inside at the sight of him, for the smaller the man, the more dangerous. They had somethin' to prove to the world, these wee fellows, and a grudge against their Maker for their paltry proportions. It could only add to my grief.

His troops stood at attention behind him, his interpreter beside him.

"I see you didn't drown after all," I said, and watched Bingham's face grow red. His thighs squeezed the sides of his horse and I saw that he'd not be gettin' down if he could help it.

"Grace O'Malley," he began in a formal voice, too high and shrill for a man.

"That's me," I said. "What have you come for, and are those my cows?"

"*I* will ask the questions here," he fairly spat, but then fell silent and confused, as though that was not what he'd meant to say. The man was simmering like a thick stew, and I wished to provoke him further.

"I understand you have prisoners," I said. "Who are they?"

When the interpreter repeated my query, Richard Bingham finally smiled. His teeth were small and straight and white, but their perfection made him look all the more peevish. With a tiny wave of his hand, the English ranks opened and the prisoners were brought through. 'Twas then that my heart sank, and I knew the trouble that lay ahead.

They were all Burkes, greater and lesser chiefs, and they'd all been beaten. They were filthy with blood and vomit caked in their hair and what ragged clothing they wore. Four soldiers carried a litter and dropped it at my feet. Stretched out upon it was a pitiful creature. Old Edmund Burke had been tortured horribly. Both legs were broken, the bone of his right shin piercing the skin. His bare feet were charred black, and they'd branded his chest and arms with an iron. Most of his teeth were gone from his mouth and his eyes were swollen shut.

"Edmund," I said, never expectin' a reply.

But the old codger's lips moved and he said, "Who is it then?"

"It's Grace," I answered.

"They . . . they . . ." I leaned down to hear him better. "They forced Morag," he whispered. "A dozen of 'em, right in front of my eyes. They would have killed her, but she died of shame before they could."

I glared up at Bingham on his horse. He wore a smug smile and I wished to slap it from his weasel face. "Why have you done this?" I said, and waved my arm toward the Burke prisoners. "Why have you brought them here?"

"To hang them," he answered. "To hang you." He flicked his fingers again and two of his soldiers grabbed my arms as a third clapped my hands and feet in chains.

"Grace O'Malley, I arrest you in the name of Her Majesty Queen Elizabeth."

"On what charges?" I demanded.

"Let me see," he said, tapping a bejeweled and manicured finger on his lips. "Treason against the Crown perhaps." His gaze had begun to wander over the village and to the fields beyond where grazed the greatest part of my herd, more than a thousand in all. He beckoned an officer to him and spoke quite loudly. "Confiscate the cattle," he said. "The horses too."

I was speechless, seething. The cattle—aside from my fleet—were the only source of my wealth. He fixed me with an ugly leer.

"You won't be needing them . . . in Hell."

With that he wheeled on his mount and pranced away. We were dragged—myself and Edmund and the other prisoners—to Rockfleet's great hall where we sat on the floor in the dark and listened as the English soldiers sawed and pounded and built our gallows.

After a day the pounding stopped, but there were no hangings. We waited, the agony compounded by the grievousness of Edmund Burke's condition. He was brave and suffered in silence, but we all prayed in the dark hall that he'd die and steal from Richard Bingham the pleasure of murdering him.

Finally the doors were thrown open and the soldiers marched us out into the sunlight. There were seventeen gallows, one for each of us. The villagers had been pulled from their homes to watch the hangings, and the troops had convened as well. Captain Bingham, finally with his feet on the ground, was stridin' around most important in his miniature strides. But he was nervous as well, looking time after time at the road leadin' to the village, as though expectin' someone.

An officer came, leaned down and whispered in his ear. Bingham smiled that tight-lipped smile and quick gave the signal. We were led, each of us, to our own gallows. Poor old Edmund, still hangin' on to life, was lifted by two soldiers—one under each arm—and dragged across the yard screamin' with the pain of his broken legs.

I could scarce believe my life would end this way, hanged as a traitor in Rockfleet yard at the hands of an English dwarf. From the scaffold I could see Bingham, whose eyes were fastened on the road, and I wondered who he was waitin' to see. But then I felt the rope put over my head, and its weight as it lay heavy on my shoulders. I looked round me and saw the others—fine Burke chieftains, nooses on their necks, their lips movin' in silent prayer.

I gazed once more at Bingham and at just that moment I saw him turn and smile, and I heard the clattering of hoofbeats. A lone figure rode hell-bent into the yard and reigned in his horse in a cloud of dust. Who was it that Bingham had waited for? The rider dismounted and emerged from the dust.

'Twas Devil's Hook, all afire. He looked round the yard with no surprise and found me on my scaffold. Then he saw Bingham and strode in his direction. Soldiers moved to block his path but Bingham shooed them away. He'd been waitin' for Hook. For his grand entrance.

The English captain took his place on a raised field stool, which barely brought him eye to eye with my son-in-law. I could not hear their words but I knew Devil's Hook was pleadin' for my life, and that smug look of Bingham's never changed for a moment. As Hook spoke, the little man waved his jeweled hand and one by one the best of the Burkes' manhood died kickin' at the end of a rope. Finally, despite Hook's frantic pleading, all that were left alive were myself and Edmund Burke, he moanin' in the soldiers' arms.

Like Julius Caesar—only smaller—Bingham stood from his camp stool to signal Edmund's execution, and a moment later the old man was gone, out of his misery.

There was silence in the yard and all eyes were fastened on me. Bingham stepped down and walked to my wooden gallows, Devil's Hook trailing after.

"I accept your offer," Bingham finally said to Hook, whose body sagged with relief.

"What have you done?" I asked the man I'd come to love as well as my own sons.

"Offered myself as hostage for you," Hook said.

I looked at Bingham, who was mightily pleased at the bargain, and I saw then it had been his plan all along. He never meant to hang me, only to frighten me, make me squirm. He was playing, as a mouser sometimes does with its prey before bitin' off its head.

With hardly a word they released me and clapped Hook in chains. Sixteen Burke chieftains were thrown in a pile in the Rockfleet yard. Bingham led his troops from the village along with my only daughter's husband, bound hand and foot, and every head of cattle I owned. I'd not lost my life, but half my fortune was gone. All that was left was my fleet.

Now dread overwhelmed me. Hook was in Bingham's hands, my good conduct all that kept him alive. And my other children—safe for the moment—were surely his next targets. What should I do to protect them?

So, 'twas Hook who saved me from death, and I blessed him daily for it. You could say Bingham used him, knew my son-in-law would offer himself as hostage for me. But that makes the act no less valiant in my eyes. I had my freedom, and though shorn of my wealth on land, still claimed as mine my fleet, brave sailors, and the sea.

The day I learned Devil's Hook had liberated himself from Bingham's clutches I drank in celebration of his escaping. Then I quick called my captains to Rockfleet Keep. We'd be leavin' day after next, I told them, for the pledge of my own good conduct had rebelled, and Bingham would be here in a heartbeat.

There was no choice to our direction. We had no cargo to trade with Spain and Portugal, and it bein' winter, fishing was out of the question. Besides, Ireland was trapped in conflict, Bingham at large in the land. Now was no time for commerce. If I wished to help my children a'tall, I must move toward power.

And so I sailed north. To Ulster.

I was welcomed most heartily in the north-coast town of Dunluce by the county's two great families, the O'Donnells of the northwest and the O'Neills of the northeast. I found them in the midst of celebration, a betrothal of two children of their clans. Never were two neighbors so deeply entwined by marriage as the O'Neills and O'Donnells, and to such marvelous effect.

What can I say about Old Hugh O'Donnell? He was the chief of his clan and deft enough, I suppose. The O'Donnell was known by foreigners as "King of the Fish in Ireland," and he did trade volubly with Spain for wine. But in Irish eyes he was feeble in his rule, in all but two respects, that is, his wife, Ineen, and his son, Red Hugh.

Ineen Dubh was a Scot and a MacDonald, tough as iron and afraid of no one. They say she'd been a beauty at the Court of Queen Mary Stuart, but her marriage to an Irish chieftain would in two ways change the fate of Ireland, for she brought by her influence all the Scots Gallowglass to fight our wars. And she gave birth to Red Hugh O'Donnell. What a child he was! From his earliest days we knew him for a leader. Came as natural as breathing, rulership did. Fought his first battle at the age of twelve.

Hugh O'Neill, with his English title, the Earl of Tyrone, was old enough to be Red Hugh's father, but he saw, as all did, the strength in the child. And wished alliance with him. Already O'Neill was married to Red Hugh's sister, Siobhan, but closer still he meant to pull the families. The O'Neills had a daughter, Rose. She was twelve and as beautiful as her name. To everyone's great joy he promised her in marriage to Red Hugh, fourteen and already more than half a man.

I'd fled Connaught and found refuge in Dunluce just as festivities were about to begin. The clans were gathering, the weeks of feasting and games bein' prepared. Those who had come some distance sheltered with their Dunluce kin, or camped in the common rooms of the castle. Rathlin Island was just across a wee channel. This was home to the Mac-

Donalds, and so the Scots relatives gathered there. No one'd forgotten the terrible massacre, just ten years past, when the two Walters—Devereaux, the first Earl of Essex, and Raleigh—came ashore and slaughtered all its Scots inhabitants, men, women, and children alike. But nothin' was said of it, for this was a time for rejoicing.

Room was made for me as Ineen's honored guest in a cozy corner of Dunluce Keep. We'd always done business together, Ineen and me. Always, when I needed Gallowglass, she was there. If I didn't feel welcome enough, there was Hugh O'Neill himself, a great man and a great friend. English bred he was, but an Irishman through and through.

I can hardly express the joy of that occasion, for more than alliances were gained in that match. Sure it strengthened the claim of Hugh O'Neill and Hugh O'Donnell against their rival, Turlough Luineach, then High Chief of the O'Neill clan. The two Hughs uniting against Turlough was unbeatable. But the two children *loved* each other, could barely wait for the time that they'd wed. So as strong as politics reigned o'er the gathering, youthful passion outshone it altogether.

I sat at the long feast table before the roast at Ineen's left hand and across from Hugh O'Neill. His wife, Siobhan, pregnant with his second son, was Hugh O'Donnell's own daughter. That marriage—O'Neill with the ruling *sept* of O'Donnells—proved a great boon for him. Like I said, the family ties were close, soon to grow closer. We were lookin' out at the floor where the young ones danced.

"They lust after each other, Rose and Red Hugh," I said.

"Aye, 'tis a good match," said Ineen. "In every way."

Hugh O'Neill smiled. A handsome man he is, who lights up a room with his very presence. "Do you sometimes wonder, Ineen," he said, "why Red Hugh grew so strong so young?"

"I wouldn't wonder, with Ineen's blood runnin' in his veins," I said to answer him. "Has he learned his Latin?"

"Aye, and English too." Ineen answered, then looked at Hugh O'Neill. "His soon-to-be father-in-law insisted."

"If Red Hugh's to be the great leader we hope him to be, he'll need it," said O'Neill, "for to know the English mind you need to know the English language."

"You learned it as a boy in Henry Sidney's house, and it's held you in good stead," I said. "You're goin' to London again, I hear."

"Aye. I'll stay with my friend Tom Ormond."

"And what will he do for you at Court?"

"He's promised me a meeting with the queen."

"You're much loved by the English," I said.

"They know me for an ally."

Hugh O'Neill bore no shame for his friendship with the Crown. But my face hid little of my hatred for Connaught's new invaders.

"Richard Bingham brings you grief," he said, hardly a question.

"He's hung half the chieftains in Mayo," I replied.

"You need some Scotsmen, Grace." 'Twas Ineen speaking, with a wicked look in her eye. "Tell me how many fighters you need and I'll have them for you—a new batch, young and crazy."

"And what will I pay them with? Fish?"

"He took your herd, did he?" said Hugh O'Neill.

"Aye. And he means to take more, I'm sure of it. He's an evil little midget, and he thinks he'll bring me down."

"Well, he doesn't know you then, does he?" said Ineen with a smile. But then she grew serious. "Does he hate you for your womanhood, Grace?"

"That's a good part of it. And I trounced him first time out."

"He doesn't know who he's up against," she said, "and I don't like his chances."

"I'll lay a wager on Grace!" cried O'Neill and slapped a coin on the table.

Ineen Dubh did the same.

We all laughed.

YOU NEEDN'T GO on if you . . ."

"No, Your Majesty." Grace's face was suddenly pale and slack. "I want you to hear how your Captain Bingham murdered my son." She leaned forward, her body a tight coil, her face hovering inches from the queen's. "Do you want to know?" she asked.

"Back away, Mistress O'Malley." The sympathy had evaporated from Elizabeth's voice. Grace slid back in her chair. "Perhaps," said the queen, "I've allowed you too many liberties."

Grace strove to compose herself, resetting her features and resuming a peaceful posture. "Forgive me, Your Majesty." The apology was forced but altogether necessary, for the unspoken prize of Tibbot Burke's freedom hung in the balance. She bit her tongue, as she wished to cry out, "How would you know about losin' a child!" Instead she said, "I was still in Ulster, nearin' the end of my third month there . . ."

<hr/>

DURING THE NEXT WEEKS, we held council together—the two Hughs, Ineen, and myself. We argued endlessly over Spain and England, the invasion we all knew would happen one day. We spoke of Francis Drake's ships harrying the Spanish coasts, and the great armada anchored at the port cities. Sure we wondered if Philip's armies would come to Ireland, use the island for its jumping-off point to western England. We prayed for the invasion, for it would keep the English otherwise occupied and perhaps defeated, but we had no way of knowing, busy as we were with our own battles, and no great spy network like your Francis Walsingham had on the continent.

I was shocked altogether when I looked up one day to see Devil's Hook in the room, and by his expression alone I knew someone had died. He came and put his arms about me and I thought, *Oh Jesus, it's Margaret. She's died in childbirth.*

"Owen is dead," he whispered in my ear.

I pushed him away. "Owen? How!"

" 'Twas Bingham, Grace."

"But Owen was no rebel, and well out of the fight," I said. "My God, he refused to rise in defense of his own father-in-law!"

"It didn't matter. Bingham had his plans. He was coming with five hundred soldiers to Bunowen, and when Owen heard of it, he took his people and his tenants and swam his cattle out across the narrow channel to Near Island for their safety. When Bingham arrived he found them gone. What he did was pose as a poor captain who could not feed his troops, who were starving. And Owen, sweet fool that he was, believed him. He sent boats to ferry the soldiers over to the island. Then he entertained them"—Hook's mouth quivered—"with the best cheer he had. They were well fed and deep in their cups when the English turned on Owen, and at swordpoint bound and arrested him—he and eighteen of his best men. Next morning they drew out of the island four thousand cows, five hundred horses, and a thousand sheep, leaving those men remaining on the island altogether naked in the world. Owen and his followers were marched cross-country to Ballinahinch and brought before Bingham, who'd been waiting there for his prize. He made Owen watch as all eighteen of his men were hanged, some drawn and quartered in the English style. He enjoys that, Bingham does, forcing you to watch your loved ones die." Hook was raking his fingers through his hair over and over again, loath to report the cruel ending of his story.

"Tell me, son," I said, very gentle like, "how did Owen die?"

"They'd thrown him in a cottage, still bound hand and foot, and left alone to curse his own stupidity. By that night he'd already died eighteen times over when those English bastards burst in and fell on him with knives. He was altogether helpless as they struck and struck again. Twelve deadly wounds he suffered. Poor Owen."

He looked at me then, but I was still as a statue and dry-eyed.

"Grace," he said, "there's more."

"More? How can there be more than my firstborn son's murder!"

"Bingham marched to Burrishoole—"

"No—"

"He did, and he took Tibbot hostage. He's all right, Grace. He's in no danger."

"No danger! In the home of that monster?" I made for the door.

"Wait, wait," cried Hook. "Tibbot's being well cared for, I promise you. There are other children in the household at Ballymote. He's learning English."

My heart lurched then, recalling Tibbot's "trait." What *else* would he learn, and what would he forget?

"I've come for reinforcements," Hook said. "Gallowglass. *Your* hands are tied, Grace, with Tibbot your pledge of good conduct. But mine are not. I'll fight the Burkes' rebellion for you, for I love your family as my own."

Well, that was how it was. One son dead, another in English custody. All the places I called home crawlin' with Crown soldiers. I was forced to fish and trade and plunder with no safe haven to anchor. Even ferrying Ineen Dubh's crazy Scotsmen to the Connaught rebellion was risky, for if Bingham gathered proof of such a thing, my Tibbot could be hanged in his mother's place.

Well, I was more than heartsick, you can imagine. To lose a child of my own body—and so gentle a man as Owen O'Flaherty was—to as ruthless a creature as Bingham, turned my days and my dreams to nightmares. I desired the bloodiest revenge on the Englishman, but for the first time in my life, I was helpless. One false move and Tibbot would himself die. I was forced to let the months pass with no word from the boy, and my letters to him were surely burnt before he saw them. Bingham's household servants were all English and loyal to their master, so with no spies therein, news of Tibbot was scarce indeed.

Then came the report that rocked all of Ireland. The English had kidnapped Red Hugh O'Donnell, lured him aboard their ship with the promise of entertainments and fine Spanish wine. 'Twas appalling how easily he'd been tricked—Red Hugh, "Savior of Ulster"—and terrible to imagine him rotting in Dublin Prison. The Crown knew, as we all did, what a force the boy was in northern Ireland, and they wished to forestall the rebellion they knew he'd bring. But the act made clear to the Irish—loyalist and rebel alike—how treacherous were the English, and from that day on all were leery, and we all protected our backs.

Soon after Red Hugh's abduction I learned that a Ballymote miller had just delivered a great quantity of his goods to Bingham's house, and the same with a local butcher. So I went to Ballymote Town and snooped round a bit, only to find that a marriage was taking place at the castle. The groom was my own son Tibbot.

I was destroyed by the news, for 'twas not just the thought of my child's future being wrenched from his mother's control, but the choice of his wife in particular. Maeve was niece to Donal O'Connor Sligo, a North Mayo chieftain. He was not much of a man, but worse, he'd been loyal to the Crown for thirty years. My son was marrying into the family of my enemy, and there was naught to be done to stop it.

Perhaps 'twas something perverse in myself, but I wished to be present for that terrible moment, and perhaps more than that I desired a glimpse of my boy. So I contrived a disguise—the one I carried off to the best effect, a man—and for Tibbot's wedding day, friend of O'Connor Sligo's. Guards were abounding that sunny morning, posted at the castle gate and all through the gardens, which were milling with English settlers and their Irish sympathizers. But my manner was calm and subdued, and I slipped in with no fuss a'tall, with not a soul recognizing me for who I was.

I found myself a seat near the front of the chapel and prayed that the fierce beating of my heart would not be heard by everyone. O'Connor Sligo was there with his brother and wife—parents of the bride—and Richard Bingham, matchmaker, with whom they were chuckling under their breath. I wanted to jump up and wring their miserable necks. But now came the bride and groom to the altar—the Protestant altar—and they knelt before the horse-faced chaplain who, in his bloodless tones, joined the two children as man and wife. I could see half of Tibbot's face, for he'd turned it to look at Maeve . . . and the look was pure adoration. She was beautiful, with hair the color of gold, and fine pale skin touched with roses on cheek and lip. I saw in that moment he loved her, and knew he'd forgotten me, his family and clan, and what a betrayal this marriage was to us all.

Once joined in matrimony they swept—a golden pair—down the aisle and into the sunlit garden for the wedding feast. 'Twas a grand affair that I haven't the heart to describe. Several times I moved to speak with Tibbot, but at every turn he was thronged with well-wishers. I never took my eyes from him that day, hopin' to see a glimmer of unease or misery at his plight, but to be honest there was none a'tall. He spoke in English, the speedy learning of that language another blow to me. But when Richard Bingham came, throwin' his arm round Tibbot's shoulders, and my son's smile faltered not at all, I was forced to turn away, and I fled that place, for a weeping man was sure ruination of my disguise.

As I rode away I was all of a sudden brought to mind of a strange creature I'd seen in a Portuguese factor's home when I was a child. 'Twas called a "chameleon," an animal whose color would change in a trice to whatever color upon which he sat. Tibbot was that—a chameleon. I was wretched at the thought, but only for a moment, for I knew then the action I must take. I'd learnt in my life that no matter the circumstance, action is the best cure for wretchedness, as surely as mulberry is for a fever.

'Twas a simple matter, after all was said and done, to spring the boy from Bingham's clutches, though 'twas half a year more before the plan was carried out. I'd stayed round Ballymote Town in my disguise, takin' rooms at the local inn. Over time I learned Tibbot's movements and his favorite haunts. When I thought I knew his comings and goings, I sent word to Devil's Hook to come with a dozen men. On an overcast day in September, I had reckoned he'd come alone, and we lay in wait in the greenwood where the boy would ride out to hunt and hawk. This day Tibbot did not come alone. Maeve was with him.

But the moment had arrived to act. The couple rode into our trap, and with no sound save the commotion of our horses, we shot from our hiding places, cutting them off and surrounding them. Maeve screamed and Tibbot's horse reared in surprise. I took that moment to plant myself in front of him and pulled off my hat, letting my hair fall down round my shoulders so he should see very quickly who his abductors were.

He stared at me for a long moment. "Mam!" he cried. "What are you doin' here?"

"What do you think I'm doin' here?" I said, annoyed. "I've come to take you home."

The look of confusion on Tibbot's face was so complete 'twould have made me laugh had it not been such a dire moment. "Well, are you comin' with us, or do you prefer Richard Bingham's house to mine?"

"Of course I'll come!" he cried, but then looked wildly toward Maeve. She in turn was starin' at me as though she'd seen the Devil on horseback. "What about Maeve?" Tibbot said. "She's my wife."

"I know," I said. "I saw you married." His shock was evident. "'Tis a long story, Tibbot. I'll tell you later. But will she come of her own accord and without a fuss? For we can't afford a wiggling girl while we're escaping."

Well, he talked to her then, in whispers, all the time touchin' her hand

or her face, and I saw that they truly loved each other, and 'twas no surprise when Tibbot turned back with a smile that stretched from ear to ear.

"She'll come, Mam!" he cried. "She'll come with us gladly."

The rest was easy, though the two of them had to squeeze in the space
made for one amidst baskets of vegetables in the rude farmer's cart we
had waitin' at the edge of the wood.

Richard Bingham was fit to be tied at the loss of his hostage, but lucky
for me there was no time for retribution. Philip of Spain had recovered
from Drake's raid on Cadiz and was threatening to launch his armada on
England. No one knew their landing place, and some believed 'twas the
south coast of Munster. Bingham and the other captains had their hands
full, and in those months much of Connaught fell back into the hands of
its own people.

Meanwhile, my chameleon son had, with the greatest ease, changed
his colors and stripes once again. English pretense was gone and Gaelic
fire burned in his eyes. Of all people, *I* was his idol—rebel, pirate, leader
of loyal men. I had so much to teach him, he said, and he would be my
faithful student. He begged me to give him a ship of his own to captain,
and how could I refuse him? He was grateful beyond measure and easy
in his new life on the sea. "Tibbot of the Boats" he'd remind me was his
name, and never was there mention of the two years in Richard Bingham's house.

He did insist on teachin' me English. I recalled what Hugh O'Neill
had said, that to know the English mind you must know the language. I
took to it easy enough—like mother, like son, I suppose—and had no
regrets for the knowledge gained.

Of all people, I needn't tell you about the coming of the Spanish
Armada. We in Ireland rejoiced, for we saw that you English finally
knew the fear of foreign invasion. Of course 'twas short-lived, not like
our own that had gone on for twenty years by now. And your fear turned
to joy and celebration when victory was gifted you by the Fates and the
north wind. Soon what was left of King Philip's fleet was limping round
the north of Scotland, and down its western coast to Connaught. We'd
been told—ordered in fact—to give no succor to the Spaniard washed
up on our shores. 'Twould be treason, your edicts claimed. Help England's enemy, it said, and suffer death ourselves. And Richard Bing-

ham, fired by a burnin' hatred of Spain, would see to it that Connaught obeyed to the letter of the law that bloody edict.

It pains me to recall that terrible autumn. The seas along the western coast of Ireland had never been so stormy as they were that year. Here they came, the ships of the Spanish fleet, one by one straggling with tattered sails and broken masts, hugging the shore as close as they dared. Little did they know that waitin' there for any hapless ship washed up upon the beach, or broken on rocky shoals, were hoards of desperate Irish men, women, children—themselves battered by years of English occupation. They were near starving, they were ragged and ill, and they feared further retribution should they disobey their masters. And too, waiting on the craggy headlands like vultures for their next meal, were the chieftains, the once proud Gaelic headmen, now of divided minds, the largest part greed and expediency. The poor sailors were massacred, their bodies stripped of clothing, jewels, and money.

But worse was yet to come. Streaming out of the forests and glens and down to the beaches were English troops in their numbers who, with drawn sword and pistol, slaughtered the miserable castaways in terrible numbers—seven thousand when all was said and done. The truth is, more of Philip's troops were slain in obscurity on the shores of western Ireland than in the famous battle in your English Channel.

Not all of us took part in that despicable mayhem. Hugh O'Neill. The Devil's Hook. But the greatest surprise of all was Murrough ne Doe O'Flaherty, twenty years loyal to the English for putting him at the head of his clan. Even though his eldest son was held as hostage by Bingham, he came to our side, God bless him.

I myself had taken up residence again at Rockfleet, and my own small armada was in fine repair. Tibbot, back at Burrishoole with Maeve and his firstborn, Miles, was also waiting, prepared with his ships, which, by this time numbered seven. Like me, he bore the Spanish only good will, for while under my tutelage he'd seen me trade and pilot and befriend our southern neighbors. We watched the procession of doomed ships coast along our shores. If weather allowed it, we'd leave our sheltered harbors to guide the Spanish ships round our treacherous coastline, leading 'em to the Bay of Biscay to fend for themselves.

Finally, in November of 1588, standing on the windy battlements of

Rockfleet Keep, I spied through my glass a great ship braving the monstrous seas on its way south. I wondered that it sailed at all, for its sheets were in shreds and its mainsail gone altogether. At the harbor's mouth it turned.

I rushed to the Rockfleet beach where villagers had gathered, armed with knives and pitchforks and clubs. I could see hunger in their faces and hope for salvation. Aye, "salvation" from salvaged booty. But I went to them, walked among them, even as the great ship limped closer to shore.

"Look," I said. "I know you wish for some good to come from this fine vessel owned by the King of Spain himself. To be sure there'll be treasures aboard her, and I won't begrudge you those treasures. God knows I've lifted some booty in my life." Some laughed at that, though most were too desperate for levity. "All I'm sayin' is, there's hundreds of poor souls aboard that ship. They've suffered somethin' terrible. They're starvin', like you are, and I doubt they'd put up much of a fight. So let us welcome them, as our brothers." There were great moans and cries of disagreement, but I pressed on. "I will speak with the captain who, I promise you, will be most grateful for our mercy, and I will see what he *trades* for that mercy. There will be guns, no doubt, which are in short supply with us, you know. There may be gold, which the captain might be persuaded to release to his new Connaught allies. But I have no wish for a massacre on this beach."

I looked round at the faces of my people, and my words echoed in my ears. All of a sudden I could hear myself begging for the trust of my first crew, the one Gilleduff O'Flaherty had gifted me with. How the times had changed, but I felt now, as I'd felt then, a strange certainty of action. Leading men was my fate, and leading men *well* my desire. I'm sure you know what I mean.

In the end we let them land peacefully. Much to my surprise and delight, the ship was the *San Martin* and its captain the High Admiral of the Armada itself, the Duke of Medina-Sidonia. Grateful could not begin to describe his mien. The poor man had suffered terribly from the first moment of his appointment by Philip, a commission he'd begged, on grounds of incompetence, not to receive. But the King of Spain had been adamant, forced the position upon him, and then turned a deaf ear to all the duke's pleadings against Philip's clearly doomed invasion plans.

"Voyage of the damned," the duke had called the fleet's trip round Scotland after their defeat in the English Channel. They'd been battered the whole way, and the men's morale, already shattered by their defeat, died altogether when the food ran out and disease took hold. Indeed, they'd watched with helpless horror as their sister ships were dashed on foreign shores, their brothers hacked savagely to pieces by English troops and Irish villagers alike. Rockfleet's kind welcome had been the first and only blessing in their long, monstrous journey.

We struck a deal, the Duke of Medina-Sidonia and I. We would get guns and money. The bulk of his crew, with no food for their long voyage to Spain, stayed behind to fight the English at our side. He and a skeleton crew I piloted safely out of Irish waters.

Rockfleet opened its arms to those once proud soldiers, now reduced to skin and bones and scurvy. Soon they were guests no more, but part of village life, training with the local rebels, makin' eyes at the local girls, and learnin' a few words of Irish. All in all, Rockfleet thanked me for the deal I'd struck with the Duke of Medina-Sidonia.

But that was not the case with Richard Bingham.

A right Fury, he was. 'Twas not just our harboring the Spanish that maddened him, though that in itself was sufficient treason. But the Burkes, led by myself and Tibbot, had turned the Connaught chiefs—once subdued by the English—back to the Irish cause. Bingham'd made a mistake in murdering Murrough ne Doe's son—his hostage—for when Murrough came to our aid, he came with revenge on his mind, and all the O'Flaherty clans at his side. All, that is, but my O'Flaherty *son* Murrough.

The O'Flahertys rose in rebellion against the Crown, and they did it with a fierceness that swelled my heart with pride. The many great chieftains were as old as myself, at sixty, so my boy Tibbot, just past twenty, was new blood, and was looked to as the great hope of Connaught. Our two fleets together as one, we'd ferried thousands of Ineen Dubh's Gallowglass to our shores. And every day a new battle was won. One by one towns and villages were retaken by the people who rightly owned them.

But that was not the worst of it for Bingham. Prick that he was, he'd made more enemies than the Irish. Aye, your own Lord Deputy Perrot hated the man, suspected his misconduct and schemed to bring him down. Imagine our delight to learn Bingham had been put on trial in Dublin for his brutal deeds in Connaught! Forbidden, he was, to take the field against us.

We rejoiced in several ways. First with our own "Book of Complaints" against Bingham. Tibbot and I, using the English language, compiled the book, charging him with injustices in his rule of the province. There were more examples of murder, cruelty, repression, and extortion than I wish to remember. 'Twas a fine document though, and the council in Dublin, and Lord Deputy Perrot himself, read it with great interest.

While Bingham was thus engaged, and the Burkes enjoyed a great swelling of power, we elected a new Burkes' MacWilliam a man they called—"the Blind Abbot." Of course we knew the English would object, for they believed the title dead and buried. Tibbot and I therefore sailed off to Scotland for reinforcements, with hopes that the tide had finally turned in our favor.

How wrong we were.

Looking back, I see how foolish it was. To think the Crown would find in favor of Ireland over Richard Bingham, one of its own. That was dreaming. Bingham was acquitted by the court in Dublin and sent out with new determination and a large army to quell the "Great Connaught Uprising." And Grace O'Malley, whom he named "the Nurse of all Rebellions in Ireland," was his prime target.

We returned from Scotland heading first for Burrishoole, for Tibbot to see his family. But as we approached from the north, I could see from the deck of the *Dorcas* smoke rising from the place where the village stood. We were filled with dread as we sailed our combined fleet into Burrishoole Harbor, an unnatural silence and the smell of burning wood and flesh churning our stomachs.

The place was burnt to the ground. Men, women, children, even animals had been slaughtered, every one. Tibbot was running through the charred rubble to the keep, dead men hanging from the battlements, though the castle was strangely intact amidst the destruction. He pounded frantically on the heavy door, callin' for his wife. He cried and pounded till his voice was hoarse and his fists were bloody, but to no avail. Finally he fell to the ground with his back against the door and wept like a child. Then, all of a sudden, like a miracle, the door creaked open and there stood Maeve, with little Miles on her hip. When he saw his father in such a condition, the child began to scream bloody murder, but the family was reunited with great joy and relief.

That night Maeve, roses gone from her lovely face, told us of the massacre. They'd come in force, with a purpose. Bingham himself had led the attack. Tibbot's loyal men—those who hadn't charged out amongst the ravening English soldiers—had manned the battlements of the keep.

One by one the men were shot and killed till finally the last man, horribly wounded, had come to Maeve with the dreadful news. The town was afire and all were dead. But he would protect Tibbot Burke's wife and son with his last breath. Then he'd fallen dead at her feet. By now the keep was filling with black smoke, and Maeve could not think whether she more feared the two of them chokin' to death, or being hacked to pieces by Bingham's soldiers. She hid herself and little Miles in a Spanish cargo chest, knowing it was a poor protection, and waited for the end to come.

She thought she was dreaming when she heard Tibbot crying from afar. It took her a wee while to unbend from the confines of the chest, and to wake little Miles, who'd fallen asleep in his mother's arms.

Outraged as we were at the loss of Burrishoole, there was more bad news that night. A rebel courier seeking reinforcements from the village arrived to find it destroyed. He brought with him grim tidings. The Blind Abbot, engaged in battle with Richard Bingham, had been gravely injured, his foot cut off entirely. All who heard the news moaned aloud, for the man around whom the great Burkes' Rebellion had rallied was now—with his foot gone—reckoned as good as a dead man.

That was it. Richard Bingham's head was mine. I would kill him or I would die trying.

I learned from the courier the last known position of Bingham and his troops. They were camped in a glen, but half a night's march from Burrishoole. There was no time to lose.

Our Scotsmen were fresh for battle and felt my fervor, makin' it their own. We covered the distance in record time, and before dawn we lay in wait outside the English camp. There were some tents in the camp, but very few. Most soldiers slept on the hard ground, round smoldering fires. Centered in the camp was one large tent, no doubt their Captain Bingham's, he sleepin' in comfort on his cot. I hoped he was sleeping soundly, for a shock in that state makes the heart pound hard and painful in nameless fear. And I wanted the bastard to know as much fear before death as humanly possible.

The signal was given and with banshee cries we fell, in our numbers, on the English. Fighting was hard and men were dyin' all round as I strode through the camp, sword drawn and quivering in my hand.

A fierce battle was being fought round Bingham's tent and inside as well, I knew, from the shouts and grunts and sounds of clashing metal coming from within it. I pulled back the door flap to see Bingham reloading his pistol, with two of his soldiers flanking him—their backs to me—fighting two of my Gallowglass Scots. Bingham looked up and saw me. Then, with a wee smile, he pointed his gun not at me, but at the Scotsman to his left. He blew the man's head clean off his neck, and the fountain of gore drenched the soldier the Scotsman had been fighting. That man turned now. Turned, and I saw his bloodstained face.

'Twas my son Murrough. *He was fightin' at Bingham's side!*

I felt the earth move under me and I lost my breath. The strength went out of my hand and the sword in it fell to the ground. I don't remember what happened then. . . .

When I came to my senses, Bingham was gone, and Murrough too. A hole, through which they'd escaped, had been cut in the tent. Outside, Tibbot had led his men to a great victory, with every Englishman slain and few Scotsmen worse for the wear.

From that day forward, Tibbot was seen as high commander of the Burkes' Rebellion, he as famous in Connaught as Red Hugh O'Donnell in Ulster was.

But I was destroyed.

How, I asked myself, could a son so betray his mother? Bingham had murdered Murrough's own brother, kidnapped my youngest child, massacred the poor people of Burrishoole, hanged the great chieftains of Connaught, threatened to hang me, and relieved me of my cattle! What was Murrough thinking? How had he grown to hate me so?

For a time I went mad, some days with grieving, some with anger. On a day of anger I sailed into Murrough's lands and plundered his herd and castle. He was absent at the time and I was later glad of it, for those men who resisted we killed, and furious as I was, I could never take the life of my own child.

I had held the years at bay for so long, feeling a young, strong woman despite my aging shell, but now I grew old with sadness. My bones began to ache and my once beloved keeps felt cold with their drafts and seeping fog.

And Richard Bingham was not done with me yet. I began to believe I'd been spared for an evil purpose the year the English shipping descended on Clew Bay. The purpose, slow torture of a notorious rebel and pirate, one who was to the Englishman a mockery of womanhood. All that was left to me was my fleet. 'Twas my wealth and my freedom and the only maintenance left to me.

The invasion was peaceful enough, I suppose—forty ships, some for fishing, some for trade, some for patrolling the waters. There were troop ships as well, and these quietly harried my own, from without and within. Aye, Bingham even ordered my ships boarded by his men who kept us from all "illegal" activity. Soon we'd lost the right of way in our own waters. The English ships refused to pay tolls foreign ships had paid the O'Malleys and O'Flahertys for hundreds of years. At their will, their ships barred mine from sailin' out to the fishing grounds, and plundered the grounds themselves. My trading vessels bound for Spain and Portugal were boarded at every turn, searched and denied exit from Clew Bay on the grounds that we carried spies, or supplies for Philip's Second Armada. Even foreign vessels that had once relied upon my services piloting them through the treacherous Irish waters now braved the open sea rather than risk trouble with the English.

My people looked to me for help, but I was helpless, and for the first time poor. That was when I wrote to you, Bess. Told you of my plight and asked for your help. Return my livelihood, I said. Not only for me but for my people, who were starving and wretched. You wrote back with your eighteen questions. I answered those questions and I waited for some reply. I was still waiting when the final blow fell.

In Ulster, Red Hugh O'Donnell—himself escaped from Dublin

prison—had been restored to leadership and was moving from strength to strength. Tibbot knew the boy would be callin' upon himself for support, as the two families had helped one another for so many years. Then my son took it upon himself to write a letter. 'Twas a daft thing to do, proposing that Tibbot and Devil's Hook and some Scots should join Red Hugh and O'Neill and raise a new rebellion in Connaught. Wouldn't you know Bingham intercepted the letter and arrested Tibbot on charges of treason.

S O THAT'S HOW the boy's come to be in your English prison," said Grace to the queen. "They're torturing him, threatening him with hanging, for Jesus' sake! And the western waters are swarming so thick with Bingham's ships I had to sneak away and be ferried out, a passenger on somebody else's boat." Grace sat forward in her chair. "Your Majesty, you've heard my story. Perhaps you've heard more than you bargained for. But now you know what a low prick Richard Bingham is. And you know that Tibbot is the only son I have left. So I'm beggin' you, Bess, give me back Tibbot. Remove Bingham from Ireland, and return me the freedom of my ships. I'd get on my knees, but I fear I'd not get up again, and wouldn't that be a sight?"

Elizabeth leaned forward and gazed at Grace's careworn face. "I'm Queen of England, and yet . . . I can see you do not envy me."

"How could I?" said Grace. "I've traveled the world and I've known the love of a father, a good man, and several children. Men cleave to me as loyally as they do to you, but not out of fear, and not for my favors. I do wish for your wealth, I'll admit that. But it hasn't brought you what you truly wished for above all else. And for that I pity you. People get their heads whacked off for sayin' such things, but I'm a gambling woman, and I'll wager that mine is safe enough on my neck."

Elizabeth smiled indulgently. She spoke slowly, twisting the heavy gold Ring of State that she wore on her first finger. "I'll admit I'm well disposed to your several requests, and yet . . . you have proven your inconstancy many times over."

"I told you what I told Captain Maltby—"

"Wait! If you wish to explain yourself by claiming the submission to Henry Sidney as your husband's alone, I'll have none of it." Elizabeth's tone was suddenly brusque, and she regained her regal posture. "Clearly you meant Lord Sidney to believe your loyalty as well, and clearly you broke your promise. I believe you would do *anything* to save the life of your son."

"I wouldn't deny it. But I swear to you now, give me what I request and I will become your true and dedicated servant. I'll fight your battles on land and sea . . . against all of the world, Your Majesty. I give you my word."

They were locked into each other's eyes, each taking the truest measure of the other.

Finally Grace spoke. "Look at us. Two old birds fightin' for the same feckin' worm." She sighed. "These are strange times we live in."

"Strange times . . . ," Elizabeth's voice trailed off and she gazed away absently. "Take your leave now, Grace. My Lord Essex will escort you back to your ship. You shall have your answer by sundown today."

Grace rose from her chair and Elizabeth too came to her feet.

"I thought your arse would be sore by now," said Grace.

"It is a bit."

"You have to be careful when you ask the Irish to tell you a story."

# 6

"T IS ESSEX!" A sharp cry rang out from the crowd now emerging from the Southwark Theatre, the throng made even louder and more unruly by the raucous performance it had just enjoyed of Will Shakespeare's *The Taming of the Shrew*.

"Ho! Lord Robert!" This voice was decidedly a drunken roar, and the friends surrounding Essex—Southampton and the Bacon brothers—instinctively drew in closer about him.

But it was too late.

" 'Tis he!"

"Essex! Essex!"

Their hero raised his arm in a fisted salute and smiled broadly.

"Don't encourage them, Robert," Francis Bacon whispered in Essex's ear.

"They're harmless," he answered. "And what choice have we? We're surrounded."

Indeed, the rabble was moving on all sides of them now and hands began darting in toward Essex's person, tugging at the fabric of his doublet, fingers attempting to pluck off a button or length of braid. With a high whoop a young boy perched atop his father's shoulders swiped the feathered cap off Essex's head.

"Here now!" Southampton cried, outraged, trying to retrieve the hat, but the boy had jumped to the ground and disappeared into the throng.

"You'll have me as naked as the day I was born!" was Essex's good-natured retort. The crowd, delighted, broke into laughter and familiar banter with their favorite nobleman.

"How's the queen?" one wanted to know.

"Sharp as a pin and twice as narrow!" Essex cried back.

More laughter rumbled around them.

"Go back to Spain, why don'tcha, and pluck out King Philip's eyes!" came another voice.

"You who said that," Essex called out, "come to Greenwich Castle with me and *you* convince the queen to send me, for I haven't had any luck myself!" As an aside to Southampton he whispered, "There's Will. Grab him and meet us at the dock."

Finally extricating themselves from the mob, Essex and the Bacons made it down to the Southwark quay where Henry Cuffe beckoned them onto the dinghy that, with the bribe of a fat purse, he'd secured for the group. Southampton and Master Shakespeare were last to board before they shoved off. As they lost themselves in the dark, thick river fog, lit by only a single lamp, they relaxed and began an amiable chatter.

"Tell us, Will, was your Katerina fashioned after Lady Essex?"

"How you speak of my mother!" cried Robert Devereaux, feigning indignation at Southampton's jibe. "We should deserve our 'nest of vipers' for comments such as that."

"Really, I must know." Southampton grasped the playwright's arm and peered at him in the lamplight. "Was it Lettice who inspired your shrew?"

"He's on the spot now," said Henry Cuffe.

"No matter how cuntish the woman," Francis Bacon offered, "a man's mother is sacrosanct."

"Apparently not *my* mother," said Essex. "Will, I forbid you to answer."

"*I'd* like to hear his answer!" came a rough voice from the dark, at the dinghy's bow. When the men realized it was the Cheapside oarsman who'd spoken, they all roared laughing.

"Look," cried Cuffe, "the Gnome and Mrs Blabby."

This was a fortuitous diversion and an escape for Will Shakespeare, for they all turned to see Robert Cecil and his wife, Margaret, being rowed to the north shore not twenty yards away. Mrs Cecil was infamous for her long, excruciatingly boring monologues.

"I saw them come into the queen's box," said Essex. "Late."

"Always at the queen's business," Francis observed, a begrudging compliment to Robert Cecil.

"Ho, Robert, Margaret!" Essex waved at the couple. Cecil returned the greeting with a pinched smile and a reserved wave at the boatload of his least favorite of Elizabeth's courtiers.

"He's an avid theatergoer," Shakespeare offered. "He's never missed one of my plays."

"A new patron for Will!" cried a teasing Southampton. "I am off the hook. Tell us, Robert, is the Gnome planning to wrest his father's position from the old man before he's even dead?"

But Essex was elsewhere occupied. His eyes were fixed on the large vessel that had for the moment halted the crosswise traffic on the Thames as it moved downriver with the tide. It was Murrough ne Doe's galley starting its voyage back to Ireland, he realized. He knew the ship well by now, having come and gone several times in recent days, in his latest visit bearing two documents from the queen to Grace O'Malley. Though she was nowhere visible, Grace was surely aboard.

"Robert."

"What?"

"Have you gone deaf?"

"No, no . . . I . . . ." His words trailed off as he watched the ship disappear into the darkness and fog. He'd still not recovered his senses as they reached the water stairs on the north bank, but his friends, used to the young earl's sudden bouts of moodiness, went on with their idle chatter unperturbed.

It wasn't until they'd been seated at their regular table at the Mermaid Tavern—Essex wholly oblivious to the raucous greeting given London's most beloved nobleman—that he regained the present moment. The tavern was crowded and noisy, and a bluish smoke hung round their heads. Tobacco from America was all the rage, and nearly every man in the place puffed a pipe of it. His friends were involved in a heated debate.

". . . right where that great ox of a man is standing," said Cuffe.

"I was here that night, Henry," Southampton insisted, "and I witnessed the brawl. I *saw* where Marlowe fell. Were you here that night, Will?"

"No," the playwright answered, subdued and miserable. "I wish I had been."

"You couldn't have stopped him dying." Southampton placed a comforting hand on Shakespeare's arm.

"He might have been embroiled with *me* in an argument, and not the ruffians who—"

" 'Twas his destiny to die," said Essex, startling them all with his sudden return to the conversation. "Think you," he continued, his eyes unfocused, dreamy, "that 'tis Ireland's destiny to be conquered?"

"Ireland?" Henry Cuffe exclaimed, thrown off entirely by the sudden change in subject.

Francis Bacon, aware of the Irish rebel woman at Court, as the others were perhaps not, obliged his master's turn of thought. "There's no doubt the colonization will continue despite the difficulties. 'The last of Europe's daughters,' " he went on with a more theatrical flourish than he was normally wont to employ, 'is waiting to be reclaimed from desolation, from savage and barbarous customs, to humanity and civilization.' "

"Are *we* not savage in our treatment of the Irish?" Essex demanded.

"We give what we get," Southampton answered. "Spencer was there, forced to fortify his house in Munster against the wildmen, behind high walls and locked gates." He lifted his eyes, remembering the poet's famous verse.

> . . . *with outrageous cry*
> *a thousand villiens round about them swarmed*
> *out of the rocks and caves ajoining nye;*
> *Vile caitive wretches, ragged, rude, deformed,*
> *All threatening death, all in strange manner armed;*
> *Some with unwieldy clubs, some with long spears,*
> *Some rusty knives, some staves in fire warmed.*

"Sounds exactly like last month's tilt at Nonesuch," said Cuffe. "Men dressed as 'Wild Irish' staged a mock fight for the queen. Their matted hair all down round their faces, saffron tunics, furred cloaks, battle-axes and terrible screams. 'Twas frightening, I tell you, even though we knew it was arranged."

"Henry Sidney—and who knows better than he?—believes the Irish *wish* for direct rule," Bacon insisted. "The gentlemen of Cork are begging for it, he says. 'With open mouths and hands held up to heaven, crying out for justice.' "

" 'Tis an evil place," Southampton agreed. "It corrupts and debases everyone who's sent there to tame it. Men become infected with the 'Irish Disease.' You should know that, Robert, your father died there." He looked closely at Essex. "Surely you're not thinking—"

"I need a battle." Essex's eyes were distant and vaguely haunted. "Perhaps I *should* go to Ireland."

"And play right into the Cecils' hands?" Bacon argued. "They enjoy pushing you into dangerous military campaigns, hoping you'll be killed or disgrace yourself. Or spend all your money the way you did in France and Portugal."

"The queen does seem determined to establish our legal system in Ireland," said Southampton.

"And just as determined to spend as little money as possible to do so," Bacon added. "I say her meanness is Ireland's only hope of evading England's clutches."

"My Lord Essex." A new voice, younger and less bold than the others, interrupted. They looked up to see a page, one of Elizabeth's pretty young men. "The queen wishes your immediate attendance on her."

"At this hour?" said Essex.

"Yes, my lord."

"Ooh, what have you done now?" Southampton said, teasing.

"I don't like your chances for a happy occasion," Francis Bacon agreed.

"He's still her favorite, is he not?" Will Shakespeare piped up. "I say she craves the man's company. And why not? We do."

"Well said, Will." Essex clapped the poet on the back, then stood. He pulled at his doublet to straighten it, and Southampton gave his hose a playful tug above the buttocks, receiving a smack on the head for his efforts. Everyone laughed and the earl exited the tavern with his usual grace, amidst good-natured good-byes and happily drunken shouts from the throng of his general admirers.

No one noticed as he departed that his smile was more plastered on than genuine, nor the lines of worry that creased his handsome forehead.

◆◇◆◇◆

GOOD EVENING, Robin," she said in a mild tone, and with an expression so even that Essex could determine nothing from it. He had come, where he was bidden, to her bedchamber.

"Good evening, Your Majesty," he replied with more formality than he was normally wont to assume. His bow was low but lacked the flamboyant flourishes that might be construed as levity. He realized he was barely breathing.

"Come, let us walk," she said, and taking his arm, went with him to the door.

As they moved into the silent corridor, he stifled the urge to ask why they might be strolling at so late an hour, as they often did in order to see and be seen by the queen's courtiers and ladies. But there was no one about in Greenwich Castle save the palace guard at several doorways.

"Did you enjoy the play?" Elizabeth inquired. She was still maddeningly noncommittal, neither friendly nor unpleasant.

"Very much. One of the characters was a shrew. You would have enjoyed the comparisons afterward between her and my mother."

Essex thought he perceived the barest hint of a smile cracking Elizabeth's thin, painted lips, but he was loath to take further liberties.

They had turned a corner in the rambling palace, and now ahead of them stood a pair of double doors, those leading to a long hallway connecting the west to the east wing. He looked to the queen with silent question, but she refused to oblige him with an answer. Instead, with a mysterious expression she moved forward and knocked with her knuckles, twice, on the door.

Slowly, silently they swept open to reveal the corridor. Essex's eyes widened at the sight before him. It was quite as extraordinary as anything he had ever seen. Both sides were lined with tapers, large and small, upright torches and candelabrum—hundreds, perhaps thousands of them, illuminating the hallway into a brilliance that matched sunlight.

He turned to Elizabeth, smiling delightedly in his astonishment. He opened his mouth, but she closed it with a gentle finger to his lips, then tugged at his arm, a signal that they should move forward into the spectacle itself.

It was magic, walking with the queen through the candlelight. He could not help but glance at her, and bathed in the bright warm glow she was as lovely as he had ever known her, the lines on her face erased by the light, white points—like stars—reflected in her dark eyes.

When she spoke, she spoke quietly and carefully, as though to preserve the mystery of the moment. "This is your future as I see it, Robin. Brilliant. Perfect. Filled with light."

Essex drew in a long breath and, closing his eyes, released it, relief and joy in equal measures flooding his soul. He knew the queen's next words even before she spoke them.

"The Farm of Sweet Wines is yours, my lord Essex. You will use it wisely, I expect, and you will cease all further suits for monetary favors from your queen."

Essex, overcome, fell to his knees at Elizabeth's feet. "When Your Majesty thinks that Heaven is too good for me," he whispered, "I will not fall like a star, but be consumed like a vapor by the same sun that drew me up to such a height."

He felt her touch the top of his head, and he reached up, taking her hands in his. He began to kiss them, again and again, whimpering with small cries of gratitude, inhaling the soft fragrance of the long white fingers, tasting the warm salt of his tears.

THEY HAD DECIDED TO set out before midnight, for though the queen had given Murrough ne Doe a letter of safe conduct, there were fewer chances of a hostile boarding at this hour.

Grace climbed the stairs and felt the thick mist envelop her as she strode out onto the deck and headed for the bow. The ship's progress was slow, letting the tide take it downriver, but the pace seemed just right to her. Natural. And her heart felt light for the first time in so many years.

The Queen of England had granted all of her requests. Grace had stowed Elizabeth's letters in the chest above the cabin bed. She would present one to Bingham as soon as she returned home. Or perhaps he would have been relieved of his post before she arrived—as the second letter promised he would be—though that was perhaps too much to hope for. In fact, she would relish the sight of Richard Bingham's face as he read of Tibbot's pardon, written in Elizabeth's own hand, and a directive for him to arrange for Grace's pension. There was time enough for his removal. It was hard not to gloat, she thought, smiling in the dark.

Now she felt Murrough ne Doe joining her at the rail. He stood beside her gazing out in wonder at the traffic on the Thames at such an hour.

"So you're pleased with your visit to London?" he said.

"I am. Very pleased indeed."

"You'll have your boy back. Your fleet. And good riddance to Richard Bingham."

" 'Tis hard to believe."

"Will you keep your promise to the queen?" he said.

"Which one?"

Murrough ne Doe laughed. "Grace, there's no one like you."

"I should hope not."

"Will you keep it?" he insisted.

"My promise to live dutifully as the English queen's subject, and fight her quarrels with all the world?"

"Yes, that one."

Grace sighed and peered out onto the river before her, straining to make sense of the darkness. "I'll keep my promises," she said, "for as long as Elizabeth keeps hers."

"Is it likely she will?" he asked.

Grace was silent, recalling the queen's soft expression of sympathy for her loss of Eric, and the guileless admission of desire to hear the adventures of one more traveled than herself. She had felt fleeting moments of understanding, even kinship with the woman . . . and she had in the end granted Grace her heart's desires.

Yet she was Elizabeth, Queen of England, chief vanquisher of Ireland. She was strong and cunning enough to have held her throne for thirty-five years.

"Is it likely she'll keep her promises to me?" said Grace. "I'm afraid only Jesus knows, my friend. I'm afraid only Jesus knows."

1596

# 7

He was scrambling effortlessly up the rigging, surefooted and fear-less. The wind was stiff, and coming, it seemed, from every direction, but his eight-year-old limbs felt strong and sure, and the crow's nest was not far above him, though a good twenty feet aft. Sure it was a long way, but so what? He'd have to jump, that was all there was to it.

"Tibbot, come down from there, you little monkey!"

He looked down to see his mother standing on the deck below, legs planted far apart, hands akimbo in that mannish stance of hers. Her neck was craning up to watch his progress amidst the masts and sails and rope rigging of the *Dorcas*.

"You come down from there this minute!"

Why was she nagging him? he thought petulantly, and why did he detect fear in her voice? She never used to nag him for such antics. He was her little monkey and she was proud of his agility, his speed and grace.

He crouched, winding tension up in his knees, set his eyes on the empty crow's nest, and sprang. For a moment he was flying, terror and exhilaration pumping through his veins in equal measure. His fingers caught the lip of the large bucket and he hauled himself up and over.

He was standing tall, gazing out over the whitecapped sea. Stand-ing very tall indeed——too tall for an eight-year-old. Ah, he'd become a man, had grown up very quickly. But his mother was still standing below, on deck, silent now. 'Twas only her presence that nagged at him. He would ignore her, he thought, then chuckled, as if it were possible to ignore Grace O'Malley.

His sights turned to the coastline. Ireland, the northwest coast—rocky islands and sand spits, harbors jutting deep inland. He could see that the countryside was scorched, fields bare, forests of skeletal trees, blackened and dead. His throat tightened at the sight, and rage filled him, hatred for the men responsible. *The English*. What had they done to his home, his beautiful home?

But wait, were those voices he was hearing? Yes, women's voices, and they were singing. Oh, 'twas a lovely melody, soft and sweet, and a harp playing besides. It soothed him, the distant singing, though as the *Dorcas* neared land it was louder, more distinct. There must be a dozen women singing their siren song. Yes, that's what it was, the siren song from Homer's story. But then he must take care, mustn't he? He should. They would lure him to destruction. But look!! The ruined countryside was green and fecund here. Great herds of cattle grazing on the hillside, as if the singers and their song had *healed* the land. Mayo was as it had been in his youth. Oh, sweet Ireland!

And now he could see Sligo Castle, such a beautiful place. The place where love lived. His heart filled suddenly with joy, filled so full he thought it might burst. Maeve would be waiting for him there. It was Maeve's home, and perhaps she was among the singers of the lovely song. No need to fear his beautiful wife.

As if by magic the *Dorcas* steered itself through the waves and toward Sligo Castle. His mother was below, arguing with the mate. No, she would not take the helm. She stood there, arms crossed over her chest with a disapproving frown. But who was she to disapprove of her son sailing into the arms of love? Maeve was his wife. And Sligo Castle her childhood home.

"Da!" At once he recognized his son's voice calling from below. He looked down. Why hadn't he seen Miles before? He was climbing up the rigging, not so surefooted as he himself had been. This was dangerous. The boy was inexperienced. He could fall, could be killed. But the singing voices were louder now. Very loud. He tore his gaze from Miles to the shore and Sligo Castle.

He could see the dock, and a dozen figures standing there. But wait! They were *men* . . . soldiers, soldiers wearing robin's-egg-blue livery. Where was Maeve? he wondered. What had they done to her? The fucking English! He opened his mouth and shouted, "You bastards, where is my wife? Where is my wife!"

A gentle hand was shaking him and Maeve's sweet breath blew softly across his face. Tibbot opened his eyes.

"Da? Is Da all right?" He could hear Miles's voice, half asleep. The boy was in a bed next to them.

"He's fine, son," said Maeve. "Just dreaming out loud."

Tibbot could see only the outlines of Maeve's face in the dark, but he reached up and stroked her cheek, still unable to speak. He was trying to remember the strange dream that was quickly receding from his memory.

Maeve leaned down and kissed his lips. "You *are* all right, Tibbot?" she whispered. "You were calling out for me."

"I'm all right," he finally managed. "You were one of Homer's sirens, or I thought you were. But then you turned out to be a soldier. An English soldier."

"Was I in the dream too, Da?"

"You were," said Tibbot, "climbing in the riggings of your grandmammy's boat."

With another kiss Maeve snuggled down under the covers, her body warm and comfortable next to his. It was all starting to make sense now, Tibbot thought. The three of them—he, Maeve, and Miles—had arrived at Sligo Castle yesterday. It was a place he loved to visit, for many reasons. First and foremost it was his wife's childhood home— *where love lived*. It was still beautiful, the countryside surrounding the castle, as yet untouched by war. This, Tibbot knew, was the result of Maeve's uncle O'Connor Sligo's longtime loyalty to the English. It had served as protection against the blight of warfare that had ruined the rest of Connaught, and Munster too. He loved the castle for another reason, one that he would never utter aloud in front of his mother. O'Connor had, over the years, brought the best of England into Sligo—a decent school for the children, furniture, hangings, plate. There was even a small gallery of portraits he'd had painted of his family, hanging in the great hall. *Refinement*, that's what it was. Tibbot did have a love for things English, gained from his years living in an English home. That was what his mother would hate to hear. And worse—all of them knew but did not say it aloud—he and Maeve bore a great debt of gratitude toward Richard Bingham himself. For it had been Grace's nemesis who had brought the pair together. Theirs had proven a love match from the beginning, despite the crass political reasons for which the marriage had been arranged.

Finally, he loved Sligo Castle for its importance in the scheme of things. By virtue of its very placement on the map of Ireland—set near a fine harbor and lying close to the borders of both Connaught and Ulster—it was known as the gateway between the two provinces, a vital stronghold worth a good fight.

Thankfully there had been little fighting up till now, aside from the usual squabbling and cattle raiding amongst the petty chieftains. O'Connor Sligo had for decades kept his territories peaceful, though many, including Tibbot's mother, believed the price was too high. English loyalty meant English occupation, and as the rebellion grew, so too had the numbers of Crown soldiers increased in Sligo.

Still, when Tibbot and his family had arrived the previous day he'd been surprised to find Sligo Castle guarded by Richard Bingham's guard—*the distinctive blue livery*—and inside a good-size garrison of his soldiers.

They'd been greeted warmly by Maeve's elder brother, Donal O'Connor Sligo. He was Tibbot's age, but a much softer man, he and his family never having had to fight for their very survival against an encroaching enemy. Early on, Donal's guardian, Uncle O'Connor, had submitted to the English—a submission that, unlike most chieftains' surrenders, had been altogether sincere. He'd come to be known as one of the Crown's most loyal adherents. And after that, life had proven easy. Tibbot always believed Maeve's sweet temperament was born of that cultured, carefree childhood, so different from his own roughneck youth.

Donal had informed them on their arrival that the old man was sick and abed, suffering agonies with the stone. The castle was presently secured by Bingham's garrison, led by an Irishman—another Crown loyalist—Lord Clanrickard's son, Ulick Burke.

"My least favorite cousin," Tibbot had remarked, for Ulick Burke had always been a bully, and a stupid boy at that. *Stupid and a bully—a deadly combination.* The same, his mother would say, as her first husband, Donal O'Flaherty. They'd had some words—Tibbot and Ulick—shortly after his arrival at Sligo, and they'd been far from pleasant. Sure Tibbot had goaded the young man, teasing him about his pretty uniform matching his pretty blue eyes, but Ulick had lashed back with outright insults and threats. Donal had placed his pudgy body between the two men. He hated unpleasantness. Couldn't the two Burke cousins attempt to get along?

Once Ulick had stomped off, Donal had whispered to his brother-in-law that he feared "a situation" was developing. He did not know what it was exactly, but from what his spies were saying, Ulick Burke was at its center, and it would be happening sooner rather than later. Donal was glad Tibbot would be here for its development, but Tibbot had been annoyed. Maeve and Miles were with him. This "situation" could turn ugly, and Tibbot did not wish to place his family in harm's way. *The Sirens' singing,* he mused. *The beautiful turning deadly.* In fact, on the morrow he would inform Donal that their plans had changed. They would leave Sligo Castle and head south for a visit with his mother. She'd be cheered seeing them. Grace was more forlorn than Tibbot had ever known her, exiled for the first time in her life from beloved Connaught by Richard Bingham's interference, and a virtual prisoner at his hands.

Tibbot's own fortunes had taken a downward shift as well. Under the Composition of Connaught, he had lost Burrishoole to Tom of Ormond. Now he was a tenant on his own land—a *tenant*! If that wasn't bad enough, Richard Bingham was having Tibbot's fleet watched too closely for any real freedom. All of the Burkes' chieftains and clansmen who had once looked to him for leadership were now looking away. It was no wonder his confusion had grown. *Were the English his friends or enemies? His patrons or destroyers of all that he loved?* He simply didn't know anymore.

Indeed, things were changing fast all over Ireland. The Munster Plantations were thriving under the administration of their English settlers, though in the north—Ulster—trouble was clearly brewing. Hugh O'Neill was building an army there—a huge army—and he was funding it with English subsidies. Sure O'Neill's upbringing in Henry Sidney's home should have guaranteed his loyalty to the Crown—at least that was the queen's thinking—but by now he had broken that loyalty half a dozen times, leading his rebels against English armies. And each time, by simply begging their pardon, he had been forgiven. Truces were set in place and more English money poured into his coffers. In fact, the man had broken his eighteen-year-old son-in-law, Red Hugh O'Donnell, out of Dublin Prison. Everyone knew O'Neill had been behind it, but the English—outraged—had held their tongues. Then O'Neill had formed an alliance with the boy that had, in a stroke, unified the entire north. The beloved young rebel—"the Fighting Prince," Red Hugh was now called—pulled together his own terrifying army out of O'Donnell clansmen and his mother Ineen Dubh's Scots Gallowglass. Together with Hugh O'Neill's English-backed army they were sweeping across the north striking fear into every English heart. Were the English blind? Tibbot wondered. Or did their hopes and wishes for their good "Earl of Tyrone" blind them to the truth about his loyalty?

Tibbot had nearly dozed off into sleep when he heard men shouting, shots fired. Then Maeve was shaking him, whispering, "Tibbot, sweetheart. Something's happening." He was up on his feet in seconds, moving to the window of the cottage within the courtyard of Sligo Castle. He could see chaotic movement in the torchlit yard. Donal's "situation," he surmised, had developed more quickly than either of them had imagined.

"Get dressed," he hissed to Maeve and Miles, then a moment later came a pounding at the door.

"Come out, all of you!" It was a soldier's commanding voice.

Tibbot pulled on his breeches and jacket and grabbed his pistol. Holding his wife and son close behind him and with his gun at the ready, he carefully opened the door. The blue-clad soldier was standing at attention.

"Put your gun away, sir," he said, "and all of you accompany me."

Tibbot realized that the soldier had spoken in Irish, and not the English language.

All the residents of Sligo Castle, still in their nightclothes, had been assembled in the courtyard. Even old O'Connor Sligo was dragged from his sickbed looking mightily aggrieved. Donal Sligo was likewise shivering in his nightshirt, his household gathered round him. All of them watched as soldiers carried the still bleeding bodies of their garrison mates into the yard, laying them out in two neat rows. There were forty-two dead soldiers, the only casualties of what Tibbot soon realized was Ulick Burke's "mutiny." It was soon apparent that all the living soldiers were Irish and all the dead English, and it struck Tibbot once again how mad was the English policy of filling the Crown's ranks with so many Irish. His countrymen had shown time and again that loyalty was to be measured at any given moment by which side was winning.

Now Tibbot could see Ulick Burke striding importantly about the yard conferring with his fellow mutineers. Donal Sligo started to move forward for a word with him but was halted by two soldiers with drawn swords. Ulick was clearly enjoying the scene—this small, bloody victory, the utter surprise and confusion of the castle's residents. But in the next moment, with Ulick's signal that opened the gate and lowered the moat bridge, the "great plan" was revealed to all. Clattering over the draw-bridge rode Red Hugh O'Donnell and a rowdy company of Ulstermen.

Tibbot could see that the three years in Dublin Prison and the three leading a rebellion had hardened the fun-loving lad he'd known since childhood into a fierce and angry man. Red Hugh gracefully dismounted and removed his helmet, revealing a wavy red-gold mop of hair as he strode to face Ulick Burke. Their smiles were little more than leers, and their embrace more for victory than affection. What was left of Bing-ham's garrison cheered.

Then Ulick raised a hand to silence the soldiers. The flickering torches playing on the courtyard lent an eeriness to his shouted announcement. "I hereby deliver the Castle Sligo to you, my lord O'Donnell, and to all the rebels of Ireland!"

The soldiers cheered again, though silence pervaded the members of the O'Connor Sligo family and household, who were all at a loss for a reaction.

Red Hugh swept the courtyard with eyes that flashed yellow in the firelight. "Are you not Irish first?" he demanded of them all. "And should you not celebrate the freeing of your lands and castle from En-glish tyranny?"

There were a few weak "huzzahs" from a clutch of servants standing huddled together, but not a sound from O'Connor nor his nephew Donal Sligo. Red Hugh found the old man in the shadows and moved to face him.

"You've been loyal to the Crown for so long you don't know what freedom is," he said with a withering gaze. "How do you sleep at night?" Without awaiting reply he moved to Donal and eyed him with disgust. "You're a young man, Donal. You've no excuse for siding with the English."

"They've been good to us here," Donal said, proudly defiant. "And you've no right to take this castle. 'Tis my family's, and has been for two hundred years!"

"Sligo Castle is necessary for the defense of the West Country against the Crown's army," Hugh announced with stern finality.

Then a voice rang out in the otherwise silent yard. "Are you sure you're not taking it for your own pleasure?"

"Who spoke?"

"Tibbot Burke."

"Tibbot!" Red Hugh moved eagerly toward the voice. "I didn't know you were here."

The two young men stood face-to-face, sizing each other up, having not laid eyes on each other for several years.

"You look well, Tibbot."

"You look well yourself. Rebellion seems to agree with you."

Red Hugh laughed. "It does, it feels right, Tibbot. *You* know that from the times you fought on our side. But you forget it again whenever you fight for the English. Do you not think it's time you stood your ground? Stood for Ireland?"

Tibbot stared hard at his old friend. "I suppose you want us all to believe you're taking this castle for the good of the rebellion."

"Yes, I do."

"Well, I say you've no right. This is Connaught, not Ulster. And when you steal from the lords of Connaught, you're just as worthy of contempt as the English are. You're no different. You just want to rule us."

"You're wrong about that." Red Hugh held Tibbot's eye. "I mean to reestablish the hereditary rights in Connaught that England has forbidden. I'm arranging for a new election of The MacWilliam."

The news so stunned Tibbot that it rendered him silent.

"You like that, do you?" Red Hugh was smiling. "Well, you should, for who is more worthy of the Burke MacWilliamship than you? Would you like that, Tibbot? The title you were born to hold?" When Tibbot did not quickly answer him, Red Hugh turned on his heels as if he had not a minute of his precious time to waste on hesitant men, and again faced the Sligo residents. "Of course the lords O'Connor and Donal Sligo must relinquish residency in this castle," he announced, "but those of you who pledge your support of the rebel troops that I garrison here may stay."

Before he strode from the yard, Red Hugh stopped again before Tibbot. "You and your family will leave tonight. Await news of the election. 'Twill be soon." He turned to go, but glanced back over his shoulder. "And send my respects to your mother. She is a great rebel."

<hr />

WELL, SHE HAD SLIPPED line and sailed out of Tralee Harbor undetected by the English guard, and her voyage to Spain had proven more than successful, but now Grace O'Malley was left to face the unpleasantness of her premature return. At the helm of her galley *Owl*, she could see a whole company of the queen's soldiers standing at attention on the harbor dock. They'd be waiting for *her*, that was sure, and the prissy Captain Brady would be well armed with complaints, and threats of imprisonment for her treasonous offenses against the Crown. First he would chastise her for setting fire to the English barracks one night several months before. It had been a necessary distraction, one used to draw away the soldiers guarding her person and vessels. She would also be accused—rightly—of boring holes below the waterline of the queen's carracks, scuttling them and making it impossible to give chase to her fleet when it slipped its moorings in the flickering light of the barracks fire and sailed away.

Grace knew that the full wrath of Brady's commander, Richard Bingham, would shortly fall upon her head, but the truth of it was, she was past caring. What more could he do to her that he'd not already done? He had deprived her of her homes in Mayo, murdered one son, ruined another, and laid waste to everything he touched. Now, despite the queen's instructions to Bingham that Grace be left to her own devices, he had cessed a company of English troops on her, ensuring that her movements and activities were severely restricted.

She had for a time succumbed to self-pitying depression, allowed herself to wallow in it like a pig in swill. A message had come from O'Neill—his revolt in the north was strengthening every day, but without aid from Spain, it could never in the end hope to succeed. He urgently needed her help. Grace had been dumbstruck. The first chieftain since Brian Boru to unite all of Ireland behind him was asking her for help, and she—a virtual prisoner in the midst of Bingham's soldiers and spies—was helpless, her hands securely tied. Each cargo was searched. Each voyage must be approved by Brady. And to enforce the Crown's strictures, at least twenty English soldiers accompanied her crews when any of her ships left port. She could not possibly offer The O'Neill her services.

One wind-whipped Munster night, alone in the drafty stone house, Grace had drunk herself into a stupor. It was the next afternoon, the sun about to set over a gold and iron sea, that she awoke sick and sodden and altogether ashamed. *She'd been granted a brilliant life, and freedom beyond reason. Yes, she had suffered some losses, but who had not? She was older and wiser than that dandy captain and his garrison full of men who wished desperately to be anywhere in the world but the cold, miserable coast of western Ireland. Surely there was some way, with the help of her clever and devoted crews, that Brady's garrison could be duped while she and her men made their escape.*

It had proven easier than she'd imagined, the English even more gullible and careless than she had hoped. When "Fire!" had been called in the barracks on the far side of Tralee Village, all but four of the soldiers guarding the fleet were ordered to fight the blaze. Those four were easily disabled, and there was more than sufficient time to drill the hulls of the English vessels full of holes. By the time the fire was out, Grace and her fleet had cleared the harbor. The soldiers returning to their dockside post would have been gobsmacked to find their prisoners escaped and their own ships listing in the water.

All of Grace's vessels made it safely to the high seas and well into the Bay of Biscaye before the English could take out after them.

Now she could take pleasure in knowing that all her ships but the *Owl* were bound for Ulster ports, loaded with Spanish guns and ammunition for Hugh O'Neill's army. By a rare stroke of ill fortune, her own ship had been intercepted off the Scilly Isles by the queen's navy, and now their large escort was making escape impossible.

As the hull scraped the wooden dock at Tralee, a mate gave Grace his hand and helped her down from the *Owl*'s deck. She could see the company of English soldiers still standing at rigid attention. They would have been tongue-lashed, or more probably punished for their stupidity in allowing the rebels' escape. Of course it would have been Brady's ill-conceived orders that had left the fleet all but unguarded, but officers like Brady never claimed responsibility for their blunders when there were perfectly good underlings to take the fall. There he was—the good captain coming forward to meet Grace as she disembarked. *He's smiling*, Grace thought. *Why is he smiling?* Then she saw, walking by his side, yet another surprise. It was her son Tibbot with Captain Brady, and the two men were chatting amiably.

Her boy was looking more manly and handsome than she'd ever known him, and it was he who extended his hand to help her from the deck. "Mother," he said, and embraced her. The English captain looked on with a hardly disguised grimace.

"Hello, son," she said. "Good to see you." Then to Brady, "Good afternoon, Captain."

"Welcome home, Mistress O'Malley. We've missed you."

"As I have you," she said, growing more perplexed by the moment. The storm, if it was to break, must surely break soon. But Brady simply accompanied Grace and Tibbot to the wagon that awaited them. From the corner of her eye, she could see the soldiers in a calm and orderly fashion boarding the *Owl* to search it. They would come up empty-handed, she knew, which would only add to their frustration.

Tibbot had chosen to drive his mother, so in moments they were alone, a pair of ponies hauling the wagon up the track to Tralee Village and Grace's stone house.

"What was that all about?" she said.

"Rather a happy surprise?"

"I'd say so. What's happened?"

"Richard Bingham's been brought up on charges."

"No . . ."

"By his own countrymen. Fenton and Perrot are as keen to be done with him as you are. He's in Dublin now, facing an inquiry."

"Jesus be praised."

"Captain Brady was happily left to his own devices after he let you slip away," said Tibbot. "With the flap about Bingham, hardly anyone noticed your escape. Even though your fleet has gone missing—doing who knows what mischief—at least he has the 'rebel woman' in his hands again. Whatever harsh measures he might have taken against you have been, well, *softened* by my influence."

"Then your influence must have grown substantially in my absence."

"You could say that. Word has it that while Grace O'Malley can always be counted on to make trouble, her son's loyalty to the Crown may still be winnable."

Grace was rendered silent by the thought, one that constantly troubled her. It had become clear in recent years that while Tibbot loved her very dearly, she carried no influence in the matter of his loyalties. Now she worried that his ambitions, together with his chameleonlike changeability, would lead him astray.

"I've just come from Sligo Castle," he went on, unrepentant for the stance he knew annoyed her. "There's been a rather interesting development."

"Oh?"

"Ulick Burke has mutinied and handed the castle over to Red Hugh."

*So Ulick Burke was taking a stand against* his *father, a longtime loyalist to the English—yet another Irish family sundered by this never-ending conflict.* "Has he now?" said Grace. "What of O'Connor and Donal Sligo?"

"Put out of the castle."

Grace sat silently, digesting the intelligence. Finally she said, "And where do you stand in all of it?"

They'd reached the stone house, and Tibbot helped his mother from the carriage. 'Twas he who was silent now, carefully considering her question. With no answer forthcoming, she walked ahead of him up the stone path and entered the dark, frigid residence, then went about lighting the lamps as Tibbot followed her in.

"Your cook's gone to market," he said. "She should be back soon with our dinner."

"Don't change the subject, Tibbot. Where do you stand?"

"I haven't yet decided," he said. "O'Connor and Donal are Maeve's kin, and they've been good to me."

*That they were English sympathizers was hardly mentionable*, thought Grace.

"On the one hand, Red Hugh has no right to be invading Connaught," Tibbot continued. "On the other . . ."

Grace could see a light beginning to burn behind her son's eyes.

". . . he's proposed an election for the MacWilliamship, and he says that no one is more qualified than myself for the title."

"Let me get this straight. An O'Donnell from Ulster is calling for the election of the Burkes' MacWilliam in Connaught. And you believe, by Red Hugh's influence, you'll be elected?"

"I do."

"And as Red Hugh's MacWilliam, would you fight as an Irish rebel?"

"I'll never be *Red Hugh's* MacWilliam, Mother. When I'm elected I'll be my own man, the chieftain I was always meant to be. And yes, I'd fight for Ireland."

"For as long as the rebels were victorious," said Grace.

"There's a good chance they'll prevail."

"Do you really think Red Hugh would ever, in a thousand years, back *you* for the MacWilliamship? You're too strong a leader in Mayo, Tibbot. What Hugh needs is a follower, someone with no ambition of his own."

"You couldn't be more wrong," Tibbot argued.

Grace's head was beginning to ache. She lowered herself into an armchair. "Light the fire for your mam, will you, son?" That was all she would say on the subject. She would refrain from nagging him. She hated nagging women, and besides, she knew that, in any event, it was futile.

Relieved of Grace's inquisition Tibbot became industrious, carefully laying the peat bricks in the hearth and setting them to light. It was not long before the heat began to ease her bones, and after Tibbot placed a pillow at her back, Grace settled comfortably into the chair.

"Have you had a letter back from the queen on your complaints?" he asked.

"I've heard nothing myself from England. Just rumors that she refuses to send sufficient troops here, or to properly supply the ones she does send."

"Good news for us."

"Aye, Elizabeth is blind when it comes to Ireland. And deaf. And stupid."

"She speaks well of *you*," said Tibbot with a teasing smile.

"She ordered your release," said Grace, "and I appreciated that. But I got the feeling she was moved to free you not from a queenly place in her mind, but from somewhere softer—in her heart. If I didn't know better, I'd say it came from a *mother's* heart. Who knows, maybe those stories were true about her and Dudley's son. When I was in the Spanish Court, I heard a strange tale of an English spy captured in the north of Spain— a man callin' himself Arthur Dudley, the queen's bastard. King Philip wasn't sure the man was who he claimed to be, but was cautious enough to chuck young Arthur Dudley in the Madrid Gaol and throw away the key. If he's who he says he is, he's the rightful heir to the English throne." Grace's eyes narrowed. "Arthur would have been your age, Tibbot, or thereabouts. Perhaps the queen's fine gesture releasing you was as one mother to another."

"That's a fine story, Mother," said Tibbot, amused, "one that only a romantic would believe. Who would have thought Grace O'Malley a romantic? I think I'm the only one who knows it."

"Well, Tibbot, you're the only man in the world I love. Who better to know my weak side?"

"You trust me then?"

"I trust you would never betray your mother."

"Like my brother did?"

Grace was silent, her eyes suddenly hard.

"Are you sure you won't see Murrough?" Tibbot ventured.

"I've never been more sure of anything in my life."

"He's your son."

"And he was ready to whack my head off!"

"That's not true. He was simply fighting alongside Bingham. He had no idea you would show up in that tent."

"But that's the point, Tibbot. He was fighting alongside *Bingham*. That bastard murdered his brother Owen! There's fighting for England for expediency's sake, and there's fighting with the Devil himself. What Murrough did was inexcusable. I may be his mother, but there's a limit to how much I can tolerate. And don't be standin' up for him!"

"He's a brilliant fighter," Tibbot persisted. "And I would do well to keep him by my side."

"Aye, he takes after his father like that. So keep Murrough at your side—if you must. Just watch your *back,* brother or not."

"Yes, Mother."

"I don't like your patronizing tone when you say that."

"No patronizing intended. Look, forget about Murrough and tell me about Spain."

"Aye, Spain. 'Twill be Ireland's savior if she keeps her promises. I met the king."

"You met King Philip?"

"I did, at the Escorial. I'm Hugh O'Neill's messenger now," she said with an amused smile.

"What were you sent to say?"

"Oh, I offered him the crown of Ireland in return for his help with the rebels."

"What did he think of the offer, coming from the mouth of a woman?"

"I didn't ask him that, but I suspect it surprised him. He was most solicitous, though, for he wants Ireland badly. Poor old bastard. Very shriveled, with knee joints swollen to the size of melons. His skin is like parchment and covered in oozing sores. They say he eats nothing but meat, and that's causin' him to rot from the inside out."

"So you offered him O'Neill's crown. And then what?"

"Well, he looked in my eyes very long and hard, silent like, and then he stood and hobbled out the door of his bedchamber, where I'd been taken to see him. He hasn't a throne room in that mausoleum he calls a castle, but lives in a Spartan little room with only a bed and a chair and a table—the King of Spain! So he rises with those wretched knees and opens a door, beckoning me after him into—if you can believe it—a great, soaring chapel. He can lie in his bed, he tells me, with the door open and stare in at a huge painted Jesus hangin' on the cross above a gilded altar. It brings him peace, he says.

"So down on the marble on his poor knees he goes—enjoyin' the agony, if you ask me—and he points to the floor beside him. Well, I kneel there too, and for the longest time King Philip prays his heart out for guidance from the Lord. All of a sudden he cries out like somebody's stabbed him, but he's all right, and he turns to me and says, 'The Lord has spoken, and he entreats me to help my brethren bring back the true religion to Ireland.' Of course I don't tell him that the last thing on Hugh O'Neill's mind is the Catholic Church. He'll do or say *anything* to be granted King Philip's aid against Elizabeth. Who better to ask than the man who named her a heretic, and England the 'Scarlet Whore of the World'? 'Oh yes,' he says, 'God is on Ireland's side, as he is on Spain's, and we will have a great victory in the name of Jesus Christ our Lord.' I didn't say, 'Where were God and Jesus in the English Channel? How could he let your armada founder, and your soldiers die like dogs on the coast of Ireland?' I didn't say that. I just let him rave on until he was ready to sign the requisitions for guns and shot and powder. And then he blessed me—as though he was some sort of holy man himself—and sent me on my way.

"I've met all kinds of people, Tibbot. Ones with war and killing on the brain, ones who think of nothing but love, and what goes on between the covers. Some are devoted to learning, others to great art, or story-telling, or the makin' of fine wine. But never in my life have I met any-one—layman or clergy or saint—who has been so one-minded about God as the King of Spain is. Devotion is fine, but with him I fear 'tis a sickness. And while Ireland owes him a debt of gratitude for all he's given, and promises to give in the future, I fear his religious disease may infect our cause and bring us to grief."

"You worry too much, Mother. Just take his gifts and never look back. For my part, your story gives me great hope for the rebellion." Tibbot's eyes were shining again. "All of a sudden it feels possible.

When I'm The MacWilliam, I'll join with Red Hugh and Hugh O'Neill and we'll take back Ireland. Take it back from the heretic queen!"

"Will you?" said Grace very quietly.

Tibbot Burke was too lost in his dreams of triumph to hear the sarcastic tinge to his mother's voice, the worry that her fickle son was less a man of his word than his changing passions, and that one day he would break her heart.

# 8

ANOTHER BLANKET, damn you! Throw me in another blanket!" Tibbot Burke could hear himself shouting at the door of his dark, reeking prison cell, and he feared that a touch of desperation had crept into his voice. *Sweet Jesus, he could not, would not allow his captors to see his weakness.* But if he didn't get another blanket and some decent food in his belly, he would die in this black hole, and that, Tibbot thought with sudden defiance, was simply not his destiny.

He would kill Red Hugh O'Donnell the next time he saw him, throttle him with his bare hands. This was *his* prison. *His* wretched guards—in a far-flung outpost in southwest Ulster, just over the border from Sligo.

Tibbot slumped down on his vermin-infested straw pallet thrown in the corner, and wrapped the one ragged blanket they'd given him round his bony shoulders, trying to keep his teeth from chattering. The cold was wicked and had been constant for the whole two months he'd been imprisoned . . . or maybe it had been longer. Tibbot had, in the windowless hut, lost track of time, the days and nights much the same, the only sunlight falling through when the heavy door was opened and a bowl of watery oat gruel pushed through. Would he be blind, like a mole, when he was finally freed? A blind, bug-bitten skeleton with skin hanging off his bones?

"Another bloody blanket!" he shouted.

The next moment the door was flung wide open, letting in a gray light dulled further by heavy snowfall. Tibbot shielded his eyes, squinting to see who was clomping heavily into the tiny hut. But even when he saw the square, red-bearded face that topped the burly form he did not recognize it.

"Tibbot Burke?" the man said.

"Who else would it be?" he replied irritably.

The man leaned over and grabbed Tibbot by the arm more roughly than was necessary, perhaps in answer to the prisoner's rudeness, and pulling him to his feet, marched him outside. Tibbot felt an unseen pair of hands throw a heavy cloak over his shoulders, and now another man was leading an old sag-backed horse toward him.

"You're free to go," said the burly, bearded man. 'Twas a simple statement delivered in a tone of disinterest, even boredom.

Tibbot found himself momentarily paralyzed. "Are you Red Hugh's men?" he finally demanded, desperate that his shaking knees stay rigid and his body upright.

"Who else would we be?" said one, mildly amused.

"Then he's sent orders for my release?"

They regarded him blankly, the snow swirling round them.

"Why are you letting me go?"

"Would you rather not be let go?" said the man with the horse. "We'd be glad to throw you back in your dunghole if that's what you want."

They all laughed.

"You better help him onto his horse," said the red-bearded man. "I don't think our food agreed with him. He's gotten very thin."

They laughed again and a moment later Tibbot, four hands grappling with him, found himself seated on the horse's back. The cloth saddle was damp and cold under his thin breeches. Still shocked by his abrupt release and fighting mental confusion, Tibbot sat as tall as he was able, but never moving.

"Go on, get out of here," said the bearded man, "or we'll shoot you and be done with it."

"Which way is south?" Tibbot asked.

As the three men turned away, one of them bothered to point, and the other slapped the horse's rump. It began a slow plodding in the wrong direction and Tibbot, with some effort, turned the poor creature around. A moment later the three Ulstermen had disappeared into the snowstorm and Tibbot was alone.

Of all the miseries of his capture and hellish imprisonment of the last months, this moment, he realized, blinking back tears, had been the most humiliating. And Red Hugh O'Donnell had arranged for his humiliation. The man would pay, Tibbot promised himself as he headed south to Connaught and freedom. He would surely have to pay.

◈◈◈

NEVER, OBSERVED TIBBOT, had his thoughts been so black. He was alone in the dead of winter, riding south out of Ulster across the borderlands into Mayo, and neither his recently regained freedom nor the magnificence of the Sligo countryside could lift his spirits. *His spirits . . . what was left of them. Oh why had he not listened to his mother?* She had tried to warn him of Red Hugh's true intentions, but he'd been pigheaded, choosing to believe what he wished to believe— that the "Fighting Prince" was his ally. That he would support Tibbot's bid, even over other Burkes who might have held superiority in years and qualifications. If only he'd heeded Grace's warnings . . .

Instead he'd traveled with all the Connaught clans to the Rath of Eassacaoide in Kilmaine—the ancient inaugural place—to what had been meant to be a true celebration of resistance, the MacWilliamship having for some years been outlawed by the English. All the clans had gathered in their numbers in peaceful anticipation when, to the sound of pipe and drum, in rode Red Hugh O'Donnell with eighteen hundred of his soldiers and Gallowglass. It was true that he'd convened the election, and for that had earned the respect of the congregation. But he'd gone too far when he'd strode importantly with his bodyguard of burly Scots to the summit of the rath and taken a stand there like some Greek god, enclosing himself even further with a wide ring of armed protection. The Burkes found themselves roughly excluded from this inner circle of power, and no one was permitted into Red Hugh's presence unless he was summoned. All of Tibbot's demands to speak with his old friend—

his *patron*—had been summarily dismissed, and he began to worry that things might not go as he'd planned.

Despite Red Hugh's rude entrance, the elections had gone on as scheduled, with as much of the traditional fistfighting and shoving as serious deliberation. Red Hugh, as most expected he would, had refrained from interference, though Tibbot's hopes for his help had been altogether dashed. Nevertheless, Tibbot—on his own merit—and three other men had been set apart as the most eligible candidates. But when all the votes had finally been cast and counted, William of Shrule had been chosen The MacWilliam. Tibbot was shocked and dismayed by the outcome, but it had been a fair election. Nothing, however, prepared him—indeed, prepared any of them—for what happened next.

In the midst of the celebration of backslapping and congratulations, Red Hugh O'Donnell descended from the rath's summit and shouldered his way in amongst the Connaughtmen. His guard unsheathed their swords and raised their pistols. He shouted above the outcry that The MacWilliam had been selected, but that William of Shrule was not that man. Theobald Ciotach would stand as the Burkes' chieftain, and if anyone objected, they could fight him and his army right here, right now.

Of course no one had been prepared for a battle, and they were quite outnumbered in men and arms. But as the arrogant Red Hugh marched "his" MacWilliam to the top of the rath, dozens of skirmishes broke out in the mass of clansmen and soldiers. Many were shouting in fury that Theobald Ciotach was but a green boy—a puppet who could never lead the Burkes but would gladly do his master's bidding. Most turned away and spat in disgust as Red Hugh lay the ancient MacWilliam mantle round Theobald's shoulders and raised the young man's hand in hollow triumph. Domination by the English was repugnant, but it was clear to all that as the new Burkes' chieftain would be ruled by an Ulster overlord, so too would Red Hugh expect to rule *all* the Connaught Burkes. They'd been tricked by Hugh's promises of restoring their age-old title, first usurped by the Crown, now debased by one of their own.

But among the clansmen there at the Rath of Eassacaoide that day, Tibbot Burke felt the most badly betrayed. His mother, God love her, had been right about Red Hugh O'Donnell.

And in the following weeks Tibbot saw that she'd been right in another respect. The Queen of England had stupidly allowed her forces in Connaught to dwindle to nearly nothing, this at a time when Red Hugh's army had grown to enormous proportions. But the effect of their diminishment had proven a blessing for Tibbot. *The English needed him more than ever.* He was the only Irishman with a fleet of ships who knew the treacherous coastal waters, who could pilot their troop and supply ships safely into harbor. Grace O'Malley had as large a fleet as his, but it was well known that her sympathies lay with the rebels. With gentle handling and bribery—the English had come to believe—Tibbot Burke might still be wooed to their cause.

Indeed, he had given them reason to believe his sincerity. Within weeks of the false election, Tibbot had led his own forces against Theobald Ciotach's soldiers. They'd been little more than skirmishes, but Tibbot's persistence had demonstrated to Red Hugh his fierce defiance, and shown the English that Tibbot was willing to fight one of the Crown's most dangerous enemies. Red Hugh had not been unaware of England's interest in Tibbot and—conveniently forgetting his betrayal of his old friend—himself began to woo Tibbot to his side, to "the side of the rebellion," he continued to insist. But Tibbot had decided he would not be fooled again by the "Fighting Prince of Ulster," and indeed for many months enjoyed playing one enemy against the other. With clever maneuvering he kept the English fearing that he would side with O'Donnell, and O'Donnell worrying that Tibbot might defect to the Crown.

But luck has a way of abandoning even the most worthy, and during one of the skirmishes near the border, Tibbot had been unhorsed and captured by Theobald Ciotach's rebels. Disbelieving the Fates, he had been marched in chains through freezing, muddy bogs over the border into Ulster and a small encampment of Red Hugh's army. He was thrown unceremoniously into a makeshift prison cell and left to rot, in total isolation. As the weeks dragged by, Tibbot realized that this incarceration was even more wretched than the one he'd suffered at Bingham's hands a few years back. In the English prison—even with the beatings and torture that had nearly crippled him—Tibbot had consoled himself with the knowledge that he was a political prisoner in a good fight. But now he languished in obscurity, his own countryman's captive.

Never once had Tibbot been sent word from Red Hugh acknowledging that his respected opponent was in his custody. He had simply been abandoned and ignored.

In late December, traveling south into Connaught, the weather had gone from appalling to murderous. The pony had dropped dead under him, and Tibbot had been forced to trudge through thigh-deep snow for endless miles to the nearest settlement. The villagers had been hospitable enough for the week it took him to regain his strength, but they were loath to relinquish even one of their precious horses to him. It was only by revealing his identity and promising that Tibbot Burke would lead their men and the rest of Connaught to victory against the tyrannical Red Hugh O'Donnell that secured him a mount. There *had* been one tidbit of cheerful news to come out of the village. Sligo Castle was back in the hands of O'Connor and Donal Sligo, though the details of that triumph were unknown to his hosts.

Finally the blessed castle was within sight and Tibbot's battered spirits soared. He could see that English soldiers were again garrisoned and guarding the moated castle, but this time they wore no blue livery, just the usual makeshift uniforms of the queen's army. At the gate he stated his name and was instantly granted entry, and once again found himself being greeted warmly by his brother-in-law, who had thankfully not fussed over him, or harped on his scrawny condition. There were a few questions about his captivity, but Donal Sligo seemed rather relieved that Tibbot had little to say of it. In fact, once the obligatory questions about the state of Tibbot's family were concluded, Donal Sligo got straight down to business.

"Come with me," he said. "You must meet our savior and—you'll be most pleased to know—Richard Bingham's replacement."

"Bingham's *gone*?"

"No, but seriously demoted. Sir Conyers Clifford is the new governor of Connaught, and he's brilliant. I promise you'll like him very well."

They walked shoulder to shoulder to the garrison, Donal using the time to cram as much intelligence into Tibbot as the time allowed—how the Englishman, Conyers Clifford, despite his unquestionable loyalty to the Crown, had become a true friend of Connaught. He had thrown out Bingham's brutal policies and done right by the Irish instead.

In the garrison office a well-built man of thirty stood poring over a map on a table. His long, sandy hair and tanned, even-featured countenance was very pleasing to behold.

"Captain Clifford, may I present my brother-in-law, Tibbot Burke, newly released from his captivity."

Clifford smiled, revealing white, even teeth, and when he spoke it was with a rich and modulated voice. "Wonderful! Most honored to meet you," Clifford exclaimed with what appeared to be the most genuine sincerity. They bowed to each other in the curt, military style of the English.

Tibbot was unprepared for the warmth with which he was being received by the man. "I'm very happy to be here," he said, "and happier still to meet you, my lord."

"No more pleased than the Privy Councils here and in England will be to know you've escaped Red Hugh O'Donnell's clutches."

Tibbot quietly decided that it would serve no purpose to disabuse the Englishman of the true and pathetic circumstances of his release. He wondered briefly if he should, in fact, fabricate a story of an heroic breakout. But it proved wholly unnecessary. Tibbot, it appeared, was already thought a hero by the English.

"You've come home at a crucial time, Tibbot," Conyers went on. "We've taken back much of the territory Red Hugh so boldly claimed for himself. Friends like Donal here are working with Her Majesty's army to push them out of Mayo, and Connaught entirely."

Though he was able to hide it well, Tibbot felt himself momentarily confused. *Of course he wished the arrogant Red Hugh expelled from Connaught and punished for the miserable treatment he'd inflicted on him. But Tibbot had not yet decided whether to fight on the side of the English, or not. He needed time to think, and perhaps his mother's advice . . .* "Have you news of my fleet?" he said, composing himself.

"Happy news indeed," said Clifford. "All your ships lie in harbor, altogether intact at Burrishoole. I will send word to their captains of your return."

Tibbot beamed with pleasure. The thought of reuniting with his crews cheered him immensely.

"I shall also messenger the Council in Dublin," said Clifford. "You've been the subject of considerable discussion there."

"Have I?"

"It was decided that if you were somehow to escape O'Donnell, we should be prepared to make you an offer you would no doubt find pleasing."

Donal shot Tibbot an encouraging smile.

"What is this offer?"

"Actually, we thought that *you* might compose a list of requests that would, of course, include a reparation of lands taken from you, a suitable title, and perhaps a small army of your own, paid for by the Crown. Of course Red Hugh's MacWilliam would—with our help—be banished from Connaught."

Now Tibbot found himself quite speechless. He was being offered the very world by the English. He'd known he was valuable to them, but never dreamt the extent of that valuation.

"What would the Crown demand in return?"

"Use of your fleet in bringing our troops and supply ships safely through Irish waters and into port. Your full support and loyalty to Her Majesty." Clifford cleared his throat. "Of course such a generous offer would require a promise of good conduct."

"A hostage." Tibbot's words were a whisper. There was silence, as all three men knew exactly who the hostage must be.

This was a moment fraught with danger for Conyers Clifford, Tibbot realized. He clearly—no, *desperately*—wanted this Connaught rebel on his side, though now he'd been forced to demand a thing that could altogether quash the deal. But when Clifford next spoke, his warmth and honesty banished the chill in Tibbot's heart.

"Of course Miles would be treated with the greatest dignity and respect, that befitting the son of a great chieftain. And there is no way to place a value on the education he would receive under an English roof— as you did. I'm sure you wish such a privilege for your son."

Tibbot's mind was whirling again. *Miles given as a hostage. How would Maeve feel? What would his mother say? And of course, there was the nagging dilemma of choosing sides. He meant to be on the winning side, of that there was no doubt. The English were strong, but O'Donnell and O'Neill now had the backing of Spain, and the cause of freedom spurring them on. They might very well prove victorious.*

Conyers Clifford's soothing voice interrupted Tibbot's ruminations. "You needn't decide now, my friend. There'll be time to think on it, discuss it with your wife. But if you will, come here and have a look at this." He waved a hand over the map on his table. Donal Sligo with no hesitation, moved to Clifford's side, smiling with encouragement to Tibbot.

"We're well into a strategy for removing Red Hugh from any remaining holdings in Mayo, then unseating Theobald Ciotach from the MacWilliamship," Donal explained. "Till now we've been at a disadvantage, with the Crown's troops here so depleted. But with your return, Tibbot, I tell you all the Connaught chieftains will rise up behind you. They're outraged at Red Hugh's incursions, and with you at their head they will fight!"

Suddenly clarity, hope, and then joy swept over Tibbot like a set of rolling breakers. *Nothing could be accomplished until that arrogant rogue O'Donnell was put in his place. Tibbot would give his aid to the English now, when they needed it most. He would make himself indispensable to them. Accept their rich gifts and give his son a brilliant education. He would never be in this enviable position himself had he not been held hostage in Richard Bingham's home. One discounted the might of England at his own risk. He would not make that mistake. On the other hand, he would hold in reserve his prerogative to take the side of his countrymen when, and if, it suited his purposes. And who was his mother to censure him for his decisions? She had always done what had been necessary for her own survival. Now he would do the same.*

"Make room," said Tibbot with a boyish grin as he moved to Clifford's table. "Let me see how you plan to scourge Red Hugh O'Donnell from Connaught."

1598

# 9

**B**Y GOD, Robert, how much more loathsome can one man's mood become!" Southampton glared at his companion slouching in the dark carriage now jouncing along the narrow cobbled lane.

"Shall I show you?" Essex snarled back and made as if to lunge at his friend.

Southampton sighed, resigned to Robert's petulance and abusive tongue. It was strange, however, to see the Earl of Essex in such somber garb traveling incognito about the rough streets of London in this rude coach. But where they were going, neither of them could afford to be recognized. Indeed, 'twas their destination itself that had much to do with his friend's foul temper.

"You're so sure it's the French pox," Essex said. "Why not the clap?"

"The rash. The aching limbs. I've seen it before. And you admitted to the chancre on your prick."

"I suppose you would like to have examined it yourself. Closely."

"How rude of you to say. But don't flatter yourself, Robert," Southampton sniffed indignantly. "I prefer my pricks large and healthy. Right at this corner, driver!"

The carriage wheeled about in such an extreme turn that Southampton was flung into Essex's lap. Having righted himself, Robert—red faced and muttering low curses—thrust himself bodily from the coach window and began shrieking loud threats of death and dismemberment at the driver. Southampton hauled him back in.

"Just calm yourself, man. We'll be there soon enough."

Essex curled up in his corner and fumed silently.

How had it come to this? Southampton wondered. A few short years ago Robert Devereaux had been a national hero—youngest of the Privy councilors, beloved by the queen; now his physical constitution was alarmingly weakened. And his list of enemies at Court was growing daily. But it was understandable, Southampton supposed. Robert had suffered more than his share of shattering setbacks in the past several years . . . and the queen had played a role in all of them.

First there had been the Calais fiasco. The Spanish king had sent his fleet to capture Calais, that spit of France within sight of the Dover cliffs, and too close for comfort should Philip prove victorious. Plans had quickly been set in motion for an English counterattack, but on the eve of departure, Elizabeth had scuttled the relief expedition, complaining that the French king still had not repaid a large loan she'd made him, and was refusing to agree to a permanent garrison of English troops in Calais should her army prove successful. After desperate pleading by Essex, as well as her admirals and Privy councilors, the queen relented and the mission plans were resumed.

But once again, at the eleventh hour, she vacillated, canceled the expedition and insisted on waiting for the French king's assurances that her demands would be met. Essex had, on bended knee, begged her to allow the English fleet to sail. Spanish occupation of Calais was an unacceptable risk to England. Peevish and complaining, she'd finally agreed. But she had delayed too long. The Spaniards had landed at Calais and won a resounding victory before the English fleet could intercept them.

Elizabeth's dealings with Spain had proved an even more maddening example of the queen's indecisiveness. It was widely believed that Her Majesty's "pinprick raids" and halfhearted measures had taught their enemy precisely how to defend itself against England. Essex had been the most outspoken of her Privy councilors, arguing passionately for the necessity of a direct and devastating offensive against the Second Armada before it could strike again. Anthony Bacon's spies in the Spanish ports were reporting the grim facts. A new, larger, and more well-prepared fleet was assembling, and the target might just as easily be Ireland as England. That small green island with its rebellious chieftains would be well pleased to invite Philip's soldiers in. The Irish were already said to be receiving shipments of arms from Spain. They would be happy to return the favor by opening a back door to England's largely unfortified west coast.

Therefore, a preemptive strike on Philip's largest port—Cadiz—was planned for the June of '96. Essex, along with Raleigh and High Admiral Howard, would command the largest English force yet gathered for a combined naval and military operation—eleven thousand men and one hundred ships, and enough supplies and ordnance for a five-month voyage.

Essex had traveled to the fleet at Plymouth to organize this mammoth effort. And he had outdone himself. His organizational skills had impressed even his most virulent detractors. He'd not hesitated to finance a large part of the operation out of his own coffers, though he had complained to his friends that he had "a little world eating at my house."

Six months later—days before departure—Elizabeth, unbelievably, had recalled all three of her commanders. She'd changed her mind, she announced in a voice that was growing more shrill every day. The risk was too great. The expense unacceptable. She canceled the Cadiz adventure altogether, snapping the royal purse strings shut.

Essex had been livid, but he'd not stood alone. He was joined in outrage by his fellow officers and much of the Privy Council. *Was the expedition not meant to forestall Spain from assisting the Irish in their rebellion that was every day growing more costly and dangerous? How weak and harebrained would England appear in the eyes of the world?*

In the end it had been Essex who turned the tide, once again crawled at the foolish old woman's feet, begging her permission to allow the expedition to proceed. She grudgingly agreed. But her wild unpredictability had become apparent to all, and everyone at Court now worried that Elizabeth's critical faculties, once impeccable, had begun disintegrating with age.

The attack on Cadiz, mused Southampton, should have been a glorious victory for Essex, the pinnacle of his career. The Spanish warships guarding the mouth of the famous Spanish harbor had easily been overcome. With God Himself smiling down, the city had been taken entirely by surprise. And Robert Devereaux, at his most magnificent, led his troops into the fortress with unerring strategies and with bravery lauded by his men and his fellow officers. The loss of English life had barely reached one hundred men, and to everyone's surprise, the sack of Cadiz, under Essex's command, was carried out with unheard-of restraint and humanity.

Alas, Philip's huge merchant fleet, anchored at the far end of the harbor, had been saved from English capture. The Duke of Medina-Sidonia—disgraced High Admiral of the first armada—was at the time of the attack governor of Cadiz. In what was surely a bittersweet triumph, Medina-Sidonia had torched the heavily laden merchant fleet, burning it to the waterline and robbing the English of twelve million ducats' worth of goods. It had been an unforeseen accident, and at the time no blame had been laid at Essex's feet.

Indeed, no one—despite his stunning victory—was paying heed to Essex at all. His pleas that the English fleet should stay in Cadiz, laying in wait for the imminent return of Philip's New World Treasure Fleet, had been shouted down by Raleigh and Howard and, maddeningly, by Elizabeth's long-distance communiqués as well. No one could be convinced of the obvious—that capturing the fifty ships laden with gold would have made frivolous the loss of the merchantmen cargoes.

Instead everyone, groaning under the weight of their personal spoils, wished to return home at once. All Robert's instincts had screamed that they should have jumped at the chance to loot the treasure fleet, if not in Cadiz, then by sailing to the Azores to intercept it. Essex had argued this even after the English fleet had weighed anchor for home. He'd argued as they sailed north along the Portuguese coast, and become even more forceful as they'd approached Lisbon. That city's harbor was another stopping-off place for the Treasure Fleet. By his calculations the gold-laden ships should be only days away. To his utter dismay all his arguments and pleas had been overwhelmingly dismissed.

The English fleet had sailed home expecting uproarious congratulations, and while the public widely celebrated Essex's capture of Cadiz with feasting and fireworks, the queen had offered nothing but the back of her hand. She was furious that Essex had lost the merchant fleet, and nearly apoplectic that he'd dared to knight sixty-eight gentlemen for their bravery in battle. The creating of knights was the divine authority of a monarch, Elizabeth had haughtily declared. But worst of all, said the queen, stamping her feet like a spoilt child, she had made no money on the venture. Everyone else had done splendidly—even the lowliest soldier had shared in the spoils. But what return had she had on her fifty-thousand-pound investment? As far as she was concerned, the expedition was a grievous failure. Essex was an incompetent and should consider himself disgraced. Raleigh and Howard would take credit, if any were to be had.

But even worse injury had been done. Elizabeth, during Essex's absence, had named Robert Cecil to the post of Queen's Principal Secretary. Essex's constant fears that his enemies would make hay when he was gone from Court had been proven out. But the final blow came when the news that Philip's treasure fleet had blown into Lisbon Harbor unmolested, *not forty-eight hours* after the English ships—racing like rats for the safety of their Plymouth homecoming—had sailed right by that city! Even then Elizabeth refused to relent in her rebukes and criticisms of Essex. His military judgments had been well and truly vindicated in everyone's eyes. Everyone's but the queen's.

It was then that the two of them—Essex and Elizabeth—began their most bizarre dance. They argued. About anything. About everything. He would rage and sulk and retire to the country, claiming illness. She would fly to his bedside and nurse him like a loving mother. Fences would be mended until the next explosion, the next flight to Wanstead House, the next reconciliation. Essex dallied during these months, not with the ladies of the Court, but with low whores whenever and wherever he could find them, making no attempt to hide his debauchery from the queen. Southampton suspected his intercourse with those base women was what had caused the syphilitic pox that was now afflicting his friend.

When the queen announced promotions for Raleigh and Howard, but not Essex, his resulting outburst shook the palace walls. In turn, Elizabeth, stomping through Greenwich like a crazed harridan, proclaimed that she was done with Essex. She would break him of his will, "pull down his great heart."

The illness that followed—an incapacitating dysentery—precipitated the queen's softening and relenting, and the offering to her favorite of a plum post—Master of Ordnance. Then came the ultimate announcement—his most lofty military commission. Not only was it to be his first sole command, but the next year's most politically vital expedition. The English fleet would sail to the northern Spanish port of Ferrol, where they would crush the New Armada, known to be waiting for fair weather to try again for an invasion of England. Once the Armada had been incapacitated, read the orders, Essex would take his ships to the Azore Islands—stopping-off place of Philip's Treasure Fleet before its return to Spain. Here Essex would be positioned for a second chance to win the greatest prize of them all.

But foul weather had cursed the first leg of the expedition. Incessant gales had driven the English fleet back from Ferrol—*three different times*—and attack had proven impossible. This had been a great failure, but all might have been saved, forgiven, thought Southampton, had the "Islands Voyage" following Ferrol been successful. It had, unfortunately, proven an unprecedented disaster. Raleigh, though relegated to second in command, clashed incessantly with Essex. And while Robert Devereaux waited at anchor amongst the Spanish-held isles, the full extent of his erratic behavior became all too apparent. The weeks were punctuated by a halfhearted landing here, a feeble incursion there. There was disturbing evidence of his inability to coordinate attacks. Time and again his judgment proved faulty and his faculties diminished. He and his men blundered around attacking the wrong places, always maddeningly off in their timing.

They took up residence in the town of Villa Franca, drinking and whoring. And his soldiers and officers showed no desire whatsoever to leave their very pleasant accommodations. Worse still, Essex several times forgot to inform Raleigh of his changes of plan. And there was no shortage of men trying to stir up trouble between the two rivals. Finally, after weeks of lying in wait, *Essex altogether missed the coming of the Treasure Fleet*—fifty-five galleons loaded down with unimaginable quantities of gold. They slipped past the English fleet and safely unloaded their cargoes in the islands' strongest fortification.

When word reached London, Elizabeth had raged. Another waste of her time and money. Essex had been inconsolable. Stung by the queen's rebukes and insults—this time well deserved—Robert had shut himself up in his rooms at Essex House, drowning in melancholy. He refused to eat. His eyes sank deep in his pale face. He began acting like a madman, wrapping his head in blankets so he looked a proper Turk in a turban. The game was always played to extremes. But just when most had admitted that the Earl of Essex had finally fallen from the queen's favor, news flew from Court that Elizabeth had named the disgraced man Master of Ordnance, as well as Earl Marshal of England—the highest military title in the land. As if nothing had ever come between them, Essex had burst from his rooms ecstatically, a new and happy man.

Francis Bacon had tried to warn him that his behavior was inflammatory. And even Southampton, usually wild and game for anything, had whispered caution in Robert's ear, but he remained obstinate, oblivious. His companions grew alarmed whenever Will Shakespeare's *The Tragedy of King Richard the Second* played at the Globe, for they knew that Essex would invariably be there in the audience, loudly cheering and stamping during the scene where Lord Bolingbroke seizes the throne from his king.

But this disease, thought Southampton, was worse still. He knew the French pox had caused men to go insane, and Essex was displaying all the classic symptoms. He would do anything to save his friend from that fate, for his own advancement and destiny were deeply and irrevocably entwined with Essex's—for better or worse.

The carriage lurched to a sudden stop, throwing its passengers against the opposite seat, the ride's final indignity. By the time the two shaken men had reached the door of Crosley's Apothecary, Robert Devereaux was apple red, veins bulging in his forehead. It would be a waste, Southampton knew, to suggest Essex calm himself. Instead he pushed open the door, causing the bell above it to jangle merrily, announcing their arrival in the tiny, aromatic shop. As his friend followed Southampton in, Essex reached up and grabbed the irritating bell, nearly ripping it off the lintel. Southampton apologized with a silent gesture to the startled apothecary, a plump, bespectacled man now tidying the brown vials and paper packets on the marble counter behind which he stood.

"Good day, gentlemen," he said, "good day, good day, good day."

Southampton groaned inwardly. Crosley, it appeared, was the type of man who used ten words when one would suffice. Still, he was making a valiant attempt to pretend he had not recognized Essex, London's most famous nobleman. Southampton graced the chemist with a small, grateful smile.

"My friend has a problem, Master Crosley. Would you be so kind as to see us more privately?" Southampton gestured with a slight tilt of his chin to the door behind the counter.

Crosley opened the hinged counter and showed them through into his workroom, a den of alchemy, its walls lined with shelves full of bottles and mysteries and foul-smelling miracles. Southampton could see panic rising in Essex's eyes. He would bolt if their business could not be quickly accomplished.

Southampton began, "My friend Master Chambers, I fear, has contracted—"

"The great pox. Yes, I can see it in his complexion, his eyes," Crosley interrupted. "Have you had the rash, sir?" He spoke directly to Essex, who nodded once. "The fever, the headaches, the general malaise?" Essex nodded again. Crosley whispered discreetly now. "The *grand-gore*?"

"The what?" Essex snapped.

"The large sore."

"Yes, I have."

"Pain in the liver? Just here." The apothecary pointed to Essex's right-upper abdomen. "May I see?" The earl lifted his jerkin.

"Uhm. Enlarged. Well, you're in fine company, sir. Good King Harry. Francis of France."

"Will's King Lear," Southampton whispered in Essex's ear. Robert was neither amused nor comforted.

" 'The serpentine sickness,' " said Crosley. "Brought over from the New World by Chris Columbus, some say. But it depends on who you hate the most, what it's called. The French say 'Disease of Naples.' The Italians 'the French pox.' We English named it the 'Spanish pox' or 'Spanish needle' or 'Spanish gout.' The Calvinists, of course, swear it's God's new plague sent down from Heaven to punish debauchery. And the Puritans—"

"In any event," Southampton interrupted, "there *is* a treatment?"

"There are several," said Crosley with maddening calm. "Take your pick. Some favor zinc, borax, and alum. Mild to the system but—by and large—ineffective."

"What else?" said Essex, his eyes desperate.

"Well, the mercury, of course, a well-known treatment favored by the Turks. It tends to loosen your teeth, and I see you have nice teeth . . . Master Chambers. And I'm afraid it poisons you to a certain extent, and produces copious saliva."

"Wonderful. I shall drool on the queen's bosom," said Essex, uncaring that the man would know for certain his identity.

"There's the 'virgin cure,'" said the chemist with a sudden lascivious smile. "Swive one who's young and never been done before, and God's curse is lifted." He noticed the scowls of the two gentlemen and quickly added, "I myself put no credence in it, but it might be delightful trying."

"There must be something else," Southampton said, beginning to lose patience himself.

"Indeed. A very popular treatment." Crosley shuffled over to his shelves and reached up for a large, tall glass jar that held thick scrolls of what appeared to be reddish-brown tree bark. He carried the jar to his worktable and with a small flourish untied its leather top. A pungent, earthy aroma filled the room. "*Guaiacum* bark, from a hardwood tree in the New World. Fitting, don't you think? As that's where the pox comes from."

"They call this 'holy wood,' do they not?" asked Southampton. "I've seen it hung in churches."

"The very thing."

"'Tis expensive . . . ," Crosley said, looking sideways, knowing such patrons could well afford the treatment.

"Just tell me how it works," Essex said, hysteria creeping into his voice.

"Well, I will grind the bark into a powder, you see, and send it home with you in a packet. You pour the contents of the packet into four cups of clear water and boil it for an hour. You'll let it cool. Then you'll drink it. It will taste like bear shit, or worse. You will drink all of it. Then you will lock yourself in a sealed chamber and light the largest fire you can.

Keep it up all day and night. You will sweat like you've never sweat before, and all the poisonous humors will pour out of you."

It sounded logical, thought Southampton, and this was the first time in weeks he'd seen Robert even remotely calm.

"Only one treatment is needed?" Essex asked.

"One is all a body can stand," said Crosley.

"But will it cure me?"

The apothecary shifted on his feet. "It cures a good many, sir."

"Give it to me," said Essex, his eyes cold. "And I was never here. You understand?"

"Perfectly, my lord. Perfectly."

⬥⬥⬥⬥⬥

D AMN CROSLEY, *damn the man!*
Despite the fire blazing in the hearth and the red heat of several braziers set about his room, Essex, wrapped in rugs and furs and lying in his bed, was shuddering with cold. Moments before he'd poured sweat, then vomited the contents of his stomach into the fire. He prayed he'd not purged himself of the medicine—more foul tasting than the apothecary had warned—for despite his current misery, the effects of the pox were worse still. He'd seen men die of it—wasted, gibbering madmen, shunned even by their families.

And there were signs in himself, Essex was forced to admit, terrifying portents of the disease. His mind, once a razor's edge of wit and logic, now succumbed periodically to prolonged bouts of fuzziness, times when his ill-conceived desires overwhelmed his intellect and good sense. Much as he hated to admit it, he had bungled the Azores expedition. Bungled it dreadfully. At the time it had seemed perfectly reasonable to garrison himself and his men in Villa Franca while waiting for the Spanish Treasure Fleet. And his annoyance with Raleigh, which had risen to a screaming pitch in which he had raged at the man, leveling the most execrable curses on him and his family, had also seemed at the time altogether justified.

When news had reached Essex's party that Philip's treasure ships had slipped past the English fleet and were safely unloading their cargo—

gold which he had sworn to Elizabeth would soon be overflowing *her* coffers—his wild bingeing had been extinguished by a long, cold wave of terror. *What could he have been thinking?* Recalling the preceding days of drunkenness and debauchery with the local prostitutes, Essex realized he'd not *been* thinking. No. He'd been no more than a stuporous passenger flying along a cliff-side road in a driverless carriage led by a team of insane horses.

Now, lying in his bed, Essex found himself overcome by a sudden and devastating fatigue. His body grew limp and he was about to close his eyes when, in the shadows, he heard muted, muttering voices, snide whispers, laughter. In the fireplace, goblins were dancing amidst the flames. They were hideous, their garments all afire, their skin crackling and peeling black, yet still they danced, their high, shrill laughter aimed at the pathetic creature huddled on the canopied bed.

For he was weeping like a child, weeping in terror. Altogether doomed.

◈◈◈

"GENTLEMEN ADVENTURERS'? How very condescending of you, Francis. Most would call us soldiers." Essex was hurrying across Whitehall's courtyard with Francis Bacon at his side, Bacon struggling to keep up with his patron's long strides.

"I do find your recent companions difficult to take seriously, my lord. You seem to have abandoned your more substantial friends for a pack of puffed-up ruffians."

"And you, Francis, have abandoned *me*."

"I've done no such thing!"

"Do you think I'd not heard of the simpering letter you recently wrote to Burleigh?" Essex never slowed his pace for a moment, nor would he meet Bacon's eye. "You're too ambitious a man to align yourself with the losing side at Court. And I have become just that, haven't I? I'm well aware that you mean to switch your allegiances."

"I mean nothing of the sort," Bacon spluttered. "But if I did I would have just cause. Your behavior has been consistently appalling—"

"I've been ill," Essex offered, a weak excuse, "but I've completed a treatment I'm assured will cure me." Now Essex stopped and turned on Francis Bacon. "I believe you hold me responsible for the Attorney Generalship you were denied. And the Solicitor General post as well."

"Untrue!"

"True enough! I tried *everything*, Francis. I begged and cajoled, went down on my knees to that damned woman—"

"Shhh, Robert!"

"Well, I did, and it made no difference. She never forgave you your arguments against her subsidy, and she cannot stomach your love for other men. Can you not at least do as Southampton has done and take a mistress?"

"I could take a mistress," replied Bacon, "but I could not—as our friend has so easily done—get her with child. My prick will simply not perform for a woman. Believe me, I have tried. But you've changed the subject, Robert. We are speaking of *you*."

"Indeed, and why you cannot believe that I did everything in my power—"

"I know that, and *I do not hold you responsible*, I swear it."

"Then why have you turned against me?"

Francis Bacon was silenced by the question, the truth of which he could no longer deny. Finally he spoke. "Why? Because you refuse to listen to me, Robert. My best advice is altogether lost on you. I clearly warned you to deal gently with the queen. To downplay your popularity, which makes her jealous. And to curb your military zeal. Yet you flounce indignantly from Court at the smallest perceived slight. You blatantly court public affection, and you have accepted not one but *two* of the highest military titles in the land."

"Look, I really must go," said Essex, turning to continue on to the castle's north entrance. "I've a Council meeting to attend, and I'm already late."

Bacon caught up with Essex, curiosity overcoming his indignation at the brush-off. "Are you discussing Ireland?" he asked.

"Is there much else the Council discusses these days?"

"I've told you I think that throwing yourself wholeheartedly into the 'Irish question' behooves you politically. Your father made his mark there, and there is nothing more important to the state just now. Whoever triumphs in Ireland will be forever bathed in glory as well as Her Majesty's favor. 'Tis shocking to admit, but even Spain is eclipsed by the damned Irish Rebellion. Will you discuss Lord Burgh's replacement?" Bacon persisted.

"Is there *anything* goes on at Court that you do not know about?"

"Very little."

"Then you must know I'm putting George Carew forward for the post."

"For Lord Deputy of Ireland?" Bacon was incredulous.

Essex smiled, pleased he had managed to surprise.

"What better way to rid myself of an enemy?" said Essex. "Send him to the hellhole that eats men alive, and let the Devil take him."

"But Carew is Robert Cecil's dearest friend," Bacon argued. "Your motives will be utterly transparent. You'll look a fool, Robert."

"You're growing very tiresome, Francis. I really have had enough of your advice." Essex picked up his pace and lengthened his stride, leaving Bacon behind.

Francis Bacon stood and watched the Earl of Essex disappear into Whitehall Palace and sighed deeply. His patron, his friend was walking straight into trouble—trouble of the deadliest nature. And there was not a thing in the world he could do to prevent the coming disaster.

B Y GOD, *his head hurt!* It was throbbing, pounding in his ears. Essex wished desperately to just sit down, but Elizabeth, next to him at the head of the Council table, was standing, as she often did these days, refusing to be seated while she conducted the affairs of state, sometimes for hours on end. And of course her Privy Councilors—except for old Burleigh, who looked too frail even to be alive—were not permitted to sit in the queen's presence. Essex's stomach began churning and he was gripped by the fear that his bowels might suddenly turn to water right here in the Privy Council Chamber. Indeed, this rumbling and nausea had ceased only occasionally since his excruciating *Guaiacum* treatment. And his physical ills had been exacerbated by the litany of affronts and injuries that Elizabeth had already directed at him this morning. She could sense his weakness—he was sure of it—and seemed determined to push him to the edge, force him to strike out at her publicly so that she could justifiably rebuke him. Crush him. Indeed, "pull down his great heart."

And Burleigh, sitting at Elizabeth's left hand, had had a go at him as well. When Essex suggested that England needed once and for all to bring Spain to her knees with an all-out military effort, the elder Cecil had insisted that *negotiations* were the preferable road to peace. The old buzzard had fairly trembled with indignation, accusing the earl of seeking war, slaughter and bloodshed, even more than Spain did. He'd gone so far as to lay open the Bible that sat on the table before him—Essex wondered if the whole performance had been planned—and read aloud from Psalm 55. " 'Bloodthirsty and deceitful men shall not live out half their days'!" Burleigh shouted out like a Puritan minister. Using all his restraint to keep from reaching across the table and throttling the old man where he sat, Essex had skewered Burleigh with his eyes.

"How dare you accuse me of loving war? It has taken my health, stolen the lives of my brother and many dear friends, subjected my person to the rage of seas, plagues, famines, and all manner of terror and violence. Of course peace is preferable to war," Essex had continued, holding the eye of one Privy councilor after another, "especially for a trading nation like England. But I strongly object to these 'peace negotiations,' for they *will bring no peace*! Can you not see that the Spaniard has no interest in peace? These talks would only give them time and advantage—breathing space to lay their plans and rebuild their forces. *They cannot be trusted!*"

Essex was sure he'd spoken wisely and well, but all at the table just stared at him with stupid, blank expressions, as though they had forgotten King Philip's rabid obsession with turning the whole world Catholic. Forgotten the Armada of '88. Forgotten Cadiz. The Council had turned against him, he suddenly realized. *Robert Cecil must be poisoning their minds. That was the only possible explanation.*

Now the report from Ireland was dragging on incessantly, and Thomas Windbank's monotone was trying more than Essex's patience. Burleigh's eyelids were decidedly heavy, though Robert Cecil, standing next to his father, nudged him discreetly when the elder Cecil seemed in danger of nodding off. The councilors had so far learned that the Munster Plantations were thriving and relatively calm, despite the fulminating uproar in the north and west of Ireland. Tom of Ormond was, of course, still loyal to the Crown and holding his territories around Dublin and the Pale against any rebel incursions. In Connaught, Richard Bingham's replacement, Conyers Clifford, was having some limited success, and Bingham himself was imprisoned in the Fleet. He had apparently been as despised by his fellow governors as he had by the Irish, and was serving time for extortion and corruption.

Essex had come to attention at the mention of Bingham and turned his eyes to the queen, trying to discern a reaction to the name. The "Flail of Connaught" had finally been removed from his post, as she had promised Grace O'Malley he would be, but it had taken five years. But there was no reaction in Elizabeth's expression, which remained hard, the eyes lizardlike.

Red Hugh O'Donnell, who'd made a daring escape from Dublin Prison was now leading a fierce rebel force in Ulster. He was moving down across his southwest border into Connaught, where Tibbot Burke—leading the better part of the Burke clan—was resisting him. Again Essex detected no visible response in the queen at the mention of Grace O'Malley's son.

High Admiral Howard, at Essex's right, interrupted Windbank's report. "There is a rumor abroad that the Earl of Tyrone was complicit in his son-in-law's escape from Dublin Prison."

"The Earl of Tyrone is loyal to the Crown!" It was Burleigh who'd piped up, clearly less somnambulant than he appeared.

"We cannot ignore Tyrone's many local incursions," said Howard. "Especially his attack on the fort at the Blackwater River. That is England's primary stronghold in northern Ireland."

"Tyrone always submits afterward and asks for pardon," Burleigh argued.

"But his truces never hold for long." Howard was more than a little skeptical. "Indeed, a list of those broken truces is piling up rather quickly," he said. "I have also heard tell that our lord of Tyrone is raising a proper army, having Spanish arms delivered to him by the pirate woman O'Malley."

"Even if he has raised an army," Essex interjected, "we have no need to fear it. Many of the regiments we're sending into Ireland have been brilliantly trained in the Netherlands war. The Irish are not *soldiers*. They're ragged rebels." The truth was, Essex had so far failed to immerse himself in the details of Elizabeth's Irish wars, and was still only half educated about them.

"I agree that any rebel army that might be raised would be of no consequence," Admiral Howard agreed, "though I should point out that while the Netherlands contingents are good soldiers, the bulk of the men mustered from the English countryside are for the most part vagrants, convicts, and younger sons of younger brothers." The admiral turned and spoke directly to the queen. "But all of this misses the point, Your Majesty. We are arguing the Earl of Tyrone's *loyalty* to England. And I have heard a further rumor, one that greatly disturbs me. I have heard that in a sacred ceremony in the midst of a field at Tullahogue, Tyrone sat himself on the ancient rock throne and received the title of "The O'Neill."

"That would indeed be a great betrayal of our trust," said Elizabeth, "*if* proved to be true. He has sworn to eschew all Gaelic titles, especially one that would elevate him so greatly."

"If Tyrone has accepted the O'Neillship," mused Howard, "he might as well be crowned the King of Ireland."

"I tell you he is loyal!" cried Burleigh, slapping his hand on the Bible before him. "He loves England. He appreciates the many favors she has bestowed upon him, from childhood onward. He may be forced to pretend allegiance to the place of his birth, foment small rebellions here and there, even assist in the escape of his son-in-law. But like our dear cousin, Tom of Ormond, he knows his duty. More, he craves that which is English. How else do you explain his marriage to Mabel Bagenal?"

"A beautiful girl half his age? Very easily," Lord Windbank said with a smirk.

"No," insisted Burleigh. "He had the choice of any of his countrywomen, even young enough to be his granddaughter. But he pursued and married Mabel to bring the flavor of England into his household, as well as to prove his loyalty to us."

"Her family does not see it precisely that way, my lord," said Essex. "They say she was raped and abducted by Tyrone."

"Nonsense!" cried Burleigh. "Utter nonsense!"

Robert Cecil spoke now. "My father so believes in Tyrone's integrity that he has made him and his bride a handsome wedding gift."

"What have you sent my lord Tyrone?" asked the queen, placing a gentle hand on Burleigh's own gnarled one. Her indulgence toward the feeble old man seemed almost desperate.

"Tyrone wrote that he was building a proper English castle to house his new wife," Burleigh answered, "and it required a proper lead roof. I am sending him a shipment of the materials he requested."

"Will you send him my best wishes on his marriage, my lord?" Elizabeth fairly crooned, gracing Burleigh with her warmest smile.

Essex felt blood rising in his cheeks, and before he realized it he had blurted out, "With the state of the world as it is, can we afford to stand here discussing bloody wedding gifts?"

"And what would you have us next discuss, my lord Essex?" The queen's voice had grown quite cold again.

"Thomas Burgh, Lord Deputy of Ireland, a man who—through his honesty and industriousness—might well have brought an end to the conflict in Ireland, has died," said Essex. "A replacement is needed, and needed quickly. I propose George Carew for the post." There was an uncomfortable silence all round. *Francis Bacon had been right*, thought Essex. *They all saw through his devious reasoning*.

"Curious. Very curious," said Robert Cecil, putting into words the thoughts of every person in the Council chamber. "Your stepfather, Lord Leicester, did precisely the same thing twenty-two years ago. He named his enemy—your father—Lord Deputy of Ireland, just to be rid of him. George Carew is my friend. I think you wish him ill, to send him to Ireland to conveniently die as your father did."

"I object, Your Majesty!" Essex cried, but his righteous indignation fooled no one.

"*I* propose"—Elizabeth's brittle voice interposed itself between her two squabbling councilors—"William Knollys for the post. Your uncle, Robert."

Essex felt his blood beginning to boil. He thought he might jump out of his skin and he silently cursed the pox, cursed the treatment, cursed Burleigh and Cecil, and even, God help him, Elizabeth and her contemptuous jibes.

"I name George Carew for his supreme levelheadedness and administrative genius." Essex spoke directly to the queen, with cold fierceness.

"Lord Knollys is older and wiser." The statement spoken with evenness and calm closed the argument like a book being slammed shut.

But Essex was seething. All of her insults, blame for the loss of the merchant fleet at Cadiz, her methodical persecution of his friends. All undeserved. He had loved her, shown nothing but loyalty, intrepidness, and bravery.

"Lord Knollys is half as competent as Carew!" he shouted. "Half as intelligent!"

Elizabeth stiffened at his raised voice, and when she spoke it seemed the blood had frozen in her veins. "You, my lord Essex, are a *ridiculous* man."

Essex's eyes stung with unexpected tears, and a lump in his throat muted any possible response to the appalling insult. He turned on his heel with the intent of going, but found himself clutching the back of his chair, for his knees were threatening collapse.

"You dare turn your back on your queen!" he heard her shriek.

In the next moment, Essex's head exploded in pain. Elizabeth had lashed out and boxed his ear!

"Go and get hanged!" she cried.

When he wheeled round in fury, he was unaware that his hand had clapped instinctively over his sword hilt. But the gesture—threatening and treasonous—had been observed by everyone in the room.

Elizabeth's eyes widened in very real terror and she stepped back. Howard leapt at Essex, clamping his hand round Essex's sword arm, restraining any further movement. But there was no struggle in him. He'd never intended a physical assault, but his pent-up fury vomited freely from his mouth.

"This is an outrage, an *outrage!*" he shouted in Elizabeth's face. "Why should an heir of the most ancient aristocracy of England bow down to the descendant of some Welsh bishop's butler?" He was hardly aware of the shocked gasps all round him, for he was not finished. "I would not endure such vile treatment from any man," Essex snarled. "And I will certainly never endure it from a woman!"

With a violent shrug, he shook Howard off him and with a final searing glance at his fellow councilors, Essex strode from the chamber.

# 10

IT HAD BEEN A WELCOME fit for a queen, with embraces and kisses and a fine meal laid out in a tent in the midst of Hugh O'Neill's army encampment. When Grace O'Malley said as much, O'Neill had fallen like a courtier to bended knee and kissed her hand, proclaiming Grace "Queen of Ireland."

"Get up off your knees and stop mocking this poor old woman, or she'll give you a good clout on the head for your troubles."

"No mockery intended," said O'Neill, gazing up at the face that had finally begun showing its age. "I could be no more serious, Grace. Without your imported bounty, where would my rebellion be? Guns and powder from Spanish ports. Loyal Gallowglass from Scotland. Intelligence packets from Rome and Seville—"

"Then it's going well?"

Hugh O'Neill's eyes were afire. Indeed, his entire countenance bespoke brazen confidence. He pulled out a bench and helped Grace lower herself onto it. "The English have no idea of what they're marching into. None. Right under their noses I've assembled an army. 'Peacekeepers' they were meant to be, authorized and subsidized by the Crown itself. They believed my pleadings of loyalty to the queen, no matter how many times I provoked uprisings. As long as I would grovel and submit, all was forgiven. Burleigh himself sent me a huge shipment of lead, believing my story that I needed it to roof a fine 'English' castle for

Mabel. Have you any idea how much shot that melted-down lead produced for our muskets?"

Grace grew serious. "Am I the only person in Ireland who mourned that poor girl's death?"

Hugh looked away. "Don't try to shame me, Grace. I loved Mabel Bagenal at first and she loved me. But how could a pampered Englishwoman have known the life of a chieftain's wife would be so brutal?"

"You could have warned her."

"She wouldn't have listened. She was desperate to leave that appalling family of hers. Pompous fart of a father. Power monger for a brother. That's who's marching his army here tomorrow—the brother, Henry Bagenal. He claims to care for the well-being of the English soldiers garrisoned at Blackwater Fort—he *is* carrying with him arms and victuals to fortify them. But he's really come north into Ulster to seek revenge on me, his sister's abductor. Her 'murderer.' Perhaps I am. She died of misery under my care. And I think by the end she loathed me as much as her brother loathes me now."

"Well, it's over and done," said Grace. "We'll talk about happier things. You tell me about this army of yours."

"We're eight thousand strong."

"Good heavens!"

"By my runner I count Bagenal's troops at half that. And they're coming along the river road very slowly, with heavy cannon and copious supply wagons."

"Does he know what he's walkin' into?"

"He may know our numbers, but if he does, he puts no stock in it. To him, to all the English, we are as we always were—barefoot savages with battle-axes, darts, and spears. I have *four thousand* musketeers, Grace, trained to shoot more accurately than any Netherlands-trained soldiers. I have a thousand horse cavalry. They've all been drilling under my command and they're brilliantly disciplined. What's more"—O'Neill's eyes brimmed with tears—"they've a *cause*, Grace."

She placed her hand over his. "I know that, Hugh. 'Tis an 'Irish cause,' and we've never known that here before. There's not another man in Ireland—in all the world—who could have rallied them, you know that's true. A single country fighting a single enemy. I never thought I'd live to see the day. Not even Red Hugh could have done it. Where is that youngster? I know he must be here."

"Aye, with a thousand of his and his mother's best Gallowglass. But he'll stay clear of you, Grace."

"It doesn't surprise me."

"The lad is feeling his oats," said O'Neill, "and Connaught is a plum worth plucking."

"Tibbot's claim to the province is stronger," said Grace.

"I agree, it is."

"They're old friends, those boys, and I think my son would have given him his loyalty had Hugh not gone and invaded Burrishoole, and worse, named his own MacWilliam, then imprisoned Tibbot. 'Twas high-handed and vainglorious, and I think in the end Hugh will rue the day he made an enemy of Tibbot. Besides myself there's no one with a stronger Irish fleet than my son, nor a western leader more worth following." Grace looked away unhappily. "Tibbot's only other alternative for proving loyalty is to the Crown. That boy has never been so confused in his life. After his release from that English prison, he joined forces for a time with his own captor, Bingham!" Grace blinked back tears of frustration. "I know his choices were few, and Clifford was willing to uphold Tibbot's own claim to the MacWilliamship against Red Hugh's man, but he willingly gave up Miles, his only son, as a hostage to the English. And worse"—she could barely say the words—"Tibbot took his brother Murrough into his own camp. They fight together even today."

"It pains you still, Murrough's betrayal," O'Neill observed. Grace nodded miserably. "If it's any consolation," he said, "I would feel the same."

"It does console me and thank you for sayin' so. Sometimes I feel so small and petty. There are times I've taken to self-pity at my plight, though I know Owen O'Malley would be waggin' his finger at me, altogether ashamed."

"So Bingham's withheld the pension Elizabeth promised you?"

"Aye. Aside from my ships, I have nothing. No land. No cattle. I live aboard my vessels with my men, and as much as I love the sea, with my bones aching as they do, I long for a place of my own—a strong keep unmolested by the bloody English." Grace's gaze was wistful. "I was a fool to trust the queen. Sure she freed Tibbot, but her recall of Bingham was brief, and when she allowed him to return to Connaught, he was more vicious than ever. She looked away when he withheld my pension from me. With Ireland, Elizabeth always looks away."

"I promise you, Grace," said Hugh O'Neill, taking both his friend's hands into his, "that after tomorrow England will never look away from Ireland again. We'll be more than a force to be reckoned with. We'll be a shrieking banshee at her back, and they'll tremble in their boots at the power of their 'Wild Irish'! Let's drink to our country, Grace. Put up your cup and drink hearty, for tomorrow will see Ireland victorious. Tomorrow will be her finest hour!"

O'NEILL COULD SEE that Henry Bagenal's six regiments had strung themselves out like a long necklace along the road from Armagh to Blackwater Fort. The Ulster chieftain had prayed for this elongated formation—companies of English musketeers and pikemen slowed by sluggish bullocks pulling huge, ponderous cannon, and the rumbling train of carts bearing victuals and armaments for the besieged and starving inhabitants of the Blackwater garrison. The English cavalry, he had learned from his spies, was blessedly small, and the army was further burdened with its leadership.

Henry Bagenal was all that was wrong with aristocratic English manhood—pompous, self-righteous, and deeply corrupted by wealth, privilege, and the illusion of his own military might. In his eyes the Irish were unendurably low, "white monkeys," best blasted off the face of the earth, to be replaced on graceful plantations by the genteel English of Spenser's poetry. He'd been horror-struck when O'Neill had seduced his sister, Mabel—delicate flower of English womanhood—sacrificing her on the altar of pagan Irish barbarianism.

O'Neill guessed that Bagenal must have been joyful when the news arrived that Tom Ormond was needed elsewhere at the time of the relieving of Blackwater Fort, for Henry wished desperately to face his sister's debaucher, her torturer, her murderer. And O'Neill was no less eager to confront so despicable a character as Henry Bagenal.

From his hiding place in the midst of his newly trained marksmen, assembled behind a long line of hedgerows, Hugh O'Neill could see the battlefield spread out before him. The road from Armagh ran between two meadows, cutting across the Callan River, which, with its bright yellow banks, glowed in the afternoon light like a chieftain's saffron cloak.

The six regiments approaching Blackwater Fort had never drawn together—a grave tactical error, O'Neill observed, one that Bagenal would live to regret. O'Neill wondered at the sheer stupidity of this long column of Englishmen marching blithely into his trap. Bagenal *knew* O'Neill was there waiting for him—Blackwater had been under his siege for weeks. His brother-in-law must believe the scatterbrained Irish would never dare confront his well-drilled soldiers on an open field. That was, after all, not the way the rebels fought. They hid in woods and behind rows of downed trees, and ran shrieking pell-mell into the fray with mindless ferocity.

O'Neill turned to his musketeers lying in their trenches behind the hedgerows. Every eye was on him, awaiting his command. The men were trembling with eagerness and pride. They had trained passionately, and for once in their lives these soldiers had guns and powder and shot aplenty. O'Neill could feel rising off them devotion and love for him, and he knew they would lay down their lives for their high chieftain and for the new cause, only now taking shape in their heads. The cause. Unthinkable just a year before—*freedom from occupation. Freedom from oppression.*

Indeed, their heinous oppressors were approaching—English soldiers who had slaughtered their brothers, their wives, their mothers. Their children. Soldiers who had mindlessly laid waste to their home provinces. To Ireland. Never before had these men fought for the whole of this ancient land, but now they understood, and their hearts—God bless their staunch hearts—were strong and ready to fight.

Raising his sword high above his head, O'Neill, with slow deliberation, lowered it, and the glorious blue morning exploded into sound.

<hr />

CAPTAIN HENRY BAGENAL'S Second Regiment lagged just far enough behind the First to be altogether ignorant of its desperate plight. Gunfire could be heard from behind the line of hedgerows, but nothing heavier. It wasn't until Bagenal witnessed the unthinkable—scores of panicked First Regiment soldiers fleeing in terror—that he moved to action. The Second Regiment charged in through the hedgerows to support the First.

A nightmare scene awaited them.

Hundreds of men lay dead in their column, the road snarled with fallen carts and writhing animals. More soldiers thrashed about in a yellow stream running with thick ribbons of blood. Then, with a great and sudden roar, a thousand Irish rebels rose from their trenches and poured onto the field, shooting as they came. A huge company of Irish horse appeared as if from nowhere, spears and battle-axes held high above the soldiers' heads, and they too were shrieking as they came.

At that moment, and to Bagenal's horror, his men—as a body—broke from their ranks and scattered. He watched in disbelief as his cowardly regiment ran, and as they stumbled across the green meadow they were solidly raked by enemy fire. Now masses of Irish pikemen in full-drilled levies swept, a human wave, across the field toward the broken regiment. On foot at the front of the enormous square was its leader, marching directly toward him.

Bagenal stood gaping as shot whizzed by his head. It was his brother-in-law, the traitor Tyrone. And the man had spotted him as well. Fury rose in Henry Bagenal and he strode out into the field to meet the bloody Irish devil. He and Tyrone would fight hand to hand, to the death, he swore to himself. He would have his revenge for Mabel, beautiful child, lost to this wretched land.

THE BALL FROM the musket of the proud Ulster marksman found the very center of Captain Bagenal's forehead and blew out the back of the Englishman's skull. Hugh O'Neill saw his brother-in-law fall, and though a great, joyful cry rose in his throat he never missed a step, leading his pikemen onward. But he found himself smiling as he marched, savoring the irony of the moment, for the ball that had smashed open Henry Bagenal's head had been molded from the melted-down lead that old Lord Burleigh had foolishly sent for the roof of Mabel O'Neill's proper English castle.

# 11

**B**Y THE LIVING CHRIST! *Would his head never clear?*
Robert Devereaux lay sprawled on his bed, fully clothed in riding gear, remembering how, when he'd awoken that morning, his
mind had been as clean and sharp as a midwinter morning. He had
dressed himself and surprised the stablehands still rubbing sleep from
their eyes with his request for the new piebald gelding—an animal barely
broken, challenge for even the most experienced rider. The Earl of Essex
had, since his retirement to Wanstead House two months before, been
riding both infrequently and indifferently. He knew of the whispers
amongst the household and stablemen of his ill health and bouts of
melancholy, and this morning he'd felt a keen pleasure at the men's
smiles and good wishes for a hearty ride. Indeed, he'd felt strong in the
saddle and altogether well with the spirited horse pounding under him.
There'd even been brief ecstatic moments when the fresh wind stung his
cheeks, whipping back his hair, and he'd felt a boy again, ranging over
the Welsh hills with his whole bright future ahead.

But the moment he'd ridden into the yard at Wanstead he'd been
besieged with unwholesome thoughts and obsessions—the same ones
that had, of late, brought him so low. The sight of the great house itself,
so richly and lovingly restored by his stepfather, fetched back the images
of Leicester's marriage to his mother in this very house.

Robert had been eleven at the time, but even at that tender age he had understood the desperate secrecy of the ceremony. As he'd dressed for the occasion, his mother had bustled into his room to instruct him once again that Queen Elizabeth must not, for the time being, know of the marriage. The "old bitch" was still in love with Lettice's husband-to-be and remained deluded that Leicester was faithful to her—body and soul. "Stupid woman!" Lettice had hissed. For two years she and Leicester had been carrying on their affair under the queen's nose. Now she was pregnant with his child. His mother had, that morning, confided offhandedly to her little boy that she bore no real love for the Earl of Leicester, but now with her condition so advanced Elizabeth would certainly find out, and it would be safer when the explosion came if the two were already married.

Then in a perfumed cloud the great beauty who was his mother had swept out of his room. Young Robert Devereaux had finished dressing that morning filled with a vague dread. He loved the Earl of Leicester, more perhaps than he had loved his own father. Why did his mother not love the man? He was good and kind, handsome and a brave soldier. He had taken great pains to refurbish the old wreck of Wanstead Estate just for his mother's pleasure. Why did she not love Leicester? And why, Essex remembered himself thinking that morning twenty years before, did she not love *him*, her own son? He was a sweet and thoughtful child, a fine student. And he was handsome— he knew his mother liked her men handsome. Oh why could he never please her! And wasn't it fearfully dangerous to deceive the queen? Was not what his mother and Leicester planning to do treasonous? Would they both end up with their heads on pikes over London Bridge? Would *he*?

By the time Essex had finished his ride this morning and fallen fully clothed onto his bed, his mind felt as though it were a crowded cell, and he a prisoner within it. He found himself wishing for the oblivion that attended one of his feverish headaches, but instead he lay immobile while thoughts wheeled before him in a never-ending parade.

Everyone wanted him back at Court. There were cries and demands

and beseechments from every corner, yet he would oblige none of them.
How could he return? He was ill. That was his best excuse and one that
was, much of the time, true. But what was he saying? He *had* returned,
not once but twice—and both times he'd been driven back to seclusion
at Wanstead by Elizabeth's cruel obstinacy.

Of course it was understandable if she still harbored resentment
against Essex for his outrageous behavior in the Privy Council Chamber
that cursed morning two months before. He'd laid a threatening hand on
his sword, after all—an unquestionably treasonable act. All of Court had
been agog. *Essex would surely be sent to the Tower for his treachery,* it was
said. Some whispered that the block was not out of the question. Yet the
queen, to everyone's astonishment, had taken no action against him.
None whatsoever. Neither punishment nor reprimand. Instead he'd been
allowed to withdraw from Court in his own time, as though *he* had been
the injured party. Of course the incident set tongues wagging at the
implications. How intimate were the entanglements between the queen
and her favorite that she should take no action against him? What secrets
did they share? Was blackmail involved? Had Elizabeth simply been paralyzed with horror, or was she planning some terrible revenge? Surely
they were not still lovers!

It had been quite extraordinary and amazed even Essex that his act,
unconscious as it might have been, had gone unpunished. At first he'd
reveled in the power that he still held over Elizabeth. He still fascinated
her, he had decided. She must still adore him.

But once smothered by the quiet and solitude of Wanstead, his relief
and celebration quickly turned sour and his bouts of black brooding
were more and more often punctuated by fits and fevers so dangerous
that the queen had sent him her personal physician. Essex had been
forced to admit that Crosley's *Guaiacum* cure had failed. Something
would have to be done to halt the disease's progress. Perhaps mercury
after all.

*Oh God, he had chosen a terrible moment to leave Court!* In the best of
circumstances his absence benefited his enemies. There were several fac-
tions hell-bent on his destruction. But this self-imposed exile had been
severely aggravated on two accounts. Shortly after his shocking performance in the Privy Council Chamber, old Burleigh had taken to his bed.

It soon became apparent that it was his deathbed. Elizabeth had forgotten everything and run to his side. This man—her most trusted councilor for half a century—was, she insisted, her twin spirit. She sat vigil at his bedside for nearly a week, holding his withered hand, feeding him gently, like a child. When it was done, she was inconsolable, much as she had been when Leicester had died. But her grief must surely have been compounded by her age and the grinning specter of her own death.

All Essex's true friends had written, begging him to renounce his banishment and make peace with the queen, fearing her heart would harden to hatred should he prove intractable in her time of agonizing loss. So he had steeled himself, prepared his apologies and ridden into London where he had taken a conspicuous place in Burleigh's mourning procession, shrouded and hooded in a great black cloak, with all appropriate demonstrations of grieving. But they had apparently proven insufficient for Elizabeth. Perhaps she required wailing and beating of the breast, for when he had requested the audience with her that all had insisted would be needed to heal the breach between them, she had politely demurred, citing the wretchedness of her own condition, not even suggesting a future meeting.

Essex, enraged, sped back to Wanstead. But his sulking had been cut short when news arrived several days later of the appalling defeat of Elizabeth's army by the Irish rebels at Blackwater Fort—a defeat now infamously known as the Battle of the Yellow Ford. The Earl of Tyrone—indeed he *had* taken the title of The O'Neill—was being hailed as the King of Ireland, and he had quickly and with frightening ease begun bringing all of that blighted country under his control. His armies—unbelievable that they could be called armies at all—had streamed south into Leinster and Munster, overrunning the Pale and the plantations till there was hardly an English settler left in Ireland who was not dead or running for his life. All over the country the Crown's armies, foolishly packed with Irish recruits, soon found those soldiers turning coat and defecting to the other side, most of them carrying with them their English weapons.

The shock and horror of The Yellow Ford had, in one afternoon, seen Henry Bagenal and *two thousand* of his men slaughtered, and brought England to its knees. 'Twas unthinkable, but Ireland was on the brink of being lost to a pack of ragged rebels! Elizabeth, humiliated and furious, had raged at her council to *do something*. They had quickly begun scrambling about, sending out orders for muster, stepping up food and arms for the reinforcements.

But their hands were tied. They were altogether stymied and not a little embarrassed, for their Master of Ordnance—nay, *High Marshal of England*—was absent from their ranks. His cooperation was essential, as was his advice and flow of foreign news from his man Anthony Bacon's large network of spies.

And so began a trial of strength between a subject and his queen, the likes of which had never before been witnessed in England.

Elizabeth would command Essex's return to Court. He would refuse, claiming ill health. She would demand he appear in the Council Chamber. He would agree to come, as long as there was promise that she would, herself, be present. She would make no such promise. He would stand firm and break off communications.

All his friends grew alarmed, aware of how close to the fire the earl was playing. Southampton had finally come in person to Wanstead, painting in vivid detail the plots that Essex's enemies were hatching all round London. Talk permeated even the lowest of taverns, Southampton insisted. Essex was losing popular support.

"She is laying in wait to humiliate me!" Essex had cried to his friend. "'Tis a trick to seduce me back into her web. Once she has me entrapped, she'll bite off my head. I tell you, I will not go!"

In the end he had, of course, gone. England's sovereignty had been at stake. And he was yet the nation's greatest hero. With all the dignity he could muster, he had made his appearance in the Council, only to find that the queen had declined to attend that session. And the next. Gritting his teeth, he asked to see the queen privately. She refused. He had written her a lengthy letter, giving his best advice on the Irish question. She had even refused to take delivery of it.

He'd been right all along, he'd raged at Southampton. He learned that she'd spread word at Court that Essex had "played long enough on her, and she meant to play awhile on him. To stand upon her greatness as he did upon indignation." Finally and most maddeningly, Elizabeth had made it known that she expected repayment of Essex's recently accrued and substantial debts to her. Immediately.

Back to Wanstead he rode with a fire burning in his heart. He railed against the queen to his terrified servants. He shrieked abuse at her into the wind, and cried out in his angry dreams all the blackest and most heartbroken of diatribes. A few staunch friends argued against his hubris. There was no advantage to defying the queen, they said. He had antagonized everyone at Court and on the Council. By his actions he only strengthened his enemies and weakened his friends. But news filtered back that although the queen would be glad to have Essex back, she wanted him as a suppliant and not as the swaggering courtier, the presumed "equal" he had been before. He'd recoiled at such a thought, his pride suffering.

One evening, roaring drunk, he had composed a letter in his own defense. "There is no heart more humble to his superiors than I," he had scrawled across the page, "but the vilest of all indignities has been done to me. What? Cannot princes err? Cannot subjects receive wrong? Is an earthly power or authority infinite? Pardon me, pardon me, but I can never subscribe to these principles. I have received wrong and I feel it! Now you demand my return to Court, but remember, I would never have gone into exile had you not chased me from you as you did, driven me into this private kind of life. When the unhappy news came from yonder cursed country of Ireland, I knew your grief at having your armies so brutally beaten back, and my duty was strong enough to rouse me out of my deepest melancholy. I offered my attendance. Rejected. I sent a letter. Rejected. What am I to think?

"I have preferred your beauty above all things. Received no pleasure in life but by the increase of your favor toward me. But the intolerable wrong you have done me and yourself has broken all laws of affection, and done harm against the honor of your sex. I was never proud, Your Majesty, till you sought to make me base. My despair, which is great, shall be as my love was—without repentance. I fear this world is not fit for me, for she which governs it is weary of me and I, therefore, am weary of the world."

Then he had collapsed and slept the sleep of the dead. When he'd woken and looked for his writings, all he'd found were scratched-out drafts. But his seal and sealing wax had clearly been used. He rang for his servant and learned to his horror that several letters had been sent off with a courier to London in the middle of the night. Essex had broken down and wept. Such raw sentiments—sincere as they were—were pure folly, even blasphemous, and could not but lead him to a bloody end. One did not chastise a rightful ruler like a child, nor impugn her God-given authority. He was clearly out of his mind, had allowed the blasted pox to poison his thinking.

He had thereafter, with great trepidation but as much resolve, begun the "mercury cure." He ate sparingly and drank only watered-down wine. He took long walks in Wanstead Wood and breathed in the good country air. Slowly his nerves calmed and he began to see a clear light ahead. Finally, last night, he had slept peacefully and dreamed sweet dreams. This morning, fresh headed, he had ridden out on the piebald gelding and glimpsed the promise of a bright future. But when he had returned from the ride, that first sight of Wanstead House had sent him spiraling into these latest, frenzied ruminations. *No, he must not allow a relapse.*

Essex pulled himself up from bed and forced himself to his feet. He moved to the window and threw it open, gulping in the sobering air. *He must fight Elizabeth no longer,* he decided. She was simply unwilling to be conquered. If he forced her to his will, she would never forget, nor forgive him. If he yielded he'd be doing nothing unworthy. *He must sue for peace with her!* Elizabeth was a great queen and, he was forced to admit, he loved her deeply. Loved her as a son loves a mother, certainly more than his own mother. And if truth be told, he silently admitted, a blush of red rising in his cheeks, he was desperate for her love in return. And even more, for her to approve of him and all he did.

He would go to Court and by his kind persistence find a way back into the queen's presence. There he would open his heart, make his humble apologies, suffer the barbs of her deserved anger. Then gently and, in love, speak the truth to her. They would, together, take Ireland in hand and conquer it. Elizabeth was *waiting* for her wise councilor to come, he knew it. She needed him as much as he needed her. With Burleigh's death there was no one else in the whole world who could partner her in this particular and dangerous dance. Whatever it took, he would provide it. 'Twas his destiny as surely as it was hers.

Essex rang for his servant, and when the man appeared, Robert Devereaux was very calm. Calmer and more peaceful, in fact, than he had been in many a long year. A pure light burned in his eyes.

"We shall ride to London this afternoon," he said with quiet surety. "To London and the queen."

*A* SUPPLIANT SHE REQUIRED, *so a suppliant he would become.*
The razor-edged halberds at the queen's bedchamber door parted with a soft whoosh, and the two guards stood at attention, their eyes staring straight ahead. He wondered suddenly if they saw him as an enemy or a friend. Was he "Essex, great hero of Cadiz?" or "Poor syphilitic Essex," whose reputation had been washed up like so much flotsam on the shores of the Azore Isles? *But why was he worrying about the opinion of door guards?* His purpose today was to find his way back into Elizabeth's good graces, or prepare to retire permanently from Court.

He found her standing at her favorite silver-topped writing desk perusing a stack of documents to be signed. She held an ink-dipped quill in the fingers of her right hand and he found he could not take his eyes from them, still long and delicate and beautifully white. Whilst the years had taken their toll on Elizabeth's face and form, her hands had yet been untouched, and in remembering them lightly gripping his prick he felt a faint contraction there.

His face, therefore, wore a gentle, amused smile when Elizabeth turned to greet him. He could see tension in her still rod-straight spine, and jaws clenched tightly. *She is as apprehensive as I am*, he thought. Then, moving swiftly to the queen, he fell to both knees before her and bowed his head. He said nothing, for Essex was sincerely overcome, and by the faint rustling of her stiff taffeta skirts he was aware that Elizabeth too was trembling with emotion.

In this way they remained for some time, a private tableau—great, silent waves of unutterable remembrances and fathomless passions sweeping over the pair of them. Then he felt her hand on his head. Not a light, glancing touch—signal for him to rise—but the palm and fingers clutching the dome of his skull.

"Your Majesty." He found that he was overcome with emotion and his eyes were filling with tears. Any further words, he feared, would be sobs.

"Rise, Robin," she said.

As he came to his feet, Essex discreetly wiped the wetness from his cheeks and blinked back further tears. He wished to show his subservience to Elizabeth, but he refused to appear weak or sniveling. He towered over her, as he always had—as tall as she was for a woman—but her dark eyes were defiant now, as if to say, "Your superior size means nothing to the Queen of England."

"First, I wish to say thank you," he began. "Your personal physician did me a world of good. I've never been so ill as I was last month."

"I believed it was all for show at first," said Elizabeth, "to gain my sympathy. But when Robert Cecil reported you to be near death I realized"—now *her* eyes threatened to overflow—"that I did not wish to lose you just yet."

He smiled.

"And England," she went on quickly, with an added stiffness to her tone, "has need of your services. Do have a seat," she said, indicating two chairs by the fire.

Essex waited for Elizabeth to sit first, but she made no move toward the hearth, saying, "Please . . . I prefer to stand. These days," she continued, carefully laying her quill in its holder on the silver desk, "I detest sitting or lying down. It seems a great waste. Does that make sense?"

Essex thought before he answered, for he realized Elizabeth was speaking from the core of herself, and he did not wish his reply to appear frivolous or thoughtless.

"Perfect sense," he finally agreed, holding her eyes. "We will spend eternity lying down."

"Yes," she said, and her tone softened. "So you are feeling better?"

"I'm very well, Your Majesty, and more so to be in your presence again."

It seemed as though she were holding her breath, waiting for the next words to be spoken. *His words. His apology.*

"I have discovered that I cannot survive this world without your love," said Essex. He saw her chest flatten in relieved exhalation. "Indeed, I believe it was knowing that the doctor sent to care for me during my recent infirmity was your personal physician . . . *sent by you* . . . that saved my life, Your Majesty." He paused and spoke the next words carefully. "I am deeply ashamed of my behavior and beg your forgiveness."

She stood silently, gazing out the mullioned window, seeming to consider the choice of his words and the sincerity with which they had been spoken. Her tongue played about her lips, unconsciously caressing them.

"You failed to destroy Philip's fleet at Ferrol," she finally said, a shrillness having crept into her voice. "A very dangerous mistake. Spain is still liable to attack our shores, or sail to the aid of the Irish rebels."

*No, she was not quite ready to forgive him. He must yet endure her scathing abuse, and he must stay calm. Would she open the wound of the Azores? 'Twould be difficult to remain temperate speaking of that catastrophe.*

"I must refer all my accidents to God's will, Your Majesty. I attempted three times to attack the fleet at Ferrol, and *three times* He turned the fury of the heavens against us. I, above all men, knew the desperate importance of the second Armada's destruction, but I *swear* the matter was beyond the power or valor or wit of man to resist."

"God." Elizabeth uttered the single word with more sarcasm than piety. "God is a jester."

Essex barked with laughter at Elizabeth's blasphemy.

"For years," she went on, "He allowed us all to believe that He was indeed King Philip's helpmate, enriching Spain with the staggering wealth of New World gold, giving strength to Philip's ravening armies in the Netherlands, allowing the assassination of a man as saintly as William of Orange. And then, in the final hour at Gravelines, He sent the English fleet a great gale that blew the Armada into the North Sea. God must surely have laughed at such a trick."

"Then you must agree that He was behind our failure at Ferrol."

"I suppose. Yes. He presides over the terrible plagues that sweep London, and allows for Philip's Inquisition." Elizabeth's gaze grew unfocused. Essex could see her mind's eye turning backward into the past. "He was there overwatching as a king loved a woman to distraction, then allowed that love to turn swiftly to a hatred so profound that she would lose her head to a Calais swordsman"—Elizabeth found and held Essex's eyes—"and there in the bestowing of the French pox on my most vital councilor and England's greatest general."

Essex looked away, shamefaced.

"My physician confirms 'tis a syphilitic condition. Pray God you do not fall victim to its madness. You will continue the mercury cure. I know you fear its effects on your appearance. But you're no longer young, Robin. Vanity of your face and figure will mean less to you in future years. Look at Robert Cecil—your 'Gnome.' His infirmities have not stopped him from rising to great heights. You shall simply shoulder the indignities like a man, for you are too necessary to England to leave her just now. So you will continue the mercury. 'Tis a royal command."

"Yes, madam."

"I choose to believe that many of your weaknesses have been induced by the pox and will be eliminated with the cure. Of course some of the flaws in your character were forged early—by that witch of a mother who bore you, for one." Elizabeth began to pace about her chamber. "Your youth was spoiled by no fault of your own. Your father died young. Burleigh's wardship was cruel to a boy as sensitive as yourself. And your one hope—Leicester, who would have guided you brilliantly through your manhood—was lost as well. And there are inherent tendencies—arrogance and bullheadedness. And you haven't an ounce of restraint." Elizabeth moved to Essex's chair and smoothed his cheek with the back of her hand. " 'My wild horse.' You allow your dark passions to lead you. Do you wish my advice?"

"Yes, I'll listen to your advice."

"Will you take it?"

She was pushing him to the limits of his pride.

"I will take your advice."

"You must conquer yourself, Robin. You find enemies lurking in every dark corner, and you are far too proud for a man not born of royal blood."

Essex was discomfited by Elizabeth's words, for they rang uncomfortably true. "Am I to be allowed a chance to defend myself and my honor?"

"Do it gently, Robin. I have already heard how much wrong I have done you and how, by my actions, I have 'disgraced my sex.' "

"I was drunk when I wrote that, Your Majesty."

"I suppose I *have* broken all boundaries of womanhood," she said, sounding almost pleased with herself. "I have always believed that I was a man concealed beneath a woman's skin."

"You are indeed," he said, finally coming to his feet to face her. "But that is why you are great."

"Am I great, Essex?"

"Oh, Majesty, yes! Who before you—man or woman—has led so wisely and so long? Behold England and you will see the miracles that you have wrought. Your father's court was all but medieval, Edward's a fanatic perversion of Protestantism. And Mary's . . ." Essex's expression of revulsion was enough description. "Elizabeth," he said, taking her hands in his, "England under your rule has become a *fabulous* place."

"Yes, it has." Now the queen stood even taller, and she grew puffed and magnificent in her pride. "Essex, I have dreamt it, as John Dee had done so long ago—England is meant to rule the world! She will colonize the East, colonize the New World—aye, let Spain be damned! No place on this earth will be untouched by our influence." Her eyes were afire. "I will not live to see such wonders, but I tell you this. I *shall* know the conquering of Ireland. 'Tis just out of my reach now, but that will change shortly."

"It must be so," he agreed, "with such one-minded persistence."

"'Tis not at all 'one-minded' when it comes to Ireland. No, I cannot claim the scheme for my own. 'Twas my father's . . . and Thomas Cromwell's. A great plan it was. Ireland has beckoned to the English kings for centuries—a jewel well worth plucking, but none began to succeed till Henry conceived a plan."

Finally Essex felt on solid enough ground to disagree. "Surrender and Regrant was sound enough in principle, but it was based on a false assumption."

"Oh?"

Essex had piqued the queen's interest, it appeared, though he hoped not to anger her with his opinions.

"And what was that assumption?" she demanded.

"That the Irish have no pride of heredity. No character."

Elizabeth nodded, agreeing. "That is why the program must and will be altered."

Essex's confidence was growing, his powers as a sage councilor returning. "The strongest of the chieftains refuse to share power," he said, "and the people are more loyal to them than we ever conceived of. We must therefore rescind our offer for joint rule."

"Yes!" Elizabeth agreed with vehemence. "We must conquer them *absolutely*. I do mean in my lifetime to finish what my father began—Ireland under English control."

At these words Essex was struck by a sudden thought—perhaps 'twas more a memory. Grace O'Malley had once sat across the fire from Elizabeth in this very chair, the goblet of warm spiced wine in her tanned fingers fueling the great sprawl of her life story. He was tempted to remind the queen of her, but before he could, Elizabeth spoke.

"Do you remember the rebel woman Grace O'Malley?" she said.

Essex smiled. He and Elizabeth were once again racing along the same track, like a brilliant rider on a great horse, their minds moving as one.

"I know you remember her," said Elizabeth with a sly grin. "For two nights you lay on the floor of the passageway like an eavesdropping child."

Essex laughed to have been caught out so easily. "You did not mind my hearing?"

"Only in one respect," said Elizabeth, looking away. "Her life was so extraordinary. I feared you would think it more so than mine."

Essex was startled by the queen's naked honesty. "She is a great leader, Elizabeth, but she cannot compare with you."

"You'd *best* say that!"

"I mean it with all my heart!"

Elizabeth moved to the fire, warming her hands there. "I was just now remembering—besides the first clear picture she drew for me of Ireland—the great unintentional trick I played on the woman."

"Trick?"

"In the beauty of her storytelling she offered me an understanding of her country, her people—not savages as we all assumed, but bearing a humanity of a different sort, pure in their Gaelic roots. *My* Gaelic roots, Essex, and yours. It reminded me that our ancestors worshiped the same gods and goddesses as Grace O'Malley's. Once I understood the true nature of their world, the people's proud spirit, I became even more determined to possess them. She had pleaded for mercy for the Irish, but instead she'd instilled a greed in me to *own* Ireland. It would be the first of England's colonies, I decided. That emerald island teeming with fierce, great-hearted subjects whom I would somehow make love me! I instantly knew what had happened. Knew I was allowing her, with every word uttered, to dig independent Ireland's grave. That is why I granted her every request. I liked the woman, respected her, and I tricked her."

"Well, she's tricked you in return. She supplies Tyrone with Spanish weapons for his war."

"We must discuss this war . . . and Tyrone," Elizabeth said, her face growing hard with thoughts of that ignominious defeat at Yellow Ford. The only army that might halt the rebels' march into Dublin had been vanquished and was now leaderless. The Irish Privy Council had sent an embarrassing, groveling letter to Tyrone, begging him for mercy on Bagenal's remaining troops, and even Tom of Ormond had felt Elizabeth's displeasure. "It was strange to us," she had written her cousin Black Tom, "that when almost the whole force of our kingdom was sent to strike a blow against the rebels, you—a man who, by your reputation and strength of nobility should surely have carried the day—should be absent, engaged in an action of far less importance."

"Someone must be sent to defeat Tyrone, and quickly," said the queen aloud. "We can ill afford any more of his victories. Every one breeds more confidence in his army. If we fail to regain control"—Essex could see a muscle twitch above Elizabeth's eye—"Dublin will fall."

"That is impossible," he said.

"You, in your self-imposed exile, my lord, have no way of knowing how serious are the breaches in our defense. Ireland has been left without a high commander for more than eight months since my lord Burgh's death. Tom of Ormond leads as best he can but he is stymied—separated from his countrymen by his Protestant religion, and distrusted by the English in Ireland because he was born Irish." Elizabeth had very suddenly grown red and agitated. "I have discussed our choices for Lord Lieutenant with the Council, and we've agreed that Lord Mountjoy is best."

"Mountjoy!" Essex was all at once as agitated as the queen.

"Why does it not surprise me that you object to our very well-considered choice?" she said. "Your good friend. Your sister's lover."

"Lord Mountjoy is hardly a soldier, madam. He is more bookish than martial, with scant experience in the wars. He has few followers and very little estate to back him up. And we *know* that a man who commands your armies must reach deeply into his own pocket!" Essex's voice had risen an octave in the course of one sentence, and he was beginning to lose his composure. "The success you demand in Ireland requires a great noble-man, Your Majesty. One who commands respect from his soldiers and is as rich in purse as he is in experience."

"And who *is* that man, if not Lord Mountjoy?" she asked, her voice suddenly icy.

Essex felt a wrench in his gut. *Sweet Jesus, this was her trap!*

"You claim your greatness to be second in the kingdom only to my own," she went on. "I can now see that *you* are the only person capable of cleansing 'the Irish stable.' Do you not agree?"

*Yes, he did agree, but not as a military commander trudging round that wretched country, but as an* adviser—*replacement for her beloved Burleigh.* Essex saw the beginning of a smile form on Elizabeth's thin lips and he felt blood and gorge rising in him. She was still as sharp as a blade, this skinny old harridan. How could he have been so easily fooled by her? Of course, in some part of her she trusted him like no one else to vanquish the Irish rebels. But that was not all. He knew in his heart that the wily old queen was finally exacting her revenge on him, revenge for the exasperating paces he'd put her through these last years. With great glee she would send him off to that savage land and its endless, bloody conflict. 'Twas a means to rid herself of a troublesome competitor for her people's love. She had finally realized there was no way that a faded, feeble old woman could compare with a young, wildly popular soldier. A hero. A *man*. God damn the woman! She was aware that he, like so many before him, would likely fall into disgrace in Ireland. He could very well die. With her gentle concern and subtle trickery, Elizabeth had taken his boastful words, twisted them into a dangerous web, and reeled him in. Now the only honorable way out, he realized with growing horror, was passage to a blighted hellhole.

"Then you name me Lord Lieutenant of all the armed forces in Ireland?" he said.

"I do, my lord Essex. I will inform the Council of it. There is no one more suitable than yourself for the position. No one but myself and you are—by the grace of Mistress O'Malley," said the queen, smiling at her own pun, "so intimate with the workings of the Irish mind. Do you not agree?"

"Yes, Your Majesty."

Shaken by her deception Essex searched desperately to discover one last opening into the queen's softness. "Elizabeth—" he said, ashamed that his voice was pleading, but she quickly interrupted him.

"I'm very tired, Robin," she said. "You must leave me now. Call my women for me as you go."

"Of course."

Thunderstruck by this old woman's utter triumph, Essex backed to the door. As it slammed shut behind him, the guards dipped their heads in respect. But as he exited the queen's chamber shaking with rage, the new Lord Lieutenant of the Crown's army in Ireland was sure he could hear Elizabeth laughing.

*A* M I GREAT, *Essex?*
       Elizabeth's question had clung fast to his mind like a barnacle to the hull of a carrack. Now as Essex moved round his bedchamber, packing his most personal belongings in a stout wooden chest, he was struck again by the memory—the guilelessness of the queen's query, and her desperation for an answer both truthful and pleasing. He wondered why the words haunted him so, then realized one day during his preparations for departure to Ireland that he had, with this commission, finally been given the opportunity to prove his *own* greatness.

That idea, of late, had kept him awake more nights than he could remember, Frances lying beside him in that irritatingly sound sleep of hers. She possessed the same imperturbable quality in the daytime as well, and he supposed that without it their marriage would never have survived as it had. She was not unaware of his present obsession and his great, simmering cauldron of fears, but she refused to allow him to endlessly stir the pot in her presence. She had married him, borne his child. She suffered his absences, his mistresses, his transparent lack of love for her, and now his disease. As far as this good wife was concerned, Robert Devereaux had made his bed, and now he could very well lie in it.

Francis Bacon, so long his adviser, had fallen away from Essex's orbit. He had raged to hear that Francis was fiercely opposed to Robert's command in Ireland. Only months before, Bacon had advised him that nothing could be better for England, or his friend's career. But since news of his commission, all his attempts to speak to Francis had failed, for the man had invented one excuse after another to be absent from Court.

Southampton might have served as his constant confessor, but he had fled to France after his secret impregnation of and marriage to the queen's waiting lady Elizabeth Vernon, and on his return had been locked in Fleet Prison—Elizabeth's punishment for his disgraceful behavior. Essex had been upset at the thought of Ireland without Southampton beside him, and it had been with the greatest relief that just days ago he'd learned of his friend's early release from prison. Elizabeth had simply wished to show the extremity of her displeasure with her recalcitrant earl.

Essex, and Lady Southampton—whom he had taken into his home with her infant son during Southampton's exile to France, and later, his incarceration—had gone to Fleet to meet the prisoner at his liberty. It had been a joyful reunion, but there'd been no time in the days since to lay open his heart to Southampton. Instead he'd spent his time embroiled in a battle with the queen to have his friend named Essex's Master of Horse in Ireland. Elizabeth had been resolutely against the proposal—as she had been to his request for Robert's young father-in-law, Christopher Blount, as an Irish Privy Councilor. The idea that Essex, in the coming military adventures, might be surrounded by strangers, and not his dearest friends, made him even more frantic.

Indeed, Elizabeth was making everything very, very difficult. One imagined she would offer Essex—her last hope for success in Ireland—every possible means to that success. Instead she had pioneered pitfalls at every turn, the worst of which was her denial of his trusted friends as his high officers and councilors.

It was vainglorious, he knew, but Essex could not help but think of himself as England's savior, willing sacrifice for an ungracious sovereign who would never realize his worth until he was dead. "If by my death," he had written to Elizabeth the previous week, "I either quench the great fire of rebellion in Ireland, or divert these foreign enemies, I should enjoy such a sacrifice. However much you despise me, you will know you have lost a man who, for your safety, would make danger a sport and death a feast." Her answer to his passionate missive had been an offhanded refusal of his request for an increasing of supplies and provisions for his troops. They would do well enough with the agreed upon amounts, she'd said, and victuals could be supplemented with local spoils. Even more maddeningly, she had insisted that he not be allowed to return from Ireland to England as he saw fit, even if his troops were secured. He had objected forcefully to her absurd ruling. "What do you think, madam," he had argued, face-to-face. "That I would use your army against you?" She had fought bitterly with him on the point, refusing to offer reasons for the prohibitions.

Only yesterday had Elizabeth signed a paper finally granting him the privilege of returning to England of his own volition.

Such irrational decisions—and there were too many to enumerate—further robbed Essex of sleep. Sometimes, despite Elizabeth's protestations that subjugating the Irish must be the last great accomplishment of her reign, he wondered at her blatant acts of self-defeat.

But there were other, more personal misgivings about the Irish Expedition. His health, for one. Though the mercury cure seemed to have halted the pox's progress in his mind and body, much damage had already been done. He was generally weakened, and fell victim to myriad agues and rheums and fevers. His bowels were constantly in an uproar, and a flux had fallen on his left eye. *All these symptoms*, he mused, *and I am embraced in the comfort of my own home*. So frightened by the prospect of illness in the distant, miasmic bogs of Ireland, Essex had contracted for an apothecary as well as his personal physician to accompany him for the duration of the war.

Perhaps the most troubling were his lapses in judgment. In his military career there had been moments of brilliance, when instinct and action were one, and outrageous chances were transformed into magnificent victories. But there was no denying that lately he had floundered, the Azores proving his nadir.

Worst of all Essex lacked confidence in his assessment of Tyrone. Now he cursed his laziness in not studying the "Irish question" more rigorously, and he wished that Grace O'Malley had spoken at greater length about Elizabeth's once loyal earl who had donned the mantle of The O'Neill, then blithely snatched Ireland from England's grasp. Essex had already underestimated the Earl of Tyrone once, disparaging his "ragtag army." The battle at the Yellow Ford had proven his judgment appallingly misguided. Essex could simply not afford to make the same mistake again.

Downstairs he could hear the household bustling with last-minute preparations for his departure. Much of the family had gathered to see him off. Lettice and Christopher, his sister, Penelope, and—quite blatantly—her longtime lover, Lord Mountjoy, rather than her husband, Lord Rich. Mountjoy had fought beside Robert many times and recently had proven quite the gentleman, considering that Essex had wrenched the Irish command from his old friend's grasp.

At the sharp rapping on his door, Essex looked up from his packing. "Come in," he said, wondering who in his family would have manners enough to knock before entering. "Francis!" he cried, openly delighted by the sight of the elder Bacon brother.

"I could not allow my lord Lieutenant to leave without a good-bye." The words were sincere, but Francis Bacon's attempts at mildness and levity were an immediate failure, and Robert's happy surprise dissolved under Bacon's lugubrious gaze.

"Come and sit down, Francis. I must finish packing before noon. My officers are coming to fetch me, and I mustn't keep them waiting."

"Yes, yes, go on with your business," said Bacon, who moved into the room, carefully shutting the door behind him.

"If you're going to lecture me or tell me not to go, it's too late," said Essex.

"I know that," said Bacon, taking a seat on the bed. "I simply wish that by your going to Ireland there was even the remotest possibility of your pleasing the queen. But there is not."

Essex laid down the wool scarf Frances had embroidered for him and looked into Bacon's sad eyes. No one, he realized, better understood the impossible position into which the earl had been placed by Elizabeth, nor the contortions and convolutions of her scheming mind.

"Into Ireland I go!" Essex cried with a theatrical flourish of his hand. "The queen hath irrevocably decreed it, and the Council doth passionately urge it." The starch went out of him then and he slumped down on the bed next to Francis Bacon. He sighed deeply and the two men sat in abject silence.

"I have no one to blame but myself," Essex finally said. "I denied the position to anyone else and it fell to me. I've seen the fire burning, Francis, and I've been called to quench it. If I slip collar now, give no help, Ireland will be lost."

"You know that failing will be dangerous," Bacon said, "and succeeding too well even more so."

"It is a strange world we live in," Essex mused, "but I think 'tis better to command armies in Ireland than humors at Court."

"I worry about your enemies at home. They're sure to be advanced in your absence."

"Southampton swears that I have a hundred thousand true hearts in England."

"A lovely thought, and it may be true, but they are common men. What you need are friends here at Court—in the center of the world."

"In Ireland I mean to command well," Essex announced, but even he could hear the uncertainty in his own voice.

"Then you must harden yourself, Robert. Become insensitive to the criticism of subordinates, stifle your impulse that all must love you. I'm no soldier, but I do know that the greatest commanders are those unafraid of being lonely and hated. And you *must obey Elizabeth's rules*. I cannot stress this more strongly. Whatever you do, submit all major decisions to the approval of the Irish Privy Council. Think independently and your head will surely roll."

Essex laughed ruefully. "I fear it will roll in any case. Tyrone's rebels are the least of our enemies. Disease in that country takes more of our soldiers than guns or swords, and corruption amongst the officers is appalling—worse even than the Netherlands. If disease is survived, desertion, famine, and nakedness sap men's strength and heart. But the worst enemy of this war is the queen herself. She professes to desire victory, yet she is mean with supplies and victuals to make her army strong. Even when she sends them, she allows such poor transport they have no way to find the troops."

Now the two men sat sighing together.

"I suppose our only joy is King Philip's death," Bacon muttered.

"By God, he was a madman!"

"Is it unchristian of me to be glad of his horrible end? They say he suffered in full consciousness and excruciating pain for months, his body covered head to foot in odorous, weeping pustules. Still he prayed to God—endlessly. On his deathbed he wondered if he'd burnt enough heretics."

"As tormented as he was, I hear he wrote to Tyrone, congratulating him on the victory at Yellow Ford," said Essex. "Do you suppose Philip's son will prosecute this war with such enthusiasm?"

"No, I do not. But it makes no difference in the end. This is *Tyrone's* rebellion now. He may have Spanish guns," Bacon observed, "but it seems he has the heart and soul of the Irish people behind him. And perhaps that is all he needs."

"Good God, Francis, if I listen one more minute to you, I shall lie down and open my veins! Give me *some* encouragement."

"All right." Bacon inhaled deeply and pinched his forehead beneath his fingers as he searched for some happy thought. "Despite her deviousness and seeming ill will," he finally said, "I know that the queen still loves you very well. Above all men, Robert. *Above all men.*"

Essex felt his eyes fill with tears. He grasped Francis Bacon's hand and held it tightly. "I pray you're right, Francis, with all my heart, for I wish to be valued by her above anyone who lives. Else I am ready to forget the world and be forgotten by it."

A sudden commotion of many horses on the Strand outside Essex House announced the arrival of the Lord Lieutenant's officers. Francis Bacon stood to go. The men embraced, then held each other at arm's length, a world of futures—many of them terrifying—swirling between them.

"God speed, Robert. Bring us a great victory."

"I will. I promise it."

Bacon moved out the door and closed it gently behind him. For a too long moment Essex stood staring at the door, at nothing at all, his mind suddenly and altogether devoid of thought. Only a shout from one of the soldiers on the Strand brought him to his senses.

"Not a good sign," he whispered to himself. Then he turned back to his wooden traveling chest and finished packing.

A ND I THEREFORE name Henry Wriothesly, Earl of Southampton, as my Master of Horse!"

There were shouts and several sincere "Huzzahs!" amongst Essex's mounted officers, their horses stamping and snorting in the road in front of Essex House. Robert had, on the one hand, been thankful there'd been no tearful farewells with his family, but wondered, on the other, how it would feel to know that your mother or wife was truly sorry to see you go off to war and perhaps your death. But he had been unaccountably cheered to see the bright faces of his officers as he'd strode out amongst them and taken his horse. These were all men who, upon hearing that Essex had been named as leader of the Irish Expedition, had come forward clamoring to fight under him.

Now Southampton, his face flushed with shock and delight at the recent announcement, trotted up beside Essex and smiled broadly. "When did the queen rescind her prohibition of me as Horsemaster?" he asked.

"She never did," Essex answered with an even gaze at his friend.

Southampton's smile evaporated. "I don't understand. You simply defied her?"

"I did."

"You're mad, Robert."

"I'm afraid I may be," said Essex who, with a stiff wave above his head signaled his officers into formation. "Ride next to me at the head," he told Southampton.

"You know how desperately I wanted the post, but this is no way to begin your commission."

Essex laughed. "The truth is, there is no good way for me in Ireland." He lifted his chin and gazed up at the sky. It was clear blue and the sun bathed them in delicious warmth. "But look, today is a perfect day. You've received your commission, and I am leaving behind a world of difficult women. Is that not something to celebrate?"

Southampton's smile returned. "To Ireland," he said, giving signal for the officers to move out.

"God help us," said Essex, a hope and a prayer—both of which he rather doubted.

⋙⋘⋙⋘

INDEED THE DAY had continued with its perfectly sunny weather as Essex and his officers joined the regiments that had been awaiting them in London. They'd been mustered from towns and villages in the east and south, and would be met at the western port of Holyhead by the Welsh contingent, and troops marching in from the north.

While the rank and file had not been provided with uniforms, some who were veterans of the Netherlands war had donned whichever pieces of their old gear that were not in tatters. Every man carried a weapon and, thought Essex with some pride, the cavalry looked strong and splendid.

For five miles along the road northwest out of London, crowds had gathered in great numbers to cheer the army on its way. Children sat atop their fathers' shoulders waving to the brave soldiers marching off to war. Women were throwing kisses, and people were crying out, "God save your Lordship, God preserve your honor!" Only then had Essex allowed himself to hope that perhaps the Irish Expedition was not a doomed enterprise. That as the Almighty had assisted the English fleet at Gravelines, so too would he provide Essex with a decisive victory against Tyrone.

But the thought had scarcely crossed his mind when a very real shadow fell across his face. Looking up he was startled to see that the bright day had suddenly filled with black, roiling clouds. He felt the first soft drops of rain fall on his cheeks, but a moment later the heavens opened and the sky was rent by thunderbolts, these sending the crowds fleeing to safety across the sodden fields.

The cavalcade of soldiers, drenched and bedraggled, now marched through the dreary, deserted countryside and Essex, looking back at his troops, was overcome with wretchedness. It was not, however, until the rain hardened into egg-size hailstones that crashed down upon the queen's army, bloodying both men and animals, that the Lord Lieutenant's gloom turned to a sickening dread. How much clearer a portent of evil could have been given than this?

Robert Devereaux could think of none.

# 12

THE JOURNEY TO IRELAND had been hellish. A ferocious tempest had tossed Essex and his troop ships around the Irish Channel for days. Finally, beaten by waves the size of small castles, they'd limped back to the English port of Holyhead. Many of his soldiers had been ill with dysentery, and the apothecary Essex had hired—the man he'd secretly hoped would be the savior of "England's Savior"—had died before the expedition had even begun.

His own health had alarmed him from the start. He'd been shaken by severe chills, as if a great hand had grasped the back of his neck and shaken him out like a wet rag. A moment later his skin would scorch beneath his clothing. There'd been a constant nausea twisting his guts, and without warning his bowels would turn watery.

Worse yet, a vagueness regularly overcame him, like blunt fingers pushing at his brain. It was the most important command of his career, and yet it took all his strength to keep up appearances for his officers and men, convince them that he was fit and capable of leading. There were other fearful demons to battle—wrenching self-doubts, memories of Elizabeth's deceit and ill will, and the legion of his enemies at Court, already scheming on the wide-open field of his absence.

Without warning Essex would again feel well. His mind would clear, and strength would flood into his limbs. He would call Chris Blount and Southampton to his rooms and parade himself before them to fire their confidence. 'Twould not do for them to see him so wretched. Then the next bout of sickness would lay him low. For days they languished at Holyhead, Essex seething with worry. Only heaven knew what outrages Tyrone was perpetrating in Ulster and Munster. The downpour at Islington had indeed proven an ill omen, and if circumstances continued unfolding as they had since then, the Irish Expedition would prove an unmitigated catastrophe. *He must get to Ireland!*

Though the skies still threatened, Essex ordered the captain of the *Sea Devil* to make ready for departure. The voyage, he announced with grim determination, must under *any* circumstances be made. The very future of England depended upon it.

The *Sea Devil* had struggled for days on her crossing, plagued from the beginning by ill winds that seemed determined to keep the ship from making landfall. Even Christopher Blount, a man of exceedingly strong constitution, was green and nauseous, and when the vessel finally docked at Dublin, he fell to his knees and kissed the ground.

The day after their landing, despite his infirmities, it became necessary for Essex to rise to a most important occasion—the receiving of the Sword of State from the Irish Privy Council, as well as its report on the state of Ireland. When the new Lord Lieutenant entered Dublin Castle's Privy Council Chamber, he found that the room itself reflected the ambivalence felt for this country by the Englishmen and Irish-English lords who ruled her. It was dreary, the once lustrous paneled walls having been allowed to rot in many places, and the smell of putrid rushes was tolerated rather than addressed. Fear was palpable. A plot to seize the castle by rebels had been discovered less than a week before its carrying out. And it was understood that the whole of Ireland had been left vulnerable by leaving the country without a viceroy for a full eighteen months after Lord Burgh's death, and eight months after the battle at the Yellow Ford.

Today's occasion was so somber as to be grim, for only the day before—the same as Essex's arrival—the longtime Lord Treasurer, Henry Wallop, had died, and the rest of the Irish Privy Councilors, wearing black, were mourning him. Perhaps its most illustrious member and the most experienced in war, Black Tom Ormond, was absent. Ormond was, the disappointed Essex was told, campaigning feverishly in Munster.

Indeed, news of the rebel was not good. And the Lord Lieutenant, upon seeing the makeup of the Council—for the most part aged nobles, sour-faced officials, and purse-lipped clergy—reminded him of how desperately he wished for Christopher Blount to be sitting amongst them.

"I begged Her Majesty to grant me this one favor," he said to the men of Blount's appointment, with no attempt to hide his sarcasm, "but I must have spoken in a language that was not understood, or to a goddess not at leisure to hear prayers." There was a shocked silence all round at his criticism of the queen, and not one man cracked the faintest smile at his wit. With an inward groan Essex insisted that the reports begin.

The two arch rebels, Tyrone and Red Hugh O'Donnell, were, of course, the worst of their problems. Ulster was entirely under their control—hostage to the rebels—and all other provinces in the country had been overtaken by them or their cohorts. They were both of them charismatics, one from the old school and the other from a younger generation. They excelled in drawing a vast array of disaffected chieftains into their confederation. The great fear—one that plagued the Council every day and in their dreams—was the coming of Spanish reinforcements to the cause. Already the rebels had received shipments of arms from Philip to the most disastrous effect—the Yellow Ford.

In Munster Tyrone had installed a young Desmond, kinsman of Gerald, and Munstermen had rallied round to fight alongside him. And an English-born patriot named Richard Tyrell, now one of Tyrone's best captains, was tearing through the south as well. The plantations had fallen—their elaborate structure having collapsed—and all the settlers routed in the space of one bloody day the previous autumn. English Munster was, for the moment, quite dead. In the absence of a governor after Drury's death, Ormond had taken command of what troops remained and was struggling valiantly, but with little success, against Tyrone and his invading army.

"I toured the south after the uprising," said Archbishop Loftus, his face pinched with annoyance. Loftus was the greatest of the councilors—Lord Keeper, Lord Chancellor, and Archbishop of Armagh. "It struck me then how right Her Majesty had been when she'd ordered that when the plantations in Munster were undertaken, the Irish race should be altogether excluded from the province. Had we listened, and not hired the savages as farmhands and servants, we would never have lost those farms."

" 'Tis my understanding," said Essex, "that without the hard work of the natives there would never have *been* plantations. What Englishman would travel to this place unless he was a landholder? Would he stoop to menial work? I think not. The Irish were our slaves, and at the first opportunity they rose up against their keepers, their oppressors."

Loftus and the others stared at Essex as though he'd grown horns on the top of his head.

"That is no excuse for the atrocities they rained down upon their masters," said Sir George Carey. "The rebels have burned and looted settlers trying to run for their lives. They were stripped and robbed and some slain. I saw a gentlewoman, raped and naked, both her nostrils slit, wandering in a daze along the road. I saw bodies of mutilated planters rotting alongside their cattle in their burnt-out fields. Irish children enjoyed bowling with the severed heads of murdered Englishmen!"

"Dublin and the Pale are, for the most part, secured," insisted the creaking old Earl of Kildare. He was perhaps the only Irish nobleman besides Tom of Ormond unquestionably loyal to the Crown. "But you must realize that the Pale constitutes but one twentieth of Ireland. The rest, all the cities and towns and countryside, have been retaken by Tyrone and O'Donnell and their minions."

The chamber door, on screeching hinges, opened and a young, fair, and very handsome man entered.

"Forgive me my tardiness," the man said to the group in a voice both forthright and confident, and suddenly Essex felt a desperate desire that this bright-eyed youngblood—whoever he was—might perhaps be one of the Council. "My Lord." The stranger bowed low to the Lord Lieutenant. "I am Conyers Clifford, Governor of Connaught."

*Ah*, thought Essex, *a soldier*. He liked the man immediately.

"You're in perfect time, Clifford," said Essex. "I've heard the news of Munster. How goes the effort in the west?"

Conyers Clifford did not care to sit, rather he strode round the Privy Council Chamber as he spoke, as sure and graceful as he was attractive. Essex smiled to himself, wondering what Southampton would make of this fine figure of a man.

"Connaught was in a shocking condition when I assumed the governorship. I do not wish to demean my predecessor's character, but Richard Bingham's methods guaranteed failure. He should have known that more than any of Ireland's chieftains, those of the west country had remained free the longest, and therefore would resist our yoke even more fiercely. Instead he was brutal beyond comprehension. Of course the more violently he moved against them, the more agitated they became. Slaughter and pillage were his answer to their further resistance.

"On my arrival I found the land and the people utterly ravaged. Famine, plague, starvation. As though they'd not suffered enough at Bingham's hands, they were dealt the final indignity when Red Hugh O'Donnell, an Ulsterman, attempted to usurp the power in Connaught. They are a proud people, but they became confused by the issue of loyalties. Whatever enemy might come at them, English or Irish, many of them are now prepared to fight to the last man, the last breath. On the other hand, they do not hesitate, when it suits their purposes, to make a public show of surrender to the Crown."

"I hope you've had better luck than Richard Bingham," said Essex.

"Oh yes," the Earl of Kildare offered. "Clifford has worked wonders in Connaught."

"My policy tends toward conciliation with the Irish lords and chieftains," he said. "Of course I began by befriending the loyalists, Clanrickard and the O'Connor Sligos. But I have in recent months worked diligently to deserve the affection and friendship of Tibbot Burke, the sea captain."

"Tibbot Burke?" The sound of the name worked on Essex's brain like a strong tonic. All at once the cloudiness dispersed and he felt himself alert. "Tell me more about him."

"Well, of course you know he's the O'Malley woman's son—her youngest son, and her favorite. Indeed, another son by the name of Murrough O'Flaherty she considers her enemy. Grace O'Malley continues, at her unimaginable age, to be the prime supplier to Tyrone of guns from Spain, as well as Scots Gallowglass to swell his ranks. She's most incorrigible and has shown no interest in any of my offers of friendship. Her son Tibbot, on the other hand, has taken me into his heart."

"You claim friendship with him? Sincere friendship?"

Clifford smiled as he arranged his thoughts. "Tibbot Burke is an extraordinary man. He is a strong and dedicated soldier and a capable seaman. He's intelligent—English educated—and though he will not admit it, he loves and admires much that is English. More than anything, *ambition* drives him, and whilst that is apparent to all—he's quite transparent—he has ceased to try hiding that trait. We therefore share a more than usual honesty, for he is entirely aware of my motives as well. He knows that I know how easily he might be lured back to Red Hugh O'Donnell and the 'Irish cause.' Still, since we've met he's remained loyal to the Crown. I try, but I cannot find fault with him. Together, he and I and Donal Sligo unseated Theobald Ciotach and pushed Red Hugh out of Connaught entirely. Because of Tibbot Burke's involvement, my army received full support from virtually every Connaught chieftain for that engagement."

"Will they remain loyal when we ask for their surrender to our control?" asked Essex. "For that is our ultimate goal, is it not?"

"It is, of course it is, and I cannot promise all the Connaught chieftains' support. But I feel"—Clifford paused, holding Essex's eye with a steady gaze—"in that place where a good soldier feels future victory or defeat, that Tibbot Burke is *ours*. What I bring you today is a means to ensure his loyalty." He opened the folded leather pouch he'd carried in and extracted a parchment from it. He moved to the window for the light.

"This is the list of requests to the Council—*demands*, if you like—submitted by Tibbot Burke. If you find some of them audacious, be reminded that I encouraged him in that direction. I wished to know the full extent of his dreams and ambitions, the better to understand his mind, and knowing full well that the Council will grant only that which is reasonable and expedient to our needs. First"—Clifford began reading—"he wishes that all the lands granted through the now defunct MacWilliamship be transferred to his control." He read silently down the page. "There are numerous other land grants he desires be made to him . . . ah, he wishes an appropriate title, letters of pardon from the queen for his mother, brother, and uncle . . . a small army—" To the indignant sniffs of the councilors on the last point, Clifford interjected, "That was *my* idea."

Essex was amused. "You would give him his own army?"

"Paid for by the Crown, yes I would. And a small salary for himself."

"You really do believe his importance in Connaught," said Essex.

"Not just Connaught, my lord. In all of Ireland. That is why I urge you to satisfy him as fully as good sense allows."

Essex fixed Conyers Clifford with a steady stare.

"Further, my lord Essex, I humbly suggest that you personally make the man's acquaintance. Perhaps . . . befriend him." Clifford smiled shyly and lowered his gaze to the floor. "We are all aware of your many virtues as a soldier and high council to the queen. I do believe you would altogether charm Tibbot Burke. He would relish your friendship, and you in return would enjoy his company. He's a lively fellow. Quick witted and a boon companion. The previous generation was lucky to have the loyalty of the Irish lords Ormond and Kildare." He smiled at Kildare, who was nodding with the compliment. "I say we will be lucky in our generation to acquire the loyal service of Tibbot Burke, and it would be worth your while to pursue his friendship."

"Yes, well, I will take your suggestions into full consideration, Clifford. And thank you." All the councilors nodded their thanks to him. With another bow Conyers Clifford backed from the room.

Essex turned to face the Council. "The more pressing issue at hand today, and the queen's express desire," he began, "is the conquest of Tyrone in Ulster. I am commanded to move with the great force she has provided, north through Ulster to the coast, and to establish a permanent garrison there near the deep harbor of Lough Foyle. She wishes us to engage the traitor Tyrone, and defeat him once and forever." Essex's confident announcement, one that he fully expected would be greeted with unanimous and enthusiastic agreement, was instead met with an uncomfortable silence all round, councilors squirming like schoolboys in their chairs. Essex found himself at a loss.

"Is not Tyrone 'like a frozen snake picked up by a farmer, which, growing warm, hisses at his benefactor'? So writes our illustrious poet Spenser. 'He is a serpent,'" Essex went on quoting, "'raised out of the dust by the queen, yet encompassing the most serious of all perils to Elizabeth's rule in Ireland.' He is, is he not, gentlemen?"

"Yes, of course he is, my lord, without question the most dangerous man in Ireland. The root of all evil," Loftus agreed. "And as our own Lord Burgh so aptly observed, 'Branches will sprout as long as the root is untouched.'"

"Her Majesty," Essex insisted, "has made it quite clear in her generous mustering of the largest army she has ever assembled—sixteen thousand men and thirteen hundred horse—that she means for me to hunt down the Earl of Tyrone and destroy him, *at any cost*."

"Agreed, my lord Essex." Nicholas White, Master of the Rolls, spoke earnestly and seemed, in fact, to be speaking for the whole of the Council, who already sat nodding in somber affirmation. "The problem, you see, is one of transport and supply. 'Tis a very large army you propose taking so far north to Lough Foyle, one that requires a vast amount of food."

"Yes, I'm aware of that, my lord." Essex was beginning to feel ill again, the clarity he'd enjoyed during his conversation with Clifford dissolving into fog.

"To feed such an expedition," Lord White went on, "a great herd of cattle is necessary. Sadly, herd animals—cows in particular—have been drastically diminished in number during the previous years' hostilities. What animals we do have are in poor health—quite inedible—and would certainly die if driven north at this time of year. It would be best to wait for high summer, when pastures would be greener and the rivers necessary to cross less wild. Too, in the summer, the rebels' corn and cows might also be confiscated for our use."

"If we cannot take cows"—Essex dabbed with his handkerchief at the perspiration gathering on his upper lip—"then we shall feed the army on dry rations."

"No, no, my lord. That is impossible. You see, the winds in the Irish Sea have been most contrary—as I'm sure you yourself realize—and the transport horses that are meant to carry your biscuit and hardtack have not even left England."

Essex sighed deeply, expelling with his breath what was left of his hope that this adventure would prove successful. "What are you suggesting, my lords?"

"Well . . ."

Essex stared round the room and all at once saw himself surrounded by a cadre of timid and dithering old men. He could not hope for guidance from them, yet he was utterly constrained by them. Much as he hated to admit it, Francis Bacon had been correct. If Essex moved without consent of the Irish Privy Council—especially now—he could not hope to remain in command. There was one explosion that he'd already been forced to deal with—Southampton's appointment to Horsemaster. Elizabeth had been livid when she'd found out.

"If I do not, as the queen has expressly bade me do, press north into Ulster and cut at the 'root' of the rebel forces, what would you have me do?"

Kildare spoke up then. "If you cannot at this time make your way to the root, my lord Essex, then alternately you might take action by shaking and swaying the branches. In other words, go south into Leinster and Munster. I'm sure Lord Ormond would be grateful for your assistance there."

Essex thought, *At this moment I would be grateful for Lord Ormond's assistance here. Surely he would see the necessity of striking Tyrone when the English army was at its strongest.*

"It is now April," Kildare continued. "You have two or three months' time before you need attack Ulster."

Essex was in despair. This was ill advised and would end in disaster, he was sure of it, but there was nothing to be done. "I shall do as you advise me, my lords, but I insist you back up the request I will make of the queen and Privy Council for an additional two thousand reinforcements and appropriate supplies and horses. Many hundreds of my men are already sick or dead of dysentery, and in the coming months we will surely see more casualties. When I finally do reach Ulster, I do not wish Her Majesty's army to meet the 'King of Ireland' as a diminished force."

"Of course, my lord. We will confirm your request." There were relieved, congratulatory smiles all round the Council table.

"You have made a wise decision," said Archbishop Loftus.

"We will see about that," Essex replied. "Time will tell."

# 13

THE STENCH of the field hospital was unendurable—*What it must smell like in Hell*, thought Essex as he moved, hardly daring to breathe, through an inspection at the side of his army's chief surgeon, Elvin Meade. Whilst the surroundings were certainly more pleasant than the usual canvas tent thrown up in a meadow—this was the great hall of perhaps the finest plantation castle in Munster—the complaints of virtually all the wretched patients here were not battlefield injuries but marsh fevers and dysentery. Even the smells of blood and rotting flesh, Essex decided, were preferable to the raunch of vomit and several hundred soldiers' bowels emptied onto their cots in the overheated afternoon.

"Two hundred and forty have died this week, my lord, and dozens more are falling ill every day." The surgeon, a tall, gaunt man with a deeply pocked forehead, hid the rest of his face beneath a kerchief, though Essex doubted anything could allay the foul aroma of the place. Even so, he now regretted having refused the offer of a kerchief for himself. Most of the soldiers, gray faced, with parched, bleeding lips and eyes glazed with fever, were too far gone to appreciate seeing the uncovered countenance of their illustrious commander.

"What are our total losses to this date?" Essex asked, dreading to hear the answer.

"Battlefield deaths and injuries are negligible," Meade answered.

"Through dysentery and various fevers, twelve hundred and fifty. I never in my life dreamed I'd wish for gaping wounds and amputated limbs in my surgery. I've not seen anything like this, sir."

"Nor have I. We shall be moving on the day after next, and I will of course need you with me. Can you arrange for local nurses to look after these men?"

"I'll do my best, sir, but as you know, there are no English left in the province, and even if well paid, one wonders how carefully the Irish women will look after a company of their enemies."

"Well, we have no choice. I shall assign two of my men to stay and oversee the nurses." Essex shook his head, unable to fathom the magnitude of his losses. "This is dreadful . . . dreadful."

"How is your own health, my lord?" the doctor inquired with what Essex perceived as sincere interest.

"I wish I could say I was well," he answered. "But the air of the Irish bogs and swamps is every bit as sick making as my predecessors promised it would be. I suffer a sweat nearly every night. Or chills. And a mild but constant diarrhea."

"Keep your strength up, sir. We cannot afford to lose you."

They had reached the door. "Thank you, Meade. I'll send you the names of the two men who'll stay behind."

"Very good, my lord."

Leaving the hospital felt to Essex like an escape with his life, and he was quite suddenly overwhelmed by pity for the horrible end his countrymen would know in this strange, inhospitable land.

He had purposely withheld from Doctor Meade the details of his own fevers—the deliriums and terrifying visions from which he suffered nightly, and the blunted cognition with which he awoke nearly every morning. Sometimes it took him several hours to regain enough clarity to give cogent orders, and strength enough to mount his horse and ride. So far only Southampton and Blount were aware of his disabilities. They had been Godsent, gracefully covering for his weaknesses each day until he was fit to command.

But the days since leaving Dublin six weeks ago with his army of three thousand foot soldiers and three hundred horse—all the rest having been assigned elsewhere—had been as ghastly as the nights. For the

Irish rebels had, frustratingly, refused to engage with the English army, with only a few exceptions. In this land of mountains, with few roads and hidden fortresses, his men had been repeatedly spooked as they marched through dark forests and misty bogs filled with distant, and not so distant, howls and banshee cries, laid low by day after day of drizzle and fog, their feet moldering in soggy boots, their bowels revolting against putrid rations and thick, miasmic air.

Essex found that the enemy would rarely confront his army or allow themselves to be flushed out of their hiding places. Instead the rebels would lurk in their rocky defiles and fetid quagmires. They'd lay in wait in the woods or along the narrow entrances to their glens, having cut down several trees that they'd woven into intricate barricades, impeding the English army's progress, impossible to clear quickly. Everyone knew they were there, a silent terror that kept his army always on edge, their nerves fraying more perceptibly with every passing day.

Occasionally they would strike, fleeting but violent ambushes. First darts would come flying out of the bushes, taking out a man's eye or panicking the horses. Then the rebels themselves, half naked, long shaggy forelocks covering their faces, would descend in a great wave with terrifying battle cries that made the blood run cold, wielding clubs and battle-axes and long pikes, though many were armed with guns. They fought like madmen, any lack of technique overcome by a crazed fervor. It seemed to Essex that when they did engage, the rebels *relished* fighting, the closer and more hand to hand the better. Just as quickly as they'd come, they would fly off, disappear like an army of wizards, back to their remote fastnesses, knowing the English could never pursue them across the moist, unfirm ground that they knew so well.

From a military standpoint, Essex was forced to admit, he had nothing to show for the last six weeks but several empty skirmishes and meaningless victories—if one could even call them victories. A castle might be taken, but later it would be retaken by the rebels. He might revictualize a garrison, but the local Irish would raid it after they'd left. There had been one confrontation that might be called a campaign, this against Richard Tyrell's horse at Cashel Pass. Here the enemy had actually engaged with them. Essex had, by all accounts, led his men bravely and even brilliantly, flying like lightning from the vanguard, to the battle, to the rear guard. But even Cashel had been no true triumph, for the confrontation was diminished by the Irish who not only claimed it a victory for *themselves*, but named the battle the "Pass of the Plumes," denoting the many feathered helmets and hats the rebels had captured from their enemies when—so they'd said—the English had fled in terror.

Ironically, the reception Essex and his army had received in the few towns held by the earl of Ormond's English sympathizers had been splendid, with music and noble orations, cheers and garlands, the parade route strewn with flowers. But they had been hollow celebrations. There was nothing, after all, to celebrate. The territories that he and his armies marched through remained entirely unsubdued. Not one submission by a significant rebel chieftain had been obtained. And Essex's army day after day was evaporating into the rotten Irish air.

In their campaign across Munster, which more and more felt like meaningless ramblings, they were confronted daily by the grim remains of English Ireland. Great houses and plantations had been deserted and looted, the fields scourged of crops and cattle. Bodies of English men, women, and children lay unburied and moldering by the side of the roads upon which the poor souls had attempted to run for safety to the nearest walled cities. And what Irish still roamed here had been stricken by famine. Their hollow eyes would peer out at him from behind the rubble of village walls, and when their skeletal faces were visible, he saw their mouths were stained bright green by the nettles and dock they were forced to eat in the absence of proper food. There had been stories of old women who would light fires in the fields on a cold morning, thereby luring children to the warmth of the flames, only to murder the little ones and eat them, like proper witches would do. Essex chose not to believe those stories, sure they had been concocted by English soldiers out of misery and a growing hatred for this wretched land, and the poor savages inhabiting the destroyed countryside.

Now moving deeper into the green wilderness of Munster, Essex felt his physical strength diminish and his senses grow more vague and unaccountable, confused many times between fancy and fact. Most often in dark, misty nights he worried that he had been infected by the faerie thrall of Ireland, such that would lead him to madness and even death.

"Robert." Essex was brought up sharply by his name being spoken.

"Are you deaf, man?" He turned. It was, thankfully, Southampton, but his face betrayed a story of tragedy waiting to be told.

"Oh, don't tell me if it's horrible, Southampton."

His friend now gathered himself into a soldierly demeanor and announced, "I'm afraid you have to hear this. Henry Harrington, in the Wicklow Mountains, was attempting a march back to Dublin—"

"Harrington had a large company of Irish soldiers under his command," Essex said. "I warned him."

"Attacked by the rebels, his Irish company turned and ran, but, my lord, the English troops were just as hopeless. They panicked altogether in the face of the enemy, many of them leaving their weapons behind. It is said that Harrington's lieutenant never even dismounted in the fray. He simply wrapped the colors round his body and fled on horseback. One captain, Allerton, did try to rally our troops, riding amongst them shouting that they had only to turn back to the enemy to save their lives, but the men were dazed with fear. They broke and fled in every direction. We shall have to deal harshly with them when we return to Dublin. Do you not agree?"

"Yes, of course we will." Essex's head had begun throbbing painfully. "How long a march is it to Limerick from here?"

"With no engagements, two days. We can expect to be greeted there by a large round of festivities and—"

"I cannot bear another round of festivities," Essex snapped. "I need a rest, Southampton. Quiet. I have to *think*. My army is melting away before my eyes. And I am as far away from Lough Foyle and my reason for coming to Ireland as I can possibly be."

"Have you any word from Elizabeth on the reinforcements for the Ulster campaign?"

"Indeed I have. The queen has refused me."

"How can she refuse you!"

"She says she will send no more men until she sees results with the ones already under my command. As for my taking Cahir Castle, that was nothing more than 'wresting an Irish hold from a rabble of rogues.'"

"She's still angry with you for naming me your Horsemaster."

"She is a petulant old fool."

"But this is war!" Southampton cried. "For pity's sake, can she not see what is at stake here?"

"She did give me high command of an enormous army—"

"Yet she continues to second-guess you, insult you, and tie your hands at every turn."

"Indeed, I am armed on the breast, but not on the back." Essex sighed. "The queen simply wishes that I never forget who rules whom."

Southampton was silenced by the truth of Essex's statement and implied question, for if the answer was "Elizabeth," his friend had truly lost his will and ambition. If the answer was "Essex," he would be speaking nothing less than treason. "Well, to Limerick," he said. "Perhaps we'll find some joy in the west of Ireland."

Essex was too depressed even to hope.

# 14

HOW MUCH MORE *of this will I be forced to endure?* thought Essex as his man Blakely lifted the heavy ceremonial mantle off his shoulders. *I am a soldier in the midst of war being feted by my enemy. Were there precedents for such orgies of cynicism and hypocrisy?* From the window of his rooms at Limerick Castle, Essex could see the remnants of the water pageant that this morning had been held in his honor. Young girls in their green and saffron dancing frocks still strolled in twos and threes along the quay. Some of his officers whom he had used his vice-regal powers to knight that morning were strutting round looking very pleased with themselves. And even now a boatload of Irish chieftains who, on bended knee, had publicly surrendered to their new Lord Lieutenant an hour past were being rowed back to the vessels that would convey them home.

*What was in the heart of even the most loyal Irish lord?* Essex wondered. *How much could they love the man who had been sent by his queen to conquer them?* Even when Clanrickard and O'Connor Sligo knelt before him, men who had for so long been faithful to the Crown, he'd attempted to look behind their eyes and into their souls to see the true nature of their sentiments. He was uncertain if he believed their protestations of loyalty or not, and this left him feeling vaguely uneasy. It had not been necessary to delve that deeply with The O'Flaherty or The O'Malley. These chieftains—fierce and brash and unashamedly rough—did not bother to hide their contempt for the highest-ranked nobleman ever sent to rule Ireland. They were there for expediency's sake only—no surprise in that—and, Essex guessed, laughed at their English "masters" behind their backs.

When, to the assembled crowd of dignitaries, the Mayor of Limerick had sung their new Lord Lieutenant's praises, presenting him with the ceremonial mantle of the city, Essex had been aware of a subtle but audible grumbling amongst the chieftains. Perhaps it had been mention of the Essex name. His father, Walter, the first Lord Essex, was after all infamous in Ireland for his massacre at Rathlin Island. In an early attempt to prove English authority, he and Walter Raleigh had sailed into the community and in one afternoon slaughtered hundreds of old men, women, and children attempting to hide from their murderers in the island caves. Indeed, "Essex" was not a proud name to own in Ireland.

Essex had been engrossed in his thoughts and not heard the tapping at the door, nor even noticed when his man left off undressing him to answer it. It had startled him, therefore, to see Blakely standing before him with a wax-sealed letter. Essex opened the parchment. It was written in English in a bold hand.

*My lord Essex,*

*Our mutual friend, Conyers Clifford, wishes us to meet. He assures me that we will get on famously. I am at present in Limerick and very happily at your service.*

*Your friend,*
*Tibbot ne Long*

Essex considered the message, and the note's tone. But more interesting still was the signature. Grace O'Malley's son had signed, not Tibbot Burke, but Tibbot ne Long—"Tibbot of the Boats." Did he mean to call attention away from his Burke heritage and his consistent attempts to grab the forbidden Burkes' MacWilliamship? Or did he simply wish to call attention to his finest asset, his large fleet of galleys? *Or perhaps,* Essex mused, *he wishes me to be reminded of his maternal heritage.* Surely

Grace would have described to her son their very pleasant meetings in London five years before.

The prospect of a rendezvous with Tibbot, Essex realized, had quite suddenly cheered him. Here was a contemporary whose intimate history he knew, an educated man, ostensibly a loyalist who, it seemed by his note, wished to befriend him in this friendless country.

Essex moved to his desk, and scribbling a reply, handed it to Blakely, sending him to deliver it. Now back at the window he scanned the castle quay, eager to see if Tibbot's vessel was docked there, or farther out in the river where the ships of the lesser Irish nobility lay at anchor. Moments later Blakely came into view, note in hand, inquiring after Tibbot ne Long's conveyance. He was pointed instantly to the largest galley docked there, and closest to the wharf—a slip reserved for a man of importance, thought Essex. *A place of honor*. He found himself unaccountably happy at the idea. Perhaps, he thought, this young man—rebel or loyalist—would prove a respite from his relentless melancholy.

As he pulled on his hose and his high kid boots, Robert Devereaux found himself, for the first time in many weeks, smiling.

ESSEX HAD ANNOUNCED himself at the dock and boarded the *Granuaile*. If he remembered correctly, this was the name given Grace O'Malley as a defiant young girl who'd just chopped off her hair—"Grace the Bald." He could see it was a proud vessel in every respect, clean and polished, with a fit and varied crew—energetic boys, brawny young sailors, wiry, weathered old men—all of whom eyed this stranger with polite wariness. Tibbot Burke . . . *ne Long*—whatever he wished to be called—came striding forward. Tall, wide shouldered, and vital, he greeted the Lord Lieutenant with a formal bow, then broke into a broad grin.

"You are *most* welcome here, my lord Essex. I've long wished to make your acquaintance."

"And I am told I would do well to make yours."

To a sprightly older mate, Tibbot said, "Bring Lord Essex some wine, the Cadizian port."

"Are you still importing Spanish wine?" Essex inquired mildly.

"No. But my mother is."

This was spoken without even a hint of guile, but those few words, thought Essex, implied volumes about Grace O'Malley's continued illicit dealings with Spain. But then her loyalty to the rebel cause was no secret to anyone.

"How does your mother?"

"She is very old and very well. She is never anything but strong and well. I've not met anyone else like her."

"I have," said Essex with a wry smile. "The Queen of England. She has the constitution of a Hereford bull."

Tibbot said, straightfaced, "I shall tell her you said so."

The two men's burst of laughter was simultaneous and almost familiar, as though they had known each other from childhood.

"Come, let me show you round my ship," said Tibbot, as eager as a boy. "We'll have a cup of wine in my cabin and then perhaps we can take her out, meet my small armada."

*Again, the choice of Tibbot's words startled Essex.* "Armada" was distinctly Spanish.

"'Tis a fair day for a small voyage," said Tibbot, regarding Essex with a studied gaze. "And you, my friend, look as though you could use the air."

Y OUR VICTORY OVER Red Hugh O'Donnell and his Mac-William at Tirawley was impressive," said Essex. He leaned back in his chair, across the table from Tibbot in his captain's cabin. "I'm told you drove Theobald Ciotach to such straits that he can no longer tell upon which elbow to lean."

"'Twould have been impossible without Lord Clifford and his fourteen hundred men," Tibbot said, draining his cup and refilling it for the third time. Essex, he noticed, at first had refused more than one drink. He was careful with his health. Perhaps the rumors were true that the man suffered from more than common fevers. But he was affable and extremely witty, just as his mother had described him, and in the end had accepted several cups of the good Spanish wine.

"In any event," said Essex, "you've established yourself brilliantly in Connaught. You may lack the title, but you've the influence and power of a MacWilliam. Her Majesty is happy to have brought you to this place."

"Let us speak candidly, my lord. Her Majesty had her own reasons to support my vendetta against Red Hugh and his false MacWilliam. She knows quite well that I am the only man who can rule 'the unruly Burkes.' And besides, my son is in English custody."

"In Conyers Clifford's home, I understand."

Tibbot smiled. "Happily for us all, with Bingham gone from Ireland. If one must be a hostage, better to be one in the house of a friend. How old is *your* son, Essex?"

"Just seven." He looked wistful. "I do not know him very well."

Tibbot was genuinely perplexed. "How is it that a father does not know his own son?"

Essex seemed thoughtful and, Tibbot observed, somehow ashamed. "I have not made the time, I'm afraid—in the same way my father made little for me." He grew silent, his gaze softening. "Either we become our parents," he said, "or become their opposites."

"Ah, a philosopher as well as a statesman . . . as well as a soldier."

"You flatter me, Tibbot."

"It seems we flatter each other, my lord."

"I hope the flattery is sincere, and not born solely of our various ambitions."

"I cannot deny my ambition." Tibbot leaned forward and, filling Essex's cup, looked him hard in the eye. "But I do believe in truth between friends."

Essex regarded him carefully. "Are you saying you will always be truthful with me?"

"Aye, I will." Tibbot hesitated for a long, thoughtful moment. "It's just that the truth has a way of shifting about with the moment. And in Ireland just now, the moments come fast and furious."

"Is it true that Red Hugh continues to court your favor?"

"Yes."

"And that sometimes you consider his offers?"

"I do. But I haven't forgiven him for having me jailed. I doubt if I ever will. And, frankly, the English perquisites are far more to my liking than his."

"I understand the reasons you've chosen to be loyal to the Crown, but I cannot begin to imagine how that decision might cause you distress. You must know that I met your mother." Tibbot nodded. "She's a magnificent woman."

"That she is." Tibbot could feel a flush of pride rising in his cheeks.

"Do you not find it difficult to stomach her disapproval?"

"Spoken like the true son of a disapproving mother."

Essex smiled. "Actually," he said, "I have been blessed with *two* ball-breaking mothers."

"How is that?"

"The first is Lettice—Lady Blount—who bore me. She is quite . . . indescribable." Both men laughed at that, wine having loosened them considerably. Essex stood and removed his jacket, throwing it on the bed piled with fine wool and fur coverlets. He moved about the tiny cabin, openly examining the surroundings. Polished wood, mariners' maps and rutters, nautical instruments. "And then there is the queen," Essex added. He paused, momentarily overcome by this thought, then turned back and regarded Tibbot quizzically. "She is in many ways more a mother to me than Lettice."

Tibbot could not hide his surprise. "I know 'tis bold of me to say, but were you and the queen not lovers? That is the widespread rumor."

Essex's answer was distinctly wry. "It can be said that Oedipus had nothing on me."

Tibbot shook his head, bemused. "I somehow feel I should press you no further on that subject."

"No, no. You and I seem to suffer a similar dilemma. I *adore* Elizabeth. To be fair, she has single-handedly made me what I am."

"As my mother 'graced' me."

"Exactly. We both receive great love and devotion from our 'mothers.'" Essex sat down and reached for his cup. "Yet every day by our contrary actions we risk their wrath, which—I have no need to tell you—is considerable."

Both men fell silent, lost in drunken contemplation.

"In the end," Tibbot finally said, "for better or worse in this conflict, I shall, I *must* seek survival for myself and my family. I believe my mother understands that, wishes the best for me." Tibbot held Essex's eyes. "What do you seek for yourself, Essex, and does *your* mother wish you well?"

Essex was completely silenced by the question.

Tibbot shifted in his chair. "Now I *have* gone too far."

"No," said Essex gently. "I can answer. Aside from the obvious—triumph over Tyrone—I have not the vaguest idea what I seek for my life. As far as the queen wishing me well, I more than ever think not. And when I hear myself uttering those words, I find them very alarming indeed."

"In that case," said Tibbot, giving Essex's arm a good-natured slap, "you'd better have another drink. Maybe two."

"A fine idea."

With a tipsy smile Tibbot tipped the flagon over Essex's cup and at the moment they both realized it was empty, there came a sharp rapping at the cabin door and a muffled voice calling, "Do you need more wine, Captain?"

The pair exchanged delighted smiles.

"Come in then!" Tibbot called at the door.

"I thought you might be runnin' low," said the sailor, entering the room. Essex had not bothered to look up as the jug was set on the table between them. "I took the liberty of substitutin' the port for a malmsey. I thought the Lord Lieutenant might enjoy a bit of sweetness."

In his inebriation it took Essex a moment to discern the overt familiarity with which the sailor addressed his captain. When he looked up, he was staring into a face he had never expected to see.

"Grace O'Malley, by God! You haven't aged at all!"

"A fine compliment and a complete lie. You look handsome as ever, Robert but far too peaked for my tastes."

"I've not been well," Essex admitted somewhat ashamedly.

"You English do poorly in the Irish clime, or is it the pox, as rumor tells it?" Grace observed Essex's startled expression. "Pardon me, but I'm far too old to mince words. And I only mention it as I've remedies for that malady brought from Spain—remedies said to work wonders."

"I'm on a course of treatment at present, but worry at its efficacy. I should be grateful to try something new."

Essex was staring unabashedly at Grace.

"You're gapin' at me like I've two noses on my face."

"Forgive me. It just occurs to me that if I were doing my proper duty just now—"

"You'd be roastin' my feet over hot coals," she finished for him.

"Yes. Demanding to know when the Spanish troops Tyrone hired will arrive to fight alongside him."

"You could demand until the cows come home, Robert, but I couldn't tell you even if I wished to—which I don't—for I don't know. My job was to *request* them. The rest . . . well, the rest is in the hands of the new King of Spain, and the gods of wind and water. So tell me, how is that old bat you work for?"

Essex choked back a laugh.

"Mam!" Tibbot whispered in warning.

"Don't shush me, son. Robert here knows how intimate I am with the queen, and she with me. He listened two nights to our conversations from behind a door."

Essex glowed red with embarrassment. "Was I so transparent?"

"I would have done the same had I been you. Indeed, you would have been a fool, given such a chance, if you'd *not* listened. You are many things, Robert Devereaux, but a fool is not one of them."

Essex tried composing himself, but the wine had loosened his tongue. "Her Majesty is very unhappy just now," he began. "This once-minor rebellion has run away from her like a team of spooked horses, to become a proper war. But Elizabeth loathes war, for it forces her to levy taxes on her people. When the people are taxed, they cease to love her—or so she believes. Above all, Elizabeth lives for the love of her subjects. Therefore, war bestirs in her the most violent of emotions. Yes, she is determined to win in Ireland. To *rule* Ireland before she dies."

Grace asked sincerely, "Do you think she'll succeed?"

Tibbot was on the edge of his chair, his own movements and fate entwined in the answer.

"The queen," Essex began, his eyes unfocused, his words beginning to slur, "always gets what she wants. She has committed every resource at her command to ensure victory. But," he continued, "she has sent *me* to do her bidding." He regarded Grace with a hangdog expression. "I am so unwell."

"Tibbot," she said, "why don't you go up and tell them to head north to Bofin."

Without a word he left the cabin, shutting the door behind him.

Grace placed her hand over Essex's own and spoke to him gently. "You're in a miserable condition, son. I doubt I've ever seen anyone more in need of a respite. Why don't you let us take you away from all your troubles, just for the day."

"How do you mean, 'take me away'?"

"Look," said Grace, "do you trust me?"

He held her eyes, which, despite her age, were still bright and twinkling.

"I should not . . . but I believe I do."

"Then let's forget about the war. Just till tomorrow. Let me show you somethin'. Let me show you Ireland."

"But I've seen—"

"I know what you've seen. And it's half the reason you're sick in your soul. I want to show you a different Ireland. A different people. Just for today you'll forget who you are. A little touch of Irish magic"—she snapped her fingers—"and the Earl of Essex is no more."

He felt himself begin to smile. "Who am I then?"

"Just a friend of mine, from Italy perhaps. When you speak to me, speak in Latin. Most here speak Irish and nothin' else, but at least they'll never know you're English. What do you say? Will you do it?"

Essex regarded Grace with amused disbelief. "All right," he said, "I hereby place myself in your capable hands."

"Good!" Grace pounded her fist on the table and stood. "Well, first things first. Out of your dandified clothes, for they're a dead giveaway. You look to be about Tibbot's size." She threw open her son's cupboard. "Here," she said, thrusting a linen shirt and plain brown doublet at Essex, "give these a try."

THE MacTHOMAS'S BOOLEY would be a sight for sore eyes. Grace and "her Italian friend," riding on horseback, had been forced after leaving the *Granuaile* to pass through territories razed and blackened since her last visit, and she prayed with all her heart that the destruction of her neighbors' lands ended before the inland hills and summer pastures that were their destination. While the fields were all but bare of crops—certainly confiscated by the English—Grace's heart soared to see small garden patches and herds of black-faced sheep grazing in the long shadows of the afternoon sun.

By the time they began hearing the sound of festivities over the low hills, she saw that Essex had calmed considerably. He'd grown suspicious when Tibbot had announced that he would not be joining them for the MacThomas-O'Malley wedding feast, that he had an appointment to keep. Essex, sobered after their earlier round of wine, had gritted his teeth and even blocked Tibbot's passage from the ship, demanding to know if his new "friend" was going off to meet and scheme with Red Hugh O'Donnell. He'd grown agitated, and the pleasant game of disguising and charade was nearly forfeited to angry distrust. But Tibbot had remained calm, had looked Essex dead in the eye and sworn on his mother's life that he was not meeting with O'Donnell, or Hugh O'Neill either. That very afternoon he'd promised to speak only the truth to Essex, he said, and he would not insult his new friend nor shame himself by breaking that pledge. Essex, still beady eyed, had watched Tibbot sail off as Grace and he mounted their horses to take them off to the wedding. And the first two miles riding from the coast inland, through destroyed countryside, had done little to ease his mind.

But once the destruction was past, with green hills and thick patches of woodland looming before them, Grace saw Robert's body sag a bit, and his features soften into something just short of a smile. When they'd crested the final hill, the huge gathering of clans spread out below, she'd turned to him.

"This is what we call a 'booley'—summer grazing for our cattle."

"But there's a house," he said, perplexed.

"Well, of course there is—a booley house. Where else would the people sleep—amongst the herd?"

Essex smiled, chastised.

"You'll just have to leave off your silly conception of the 'wild Irish.' Believe it or not, we *are* civilized, even at the booley. Did you know that back in the last millennium all the European monarchs for eight hundred years insisted on Irish councilors and clergy to advise them on matters of church and state, for of all men they were the best educated and most wise? Did you know that without the Irish monks slavin' over their illuminated texts, all the great books of Roman civilization would have been lost to the barbarian hoards? No, I can see that you didn't."

A burst of applause was heard below them, and they could now see that a bard, having just completed a ballad, was taking a bow.

"So, are you ready, Roberto?"

"As I'll ever be," he said.

THERE'D BEEN SO MUCH cheering and embracing when Grace appeared that a flush of embarrassment rose in her tanned cheeks. But, she supposed, the wedding feast would not have been held at all without her sponsorship. She had begged her old neighbor Shane Mac-Thomas to lay aside his numerous woes just long enough to celebrate the wedding of his granddaughter, Margaret, to Grace's own grandnephew, Sean O'Malley. "Life goes on," she'd told MacThomas, "even in the face of death." She'd promised Shane that the O'Malleys would attend in their numbers, and she would provide all the food and the best Spanish wine. The children, hearing the offer, had pleaded with their elders, thrilled at the chance to leave behind the everyday sadness of their lives for a day of uninhibited joy.

When they'd arrived, so much had been made of "Saint Grace"—as the celebrants insisted on calling her—that little notice was taken of her companion, "the Italian fellow," as she later heard Essex referred to.

At the feast table she and Essex were led to places of honor before the roast. Grace watched with pleasure the high spirits of the bride and groom, the love and hope and sweetness emanating from them, which no barrier of language could disguise. Though she knew he could not understand a word of the Gaelic spoken there, Essex had soon fallen into a state of happy relaxation that could almost be called languorous. He laughed genuinely when others laughed, even if the exact meaning of the humor was lost on him, and when raucous songs were sung he pounded out the rhythm with his hand on the trestle.

Everyone was stuffed to their eyeballs and most were drunk as well, there having been a dearth of good wine for so many months and years, and no reason to celebrate. Even Grace felt light-headed and pleasantly tipsy. Now the harpist and bard had taken their places under the roof of the three-sided booley house, and guests were wandering from the table to hear them play and sing. Essex stood and gave Grace his arm, leaning down to help her up.

"Madam," he said.

"*Roberto*," she whispered pointedly, continuing in Latin. "Remember who you are."

"*Bene, Bene*," he said, stifling a giggle. Grace smiled to herself, realizing that under her care the Earl of Essex, Lord Lieutenant of Ireland, was drunk for the second time that day.

The celebrants gently moved Grace and Essex forward through the crowd and in moments they were standing close to the bard and harpist. The bard was an old man named Lucius whose twisted frame took nothing away from the sweetness of his voice and his clever words. He was highly regarded by all, for he'd cheated death. Richard Bingham, during one of his purges, had had Lucius hanged for the "crime" of balladeering. But he'd not died on the gallows, just suffered a broken neck and, as he liked to say, "laid a good load in his breeches." He'd been fished from the pile of dead men and nursed back to health by friends, then had fearlessly taken to the roads, when he was well, to sing even more scathing songs about the English devils come to destroy Ireland.

It took a moment for Grace to realize what Lucius was singing, a many-versed ballad about her exploits.

"He's singin' about me," she whispered in Essex's ear.

"Is that why everyone is grinning at you?" he whispered back.

"I'd say so."

There was great applause at the final refrain, and as many celebrants surrounded Lucius as they did Grace for congratulations. But before her embarrassment overwhelmed her altogether, whistles, drums, and pipes appeared from nowhere and the dancing commenced.

Young people were first on the floor, all the misery and starvation having disappeared from their glowing faces. Everyone else stood clapping and stomping to the rhythm as the girls and boys pranced and whirled so light on their toes. One young MacThomas lad did a jig so fast and furious his feet were a blur and everyone shouted at his finale—leaping into the air, spiraling, and then landing with a great flourish on his knees.

The spirited music drove everyone out on the floor. Fathers grabbed mothers, sisters grabbed brothers, and husbands and wives were now all of a congregation, moving with melodious pipes and heart-thumping drums, the sound that was purely Irish.

Grace, clapping along, watched the widow McGowan, a pretty woman who'd been devastated by the battlefield death of her husband, come shyly up to Essex and put out her hand. He turned to Grace with a look of helpless delight, then stepped into the crush of celebrants and, without hesitation, began to dance.

She saw that his eyes darted about him, learning the steps and the turns as he went. *He's good*, thought Grace, *a natural dancer*. He danced with a childlike joy buried deep in his poor heart, the very same hopefulness and joy to which her neighbors and clansmen were now giving vent. Aye, Robert Devereaux stood out on the dance floor, he with the widow McGowan. Soon there were shouts of "Roberto! Roberto! Dance lively!" and the crowd fell away till all that were left dancing were Essex and the lovely widow. He leapt like a young stag and, with his hands on her waist, twirled the woman high in the air. The clapping grew frantic, the shouts and whistles drowning out the music. The whistles and drums rose above the din, rose to a great climax and ended, all at once.

The widow McGowan fell laughing into Robert's arms and the crowd closed in around them. Moments later Essex emerged, flushed and handsome and as happy, Grace imagined, as he had ever been in his life.

The music had slowed and couples, hand in hand, were moving in stately squares round the floor. Beaming, Robert came forward and extended his hand to Grace. She felt herself suddenly as shy as a girl, but she gripped his fingers and found herself moving in relaxed step next to him.

"You made quite a spectacle of yourself out there," said Grace under her breath. His smile was happily dazed. "At least you don't look like death's companion anymore," she added.

"*Tute bene*," he said, looking grateful.

"*Tute bene*, indeed."

# 15

THE DISASTER LORD Lieutenant Essex observed as he gazed out over the south road leading to Dublin caused him to groan aloud. He sat alone on horseback on a small rise overlooking the queen's army. 'Twas not simply the vastly reduced and dispirited troops that so distressed him, though his losses so far had been staggering, but the great slew of hangers-on who now attended the troops that remained. It was nearly impossible to distinguish in the clouds of summer road dust between bedraggled soldiers and the mob of horse-boys, servants, and ordinary camp followers trudging alongside them. Bringing up the rear of the column was the most wretched sight of all—dozens of fly-ridden wagons packed full of the sick and wounded. Only God knew how many were already dead—silent, horrifying reminders of their own probable fate for the poor soldiers lying beside them.

*My God, had war always been this cruel?* he thought. The campaigns in France and Spain, even the Azores with its confusion and defeats, had never weighed so heavily on Essex's soul. Those had been days of action and fellowship and glorious heroism. But this . . .

There'd been nothing noble in the Irish engagements—what there had been of them—on their zigzagging course back from Limerick. Even in Tullamore, where there'd been some hope of confronting the rebel Tyrell, it had ended with the English taking into custody a small herd of cows and burning a stockpile of corn. The morale of his men was shockingly low, and they'd utterly disgraced themselves in Waterford, getting drunk en masse on the town's famous aqua vitae. But then it was not only *his* troops who were suffering. He had visited Sir Thomas Norris, Governor of Munster, in a field hospital where he lay amongst his soldiers, sick near to death of both a festering bullet wound and the news that two of his brothers had already died in their service to Ireland. Not a few of Essex's men had simply disappeared. The deserters had made their way to the coast and found passage back to England. Of course there was still the matter of Lord Harrington and his army of cowards to contend with once he arrived back in Dublin.

And he was haunted, constantly haunted, by his meeting with Grace O'Malley and her son. Try as he might, he could not erase from his mind several images: The sight of the pirate woman on the *granuaile*, as easy as she could be in her nautical surroundings . . . Tibbot Burke, whose warm, disarming smile Essex could never decide was friendly or deceiving . . . Sitting before the wedding roast in an open Connaught field, beating out an Irish tune on the long trestle table . . . The lovely widow McGowan lifted aloft in his arms. Why had Grace befriended him? he pondered daily. And how, in light of her loyalty to the rebellion, did she bear her favorite son's betrayal of the Irish cause? It must pain her appallingly, yet she seemed so accepting of it. So understanding.

Worse still, Essex realized, he had during his brief sojourn with the Connaught pirates conceived a small measure of affection for the Irish people—something he would never, could never, admit to a living soul. This was perhaps the most troubling of his emotions, for a soldier, he knew, must never have more than a minimal regard for his enemy. Enough, perhaps, to allow for humane treatment of the vanquished. But this went further and much deeper. When, since his day with Tibbot and Grace, he'd had occasion to kill an Irish rebel, he'd found himself tormented by visions of the widow McGowan weeping over the dead body of her husband. And every night, hollow-eyed villagers, and children with green, nettle-stained mouths visited his dreams . . .

Without warning Essex felt his head swim with a dizziness so profound that slumping forward and grabbing his horse's sides were all that kept him from tumbling to the ground. *Please God, spare me another attack!* he silently cried. But it was no use. Wave after wave of vertigo overwhelmed him, and heat began to grow in his body—heat so fierce he wondered if his blood was boiling in his veins. "Help me," he whispered helplessly into his horse's ear. "Someone help me." But as a small but brilliant white light expanded to engulf all of his vision, Robert Devereaux realized there was no help for him, no help under Heaven ever to be found.

THE PURGE THAT Essex endured for three days on his return to Dublin had been violent enough but, he thought, not nearly as unpleasant as the letter he'd found waiting for him from Elizabeth.

"Go on, read more," Southampton urged. He and Christopher Blount lay sprawled across Essex's bed in his Dublin Castle bedchamber. Still recovering from a bout of malarial fever and the treatment that had come even closer to killing him than the disease, Essex chose not to join his friends in an afternoon of drinking. Chris Blount was far from sober.

"I cannot read another word," said Essex of the queen's letter. " 'Twill make me ill again."

"Here, give it to me." Blount snatched the two large sheets of parchment from Essex's hands, pages that were filled to the edges with Elizabeth's distinctive script. The sheer volume of her sentiments was, in itself, alarming.

Blount took a swig from his flask and read silently for a moment, having difficulty reading with his bleary eyes. "She was very distressed to learn of the courts-martial of Harrington and his men. She wishes to know if you really believe that the execution of the lieutenant who ran away with the colors, and one out of every ten soldiers in the unit, was sufficient."

"Would she have me hang the entire company?"

"Ah," Blount went on, "she hopes she will not have cause to repent her employment of you"—he gave Essex a beady stare—"and she finds it *intolerable* that you dared create fifty-eight knights in Limerick." He looked up at Essex again. "She hated it when you did the same in France and Cadiz. You really should stop doing that, Robert. You've created more knights in three expeditions than exist in all of England."

"Shut up, Christopher." Southampton grabbed the parchment sheets from Blount and perused them. "Well, at least she blames the Irish Privy Council for the disastrous Munster tour. That's something."

"Hurrah," said Essex, and pulled the covers up to his neck.

"Tyrone is apparently touting his victories over the English all round the continent." Southampton went on with his paraphrasing of the queen's letter. "Oh dear."

"What is it?" Blount drunkenly demanded.

"Here's the meat of it." Southampton smiled sympathetically at Essex, whose head was thrown back on the pillow, his eyes closed. " 'Why have you left the rebel Tyrone unassailed?' " he read directly from the parchment, perfectly mimicking Elizabeth's shrill tone. " 'What of the plan to place a garrison at Lough Foyle? Have you forgotten my exhortations entirely? What in God's name can I say to induce you to proceed to the northern action!' "

"I thought she blamed the Council for my delay in going north," said Essex.

"She seems to have forgotten that for the moment," Southampton replied.

"Bitch." Christopher Blount was already half asleep.

" 'You have broken the hearts of our best troops,' " Southampton went on reading, " 'and weakened your strength upon inferior rebels. You've run out the glass of time, which can hardly be recovered. I insist you put the ax to the root of the tree—treasonable stock from which so many poisoned plants and grafts have been derived.' " Southampton went on reading in silence, then looked up with a mournful expression "She again refuses you the two thousand reinforcements you requested."

"God *damn* the woman!"

"Oh," Southampton uttered, and quietly put down the pages.

"What?" Essex demanded. "What has she said?"

Southampton seemed genuinely stricken. "Perhaps we should finish reading this when you're better."

"I'm as well as I'm going to be," Essex insisted, "which in itself is a frightening thought. Just tell me what she's written."

Southampton blew out a breath. "She's rescinded her permission allowing you to return to England at your own discretion."

"What!"

"You must first petition her in writing, stating your reasons for wishing to come, and under whose command you intend to leave your army." Southampton continued to read and paraphrase. "Then you will await her answer, in writing, before setting out for London. But under no circumstances are you to 'desert your post' without her express permission."

Essex sighed, defeated. "Does the woman sit up all night inventing new and terrible ways to insult and torture me?"

"It seems so."

"What has she done now?" said Christopher Blount, slurring his words.

"Go back to sleep," Southampton told him, an order Blount promptly obeyed.

"What am I to do?" said Essex. "What am I to do!"

There was a knock at the door.

"Who is it?" Southampton called, for Essex was too miserable even to care.

"Conyers Clifford, sir. May I come in?" came the voice through the door.

With his eyes Essex commanded Southampton to open the locked door and Clifford was admitted. He respectfully acknowledged Southampton and afterward came to the bedside, giving Essex a sharp, formal bow. Then his face softened in friendly concern. "My lord, you are still unwell. I heard you'd contracted swamp fever, but I'd hoped the purge would have cured you."

"'Tis less the fever that lays me low," said Essex, "than the betrayal of a friend. But never mind. Come, sit."

Clifford obeyed, pulling a chair up next to the bed, graciously ignoring the sight of Christopher Blount lying passed out at Essex's feet.

"You're very well, I see," said Essex. "Just looking at you makes me feel better."

"That pleases me, my lord."

Essex could see how deeply appreciated was the compliment. His officer's handsome face was aglow.

"I come bearing ill news of Connaught," Clifford began. "Our friend, O'Connor Sligo, has been besieged in his castle of Collooney, at the far end of the Curlew Mountains."

"By whom has he been besieged?" demanded Essex.

"Red Hugh O'Donnell. With your permission I will take my army—still a substantial force of three thousand foot and three hundred horse—and lift the siege. O'Connor Sligo is to my way of thinking, our greatest western loyalist. He must not go unsupported, my lord. If we succeed, I believe we will not simply be relieving O'Connor Sligo, but will once and for all break the back of the rebellion in Connaught."

"Then by all means proceed," said Essex, pleased by such optimism.

"I also expect to receive assistance in this campaign from Tibbot Burke," Clifford added.

"Oh?" Essex, intrigued, pulled himself upright in bed.

"I've ordered him to load his galleys with food and ammunition at Galway," said Clifford, "and proceed to Sligo Harbor to await my orders. By the time we fight at Collooney and make it through the Curlew Pass to the sea, we'll be in sore need of revictualizing and rearming."

"Surely Red Hugh will know Tibbot is lying at anchor there with supplies," Essex observed.

"I assume he will."

"And you trust that Tibbot will hold fast for your orders and not O'Donnell's?"

"Entirely. Tibbot Burke is my man. My friend. Our ally. I believe you met him in Limerick."

"I did."

"Did you not find him altogether trustworthy?"

Essex hesitated. "*Almost* altogether trustworthy."

"He was loyal at the battle of Ballyshannon and helped us win a victory there," Clifford said with great feeling. "For myself, I would put my life in his hands. That is how loyal I believe him to be."

"You've proven yourself again and again, Clifford, and so I bow to your judgment in this. Take your men and what supplies you need, and grab Collooney Castle back from O'Donnell." Essex put out his hand. "I wish you well."

"Thank you, my lord." Clifford stood, nodding first to Essex and then Southampton. He smiled in Blount's direction. "*He's* got the right idea."

The three men laughed familiarly and Southampton showed Clifford out the door.

"More officers like that one and we'd win this war," said Essex as Southampton returned.

"Perhaps his campaign in Connaught will distract O'Donnell and Tyrone," said Southampton. "Pull their eyes from Ulster so we might successfully invade. Collooney may be the battle that turns the tide for us."

"May heaven allow it," Essex muttered. "Something must change for the better, my friend, or we are doomed as surely as Christopher Blount is dead to the world."

Essex gazed down at his stepfather's peaceful countenance, wondering doubtfully if he, himself, would ever again know such tranquility in his life.

# 16

GALWAY WAS A CITY occupied, and it pained Grace to see it so. She had come here on a difficult mission today, but one she could ill afford to delay. Nowhere more than the docks was the occupation so noticeable, with English soldiers marching by the dozen at the wharves, searching the cargoes of every vessel anchored there. They took especial delight in rough-handling seamen and merchants alike, even had their way with any Irish girl senseless enough to venture out to the docks unescorted. This was the greatest shame, as the Galway streets had always been known as a safe haven for women of all ages. *In the old days,* Grace remembered with a stab of unaccustomed longing, *they used to be terrified of the O'Flahertys. The days before a person had to choose sides in this miserable conflict.*

She boarded the *Granuaile,* now being loaded with barrels of powder and shot and crates full of biscuit and dried fish, and was met by a chorus of warm greetings from the crew. It always surprised Grace how glad Tibbot's men were to see her, but she guessed it had to do with a hunger not unlike her longing for the old days in Galway. Grace O'Malley stood for what *had* been Connaught, and even if Tibbot promised a future on the winning side of this war, they could not help remembering.

Grace found him on the poop overseeing the loading of his ship.

"What have you here?" she demanded.

"A good day to you too, Mam," Tibbot replied without smiling.

She could see her son was burning with a short fuse this day, but she was in no mood to coddle him. "It looks to be a fine load of shot and powder and guns too. For your English friends?"

"Why do you bother to ask?" he said. "You know it is."

"I suppose I do." Gulls were wheeling about in the sky overhead and Grace suddenly envied their freedom. "Couldn't you let the English down just this one time? At least let them wonder at your loyalty."

"They *do* wonder, and for good reason. But this time I must go."

"Ah, your 'friend,' Clifford."

"Indeed my *friend* is marching to lift Red Hugh's siege on Maeve's uncle at Collooney Castle. Do you begrudge me trying to save Connaught from O'Donnell's tyranny?"

"Do you begrudge Ireland trying to save itself from the English?"

"Mam—"

"O'Neill and O'Donnell are only trying to unite us. 'Tis the only chance we have to win."

"I don't believe we have a chance under Heaven of winning."

"That's very clear."

"Look, is it so terrible to think of English rule? Bingham is gone and Clifford is well loved here."

"*Well loved.*" She sniffed at the idea.

"He is. He was more than courageous at Ballyshannon, and what's more, he governs with a fair hand."

"And when he's dead and gone, who will we get next to rule us?"

"Clifford is young and healthy and he wishes to stay on as governor."

"Oh, he's told you that, has he? You *are* good friends."

"Who are you to talk about fraternizing with the enemy? You and your Lord Lieutenant Essex—"

"I don't bring him guns!"

Grace noticed Tibbot's eyes shifting behind her shoulder. She turned and found Murrough looming over her. "Hello, son." Her voice was flat and dull.

"Mam."

"You goin' with your brother to help the English?" Grace knew as soon as the words had left her mouth that the sarcasm was stupid and weak and had probably shot straight over Murrough's head. She'd long ago lost patience with the man, and tied as they were by blood, she had nothing to say to him. Nothing at all.

Murrough, for all his size and strength, had a dim look about him, not unlike his father, Donal. Clearly he bore as little affection for his mother as she for him, and did not bother even to answer her question. Instead he looked to his brother. "I've brought with me twenty-two strong oarsmen."

"Good," said Tibbot. "Bring them aboard and settle them. We're off when the loading's done."

Murrough turned and walked away without another word.

"Where are you headed then?" said Grace, resigned.

"Up round Erris Head to Sligo Harbor. Clifford's marching through the Curlew Hills to Collooney. When they've taken the castle back, we'll meet him at Sligo."

"You be safe now, you hear me?"

"I will be safe."

Grace could feel her mouth twist with peevishness. "I'd wish you well, son, but 'twould be a false wish."

He accepted that with a sanguine expression. "God speed, Mam."

They embraced stiffly, but as she pulled away Grace could feel Tibbot clinging to her for the briefest moment, just as he had as a little boy, and a sob caught in her throat. She turned and strode across the boards, quickly taking herself down the planks and well away before anyone might see that her face was wet with tears.

THE CURLEW HILLS lay before the Governor of Connaught, green and inviting, the late afternoon light shimmering with the promise of an easy passage and a decisive victory at Collooney. *The English need a clear victory in this war,* thought Conyers Clifford. Things had gone badly in Munster for Essex. The Yellow Ford and the debacle with Harrington in the Wicklow Mountains had all but ruined the army's morale. And O'Donnell's besiegement of Collooney, the last remaining castle guarding passage from Ulster into Connaught, had been a desperate blow. Winning it back, therefore, would make all the difference. He was pleased with the province's increasing affection for him. Normally ungenerous toward their English governors, the people of Connaught had gone so far as to dub his bare escape from Red Hugh's forces at Ballyshannon "the Battle of the Heroes."

Now the same Irish bard who'd provided Clifford with the intelligence that had saved his and his army's lives and reputation in that fight had sworn to him that except for the Collooney castle and its environs, the mountains on the way there were free from Red Hugh's rebel forces—at least in any great numbers. His large, well-trained army snaked out behind him at the bottom of the hills. There was the vanguard and main body, and the rearguard, a fierce troop of John Mac-Sweeny's Gallowglass, and behind that a caravan of carts and wagons filled with enough arms and supplies to last them on their trek through Connaught till they could rendezvous with Tibbot Burke at Sligo. He would need those supplies, as well as the tools Tibbot was bringing to help him rebuild Sligo Castle, which was all but ruined.

Clifford's vanguard commander, Alex Radcliff, had lately voiced his worries at relying for such a vital resupplying on a notorious Irish pirate. Clifford had assured him of Tibbot's loyalty. "He showed his true colors at Ballyshannon, arriving with supplies and several field pieces. He'll be waiting at Sligo as promised. I'm sure of it."

"Even," Radcliff had insisted, "if it appears the battle is favoring O'Donnell? Surely Red Hugh will know Burke is lying at anchor in Sligo Harbor. Will he not attempt to lure a fellow Irishman to their common cause?"

"Anything is possible," Clifford had relented, not wishing to continue such an irritating argument. "Anything except our losing Collooney Castle."

Now Radcliff was riding up to join Clifford at the foot of the pass.

"Are your men ready?" asked the governor.

"No, my lord," said Radcliff. "They're tired and hungry. They request we camp here tonight and begin with fresh heads and bodies in the morning."

Clifford was momentarily speechless, taken by surprise at the request. "I thought we'd at least put the hills behind us before dark. 'Tis not far, and it will be cool with the sun falling behind the mountains. The enemy is weak here. 'Twill be a walk in the garden. Tell the men there'll be plenty of beef and double rations of wine when we make camp. That will please them."

"Perhaps you should tell them yourself, sir. Many of them are grumbling."

Clifford smiled his dazzling smile, one he was well aware charmed men as handily as women, then wheeled his horse about with a flourish. "I shall have a word with the troops. Meanwhile, Radcliff, you may prepare for the ascent."

"Yes, my lord."

With that Conyers Clifford rode back to his grumbling army, puffed with confident anticipation and determined that tomorrow's action at Collooney would prove a small but glorious victory in Elizabeth's Irish war.

※⋘⋙※

THE GOOD CHEER manufactured by their cheerful commander had worn thin by the time the vanguard had trekked two miles up the Curlew Pass. Stomachs rumbled. Feet ached. The prospect of cooked meat and double rations of wine seemed very far off indeed. At least there was still light on the peaceful road. And the moisture rising from the bog to the left of them, and the shadows from the fringe of tall trees to the right of them were somehow refreshing.

The pop of small arms firing, therefore, took the vanguard quite by surprise. Here and there in the column men fell, wounded and dead in their places. The fire came from the fringe of trees, and in moments, with Radcliff racing along the line shouting his orders, the men had taken what cover they could by the roadside and begun their barrage. What "weak enemy" was this? they wondered angrily. How could Clifford have led them—tired and hungry—into an ambush of rebels armed with guns?

One hour and a half later, the vanguard's powder and shot were altogether spent, and the Irish barrage continued strong and unabated. Dozens of Crown soldiers lay dead or wounded. Suddenly unable to return fire, the musketeers looked desperately to their leader for orders. They spotted him rushing headlong at the front of a small force of pikemen into a hopeless fray. They watched in horror as he was shot dead off his horse and fell to the ground, to be trampled underfoot. The sight, stunning and terrifying, served as an unspoken signal, and all at once the men were on their feet and running pell-mell down the green Curlew Pass, back the way they'd come.

But when the vanguard collided with the main body of soldiers, they found it was, itself, writhing in full panic. Together the two companies broke and ran, a mindless mob, overwhelming the rearguard, who followed in chaotic and cowardly retreat.

---

CONYERS CLIFFORD COULD scarce believe his eyes—the whole of his army was thundering out of the Curlew Pass like a herd of stampeding cattle! *It could not end this way. No! He'd regroup them. head a small but courageous force to victory. MacSweeny would back him . . . the rebel could not be so strong . . . hadn't the bard said . . . ?* Men were running, ignoring his shouts to return to formation. *Would no one fight? No one?* The ribbon of road weaving into the hills ahead was all but deserted. *He must do something, anything . . . Where was MacSweeny? Where was Radcliff? . . . Ride alone if I must . . . The shame of it,* he silently cried, *Oh, sweet Jesus, the shame of it.*

---

IT DEPRESSED TIBBOT to see Sligo Castle in ruins. Standing on the portside of the *Granuaile*, gazing at the battered stone walls through his spyglass, he thought how strange it was to be at better ease with English occupation than Irish. They were not just *any* Irishmen controlling the castle, he argued with himself, but men bound to his sworn enemy. Red Hugh had invaded his home and torched the best part of Connaught. He'd stolen the MacWilliamship and thrown Tibbot in jail. But worse, he had disrespected him. Ignored him. That was intolerable. Unforgivable.

And then there was the true friendship he'd found with Conyers Clifford. Here was a man who understood Tibbot's place in Irish politics.

Honored him. Fought for him in the highest places—the Irish Privy Council, even with the Lord Lieutenant of Ireland. And Miles was receiving the finest education a man could desire for his son.

Tibbot had begun to worry about Clifford yesterday evening. He should have sent word by yesterday morning at the latest. So large an army as he led would have had no trouble lifting the siege at Collooney. Perhaps Red Hugh had learned of the attack and fortified his rebels at the castle. Tibbot had heard talk that O'Donnell had lately received the submission of Brian O'Rourke, a man known for his viciousness, in war and out of it. If they had joined forces, northern Connaught had just become a more dangerous place.

In any event, Tibbot felt stupid and helpless waiting like this, his fleet bobbing on the swells of Sligo Harbor like so many bloody corks. Sure the supplies he carried were vital to Clifford and his army, but Tibbot longed to meet O'Donnell face-to-face. He often pictured himself, his hands round Red Hugh's neck, choking the life from him, his eyes bulging, his face turning the same color as his curly red hair. He smiled at the thought.

"There's a boat comin', Tibbot." It was his brother Murrough, who'd just now come to his side.

"Where?"

"Look starboard."

Tibbot turned his spyglass and found a small, rowed vessel making its way from the southeast. A party of ten—no, twelve—was aboard.

"Is it your man?"

"No, Murrough, 'twould not be Clifford himself." Tibbot found he was often annoyed with his dull-witted brother. He was a mighty warrior, but much of the time Murrough needed talking to as if he were a child. " 'Twould be a messenger," Tibbot explained. "But why would he send a party of men when *one* would do?" Tibbot was straining to bring the boat and its passengers into focus. The men were too far away to be recognized, and the queen's army wore no identifying uniforms. Tibbot's heart was suddenly pounding in his chest. Something was awry. He could feel it.

The boat was moving toward them at a rapid clip, for the tide was with them.

"They be carryin' some crates and a barrel," said Murrough. "Whoever it is, they look to be intent on revictualizing *us*." He laughed as if he'd made a clever jest.

A moment later Tibbot could see their faces. "Damn!" He turned to his brother, unable to hide his desperation. "It's Red Hugh."

"Whoa! What's he doin' here?"

Tibbot's mind was racing, like a fire in a cornfield, spreading in all directions at once.

"We could kill him," Murrough offered. "There's only twelve of 'em."

"No. We'll hear what he has to say."

"I thought you wanted him dead."

"Shut up, Murrough. I have to think." *By what supreme arrogance did Red Hugh O'Donnell dare to come asking to board his vessel? What had happened?* he wondered. *What could have happened?*

It was not long before the boat came alongside. A rope ladder was lowered, and preceded by the wolfish Brian O'Rourke and five huge Gallowglass guards, Red Hugh climbed aboard. He was all swagger and smiles, as though he knew how dashing a figure he cut with his broad shoulders and the sun gleaming off his fiery hair. The rest of his men came aboard, Brian O'Rourke at his right hand and the others surrounding him on three sides. Tibbot, with Murrough at his back, moved to face O'Donnell.

"Good afternoon, Tibbot. Fine day it is."

"I have to tell you I'm in no mood for fruitless chatter, Hugh. What is it you want?"

"Well, first of all I'd like permission to bring aboard some gifts. I've food—beautiful French cheese and a barrel of good wine. May I, Captain?" he said with more than necessary deference.

Tibbot strove for calm and clarity. He nodded his permission and watched as the winched net carried the crate and barrel and cloth-covered crocks up to the deck. "Can we have some privacy?" said Hugh, still demonstrating the greatest courtesy.

While suspicious, Tibbot could sense no immediate danger. "Come on then," he said, and led Red Hugh and Brian O'Rourke below, to his cabin. One crate, the wine and a crock of cheese, was delivered inside. Murrough was the last in and stood like a sentry at the door. Tibbot could see feral scowls passing between his brother and O'Rourke, guardians of their respective chieftains.

"All right then, Hugh. You have your privacy," said Tibbot. Neither he nor O'Donnell had taken seats at the table, just stood, hands on their chair backs. "Now tell me why you're here with your false smiles and your unwanted gifts."

"Tibbot," Red Hugh said gently and put out a supplicating hand. "I know you'd like to kill me where I stand, but for the love of God, man, we should be fighting on the same side!"

Tibbot bristled, but his indignation was nonetheless tempered by the whole truth of what O'Donnell was saying. *He was Grace O'Malley's son and he was serving the bloody English invaders. Surely that was wrong.* Then, unbidden, a vision of the foul prison in Ulster and his offhanded release into the December blizzard stung him, and he felt bitterness rising like bile in his throat.

"I don't need your wine and your French cheese, Hugh. Just tell me what's happened, for I know something has, or you'd not be coming here to curry my favor."

O'Donnell withdrew his hand, and his friendly expression hardened into something more sinister. "I do have news, as a matter of fact. Collooney Castle is still in my possession."

Tibbot held his own expression steady, not wishing to advertise his alarm.

"I've also received the submission of your kinsmen, O'Connor and Donal Sligo."

It was becoming difficult for Tibbot to retain any semblance of calm. "I don't believe that," he said. "They're altogether loyal to the Crown."

"I admit, 'twas a reluctant submission, but nonetheless, they've committed to O'Neill and me for the moment."

Dread was growing inside Tibbot's head. "How did this submission come about?" he said.

"Well, you see, Governor Clifford was on his way with a large army to lift the siege at Collooney . . . but of course *you* know that, Tibbot." He smiled almost pleasantly. "I sent Brian there—you know, Brian O'Rourke—with oh, say, two hundred men, and they met up with Clifford and his miserable army of English cowards in the Curlew Pass, and as they were running away, he slaughtered them. Didn't you, Brian?"

"Aye," he said, snarling. "Those we didn't kill took shelter in the abbey of Boyle. They're still there, lickin' their wounds."

"So of course the English never arrived at Collooney to lift the siege, and that's how we convinced O'Connor Sligo that he should fight on our side."

Tibbot was trembling with the shock of the news. *Could it be true?*

"I just don't know what it will take to prove to the English that we're not giving Ireland up to them." Hugh's tone was still mild. "It's them that will straggle home in defeat, not us."

Tibbot finally found his voice. "What of Conyers Clifford? Where is he now?"

"Your friend the governor?" Hugh signaled to O'Rourke and the henchman hefted the cheese crock onto the table between them. "Why, he's right here!" Hugh whipped the oilcloth cover from the tub.

It took the barest moment for Tibbot to recognize Conyers Clifford's head within it, his fair curls clotted with gore, the glazed eyes open and staring into Hell. A groan escaped Tibbot's mouth and he clutched the back of his chair to steady his shaking knees. *He must hold firm, push down the wave of nausea threatening to shame him in front of his enemy.*

Red Hugh was altogether at his ease. He sat down at the table then, ignoring the ghastly artifact before him. "Come then," he said, paying no attention to Tibbot's outrage, "we'll drink to Ireland's victory over England," as though it were the most natural thing in the world. He signaled again to Brian O'Rouke, who began pounding a spigot into the wine barrel, then turned back to his childhood friend, who was silent and still, clearly fighting to regain his composure. O'Donnell raised his eyebrows in mock surprise. "Will you not drink with me?"

Tibbot's mind was like a ship floundering in a sudden squall, his thoughts like fearsome waves crashing in upon it from every direction.

"Will you not drink with me?" Hugh demanded. *"For Ireland?"* Now the words were a clear threat.

"We'll drink with you!"

Tibbot was wrenched from the grip of paralysis by the sound of his brother's voice. He turned to see Murrough wearing a satisfied look on his stupid face. What had possessed him to speak with such authority on Tibbot's ship? But the damage—with those four words uttered—had irrevocably been done. *"We'll drink with you."* He could not very well refuse Red Hugh now. The resignation must have been all too apparent on Tibbot's face.

"Good, good! Pour the wine, Brian. Sit down, Tibbot." Hugh lifted the loathsome crock from the table and without a second thought placed it behind him on the floor. "Come, we need to talk about your cargo. I've thought of taking it from you, using it myself. But perhaps 'twould be best if you hauled it back to Galway. Let the English think you're still loyal to them."

Slowly Tibbot took his seat, but he found he could not draw his eyes away from his friend's severed head in the crock.

Red Hugh noticed. "Don't worry, Tibbot," he said, "we'll make good use of it."

"Aye," cried Brian O'Rourke, "target practice!" He and Murrough roared with laughter.

Red Hugh O'Donnell smiled and Tibbot thought with a chill that 'twas the smile of the Devil himself. And the Devil had come to his table with a bargain to be signed in Conyers Clifford's blood.

# 17

WHILST ESSEX FELT nothing but a spot of cold wetness on his back, he nevertheless cringed as his physician placed another of the loathsome brown worms to his skin. He tried not to envision a dozen of the slippery creatures now sucking the malarial poisons from his body, only the hoped for results—good health—a state he had not enjoyed for far too long now. If the leeches proved ineffective, he mused, this last resort might indeed be his last resort *ever*. 'Twas not inconceivable that he might die of malaria, as his stepfather Leicester had done. It would, he realized with a stab of macabre irony, prevent his enduring the slow, agonizing descent into syphilitic madness.

The physician leaned down and spoke into Essex's ear. "Sir Christopher asked me to let you know when ten o'clock had arrived. 'Tis just that hour now."

"Good. An excuse to have you remove these hideous suckers from my back."

"It will take only a moment, my lord."

The physician was as good as his word and moments later was helping Essex on with his shirt and doublet. "A bleeding this afternoon, my lord?"

"I don't think I could bear it."

"Very good. But I must insist on the leeches again tomorrow morning. They seem to be doing you good."

*What is doing me good*, Essex thought but did not say, *is the absence of the death and mayhem and suffering placed before my eyes every day.*

As Essex descended the stairs down to Dublin Castle's Irish Privy Council Chamber, he was joined by Southampton and Christopher Blount, both looking rather puffed up with self-importance. Essex had insisted that his two closest advisers must be present at today's war council, a meeting that would, by its timeliness and content, determine his fate, and perhaps the outcome of Elizabeth's war.

The councilors were all assembled when the trio arrived and took their seats, Southampton and Blount at the Lord Lieutenant's right and left hands. Essex was firmly set to state his case with such strength and clarity that these doddering old fools would have no choice but to accede to his wishes. He was equally determined that he would indulge in no whining or complaining, though he believed he had good cause to do so. For every letter he had received recently from Elizabeth was filled with stinging rebukes and alarming news from London. The queen complained that she was giving her Lord Lieutenant a thousand pounds a day "to go on Summer Progress." His enemies at Court were likewise delivering wound after wound, and in every way attempting to discredit and dishonor him. There were many cruel jests made at his expense. "Men marvel," ranted one Court gossip, "at how little Essex does, preferring instead to tarry in Dublin." And the unkindest cut—Francis Bacon had turned on him. Asked by the queen for his opinion of her new Irish Viceroy, Francis had warned her that placing arms and power into Essex's hands was too great a temptation, one that made him "cumbersome and unruly." *Cumbersome and unruly!* Surely Bacon had never been his friend, only pretended to be. By now Essex's reputation was in tatters.

He'd written back, beseeching Elizabeth in the most dignified terms he could muster. "How," he had asked her, "can you expect a difficult war to be successfully managed by so disgraced a minister?" All it would take, he knew, was a kind or encouraging word from the queen lauding his efforts in Ireland for the ignominious slanders to be silenced. But all he had received were diatribes against his waste and procrastination. Finally came a curt response to his third, almost begging request for two thousand reinforcements. She would send them—reluctantly—but only if he promised to use them in the north for a quick defeat of Tyrone. It was with this bit of news that he now opened the war council.

"Her Majesty has finally seen fit to grant me my reinforcements," Essex announced, "but our problems are far from over. The victuals she lately sent us are so unsavory that they would poison the soldiers who ate them. Here in Ireland the rebel is as strong as he has ever been. My intelligence informs me that Tyrone has lately had delivered to him by Grace O'Malley a large supply of arms from Spain."

There was worried murmuring amongst the Council at that report. "And as I'm sure you are all aware," Essex went on, "we have suffered a catastrophic loss in the Curlew Mountains of Connaught. Nearly half of our troops were injured or killed during a chaotic retreat, having been set upon by"—Essex found it difficult to say—"just two hundred rebels." He struggled for composure as he continued. "Lord Clifford's body was decently buried at Lough Ce, but his head, I am afraid, has not yet been recovered."

"They are wicked devils," said Archbishop Loftus.

"He was a good man. Terrible loss," Carey muttered, "terrible."

"When Red Hugh O'Donnell finally breached Collooney's walls and took the castle," Essex continued, "he forced O'Connor and Donal Sligo's submissions. This last is not so dire a piece of news as it seems, for we altogether trust these Irish allies and believe they will return to the English fold at the first possible opportunity."

"What of Tibbot Burke?" Loftus inquired of Essex.

"There are conflicting reports, my lord. We know on the one hand that he did meet with Red Hugh on his flagship after the battle in the Curlew Pass." Essex could not hide his sarcastic tone. "They finished off a barrel of wine together. On the other hand, Tibbot Burke returned all his vessels to our men at Galway with their cargoes intact."

Southampton spoke up. "They may have conspired to make it appear that Burke kept faith with the Crown, for their own purposes."

"That is possible," Essex agreed, "but only time will tell of Tibbot

Burke's true colors. But here is the point. I and my army must leave for the north immediately. Even with the reinforcements sent, my dearly reduced troops will only number five thousand foot and three hundred horse. We cannot possibly adventure as far as the northern coast and Lough Foyle. Establishing a garrison there this year is out of the question. So we must take what we have, march as far north as we can, and do as much damage to the rebel as God will allow." Essex hesitated and tried his best to sound deliberate. "As for Tyrone, we will destroy him." He looked about the Council table and saw only two sympathetic faces, Southampton's and Blount's. All else were blank stares and silence. "What am I seeing here?" he finally demanded. "Surely at this late date this is not *reluctance*?"

"I'm afraid it is, my lord Essex." This was Nicholas White speaking with eyes lowered.

"But how can you deny a northern campaign when the queen so clearly demands it!" Essex cried.

"Her Majesty must be made to understand that our concerns still outweigh her desires," Archbishop Loftus continued for White. "Our army is plagued by deserters who run back to England, and others who join with the enemy. Still others hide in the country and pretend sickness. Of those men who are strong and serviceable, we can count only four thousand at the most. That number is easily outmatched, perhaps *doubled*, by Tyrone's forces in Ulster. Our cavalry will have difficulty serving our foot, and further, revictualizing such an army will prove nightmarish."

Essex found himself reeling at Loftus's words. The pall of weakness and confusion that had troubled him in the Azores was again threatening his logic, undermining his temper. He was loath to speak, terrified his words would betray his condition.

Southampton, blessedly aware, piped up. "I believe the Lord Lieutenant sees more clearly into Her Majesty's mind than anyone here at this table, and Her Majesty's mind *is made up*. Am I correct in that, my lord?" He turned to Essex with a disingenuous smile.

"You are indeed," he uttered with all the strength and calm he could muster. "If I may read from the queen's last letter to me . . ." Essex removed a folded parchment from a pouch at his waist and scanned the page for the passage he sought.

If sickness of the army be the reason why action is not undertaken, why was there not action when the army was in better state? If winter is now approaching, why were the summer months of July and August lost? If the spring was too soon and the summer otherwise spent, if the harvest time was so neglected that nothing was done, then surely we must conclude that none of the four quarters of the year will be in season for you and your Council to agree on Tyrone's persecution—the whole reason for your expedition!

There were angry mutterings all round.

Christopher Blount silenced them all by saying, "I presume you would not like it said, my lords, that the Irish Privy Council was weak and cowardly, that they feared to confront the most fearsome of the Irish rebels, preferring inaction instead, would you?"

Loftus pounded the table with his fist. "That will never be said of us!"

"Then 'tis agreed!" Blount shouted decisively, daring them all to dispute him, upstart that he was. None did.

"Very well," said Essex, pushing back his chair, "I expect your preparedness reports by week's end." In the next moment and in perfect synchrony, Southampton and Blount moved together with such subtle force on either side of Essex that no one was aware that they had, in fact, lifted their disabled friend from his chair. The triumvirate stood thus as the councilors shuffled from the room, not bothering to whisper their angry oaths at their having been outsmarted.

When the three were finally alone, Christopher Blount closed the door and Essex, sick and alarmingly pale, collapsed back in his chair, burying his face in his hands. "What have we done?" he said. "Nothing Loftus said about this army is untrue. They are unfit for the march north and horribly outnumbered."

"You're obeying the queen's command," Southampton insisted. "We have no choice. There is nothing else to be done."

"Nothing?" Essex whispered hoarsely.

"No, my lord."

"Then I fear we are doomed, my friends," Essex said with gravity. "Altogether doomed."

*Elizabeth,*

*Even now I am putting my foot into the stirrup to rendezvous with Tyrone. From a mind delighting in sorrow; from a heart torn in pieces with passion; from a man that hates himself and all things that keep him alive, what service can Your Majesty reap? It is clear that my services past deserve no more than banishment and proscription into this most cursed of countries. So whilst it seems I cannot please you in life, perhaps my death in the service of Ireland will bring you some pleasure.*

*From your Majesty's exiled, but ever faithful servant,*
*Essex*

# 18

THERE WERE TIMES on the march north into Ulster that the feelings of dread that had held Essex like a vise let go their grip of him. His physical ills receded and a vital force flowed through his organs and limbs. They were the moments, he realized, that he had put away all thoughts of battle, administration, command, victory, and the queen. He would leave the officers' mess, make himself scarce even from Southampton and Blount, and place himself, very simply, amongst his men.

He might walk alongside his foot soldiers, shocking himself at his strength for trekking mile upon mile on the rough, rock-strewn roads. Even more, he delighted in riding with the cavalry, exchanging notes on their animals—the health and husbandry of their mounts in wartime conditions, stories of a favorite childhood horse, martial exploits in foreign lands. At first the soldiers were stiff and formal, mistrusting the familiarity of so high a nobleman, but his honest interest and natural charm soon purchased their confidence, and before long there was easy conversation, bawdy storytelling and laughter. Talk of home and family, sweethearts, the farm suffering without its farmer—he, called to arms in the queen's service, marching now to war in a strange land. Such talk and manly camaraderie soothed Essex, caused him for that time, at least, to forget his ills, forget even who he was. Soon there were changes to be seen in Essex's army. The pace and progress of the column quickened.

Soldiers walked with a lighter step. Less grumbling was heard. Men smiled.

Essex remembered, with a touch of pique, Francis Bacon's admonition—that the great generals cared little for popularity amongst their subordinates, were satisfied with a lonely existence. That was nonsense! Soldiers performed better for a commander they loved. And for the first time in his long career, Essex knew he loved the men who served him. What did Francis Bacon know of such things? He was effete. Bookish. Lost in an endless labyrinth of politics and philosophies.

Christopher Blount had chided Essex, and even Southampton questioned his fraternization with the "common stock."

"Let me be!" Essex had finally shouted at their persistent nagging.

"I swear the Irish faeries have taken possession of your mind!" Southampton cried back, throwing up his hands.

"Perhaps," Essex agreed, "I am a better man for it."

"God's blood, Essex!" Christopher Blount was the more aggravated of his two friends. "A soldier will bleed and die just as quickly if he loves his commander or loathes him. In the meanwhile, your officers are losing all respect for you."

"Bugger them," Essex replied.

"You don't mean that," Southampton said. "These are men from the noblest families, gentlemen who begged to fight under your command. You owe them your best."

"Yes I do," said Essex, finally relenting. "They suffer this war as keenly as the lowest privates do."

Blount squealed with frustration. "The pox has eaten away your brain, Robert."

Essex drained his glass. "I've noticed that," he said with a good-natured grin. "Let me have my fun, Christopher. I enjoy these men. I've enjoyed this dreadful march. Christ knows it could be my last engagement."

"Spare us, Essex," Southampton said. "Leave the high drama to Shakespeare. You will outlive us all."

Essex smiled indulgently and, cheered by his friends' concern, slept that night like a well man, long and deep, suffering neither sweats nor chills nor night terrors. But on waking the next morning, August third, a dreadful, prescient pall descended over him, as dark as the black hood pulled over a man's head before hanging.

Riding before the vanguard and quite alone—his premonition demanding quiet and solitude—Essex had marched the army to a few miles south of Dundalk where the River Lagan flowed through some low hills. It was therefore with no surprise, though no less horror, that he laid eyes for the first time on Tyrone's rebel army.

It was vast beyond even Essex's worst nightmares. By his count there were ten thousand foot and one thousand horse—together, more than doubling the numbers of the English army. His own troops—for all their recent improvements—were still, many of them, ill with dysentery and other divers distempers. Here before him stood a home-grown force of soldiers, fresh in body and roused to a fine fever of loyalty behind their new, courageous, and hitherto triumphal Irish king. The O'Neill had made them promises of victory over the English, and had *given* them promised victories—the Yellow Ford, the Wicklow Mountains, the Curlew Pass. And now he had delivered to their feet a puny and diseased enemy commanded by a broken and dangerously uncertain leader.

That which spread out before Essex in the valley in the shape of a great army was, in fact, the dreaded doom that had plagued his dreams and now informed his bleak future. And Hugh O'Neill, the Earl of Tyrone, was the Black Prince himself.

Southampton and Christopher Blount came riding abreast of Essex. Blount's horse reared up in surprise, mirroring his rider's own. The men gazed down at the boggling sight below, their always peppery banter silenced with one glimpse of the enemy.

"Leave me," Essex whispered.

Blount and Southampton exchanged a dubious glance.

Southampton spoke. "You must allow us to—"

"What, advise me?" said Essex with the utmost calm. He closed his eyes and rubbed the space between his brows. "I am beyond advice, I'm afraid. I do wish to be alone."

"May we send your physician, at least?" Blount offered.

Essex managed a weak laugh. "So you think I'll be in need of my physician?"

"The strain, the awful decisions . . . you cannot afford a relapse now," Southampton insisted.

"I am beyond doctoring, my friend."

"Robert . . ."

*"Leave me."*

Most reluctantly, Blount and Southampton wheeled about and rode back the way they'd come. Robert Devereaux found himself gazing benignly at the scene below and he wondered at his sudden calm. Such an army would surely dismember his own. Thousands would die. All that English blood soaking the Irish soil . . . Surely God and his angels were laughing at him. *Punishment*, he thought, *for a multitude of sins.*

Essex turned his horse and rode slowly past the long column of his soldiers. Those who could see the rebel army below—farmboys, towns-men, soldiers with whom he had marched, broken bread—looked to him with pleading eyes. As he trotted past them attempting to quell his rising panic, he could feel the rumble in his watery gut, feel the familiar sick heat rising in his veins, the draining of strength from his limbs.

Was this inevitable defeat his reward for so long and glorious a career? he wondered. Would his bodily weakness prevail in the next days of trial? Or perhaps death would be so kind as to snatch him from the midst of the coming catastrophe, this unbearable disgrace. But no. There were the men to consider—thousands of Englishmen under his watch. There was greatness still pounding like a heartbeat within him. A battle to be fought, and by the grace of God and His angels, won. He could not fail. *He would not fail.*

"Make camp," he said, signaling with a flick of his hand to his com-pany officers, "and raise my tent." *The temple*, he thought with equal parts hope and dread, *the temple of my final inspiration.*

BUT THE DISEASE HAD, in the end, seized Essex and shaken him like a rag doll, though in the past days there'd been moments of clarity. He'd paraded his troops in a St. Andrew's cross before Tyrone's huge rebel force, the English cavalry proudly prancing at the cross's flanks and rear, hoping that Tyrone might attack him on open ground.

That attack never came. There'd been a moment of sheer folly. He'd requested that Tyrone meet him alone on the field, that they should fight for the outcome of the whole war, two men with swords and shields. Tyrone, old enough to be Essex's father, declined more politely than Essex's lunatic request demanded. The rebel army steadfastly held their ground, refused to be drawn into battle, a maddening and embarrassing kindness that, as every day passed, caused Essex to fall more and more violently ill. He refused the physician, he refused the company of his friends. He brooded alone, suffering his fevers and chills and blinding headaches as a sinner his penance.

This day, Tyrone's messenger had come to request a parlay on the morrow between the two earls, prelude to the battle. Essex scribbled his assent, then collapsed on his cot in a deep swoon.

In his tent the night was filled with phantoms, bloody visions: *Leicester, a rotten corpse in his splendor at Elizabeth's Court; Philip Sidney dying of a festering gangrene in Zutphen. His mother appeared. She was beautiful—as she had looked in his youth—lush lips, pearly skin, blue-violet eyes. They'd not been kind eyes, however, but sharp and accusing. And Elizabeth had hovered about him, a foul, witchlike apparition with bony fingers that had caused him to cry out for help.*

"It's all right," he heard a woman say. The voice was soothing and the vision that accompanied it likewise reassuring—*Grace O'Malley's weathered face, old and unpainted but pleasing nevertheless.* He smiled to think he had conjured up the woman.

"*That's better,*" she crooned. Then the apparition of Grace O'Malley did something peculiar. She placed a cool, wet rag on Essex's forehead and gently took up his hand in hers.

"Are you real?" he whispered.

"I suppose I am," she said. "As real as anything can be."

"How did you . . . ?"

"I told them I'd been sent by the Earl of Tyrone with a message. Your servant remembered me from Limerick. You must have told him of our adventures. I doubt he saw an old lady as much of a threat. Can you sit up?"

"I don't know."

"Well, I'll help you then. We've some talkin' to do."

"Talking? Grace, I stand across the battlefield from England's gravest enemy, the 'Father of the Irish Rebellion,' and you . . . my God, you are its mother!"

Grace snaked an arm behind Essex's back and propped him against two pillows.

"You're wrong when you say that, Robert. The Irish revolt was birthed without my help. If anything, I'm its wet nurse, for I admit to giving succor to the war. Men, food, guns—necessary as mother's milk."

"Why have you come? Tyrone hasn't really sent you."

"No. I lately brought his soldiers Spanish arms. But Hugh O'Neill has no idea that I'm here with you. He thinks I've sailed back to Connaught, and I will do as much when I'm done here."

"'Done here.' That sounds menacing."

Grace chuckled. "I haven't come to murder you in your bed, if that's what you think." She grew silent and Essex, his mind gratefully clearing, searched her face for answers. "You're outnumbered, son," she finally said. "I don't have to tell you that. 'Twill be a horrible slaughter if you march out on that field to fight. Another bloodbath on Irish ground." She looked away, as if trying to remove the image from her mind. "You will lose, but many of us will die as well."

"I haven't a choice," Essex replied. "I've promised Elizabeth. She's given me everything I asked to wage this war. Now she demands action."

"Oh, she does, does she?" Grace did not attempt to hide her scorn.

Essex regarded the old woman with puzzlement. "She is the queen," he said. "She has a right to demand it."

"A *right?* Oh, you mean the 'Divine Right' given by God to all the monarchs of the world. Of course, I forgot. The queen of bloody England has the God-given right to march thousands of men to their deaths on a bright summer morning. She has the right to send her minions to a country, not her own, to pillage and burn and rape. To murder our gods and rip the living soul from the land."

Essex was staring at the woman mouthing blasphemy.

"I know who you are, Robert. You're spawn of a murderous man who thought nothing of bashing out the brains of infants against trees on Rathlin Island. You're the fine lackey of a queen whose father whacked off the heads of two of his wives. And Elizabeth in her old age is no longer averse to killing when it suits her needs. Killing to feed her pride. Killing . . . because she can!"

Essex opened his mouth to object, but no words came.

"You can say no to this battle, Robert. Don't look at me like I've grown a horn between my eyes. *You can say no!*"

"How can I? 'Tis the largest army the queen in her whole reign has ever assembled. She *must* have Tyrone's submission. She will not die till she rules Ireland!"

Grace laughed. "Then pity poor England with Methuselah's mother on the throne. Listen to me, son. I see through you. You're in great suffering, Robert, and that suffering has changed you. You *feel* what others feel—their joy, their hunger, their pain. You feel Ireland's misery as keenly as you do your own. It is a strange and terrible thing to say, but there's more human feeling in you than there is in my own son, a son of Ireland. Jesus, poor Tibbot! He's been ripped and torn from this side to that, tortured into an undreamed-of state of confusion. He's a man without a country, and sometimes, I fear, without a soul."

"Grace—"

"No, let me finish. You don't want to go out there tomorrow and fight. I can see it in your face. You don't want the blood of those poor young men on your hands. You *know* the right thing to do as well as you know your own name." She gazed at him, her eyes softening. "Ah, Robert, the world has lately been hard on you."

Essex felt his chin quiver and tears sting his eyes.

Grace reached out and pushed the damp hair off his brow. "'Tis a load that no man should be asked to carry."

"What would you have me do?" he said in a barely audible whisper.

"I don't quite know, but Hugh O'Neill is a reasonable man. If you go out on that field and fight tomorrow, he'll take you down, I can promise you that. But if you talk to him, *just talk*, perhaps he can find a way to forego the bloodshed. Save the lives of your young men."

Essex was silent, thoughtful.

"Your fever's gone," said Grace. "Do you think you can sleep?"

"Sleep?" Essex laughed ruefully. "I may never sleep again."

Grace leaned down and kissed his brow. "You're a sweet man, Robert

Devereaux. May God direct you and Jesus protect you." She rose and, wrapping her shawl about her shoulders, crossed to the tent's door and in the next moment disappeared.

Essex lay as still as stone, hardly daring to breathe. On the eve of the war's most decisive battle, he'd prayed for inspiration, and instead had listened to treason from the mouth of a notorious Irish traitor. He had neither sought to silence her nor even argue. He had accepted the touch of her cool fingers and the comfort of her sympathy. He was no better than a traitor himself.

Essex blinked back his suddenly heavy lids and realized with surprise that he was weary and could, perchance, sleep. He laid himself back down and with a bemused smile pulled the coverlet over his shoulders and closed his eyes.

Slumber took him a moment later, and his dreams when they came in the wee morning hours were as sweet and fine as an Irish faerie's wing.

⬖⬖⬖⬖⬖

THE MORNING SUN glinting off the River Lagan was beautiful but blinding. Southampton, with Blount, had ridden with Essex to a hill that rose above the river's south edge, looking down upon Bellaclynth Ford. Essex appeared hypnotized, Southampton observed, staring unblinkingly at the scene below. 'Twas the glittering water, perhaps. Robert always claimed the sight of a river calmed his soul.

But that was not it. His friend had seemed altogether calm when Southampton fetched him from his tent earlier that morning, more easy and self-possessed than he had recently seen him—perhaps *ever* seen him. And more relaxed than he had a right to be. It made no sense. Essex faced the greatest crisis of his military career this day. He'd been very ill and his army was horribly outnumbered by the Irish. And after the inevitable battle, many—if not most of his men—would be dead. Even now the arch rebel Tyrone, astride a magnificent black stallion, was making his way down to the river from the opposite hillside. It suddenly struck Southampton that Tyrone was descending the narrow track alone, his aides remaining above, watching his progress.

Christopher Blount gave voice to Southampton's thought. "Why are his men not following?"

"'Tis odd," Southampton agreed. "Robert, shall we go to meet him now?"

"Wait," said Essex. They watched curiously as Tyrone approached the river's edge and urged his horse into the water.

"What is he doing?" Blount said, truly perplexed. "Is he crossing to us?"

"I think we should—"

"Just *wait*, Southampton," Essex sternly commanded.

By now Tyrone's horse had waded so far into the rushing water that it lapped at the beast's belly. The rebel sat tall in his saddle and waited calmly, as if his behavior were entirely natural.

"I've never seen anything like it," Blount said. "These Irish—"

"You'll stay here," Essex announced, trancelike. "I'm going down."

"What?" Southampton cried. "Robert, you cannot be serious."

"I'm altogether serious. O'Neill has made his wishes known and I shall honor them."

*O'Neill?* thought Southampton. Robert had called Tyrone by his Irish name. What had gotten into him? "Essex." He grabbed for his friend's arm. "You cannot meet this man unaccompanied. You know what they're saying about you in London. Everyone is suspicious of you as it is. At best, a private conversation with Tyrone would be thought foolish. At worse, treasonous."

"He is a reasonable man," said Essex, releasing himself from Southampton's grip.

"Reasonable!" cried Blount, exasperated.

But Essex's mount was already traversing down the hillside, leaving his men behind.

"He's gone mad," said Blount.

Southampton stared, confounded, and realized with a sharp stab of grief how completely he agreed with Christopher's assessment of their dear friend.

Robert Devereaux, Earl of Essex, had finally lost his mind.

⁂

H E HAD NEVER KNOWN such sweet joyousness nor clarity of mind as he now felt, approaching the bank of the Bellaclynth Ford. The rushing stream crisped the air and the sunlight sparkling on its rippled surface brought a smile to his face. Even sight of O'Neill sitting high on his horse in the center of the Lagan River pleased Essex, for he saw not the Irish traitor and England's enemy, but the scene of his own Fate, a chance—perhaps the last of his life—to achieve something of true greatness.

O'Neill, even in his armor, was by no means a brawny man, but the sheer force of will that shone from his strong, handsome face enlarged him. And the patience and steely control behind his eyes would as easily inspire loyalty from his men as strike terror into the hearts of his enemies. Now, as Essex approached, reining his horse on the dry river edge, he saw O'Neill fold one gloved hand over the other, and dip his head in respect, a gesture so humble, so unexpected that Essex was forced to stifle a small cry of surprise. *A reasonable man*, Grace O'Malley had called him. *Grace O'Malley in the flesh*, he mused, continuing to take the measure of this man, *or a phantom called to him by a fever of the brain?*

Who would speak first? he wondered, and would O'Neill prove himself great or merely the "great dissembler," as he was known at the English Court?

"My lord Essex, I salute you," came the deep, gravelly voice across the water. O'Neill was working with his muscular legs to keep the horse beneath him steady in the fast-moving water.

"And I you, my lord O'Neill."

Essex saw an eyebrow arch in surprise. Respect had been met and matched with respect.

"Did you know I fought for your father in Ulster when I was a young man?" said the rebel.

"I'd heard as much."

"In those days I thought nothing of pledging my allegiance to the Crown if it behooved me."

"What has changed?"

O'Neill shifted in his saddle. "The stakes," he replied. "Back then I fought for my birthright, a title I believed had been stolen from me. I fought in revenge for the murders of my father and brother. These reasons seem petty now. Today the soul of Ireland is at stake." He paused for a moment before he said, "Once upon a time your Elizabeth was a great queen."

Essex found himself bristling at O'Neill's words. This surprised him, for they were recently his own unspoken sentiments.

"Once she possessed a clear knowledge of the world, understood what was in men's hearts," O'Neill continued. "She commanded the love of her lowest subjects and highest nobles. But she's grown cold in her heart, lost that part of her that was kind and human. She is altogether blind to the grief she causes in the world. Her greatness is eclipsed by her follies. And her greatest folly, her downfall, is Ireland."

"Elizabeth wished desperately to believe in your loyalty."

"Aye. She believed I *owed* her loyalty, that because I'd spent my blood for her, kept quiet for thirty years, that I was bound to serve her all my life. She believed that she had been generous to me. But Her Majesty never gave me anything but what belonged to me already, and often supported my enemies against me. As for what I've gotten, I got it by my own scratching of the world, and not from her goodness. It shocks her that I now have my own demands, offends her that she has been forced to listen to them." O'Neill skewered Essex with his eyes. "My lord, any battle fought here today will be little more than a massacre."

"I know that," said Essex. The next words came hard, though he had practiced them a hundred times since waking. "We shall have no fight today." *There! The words were out. Capitulation.* Then Essex saw O'Neill sag almost imperceptibly. The Irish chieftain's expression, however, remained firm and implacable.

"My I speak plainly, Essex?"

"You have done till this moment. Why do otherwise?"

O'Neill allowed himself a smile. "I have been in correspondence with the King of Scotland. James, as we all know—but are prohibited from saying aloud—is Elizabeth's successor. Your queen is very close to her end. James, when he comes to the English throne, is prepared to be far more lenient with Ireland than Elizabeth has been."

"So you are saying we have only to wait for Elizabeth to die to see peace in Ireland?"

"Perhaps not so long as that," O'Neill replied.

"How?"

"Conclude a truce here with me today."

Essex felt himself shaking. He'd been prepared to negotiate with O'Neill. Understood his own position of weakness. He had even taken pleasure in his thoughts of avoiding bloodshed. *But a truce* . . .

"Your expression tells me you're a stranger to making peace."

"I will not deny it," said Essex.

"If you loved this country as I do, Essex, if you felt the breadth and depth of its suffering, you would be more willing."

"I do feel its suffering!" Essex cried out unexpectedly, horrified to feel his eyes filling with tears. He whispered, "More than you know."

O'Neill spoke gently so that Essex was forced to strain to hear him across the rushing water. "Then you would make peace with me here, today?"

Essex hesitated for only a moment more, then nodded slowly.

O'Neill's face reddened with emotion. "Though you may find it hard to believe, my lord, there is great honor to be found in making peace. 'Tis far easier to wage war—an old habit so difficult to break. You own more courage than I ever dreamed you to have. Perhaps 'tis why our friend Grace O'Malley speaks so highly of you. So, we have decided! I see your men waiting yonder. Bring them down and I will bring mine. We'll set the terms of the truce and you can send your men to a much deserved rest, not their graves."

Essex, who had remained all this time on the dry shore across from O'Neill, now urged his horse forward into the glittering river. There was magic in the moment, he thought with a smile—*Irish magic*—and a fullness in his heart that he had never known. The two soldiers, side by side, clasped one another, hand and arm, and with one rough shake gave their word . . . and made peace in Ireland.

*An honorable peace*, thought Essex, the music of moving water beneath him becoming a roar. *He would convince them all—peace before war. Life before death. It was good and right and nothing would sway him from his course.*

⬖⬗⬖⬗⬖

S HE HAD WAITED until noon on the deck of the *Owl*, anchored in the harbor at Louth, gazing inland toward the low hills. She watched for the first tendrils of smoke that might grow into the thick pall of burnt powder that hung over a battlefield, listened for the booming of cannon, the pop of musket fire. But all was calm and quiet. When at last she concluded that there would be no fighting this day, she gave the signal to weigh anchor, and it was passed to all the ships in her fleet bobbing on the water round the *Owl*. Grace knew she should be feeling relief. She'd accomplished the impossible. Essex had backed down. On the long awaited day that the two great armies were to have met and clashed, no blood would spill. No widows would be made. No orphans. Why then did her heart feel so heavy? It was temporary, this peace. She knew that, of course. It was something else that burned her eyes, ached her chest.

'Twas the thought of Robert Devereaux lying on his cot—that fevered face, brown eyes so trusting . . .

*Stop!* she ordered herself. *Pull yourself together.* Essex was a good-hearted man but he was still the enemy. When he was gone there'd be another English murderer to take his place. *Rejoice, damnit!* she ordered herself. *You've stopped the bloodshed, if only for a day.*

The oarsmen picked up speed and the *Owl* led Grace O'Malley's fleet out of Louth Harbor. They were bound for Scotland, a force of Ineen Dubh's Gallowglass reinforcements waiting there.

*Was she any better than Tibbot?* she wondered suddenly—he, one moment loyal to the English, the next Ireland. And here she was, espousing peace not twelve hours ago, now en route to transport an army of mad Scotsmen to the battlefield. *Shite! The war has made hypocrites of us all. Well,* she thought, moving up the aisle between the sweeps and taking her place at the wheel, *there's nothing to be done about it except to put one foot in front of the other and pray that the world goes no crazier than it already has.*

GOOD CHRIST, *what have I done?*

Essex sat paralyzed in the saddle watching the great parade of his army retreating out of Dundalk. All of yesterday's elation had evaporated into the warm September morning, leaving him cringing with fear and desperation. *What had changed?* Yesterday it had all seemed perfectly sensible, allowing O'Neill and his people peace and freedom. Essex had been generous, but it had seemed, at the time, not overly generous. The truce had simply granted to the Irish confederates all territories that they then possessed, free passage in and out of their country, and a guarantee that no new English garrisons were to hereafter be raised in Ireland. O'Neill had promised in return a cessation of fighting for six weeks to six months, with notice given fourteen days in advance if he would wish to begin again, such periods renewable indefinitely. The rebel had been made to swear a verbal oath for keeping the agreement, whereas Essex had merely signed his name. The entire day had been a sweet dream filled with brotherhood and goodwill, and he'd gently scoffed at Blount and Southampton's horrified remonstrances that such a truce was suicidal. That if Essex signed it, his career at Elizabeth's Court would be finished.

This morning the light of a new day had illuminated the truth of their words and the awful depth of his folly. It had not been peace that he had bargained for, but defeat, dishonor. And now he was sick with shame at the travesty he had committed. Even the grateful smiles and passionate salutes of his soldiers as they passed left him cold. Worse were the cheers as he moved through clutches of Irish peasants. Women rushed forward to kiss his hands and feet. Their shouts and frenzied mutterings were unintelligible Gaelic, but he knew they must be crying out God's blessings on him, their English savior.

*How had this happened?* He was Lord Lieutenant of Ireland, England's most revered hero and favorite of the queen. Had he lost his mind to Ireland's faerie thrall as so many before him had? Had he fallen under a witch's spell?

Suddenly the visage of Grace O'Malley rose before him, sunbrowned and wrinkled skin, eyes unnaturally bright. She had come to Essex when he was ill, delirious with fever. Perhaps she'd been real, perhaps a specter. In any event she had shifted his will, softened his heart toward the enemy. The wily old cunt had bewitched him!

The thought stunned him, then infuriated him, and suddenly his skin was crawling, his clothes confining. He wished to rip them off his body and bathe in a clear, purifying stream, bathe away the revulsion, the filthy Irish infection that had sickened him, *ruined* him. His horse sensed his master's discomfiture and began to dance under him.

"Whoa!"

Essex sought to steady him, but the beast could not be comforted. He reared sharply and it was only with the greatest effort that Essex kept the saddle.

The commotion drew Southampton's attention and he rode quickly to Essex's side. He was still scowling, and there was only the merest hint of sympathy in his voice. "Are you all right?" he said.

"Far from it," Essex replied, reining his horse in hard.

Together, in silence, they watched the retreating army.

"I've made a terrible mistake," Essex said, finally.

Southampton's laugh was derisive. "A bit late to realize that."

"What shall I do? What *can* I do?"

"Christopher says we should pick a thousand of your best soldiers, ride to London, gathering reinforcements on the way, and take the throne from the queen . . ."

"What?"

". . . being sure to first remove Robert Cecil, of course."

Essex laughed miserably. "Oh that I could."

"So you've come to your senses."

"I have, and now forced to view my 'accomplishments,' wish that I could lose them again." Essex sighed. "I must see Elizabeth. Explain my actions."

"How? She's forbidden you to return to London without notice."

"She has no authority to keep me out."

*"No authority?"*

"I am Viceroy of Ireland, the highest earl in England."

"And soon to be the most disgraced."

"Not if I can speak privately to the queen. I'll name Loftus and Carew as my deputies here, and leave Tom Ormond in charge of the army. I want you with me."

"And Christopher?"

"Too hotheaded, and even less loved by the queen than you are. I need a strong, steady guard. And no one must know we're coming."

Southampton sighed. "I fear 'tis too late. The damage has been done—so grand an expedition come to so impotent an end."

"I don't need reminding! Be a pillar for me, *please!*"

Southampton looked suddenly contrite. "Forgive me, Robert. You know I'm with you."

Essex was close to weeping. "*I* am the one who needs forgiving. You've been nothing but loyal, and I've dragged you down with me."

"No. You're not finished. This is not your fate, Robert. We'll go to London and make it right again."

Essex's eyes glittered with grateful tears. "Thank you." He grasped Southampton's hand. "She'll listen to me, won't she?"

"Of course she will. The queen never stopped loving you."

These last were words Essex longed to hear. But he realized with a painful tightening of his throat that he could not be sure if they were true. Had Elizabeth sent him to Ireland as England's last and best hope for ending the rebellion, or had she simply tired of him, his childish tantrums, hoping to rid herself of the "wild horse" she had finally realized she could never tame?

There was only one way of finding out—seeing her face-to-face. Reminding her of the love they had shared and his devotion to her that, despite her miserable treatment of him, he still held in his heart. He would ride for London before anyone else could begin whispering in her ear, planting dangerous seeds with words like "cowardice" and "betrayal" and "treason." He would ride tonight, and with God as his helper, Robert Devereaux would save his own life.

◆◆◆

THE CHANNEL CROSSING and a four-day hard ride across the English isle, with scarce time for sleep, had blurred into a never-ending nightmare, as fraught with anxious fretting as chills and saddle sores. The weather had been frightful the whole time, and Essex's mud-splattered band of rough and ready swordsmen had struggled to lift their leader's spirits with fiery talk of rebellion, raucous laughter, and curses at their enemies shouted into the wind.

Essex was nearly certain that his hasty exit from Ireland had preceded any outbound messengers, but when his party reached London at dawn to ferry across the Thames at Lambeth Crossing, the ferryman—a prodigious gossip—announced that Lord Grey had just made the previous crossing. He'd been in a great hurry, on his way to Court, now sitting ten miles south at Nonsuch, and was puffed up with some important news he was bringing the queen. Grey was one of Cecil's men. The thought of his reaching the palace before Essex so alarmed him that on reaching the river's south shore he had refused to wait for his own party's horses to be conveyed across, and commandeered half a dozen mounts waiting there for the return of their owners from London.

"Their owners will be seen to!" Essex cried to the ferryman as he and his men galloped away.

"Let me ride ahead," Christopher Lawrence urged. He was the youngest and strongest of the group. "I'll catch Lord Grey up and reason with him." He raced off but soon returned, angry and disgruntled.

"Well?" Essex demanded.

"One of Grey's men was at Holyhead when we landed. He is indeed riding to Court with news of your return. I begged him to hang back and allow the Earl of Essex to announce his own arrival, but he refused, indeed refused very rudely."

"If we ride hard, might we overtake him?" Essex asked.

"I think not, my lord. Not all of us. But I could catch him up once more, and if he again refuses to stop, I'll simply kill him."

"That will shut him up," cried Peter Westin.

"And I'll have a go at the hunchback when we get to Nonsuch!" added Southampton.

The men laughed, approving the bloodthirsty plans.

"No," Essex insisted, "let us just ride as quickly as we can."

When Essex and his men reached Nonsuch, the fairy-tale palace that was, of all Elizabeth's residences, her favorite, it appeared from the shocked greetings of the guards, ladies, and courtiers he met that Grey's intelligence on the Lord Lieutenant's unexpected return from Ireland had not yet permeated the Court. Perhaps it had not reached the queen either.

Essex bounded up the stairs two at a time, nearly knocking a chambermaid off her feet. It was only then that he realized he stank of sweat—his own and his horse's—and that he was covered hat to boot in caked mud. He grabbed at his long beard and found it studded with bits of leaves and twigs. *I must look a fright*, he thought then, but by now he was mad with desperation to see the queen. He pushed open the doors to the Presence Chamber, not waiting for the startled guards to do it for him. Courtiers were already lining up for the queen's morning appearance. Guards at the next door—the Privy Council Chamber—saw Essex coming, his sword clanking at his side, but the expression on his face brooked no argument, said, *"If you do not open these doors, I shall crash through them closed*, and they flung open the doors quickly.

His heart was pounding in his chest as he faced down the final pair of guards at the door to Elizabeth's bedchamber. The two soldiers had time to exchange a wondering glance before Essex, with unnatural strength, pushed them both aside, moved through the doors, and, turning quickly, locked them from the inside. He could hear the ladies' shrieks and frightened fluttering, smell the perfumes and powders, and the scent that was particularly Elizabeth's. He took only one breath to calm himself before he turned to face her.

There sat the queen, bony arms and shoulders poking out from a thin nightdress. She was not long up from the bed, he could see, neither dressed nor powdered nor coiffed. Indeed, she was wigless, her skull barely covered with wisps of graying hair. She clutched the claw arms of the chair with her long pale fingers. Her eyes were as round as saucers, and without benefit of wig, jewels, and paint, her nose was large and sharp as a beak. The expression on Elizabeth's wrinkled, faintly pockmarked face—except that she clearly had no previous knowledge of Essex's return—was wholly unreadable. But suffering his extraordinary passion, after so arduous a journey, about to finally kneel at her feet and pour out his heart, he was at that moment sure the expression was one of delight. He failed to consider what impression he was making. Not only was he entirely unexpected, mud soaked, sweating, and wild-eyed, but worse, Essex was fully armed and perhaps dangerous. Had his thoughts been clearer he would have known the queen would be wondering why her many guards had not stopped him. Perhaps thinking he had come to take her hostage. Come to murder her. Considering that the palace might even be surrounded by rebels.

Essex, completely oblivious, fell on his knees and, grabbing both of Elizabeth's hands, kissed them with mad fervency. She was still as a stone as he spoke, almost raving. "Oh, Majesty, Majesty! The sight of you warms my chilly heart. I know I am unexpected here. I know you forbade my return without notice, but I *had* to come this way. Too much has happened!" Essex paused, suddenly remembering he still wore his hat. He tore it off but found himself tongue-tied, not knowing how he should begin explaining himself. Just then he felt the queen's gentle hand on the crown of his head, pressing down the damp, matted hair. A relieved sob escaped him, and he felt his eyes fill with tears. He laid his head down like a child on his mother's knee, and allowed himself to weep.

*Southampton had been right*, he thought, his body softening under Elizabeth's touch. *She had never stopped loving him. She would hear him out. She would be cross, of course, but she would understand how and why he had come to grief in Ireland, signed an unsanctioned treaty with Tyrone. He had been right to fly to her—great Gloriana. He would find his way back into her heart. Begin again, more humbly this time.*

"Elizabeth," he whispered, his heart bursting with love. "Elizabeth."

Blinded by his tears and joy, Essex could see neither the queen's lips clamping grimly into a straight line nor her eyes, cold as a snake's, gazing down at her once proud Robin's filthy neck.

1601

# 19

AGITATION WAS A STATE that Grace O'Malley was altogether unused to suffering. But agitated she was, her nerves frayed, her mien snappish. *But who could blame her?* she thought to herself. Here she was, once again sailing into the heart of England, her enemies teeming all round her on both shores of the Thames. She knew if they chanced to find the infamous Irish rebel woman making for their precious queen, they would rip her limb from limb, not bothering to stop and hang her first. For Grace O'Malley was known to the English as a notorious traitor, succubus to the demon Tyrone—who was the wildest Irish of them all.

But it was not thoughts of her own death that were driving her into a frenzy, she realized, watching the bustle along the docks of the river's north shore, rather the chance that the mission bringing her here today might fail, and the only blood spilled would be Robert Devereux's. And if she were honest, she'd admit she was racked with guilt, another emotion as foreign to her as a Turk's turban. Altogether, her worries had her literally trembling in her boots. "Get hold of yourself, woman!" she said aloud, not minding who might hear.

The sinister walls of the Tower of London rose before Grace, a further challenge to her temper. 'Twas here that the object of her clandestine visit was now residing as a prisoner, awaiting "the queen's pleasure" as to his fate. Poor Essex. It had been *her* doing, Grace's interference in the course of his life that had brought him to the shores of doom. No doubt he had added to his troubles by his own words and deeds, but the truce with O'Neill had been the first breach in his ship's fragile hull, and now it was sinking fast in the seething currents of English politics. Sharks were already gathering and not a drop of blood had yet been spilt. And not one man or woman of influence had come forth to speak up for Robert Devereaux, not a single soul. So the job had fallen to her—the very siren who had sung him onto the treacherous shoals, convinced him of an action thought wise only by his enemies. An action that had brought down on him such scorn and humiliation in England that his mind, already beset by devils, had slowly begun to unravel. It had to be so, thought Grace. *He had tried to seize the English throne in his own rebellion.* Had tried and failed.

Now he was behind those hideous gray walls, awaiting word of Elizabeth's signature on his death warrant. What torments must the dear man be suffering? He was a tender soul under the leathery skin of the soldier. A sweet and passionate man who had needed scant urging to resist expediency and do the right thing. He doubtless thought it was wrong now. Probably cursed her advice, believed he'd been taken unfair advantage of at a time when he was weak and ill.

Well, the truth of it was that he *had* been taken advantage of, but Grace had had no choice. She'd done what she had to do to save lives in Ireland. *Did he know how beloved he was to the Irish people?* she wondered. His name was spoken aloud with such reverence, and ballads were sung of the great English general who'd waged peace, not war, on Ireland. Perhaps such knowledge would not ease his mind. Perhaps 'twould only anger him more.

All these ruminations were crowding and jostling in Grace's brain, the very cause of her agitation. The only thought that kept her steady was the chance that she could save him. Speak with the queen, beg mercy from the only person who could stay the traitor's death—as horrible an end as the Devil himself could devise.

Of course the Devil was still stalking Ireland, though she was resisting fiercely. Grace had lately found growing in her breast a never before felt pride in her countrymen and -women. They had once been members of divers clans living their lives in far-flung provinces, their minds set on nothing more consequential than churning butter and cattle raiding from their neighbors. Now gathered in the strong arms of Hugh O'Neill—a great family united—the Irish fought as one, and their victories against England were as numerous as they were startling. Essex's truce had held for three months, but everyone had known it would not last, *could* not last. Lines had been drawn in the sand, and those lines were crossed every day. O'Neill was raiding deep into the Pale and even that English bastion, Dublin, was under constant attack.

But the ravening English meant to have their way with their poor cousins. Elizabeth had given the Irish command to Lord Mountjoy—Grace understood he was Robert's sister's lover—and the man had surprisingly proven a fearsome opponent. Mountjoy held to the belief that his best weapon was the slashing and burning of the countryside. His own troops could be revictualized from without, he reasoned, but the Irish—with neither crops nor cattle to feed them—would surely fall. And he had somehow roused the courage in the once cowardly ranks and they now rarely ran away from a fight. Indeed, the Crown's army could be praised for its discipline and even eagerness to do battle. In one Ulster field the English had routed the rebels from their trenches and killed three hundred, while only twenty of their kind had died.

Then Mountjoy invaded Ulster by sea, landing four thousand troops in the far north at Lough Foyle, and they'd given Red Hugh O'Donnell much more than a bloody nose. Even O'Neill's supremacy in Munster had been crumbling as Mountjoy's army took back one southern city after another.

But the great shining hope, that which kept the rebels fighting with such uncommon courage, was young King Philip's promise of a huge army to be sent to Ireland's shores. The thought of Spanish soldiers—the most fearsome fighting men in the world—fighting alongside the Irish made the rebels strong. "Just hold on!" was the cry. "Help is on the way!" Of course 'twas this promised help that drove Elizabeth insane, the thought of her old enemy joined with the new, against her. The bone-chilling terror that the invasion which, by Fate's intervention, had failed in '88, would now be accomplished through the "back door" of Ireland.

Grace's own life had continued its shattering under the English occupation. Even with the blighted Richard Bingham dead—he'd returned once more, this time to govern Ulster, and been struck down by disease—her losses had yet mounted. Tibbot was all but lost to her. Like a dog with a roasted bone, he'd fought Red Hugh's MacWilliam whenever a fight could be found. Her son had finally, in a stroke he believed brilliant, gone to the Rath of Eassacaoide and with the Burke clans gathered there, crowned a MacWilliam of his own choice. But to everyone's surprise it had not been himself upon whom he bestowed the long coveted title, as Henry VIII had crowned himself the Pope in England. Tibbot named Margaret and Devil's Hook's son, Richard Burke. The two MacWilliams—Red Hugh's and Tibbot's—thereafter battled each other in endless skirmishes that failed, always failed, to change the complexion of Connaught.

Sadly, Tibbot had found much pleasure and sustenance in his English employers and was even now engaged with his huge galleys in patrolling the western Irish coasts, seeking interception of the Spanish troop ships on their journey north to Ulster. Grace refused to relinquish one last hope that Tibbot's deepest loyalties would emerge in such a conflict, and he'd perhaps allow a ship or two to escape them and sail to the aid of O'Neill and the Irish cause. Well, she could hope . . .

She saw very little of Maeve and the grandchildren now. Miles was still hostage to the English, though not in Clifford's house, he dead, at O'Donnell's hand. By now Miles would be a proper English gentleman, Grace thought, trying to quell her bitterness at the thought. She lived at Rockfleet these days, slave to her aching bones. She hardly sailed with her fleet anymore, leaving the captaincies to younger men who, blessedly, remained loyal and still called themselves "Grace O'Malley's men." Her many spies and messengers were her nets flung out into the sea of the world. When she'd draw them in, bits of news, like so many glittering silver fish, could be collected and stored. So even there in her windswept isolation, the war and the world were alive, and she a part of it still.

*Seventy years old.* 'Twas hard to believe. In her mind she was still a young woman. She was lonely, yes, but allowed herself no pity for it. Of late, when the pain could not be eased by an infusion of willow bark and henbane, she would find herself dreaming of Spain. Oh 'twas so warm. The bright blue sky. Andalusian hills sizzling under a white-hot sun. And she'd remember Eric, their lazy float on the Nile barge, the great-tusked elephants playing on a reed-choked shore. She'd smile recalling the fire-works viewed from a gondola in Venice Lagoon, the feel of his sweet lips on her face. But that was another time, another place, she knew. It existed only in her mind, her memories, and would be extinguished entirely when she lay down and took her last breath.

But here she was now, in disguise again—Essex would surely be amused. "Oh, Robert, Robert," she whispered as though, so close by him, he might hear her. But now the gray walls of the Tower receded from view and Grace knew she must take herself in hand. She'd placed herself and her crew in terrible danger for this outrageous scheme, and it would be foolish to allow her weakness and sniveling to threaten Essex's one chance at rescue. Upriver at Hampton Court lay his only possible salvation. Elizabeth sat with her Court at the great palace there. Richard Tyrell—a rare Englishman born with an Irish heart—had been lent to Grace by Hugh O'Neill. He could scarcely spare his captain out of Mun-ster, but he was the only man she trusted who, with his English voice and manners, could find her a way into Elizabeth's presence without endan-gering her crew. Posing as the captain of this English cog—one Grace had conveniently lifted from its crew in the Bay of Biscay—Tyrell had already brought them through the first naval checkpoint at the mouth of the Thames, and again at Tilbury.

She would go and speak to Tyrell now, finalize their plans—the sealed letter to the queen begging for a secret audience and signed "Granuaile," a name unrecognizable to all but Elizabeth. Grace knew it was more likely that the queen would refuse the meeting—even call for her arrest—than grant yet another favor to "the mother of all the rebel-lions" in Ireland. But old as she was, Grace was still a gambler, and the odds that the queen's curiosity would outstrip her rage, though slim, were worth the risk, even of her own life.

Hampton Court—the brick square the size of a small city—was com-ing into view. She must steady herself, she thought, summon all her resources so she could speak with the wit, authority, and eloquence of an old Brehon judge.

Well, she was ready as she'd ever be. It would not be long now.

Essex had done his best for Ireland. Now she'd do her best for him.

# 20

ROBERT DEVEREAUX lay abed staring at the mildewed ceiling and realized it was perhaps the most interesting feature of his windowless cell. Then it occurred to him how sharp were his perceptions and how clearly and cogently he was thinking. Now, waiting for word from the queen as to whether he would live or die, he almost longed for the haze and confusion, violent ravings and religious melancholies that had plagued his mind for the past year, even as recently as yesterday. It seemed suddenly that the pox and his various fevers had lost their grip on his body and soul. He could see everything—the events now past, his mad behavior, follies and tribulations so clearly!

Certainly his downfall had begun with his return to England and his forced audience with the queen. No other moment, unless perhaps his failed uprising, could demonstrate his muddle and insane logic so well. Elizabeth, taken quite by storm, would of course have believed her person, and perhaps her kingdom, to be under siege. He'd come straight from the battlefield, armed, and crashed through her doors a filthy and repulsive character. And by her earlier, specific prohibition of just such an act, she had advertised her fear of it. But how strong Elizabeth had been! She'd never shown that fear for even a moment during the first audience. She'd spoken gently to him and very peacefully. After some minutes she'd suggested that he go to his apartments and freshen himself before they talked further, and when he returned they had conversed pleasantly for nearly two hours.

He'd gone down to dinner then, joining his friends at the long table, filled with joy and relief at his reception. He thanked God that after all his storms abroad, the queen had greeted him with so sweet a calm. He'd ignored the smug looks from across the hall where Robert Cecil dined with Walter Raleigh and Lord Grey, though he had wondered briefly why the Gnome had failed to warn Elizabeth of her Lord Lieutenant's imminent arrival. Now he was able to see Cecil's cold logic. *Allow Essex to show himself a reckless and dangerous villain, a man who would blithely disregard the queen's direct orders. Allow Essex to dig his own grave.*

But he'd not known that then. He'd continued in a rare state of euphoria through dinner, delighted when a page invited him back to Elizabeth's presence for continued talks that afternoon. But when he'd arrived, her demeanor had shifted considerably. Where had been warmth was now chill. Mildness had given way to sharp questioning. That steel trap of a brain was all too apparent. Suddenly the audience was over, but she demanded he be questioned by the Privy Council, who sat waiting in the next room. At that moment Essex felt the first stab of fear, that his admittedly rash actions might spawn disastrous consequences. But just how disastrous he could never have imagined.

The Council's questioning had been hard and direct. Why had Essex deserted his post and, against the queen's direct orders, returned without permission to England? How could he have possibly concluded so lenient a truce with an enemy who had broken so many treaties in the past? How had he allowed his army to deteriorate to such a pathetic condition? What had possessed him to create so many knights? Why had he ridden into Court unannounced in such roughneck company?

Essex had begun explaining with some confidence, but it had soon failed him under the endless battery of scorn and suspicion. They'd interrogated him continuously until eleven o'clock that night, and when they were done announced that he was under house arrest. Lord Egerton had taken him, under heavy guard, to York House, on the Strand, not far from Essex's own home. But the imprisonment was nevertheless complete. He was allowed no visitors, not even his wife, and he was prohibited from leaving his room even for a simple walk in the garden.

During the early days of his captivity, he'd been unable to eat, and rarely slept. When he did sleep his only dreams were nightmares. Then he fell ill—so appallingly ill that a rumor had spread through London that their favorite nobleman, Lord Essex, had died. There were church bells rung, tearful eulogies spoken from dozens of London pulpits, and even public mourning before the rumor was squelched.

His imprisonment dragged on for almost a year before he was brought before a commission in the Star Chamber to receive his official censure. While he was charged only with the minor crimes of contempt and disobedience, it had proven the most humiliating day of his life. Not one man had stood for his entrance, nor removed his cap, nor offered any sign of courtesy. Then Essex, bareheaded, had been made to kneel for hours on a stone floor before the panel as his "offenses" were read out. Several men came forward to give evidence of Lord Essex's ignominious actions. The Attorney General, that pompous buffoon Lord Coke, had called his going into Ireland "proud and ambitious," his time spent there "disobedient and contemptuous," and his leaving "notorious and dangerous."

Francis Bacon, claiming that it pained him horribly, nonetheless laid aside his longtime loyalty to the earl and read from the letter Essex had written when he'd been drunk and furious with Elizabeth. " 'Cannot princes err?' " Bacon quoted to the gasps of the court. " 'Cannot subjects suffer wrong?' " Bacon had then concluded smugly that by Common Law of England a prince 'could do no wrong.' " This had proven the most shocking and damaging evidence of all.

It had taken all of Essex's will to bear the excruciating pain in his knees and the betrayal of his peers who had—some of them—been numbered among his friends. Finally they had let him stand, then lean, then sit, but the proceedings continued. He was allowed to speak, but there had been nothing he could do but apologize. They'd been unmoved by simple apology, however, and groveling had been necessary. Weakened by his fevers and the pain of the day's ordeal, he fell to his knees once again, begging that they believe his sincere confession—his inward sorrow for the great offenses toward Her Majesty. There was no excuse for his crimes of error, negligence, and rashness—not even his youth or illness. He would tear his heart from his breast with his own hands, he'd cried, rather than lose the queen's affection.

Finally it was over and he'd been freed, allowed to return to Essex House. It was depressingly empty, all one hundred and sixty of his household staff dismissed and instructed to find other employment. But worse, he was strictly prohibited from going to Court—a sentence like unto death for a man such as himself. He was nothing without Court life, and he would soon be horrified to learn that Court life went on perfectly well without him.

Meanwhile the queen had appointed Lord Mountjoy to lead the Irish Expedition. His sister's lover—now the father of her two children—had sailed for Ireland with grievous misgivings about his command. At first he'd written to Essex, pained at the treatment his friend had received in the Star Chamber, and offered up an audacious plan. On his, Essex's, and Southampton's behalf, he would write to James of Scotland. Everyone knew that despite Elizabeth's refusal to name her successor, the Scottish king was everyone's choice. The three Englishmen would promise their support for James's claim at the time of Elizabeth's death. Perhaps, they suggested, the king would consider rescuing Essex from captivity. Mountjoy offered four thousand of his troops to join with a Scottish force coming south into England for that purpose. But once Mountjoy had experienced command in Ireland for several months, he'd surprised himself, the Council, and the queen with several victories over the rebels. And soon, with his own career flourishing under the approval of Her Majesty, he'd politely withdrawn his support for Essex's cause.

It had thereafter fallen to Essex himself to begin a correspondence with James. Perhaps—considering his recent censure—it was reckless, but Elizabeth was very old and could not have long to live. Surely it was sensible to align oneself with the next regime. He had, on good intelligence from one of his Court spies, suggested to James that Robert Cecil was conspiring with their old enemy Spain to install the infanta on the throne instead of himself. This news so alarmed the Scottish king that he took the threat quite seriously and wrote back to Essex. It was a short but encouraging note on parchment that Essex folded small, placed in a black velvet pouch, and wore round his neck day and night.

Once more his men were around him—Southampton, Blount, Henry Cuffe, and others. But rather than soothing his spirits, they tried to rouse his rebellious passions. They brought news every day from the City of London that the common people there were behind him. More and more soldiers and swordsmen and knights—veterans of the Irish wars—were riding back and filling London streets and inns. Drunken, brawling roustabouts loudly swearing their allegiance to their great and misunderstood commander, Essex.

He'd had news from another trusted source that the Sheriff of London had a thousand armed men who would come to Essex's aid at a moment's notice. Never, said the sheriff, had the common man so loved their hero. Never had they been more ready to fight. If ever the Earl of Essex chose to lead a coup, all these men would indeed stand behind him.

But Essex had been unready for such an action. He'd been badly weakened by his year-long ordeal at York House, brought low by his illness and the shock of his humiliating treatment in the Star Chamber. He clutched at the shreds of his old existence, as tattered as they were, for it soothed him to remember how lofty and magnificent he had once stood. These were the heights, he was sure, to which he might once again climb if he could but regain Elizabeth's love.

But the vultures were at his door. All his hungry and annoying creditors had come knocking, at first politely, then with growing contempt as they realized the great man had nothing with which to pay them. The clothiers, jewelers, grocers, saddlemakers, gambling partners. Everyone was demanding their due and each day their cries grew louder. Of course there was a solution. It was the *only* solution. In September his grant of the Farm of Sweet Wines was due to be renewed. 'Twas the Farm that had made him a rich man for the previous ten years, the Farm that had allowed for his elevation and the financing of his military and naval expeditions. His enemies and creditors no doubt huddled together in taverns whispering that the queen, in her displeasure with Lord Essex, would never regrant him the Farm, and he would be forever and utterly destroyed. His creditors would curse their losses. His enemies would laugh at his ruin.

He had therefore begun a campaign of letter writing to Elizabeth. Now he could look back and see how transparent his correspondence had been. All the fine words and flattery—talk of kissing her "fair correcting hand," protestations that he remained Her Majesty's humblest, most faithful, most devoted vassal, the whole world being a sepulchre till his exile from her might be ended—all had fallen on deaf ears. No, worse. They had alerted her to his wild desperation. Shown her the softest part of his underbelly, the precise spot where she might sink her blade for the deadliest effect.

But the time came and passed for the regranting of the Farm with only a maddening silence on Elizabeth's part. The delay, fraught with so much trepidation, began to bring on his fevers again. He grew alarmingly thin and his eyes were ringed with black.

Word of Mountjoy's successes against the rebels in Ireland continued filtering back to London along with his urgings of patience to Essex and his refusal to play any part in Robert's plans to restore himself to favor, save by "ordinary means." Essex cursed Mountjoy's cowardice and faithlessness, forgetting that he himself would have done the same had the tables been turned.

He was supping with Southampton and Henry Cuffe at the end of October when news of the Farm of Sweet Wines arrived at Essex House. The queen had decided to withhold it, indeed keep the revenues for her "poor shrinking treasury." It had been a moment without compare in his life. He had vomited, then slumped over the table, his arms outstretched in front of him, a thousand thoughts and images jamming his brain. He was lost, ruined, disgraced. He might be hounded from the country by his creditors or marched off to debtors' prison. All his many titles would prove empty, worthless without money to support his estate.

Elizabeth had done this to him. She was a witch, a vicious demon, an eater of men's souls. She hated him. *Why did she hate him? What had he done that had so offended her?* he'd cried to Southampton and Cuffe, who knelt helplessly beside their friend. He *had* loved her—if not as a woman for many years—as a true subject. His recent letters protesting his devotion had been sincere. But a man had to live, and Elizabeth knew very well that he lived and died by her grace alone. *Why was she punishing him so!*

Everything had turned on that terrible night. His mind, already strained, had snapped like a dry twig. Fits of hysterical laughter would suddenly turn to uncontrollable weeping. His retorts to the royal dismissal were very loud, very public, and very rude. "The queen's mind," he had announced at a crowded Essex House gathering, "is as twisted as her wretched old carcass!"

And suddenly his cohorts' schemes for rebellion seemed less farfetched. Anthony Bacon's much reduced but enthusiastic network of spies were producing evidence every day that Robert Cecil and his other enemies—Raleigh, Howard, Grey—were part of a great conspiracy, with violence against "the Essex Faction" its certain outcome. Indeed, it was these very men—his enemies—who were responsible for his misfortunes. They who had poisoned Elizabeth's mind against him.

Francis Bacon's last letter to him, one in which the lawyer, now amongst Elizabeth's closest confidants, had warned Essex one more time against his dangerous conceits. He said he was sorry that his lordship "should fly with waxen wings, doubting Icarus," but Essex, erratic and beyond reasoning, had been blind to the analogy, perhaps blinded by the same sun—Gloriana—whose furious heat would in the weeks to come melt his own waxen wings and send him crashing down to earth.

"Rebellion." He moaned aloud, the terrible word echoing in the high-ceilinged cell. How could he ever have led a rebellion against the Crown? Elizabeth was the rightful Queen of England, blood and heir of Great Henry. What could have possessed him to presume supremacy over his liege? Even the arch rebel Tyrone had bowed his head in humility to Essex as a vassal of a rightful monarch. No, there was no good excuse for his behavior. Not his illness. Not his fury nor his thirst for revenging the Farm of Sweet Wines being taken from him. He had led, and in turn, had allowed his friends and supporters, each of them a man in desperate financial straights, to lead him into the worst kind of treason. Had he been saner he would have seen clearly that all of them—Blount, Rutland, Cuffe, Southampton—had either fallen out of favor with the queen or lost his family fortune, or both. All were wild with thoughts of a new regime, their favor and titles and fortunes restored. Many of them spoke, in those weeks before the uprising, of placing Essex *himself* on the throne. That had never been his intention! He would simply relieve the tired old woman of her crown and place it on James's head. If Robert Cecil and Raleigh somehow lost their lives in the course of the coup, all the better.

Every day the Essex House courtyard had teemed with larger and more frenzied crowds of swaggering swordsmen, drinking, gambling, even sleeping there. Puritan preachers would come and shout fiery sermons to inflame listeners whilst inside Essex and his coconspirators would plot and plan in earnest. From where could more arms be procured? More rebels? Which captains would lead which companies?

The country was primed for such an uprising, Essex was every day reminded. One of his followers had ridden into Wales to the Essex family seat, going from house to house, large bands of Welsh squires joining up to fight. They had even begun marching toward London, armed and in the service of the good earl's rebellion. Londoners especially were fed up with the doddering old queen. Both Puritans and Catholics, victims of Elizabeth's "strictly conforming" Protestantism, chose to believe that Essex the king would be more lenient toward their religious leanings.

Only the final choice had to be made. *To what destination would the rebels march? The Tower of London, where the huge arsenal, if captured, would brilliantly supplement their own cache of arms? The City, just beyond the Tower, where Essex was sure he could count on the greatest number of supporters pouring from their homes to march behind him? Or the Court—the true goal of their ambitions, where the queen and her blighted councilors sat? Which was best to seize first?*

They had been so lost in their blistering arguments that Essex and his rebels had fallen oblivious to all else, unaware that the boisterous gatherings at the house on the Strand had attracted much attention. Indeed, that their plans for an uprising were public knowledge! The conspirators had become so outrageous and bold that on the first Saturday of February they'd demanded that the actors at the Globe put on a special performance of Will Shakespeare's *Richard the Second*—a play that featured in it the deposing of a rightful king. How stupid they'd been!

The play had proven the final provocation. That same night a messenger from the Privy Council was sent to Essex demanding he present himself to them for explanation. The messenger was turned away. Secretary Herbert was sent then, but he too was dismissed out of hand.

*Rebellion.* Thought of that Sunday dawn and what came after—the dismal "twelve-hour uprising"—twisted Essex's gut. All that could have gone wrong, did. But that was not surprising, he thought, even now shaking his head in disbelief. That doomed venture's captain had been insane at the time, hate maddened and fearful beyond reasoning. How many times can it be whispered in a man's ear that his friend, his love, his *mother* now conspired to kill him, before the sly rumor becomes truth? And that the crooked little Gnome was with her, nay, 'twas *he* whispering in her ear, made it all the worse. Together the Faerie Queen and wizard dreamed Lord Essex into his grave. *"Put an end to the burden he's become,"* he imagined them saying. *"Once beloved, now dangerous. Lose him."*

He had in the end truly believed they conspired to take his life. Their reasons? Clearly, Robert Cecil's heart pumped jealous blood. He was the runt of the Court, his devious mind his only weapon, for his manly worth was next to nothing. He coveted Essex's strength and beauty, secretly longed to be a soldier. He *hated* Essex.

The queen was simply a faithless woman. The Farm of Sweet Wines, flowing warm and red, had been his lifeblood. By withholding it she had struck a blow she believed was mortal. She had never loved him. Could never have loved and cut so deeply. Of this he'd been sure.

Enough reason, he'd believed, to strike before they could murder him. Lord Knollys, his uncle, and three others from the Council—of all those who sat at the Privy table, his four best friends—had braved the rabble at Essex House that Sunday morning and strode into the yard. They'd come to plead good sense, to offer a hearing for the earls' complaints. What they found was the earls of Essex and Southampton stirring a boiling cauldron of sedition. The crowd, inflamed, would have killed the delegation, torn them to pieces, but Essex had lured the party inside the house, up the stairs and into his windowed study overlooking the Thames. Once inside he'd made them prisoners, setting a guard of musketeers at the door.

By now Essex had ridden too far down the road of rebellion to return. Cries from the courtyard below—three hundred men ready to fight—loudly called for the march to begin. But march *where*? The Tower and the City beyond? The Court?

The mob made their choice. "To the Court! To the Court!" they shouted, knowing Elizabeth sat there quite unguarded but for a score of castle guards and as many courtiers ready to raise their swords in her defense.

*But hold a moment. More men and arms awaited in the City and the Tower. Would not his coup succeed better with three times more rebels and guns? Then again, how long would Elizabeth remain so poorly guarded?*

Here was his moment. That one which, in his choosing, would raise him or defeat him. And in that moment, when the scales of Fate would have tipped as easily one way as the other, a great, blanketing fog enveloped his brain, thick warm mists that blunted his senses. All round him men were shouting—his friends, the rabble, the Privy Councilors pounding on his study door to be released. As in a dream their cries began melting into a great white roar. He felt drunk, wobbly, and his men, moving with slowed motion, seemed blurred round the edges. He'd begun to panic, as though the reins of a whole team of horses had slipped from his fingers and down between a dozen thundering hooves! They were all waiting for him to speak, to command them, unaware of his desperation. Someone shouted for silence. They would hear their leader's orders. *He must speak now!*

"To the City!" Essex cried. "To the City!"

"Not the Court and the queen?" someone cried back.

But logic was absent in that courtyard. All Essex could see in his wretched state was the prospect of greater numbers. More rebels. More firepower. *A great mass of men descending on the palace might mask his deficiencies. It will work,* he thought frantically. *Get the men. Get the guns.* Then *march to Court.*

The three hundred had followed him out through the gates of Essex House, followed him through the streets to the City. The march had for a time cleared his head, but once they'd reached the City's heart, he crying, "To the queen! To the queen! A plot is laid against my life!" and no one had risen to his cries—*not one man*—he'd grown dizzy again, almost faint. They'd passed the house of the noblemen who'd been with him since the start—Bedford, Sussex, Cromwell, Mounteagle—expecting them to pour out with their troops—but they did not come. *Where were they?* But of course, he'd told himself, only half believing the voice in his head, they would all be waiting at the sheriff's house. "Reinforcements at the Sheriff of London's house!" he cried to his now grumbling army. "March on!"

But the sheriff—faithless coward—had sneaked away moments before their coming. The house was empty, the thousand troops nowhere to be found. Chaos ensued round him then. Men shouting. His captains hissing in his ear, "What now, Essex? Let us march on the queen *now!*"

But he was mind-boggled. Quite beside himself. The sheriff's house seemed a fine refuge from the madness. Quiet. He went inside, called his captains in after him. They'd leaned close, waiting for his command. Finally he spoke.

"Let us dine," he said.

Indeed, Robert Devereaux, Earl of Essex, in the critical hour of his bid for the English throne, called for a light repast to be served at the sheriff's table. Even now, lying on his cot in the dark Tower cell, Essex could feel himself blush with shame. For *three hours* the rebellion's leaders had eaten all the stores in their absent host's pantry. Essex had even changed his sweat-soaked shirt for one of the sheriff's clean ones. It had all seemed perfectly logical then. As they emptied the sheriff's finest casks, no one had contradicted their leader nor expressed his misgivings.

But at Whitehall the Council had begun to act. They'd called for faithful Londoners to surround the queen in her palace. They'd sent a strong Privy Guard to block the rebels' way home to the house on the Strand.

Then, the fog in Essex's mind lifting slightly, he perceived the mounting dangers. He'd risen, full of wine and cold meat, and strode outside still wearing his napkin tucked in the neck of his shirt. Southampton had hardly time to remove it for him when Essex cried to his troops—those brave souls foolish enough to still remain—cried in his defense that he acted only for the queen's good, fought this day against "evil atheists in Spain's employ."

With Essex leading they'd tramped through the streets for hours more, denied passage this way and that by the queen's guards. Fired some volleys. Were fired upon. Christopher Blount had been shot in the cheek. Essex fainted twice and was brought back to the world sweating and shrieking.

They were fugitives now, what few stragglers were left loyal to the madman. Some pitying Londoners helped them escape to a dock on the

Thames and they'd rowed, pathetic and bedraggled, back to Essex House.

The four Privy councilors, moments before the rebels' arrival, had been set free, and the men Essex had hoped would be hostages to be bargained for by the queen—his last hope—had quietly slipped away.

He knew then that the game was up. He'd frantically burned his papers and diaries, hoping to save his friends from incrimination. He'd thrown the velvet pouch with King James's letter into the fire and watched even that hope turn to ash.

Soon royal troops were sniping at his windows. Essex House surrounded, he was a cornered animal. Only Southampton stayed by his side. The guard was calling for surrender. Southampton and he had climbed to the roof and, with no hope left, his friend shouted down at the soldiers their terms for such a surrender. But Essex, sick and crazed, was shouting too—he, his mad protestations of loyalty to the queen. "I moved only to root out the atheists and caterpillars!" he'd cried. "Atheists and caterpillars!"

The rest had been a blur—their arrest, incarceration at Lambeth Castle till the tide had turned, and transportation to the Tower of London in the wee hours of Monday morning. Essex had fainted once again when they'd rowed through the Traitor's Gate. Fainted dead away. His twelve-hour rebellion had been the most shameful performance a nobleman could ever have dreamt of performing.

But there was worse to come. Once imprisoned he had fallen into a religious fervor so extreme, so terrifying—with God and his angels sitting in a heavenly Star Chamber condemning him—that he'd been reduced to a trembling milk pudding. When his trusted chaplain, Reverend Ashton, had arrived and insisted the prisoner purge his soul of all his most grievous sins, Essex—threatened with eternal damnation, and racked with shame—had vomited forth a terrible confession of every plot of which he was guilty, and every person with whom he'd conspired. Before he knew what had happened, he'd given up all the friends whom he'd previously protected. Instantly the good reverend turned on Essex and with a straight face, announced that the contents of his private confession would have to be shared with the Council. He'd been tricked! All his friends and conspirators had been quickly arrested.

His and Southampton's trial for high treason and the verdict of guilty had been a foregone conclusion. Witness after witness had come forward to denounce him, the unkindest of all Francis Bacon. He had offered a scathing indictment of the Lord Lieutenant's actions, then turned and said directly to Essex, "I know but one friend and one enemy that my lord has. That one friend is the queen. And that one enemy is yourself."

Essex protested that he'd meant the queen no harm, that he'd only wished to stand in her presence to demand assurance of the lawful succession of James, and not the Spanish infanta put forward by Robert Cecil, and for a moment those present seemed to consider the truth of such an argument. But in a moment of drama so high that even Essex gasped with awe, the Gnome—previously absent from court—had stepped out from behind a curtain where he'd been hiding, to defend himself of the blasphemous charges, and quickly demolished Essex's case against him.

But Southampton, his friend and close conspirator, had proved the gravest disappointment of all. He had admitted to the early scheming done with Essex, to capture the Court and the Tower, but then swore he knew nothing of his friend's plans on the morning of the Sunday uprising. *Why, he had never drawn his sword the whole day!* 'Twas only by virtue of his love for Essex that he had so plotted in the first place. Southampton's groveling and lies had been nothing short of obscene, and even in his woeful state, Essex felt the betrayal as a sharp blade between the ribs.

In the end they had both been found guilty of their crimes and condemned to a traitor's death—the hanging, disembowelment, drawing, quartering, and beheading that was fair punishment for such treason. But as they were noblemen, they asked the queen's mercy that they might simply suffer beheading, and that was granted forthwith.

Now here he lay, eyes fixed on the ceiling of an English traitor's last abode. In his youth he had oftentimes dreamed of rising so high as he had, but never had he envisioned his falling this low. Passion had ever guided his words and deeds, and now he could see that in good part 'twas passion to blame for his bad end. *Yet*, he pondered, *was a life lived without it worth living at all?*

But there was something else that needed admitting. He had underestimated the queen, canny old woman with a steel-trap brain. All her hesitation, indecision, dissembling was born not of womanly weakness or senile confusion. It was her way of unbalancing her enemies. Allow them to think she was muddled, unhinged. They'd lower their guard, believe they held the advantage. Then she would spring.

"I deserve death," Essex whispered aloud. There was no excuse for his treason. None but madness. He believed in the monarchy and he loved his queen despite her unkind cuts to him. Many of them had been deserved. He'd been reckless and vainglorious his whole life, and had even dared to place himself above her. A person so rash and selfish was bound to receive his comeuppance.

With a clear head that he now prayed he'd enjoy till the end of his life, Essex saw that beyond the follies of his shallow youth, his recent crimes must have been born of a sick, fevered mind. So many times he'd found himself incapable of anything more than muddle and confusion. The pox, despite his best efforts to contain it, had eaten away at his core, had sapped not only his bodily strength but his character as well. He was half of all that he had once been, had become the kind of man he'd always despised. And suddenly he knew 'twas not worth living in such a state. He should welcome death, welcome it! 'Twould spare him further agonies. If only he could hold this clarity, use the strength left to him by God's mercy so he'd not cower in the straw before his peers, a gibbering madman. He would stand tall and walk to his execution a proud nobleman. Speak his last words with calm and dignity.

All of a sudden a vision filled his head, as visions so often do, wholly unbidden and from out of nowhere. He was astride his horse, riding away from the battle at Louth, the battle that never was. His grateful soldiers and the Irish he'd spared from slaughter all saluted him. But the misery of that moment—his terror that he'd done wrong by making peace and not war—had lifted now. 'Twas instead replaced by that same celebration in the faces of those whose lives had been saved that day. All the blood—English and Irish alike—still rushing through living hearts and veins had not spilled like some unholy wine on God's apron.

He had cursed Grace O'Malley that next day, cursed her for her guidance to be merciful, to love her people and his own, and to spare them death. Now, his chest expanding with a light and easy heart, Essex found himself blessing the old woman, *his good mother,* blessing and forgiving her everything. She had led him away from the vengeful Old Testament God and onto the path of a most merciful Jesus. Without Grace he would be going to his Maker with the deaths of two thousand more souls on his conscience.

He breathed easier now and wondered at the lightness in his chest. Then he smiled, for he saw clearly that Robert Devereaux, Earl of Essex and loyal subject to his queen, had seen fit to forgive himself of his many sins, and would walk to his well-deserved death a redeemed and happy man.

# 21

RICHARD TYRELL had done his job well, and now Grace stood before Elizabeth's bedroom door. The halls of Court as she'd been led through were quiet and mournful, the gentlemen subdued, the ladies in their muted gowns no longer fluttering like flocks of painted birds. One of the guards moved to open the queen's door for "the old gentleman" and Grace entered. This was Whitehall, not Greenwich as the last time, and a different yet equally resplendent chamber dazzled her eyes. Again, two chairs had been placed by the hearth, but the blazing fire had failed to take the chill from the midwinter morning.

Elizabeth, hardly more than a gorgeously attired stick, stood with her back to Grace, staring intently at the heavy velvet curtains near her stately bed, her arm held rigidly at her side, a rusty sword gripped in her hand. She'd not heard Grace enter and was muttering angry oaths under her breath as she moved slowly down the long arras. Suddenly the skinny arm retracted and with a low grunt the queen thrust her blade through the curtain. Again and again she stabbed at the imaginary foe behind it till she was satisfied. When she turned to see Grace watching the bizarre performance, Elizabeth showed not the slightest touch of embarrassment, just murmured, "Never too careful." Then she gestured with an annoyed sweep of her hand for Grace to sit.

"I'll stand, thank you."

Elizabeth glared at her visitor's insolence, taking scornful note of

Grace's disguise. "You're a fool to have come here," she began. "Have you no fear of a traitor's death?"

"I'm no traitor, Bess. To be one implies I'm a subject of yours. I've never been one nor will I ever be."

Elizabeth came and stood before Grace, eyeing her fiercely. "Still, you gave your word to me and broke it."

"Aye, after you broke yours to me. But that's history, and I've not come to talk about an old quarrel between a couple of bad-tempered old bats." She saw Elizabeth bristle, but went on. "A friend of mine is sitting in the Tower of London waiting for execution."

"He deserves his fate."

"I thought we'd talk a wee while about that."

"And why would I deign to spend my time discussing such things with the likes of you?"

"Because my interference caused his present condition. 'Tis my duty to speak up for him."

Elizabeth's eyes narrowed suspiciously. "What conceivable part could you have played in his treachery?"

Grace moved to warm her hands by the fire. She knew the queen was watching her, taking stock of the slight stoop that her advanced age had foisted upon her. "Essex was fevered and ill the night before he met with O'Neill at Louth," she began. "He was delirious and weak as a whipped child. I went to him—he trusted me, you see—and spoke to him very comforting like, reasoned with him as to my way of thinking. He had no defenses, see. Was altogether vincible. I was gentle and kind and nursed him like a mother. He opened to me like a flower to the sun, and I thought to myself, 'Is there no one who is tender to this sweet man?' In any event I showed him a way to save the lives of his men, whom he'd come to love, and by the time I left, peace and mercy loomed large in his mind. They were still fixed there when at dawn he rode down to the River Lagan and treated with Hugh O'Neill."

Elizabeth's face twitched with fury to hear such consequential intelligence never known to her before this moment. But she pulled herself taller and assumed a proud expression. "I forgave him that," she fairly spat.

"So I'm claimin' too much credit for myself, am I? You weren't fit to be tied at the truce with O'Neill?"

"Of course I was! Essex was my choice to lead the largest army England had ever assembled. He was sent to end that ridiculous rebellion once and forever. And he disgraced himself. Disgraced *me*. Made a mockery of my war!"

"Bess," said Grace quietly, "he was outnumbered two to one. Had he fought O'Neill, thousands of your English soldiers would have died."

"They would have died *honorably*." Elizabeth turned as though her legs would no longer hold her, and tottered to one of the chairs by the fire. But she refused to sit, just used the back to keep herself upright. "As I said," she continued haughtily, "I forgave Essex that cowardly truce." She was quite insistent, though her face seemed to crumble.

Grace turned to Elizabeth and silently demanded that she say what was on her mind.

"He tried to seize my throne." The queen's outrage seemed forced.

" 'Twas not what I saw in your eyes just then. What other 'crime' did Robert Devereaux commit?"

Elizabeth refused to answer, her lips set in a stubborn line.

"Go on, tell me."

Elizabeth's eyes grew unfocused as she recalled the scene. "When he returned from Ireland, he broke into my room like a madman. I was not long out of bed, still in my shift. Unkempt. Unadorned. No wig on my head."

"So you looked a proper hag, did you?"

Elizabeth looked as though she might strike Grace, but she took a breath and continued. "He'd been my lover not so many years before, and now he saw me . . . like that. I have never known such humiliation. But"—she fell silent, as if she were putting the thoughts together for the first time—"my hideousness mattered not at all to him. I was a sexless creature. Might have been his grandmother. The crone goddess. He did not see a woman at all." Elizabeth looked haunted. "And later . . . later he said . . . that my mind was as crooked as my carcass. *Carcass!* That was the word he used to describe this body." Her lips trembled. "Dead. Shriveled. Decaying."

"For Jesus' sake, woman, you're sixty-eight years old!" Grace shook her head in disgust. "I've no pity for you or your stupid vanity. So this is the reason you're going to take the poor man's life?"

"Essex will die because he's a traitor!" Elizabeth shouted. "I am Elizabeth, lawful Queen of England." Her voice grew shrill. "I *made* the Earl of Essex, made him the great man he was. Showered him with riches. Titles. The finest commands. And how does he repay me? By rising up with three hundred rebels to usurp me! Ungrateful prick." She looked away with tears welling in her eyes.

" 'Twas wrong of him," said Grace. "Of course it was. But he's a man driven by his disease. You must know that. He falls into fits of delirium, loses control of his senses."

Elizabeth refused to meet Grace's eyes. Guilt was plain on her face.

"What is it you're not sayin'?" Grace demanded. But Elizabeth was silent. "Did you provoke him?"

"Perhaps."

"What did you do, Bess?"

"I refused to let him back to Court, or to see me."

"What else?"

Elizabeth looked down at her once slender fingers, now bloated like sausages, and twisted the last ring left on her fingers. "I withheld his only means of regaining his wealth—income from the taxation of sweet wines."

"I see." Grace fell silent, considering the impact of Elizabeth's confession. "So . . . you took the wealthiest, most popular man in England—your country's greatest hero—and in one stroke turned a proud nobleman into a pauper. And you wonder why he led an uprising against you."

Grace finally lowered herself into one of the chairs. She sighed, as one does who knows her mission is hopeless, but nevertheless she said, "Don't kill the poor man. Exile him. Send him home with me. The Irish love him." Grace gazed into the fire. "*I* love him."

The admission only inflamed Elizabeth. "He'll die in England. He'll die under the ax. I want him punished publicly. People must learn that if you rise up against your lawful prince you cannot expect to die with your head on your shoulders. Robert Devereaux is not some naughty little boy, nor even my 'wild horse.' He is a traitor and a danger to the world."

"He'll die because you hate him," Grace insisted.

"Yes, I do hate him, for he forced my hand! I have no choice but to end the life of someone I . . . I . . ." Elizabeth was shaking with rage.

"Today I may be a pitiful hag who's had to have the ring of state sawed off my bloated finger, but I have given my whole life into the service of England, and I have had a great and glorious reign! A reign that will be remembered long after we are all dead. *My* navy beat back the Spanish Armada. *My* ships sailed to the farthest shores of the New World. In my time Marlowe and Shakespeare wrote words the likes of which no men have ever in their lives heard spoken before. England has flowered under my hand! Elizabeth the Queen is revered by all, feared by all. I ruled like the best of the Tudor princes—brilliantly and absolutely. Now comes the blackest of traitors, a man who, by his unconscionable acts, offended every man of noble blood, and common blood too. He placed in jeopardy the very monarchy of England. If I were to treat such bold-faced treachery with mercy, would it not be said I had done so out of womanly love for a man? Would I not be thought weak? There is no doubt I would. I will not"—Elizabeth spluttered with outrage—"I will not be remembered as a weak prince!"

Grace regarded Elizabeth with a cool gaze, sensing the queen had more to say.

"I had long believed I was my mother's daughter—child of the staunchest, cleverest woman to wear the Tudor crown. But now I know better. 'Tis my *father's* blood rushing through my veins." Elizabeth gazed back into the past. "She called him 'the Beast.'"

"Aye. A man who murders those he loves is indeed a beast," Grace agreed. "So, you're content to be 'the Beast's Daughter,' are you, Bess? Prepared to do to your lover what your father did to your poor mother?" Elizabeth flinched visibly, but Grace went on. "Is it that same beast who suffers no qualms about murdering a *whole country?*"

"Quelling the rebellion in Ireland is in no way the same."

"I'd have to agree. It's far more heinous."

"You talk nonsense. 'Tis a monarch's prerogative to use a firm hand on unruly subjects."

"You're so sure Ireland belongs to you."

"You're being absurd."

"Your father and his wretched Cromwell conceived their rights of ownership, their 'Surrender and Regrant,' and you blindly followed suit. You thought you could simply claim the country as your own and rule it as you did England. You had no idea then, nor do you yet realize, that Ireland will not be ruled by the likes of you."

Elizabeth sneered at such a notion.

"How do you dare—a foreigner—send your governors into Ireland, your soldiers, and tell them to pillage and burn and rape and murder, and then expect the people to call you their beloved queen?"

"Tyrone would place the King of Spain on the Irish throne."

"At least the Spaniards have warm blood in their veins and not ice water like you do. You take such pride in your subjects loving you, but you've got it wrong. You've become a vindictive old bitch who's about to behead your people's favorite hero. Robert Devereaux is a poet, a passionate gentleman, the only great-hearted man in your miserable Court." Grace pushed herself to standing. "I didn't really think by comin' here I could change your mind, but Jesus knows I had to at least try."

She started for the door but turned back and went to face the queen eye to eye. "You don't own Ireland, Bess. You can have your occupation and win your battles. Turn the minds of our chieftains, establish all the plantations in the world, and you still won't own us. We are what we are in Ireland—what we've been for a thousand years. Don't you know you can force a person's hand, but you cannot force his soul? I can see in your eyes that you think I'm a daft old woman who knows nothing of the 'pre-rogatives of princes.' And I know England will come again and again to Ireland and do its worst to us. Spill our blood. Corrupt our sacred lands. And we may be bent by the might of your swords and your guns. You won't think twice of the carnage you inflict, of the wounds left festering, the ancient memories that still slumber in the glens and the hills and the western isles. But we will not be broken, Bess. And sooner or later the dreamer will awaken and *there will be hell to pay!*" Grace leaned close and whispered fiercely in Elizabeth's ear. "You . . . mark . . . my . . . words."

She pulled herself tall, and with the rage of angels straightening her spine, Grace O'Malley turned her back on the Queen of England and strode from the room. As she left she leveled the guards with a withering stare and before they could stop her she gave the huge doors a defiant shove, swinging them together with a great, bone-rattling crash.

# 22

THE COG HAD escaped unmolested from the Thames, sailing out into the Channel at Dover, then headed south for a piece, and finally west. Grace stood at the rail as the vessel coasted the waters off the Isle of Wight where the great Armada had first encountered the English fleet in '88. A gull screamed overhead and suddenly Grace imagined herself a seabird on that fateful day, watching from high above the magnificent crescent flotilla—five miles long from tip to curved tip. There would come the English vessels, so low and sleek and agile next to Philip's huge, ponderous, high-castled ships, swooping in one by one for their fierce broadside volleys of the all-but-stationary Armada, and peeling away too quickly to be damaged themselves. Though the loss of life on both sides had been small, that one sea battle had turned the world on its head. Days later, off the coast of Calais at Gravelines, the swift English fleet, assisted by the breath of God himself, had scattered Philip's mighty Armada and lifted England to a place of strength and power she would later wield as a cudgel to batter Ireland. Everything had changed in these waters south of England, thought Grace, just thirteen years ago.

Thirteen years ago the true rebellion had hardly begun. Today Robert Devereaux, poor bastard, was as good as a dead man, and what was left of her own family was lost to her as well. All at once the weight of her years settled hard on her shoulders and a deep sigh escaped her. The sound was pitiful, she had to admit, tired and defeated.

Well, she *was* tired. She'd been fighting one battle or another her whole blessed life—for freedom from a girl's life, the brainless Donal O'Flaherty, and the thick-headed Richard Burke. There'd been Turkish pirates, the hell of prison, and the cold evil of Richard Bingham. She'd fought to save her sons and fought against her sons, and nursed the whole of the Irish Rebellion.

'Twas no wonder she was tired down to the marrow of her bones. Perhaps what she needed was a rest. No one would begrudge her that. She could sail south to Spain, to Majorca, a land untouched by the cares of the world and the wars. The sun would warm her joints and she'd drink wine with every meal, sleep in a whitewashed cottage near the shore and let the waves lull her to sleep in the balmy, fragrant evenings. Aye, a rest would be just the thing. She'd earned it, after all.

"Grace, to starboard!" A hand in the nest was calling and pointing with all the excitement of a lad on his first voyage. She followed the line of his arm and beheld a great striped whale at the top of his joyful leap, then felt her heart—like the gray beast—leap nearly out of her chest with a similar joy. She shouted as he crashed down again, water exploding round his bulk, then watched him dive beneath the waves and disappear.

*Does that whale rest?* she wondered then. Or does he swim and feed, make his families, guard his precious waters till he breathes his last and sinks to the ocean floor? Does he ever weary of flight, of sailing up to the sun for that brief moment of clear light and the breath of salt air? Is that not all the respite he needs to keep him moving, moving in the depths through the long years?

A fresh breeze caught in the sails and now the cog was racing into the west wind. Salt spray wet her face and Grace's long silver hair whipped out behind her. She inhaled a slow easy breath and her old body began to sing the song of the waves and the whales and the weather, and she knew then she had no wish to rest. Not just yet. There was time enough to rest when she closed her eyes to die. For now she'd just sail on.

There was far too much left to do in the world.

game, rebelling one day, swearing his loyalty to the Crown the next. Providing Grace O'Malley as a hostage to Drury gave him some breathing space, but after the defeat and massacre of the Pope's nine hundred troops at Fort del Oro, Gerald's fortunes declined. He was proclaimed a traitor and went on the run with his wife, ELEANOR, COUNTESS OF DESMOND, and the Jesuit FATHER SANDERS. Once the richest landholder in Ireland, Gerald was now reduced to sleeping in caves and on flea-ridden straw, and stealing food to stay alive. But his flight through the Munster countryside was not a simple rebellion against the English. He was also a ruthless murderer of his own countrymen and -women— any he believed to be English sympathizers. During what came to be known as the "second Desmond rebellion," famine, plague, and skirmishes took a staggering number of lives. While in hiding, Father Sanders died of dysentery, and with him any remaining notion that the Desmond rebellion was of a religious nature. Lady Eleanor, reduced to rags, tried to beg leniency from the Crown for her husband, but by now everyone—Irish and English alike—wanted Gerald dead. In 1583, near Tralee, the earl, then a crippled old man, was discovered cowering in a corner of a rude hut by his own countrymen. He was dragged outside and, with no fanfare, executed. His head was sent to Elizabeth who, says legend, spent a whole morning gazing thoughtfully at it—all that remained of the Irish earl whom she had prayed so fervently and long to be faithful to her—before consigning it to a pike on London Bridge.

The career of RICHARD BINGHAM—despised by Irish and English alike—was checkered at best. "The Flail of Connaught," while successfully subduing the province, was twice recalled by the Crown, placed on trial for his mismanagement, and even imprisoned at the Fleet. But the queen, either eternally hopeful or made desperate by the dearth of men willing to serve in Ireland, sent him back one more time after the battle of the Yellow Ford to govern Ulster. He died of the "Irish disease" several months later.

LORD MOUNTJOY (CHARLES BLOUNT), despite his "bookishness," his dearth of experience with large bodies of troops, his poor health, and his hypochondria (he'd wear three pairs of stockings and three waistcoats in winter), became Elizabeth's great hero in Ireland. Within two years he had taken back cities, towns, and provinces from the rebels, and won a decisive battle at Kinsale that ended O'Neill's supremacy forever. Mountjoy marched into Ulster, and at Tullahogue—in a highly symbolic gesture— broke apart the ancient throne where The O'Neills, for hundreds of years, had been created. In 1605 Essex's sister, Penelope, left her husband, Lord Rich, to marry her longtime lover, and the father of her children— Lord Mountjoy. He died suddenly of pneumonia the next year.

On his march to meet with the long-promised Spanish reinforcements at Kinsale, RED HUGH O'DONNELL, the still young and arrogant rebel leader, unaccountably laid waste to the Munster countryside, burning and plundering a land inhabited only by his countrymen and fellow Catholics. After the defeat at Kinsale, Hugh O'Neill sent O'Donnell to Spain to beg a new army from Philip III but was unsuccessful in regaining the king's support. He never returned to Ireland, dying within the year, some say poisoned by an English agent.

Not surprisingly, the truce HUGH O'NEILL, EARL OF TYRONE, negotiated with the Earl of Essex held only long enough for the English, under Lord Mountjoy, to gain the strength they needed to pursue Elizabeth's objectives in Ireland. While O'Neill fought valiantly with his rebels to hold on to his gains, and continued to pray for the queen's death, which he believed would alleviate his and Ireland's problems, he began to lose ground. Though he was well aware that Spain's motives for helping Ireland had more to do with unseating the "Heretic Queen" than assisting Ireland in its bid for sovereignty, O'Neill persisted in suing for their aid. In 1601 it finally arrived—a four-thousand-man invasion force bound for the eastern port of Cork. Due to high wind and surf, the Spaniards landed a few miles south at the town of Kinsale, which Mountjoy quickly surrounded and besieged.

O'Neill and his army marched south from Ulster to meet the enemy while his ally Red Hugh O'Donnell marched in from the west. But once the Irish armies were in place, O'Neill and O'Donnell began arguing as to which of them should begin the attack. This delay proved fatal as the agreed upon hour of rendezvous with the Spaniards passed, and the window of opportunity for an Irish victory slammed shut. The Battle of Kinsale lasted three months, and in the end O'Neill was unable to defeat Mountjoy's siege lines. Finally the Spanish troops surrendered to the English and sailed home. Thousands of Irish rebels died in the fighting or, taken prisoner, were hung.

Hugh O'Neill was forced to submit to the English conquerors in a series of humiliating ceremonies, first on his knees to Mountjoy, then to the Lord Deputy and the Irish Privy Council. It was only after he'd put his submission in writing, renouncing his title of "The O'Neill and his allegiance to Spain, as well as protesting loyalty to the Crown, was he told that Elizabeth had died six days before. Mountjoy had tricked him. It was said that O'Neill wept openly and copiously for both his personal defeat and the ruination of the "Irish cause."

The rebel leader retreated to Ulster, and by the good graces of the new king of England, was pardoned once again, and his lands restored to him. He took up residency in his luxurious home, but spurred by a series of dangerous events and the realization that no hope was left for a free Ireland, O'Neill and a handful of Irish overlords and their families sailed from their homeland in 1607. The tragic "Flight of the Earls" ended the most tumultuous century in Ireland's history.

Tyrone, after wandering with his family through France, the Netherlands, and Germany, finally took up residence in Italy, subsidized by the Pope. Every night, deep in his cups, he would brag that come Hell or high water he would die in Ireland. In 1616 the great rebel O'Neill passed away, a frustrated exile, in Venice.

TIBBOT NE LONG BURKE, hard-pressed to choose sides in the Irish rebellion, finally made his decision at the battle of Kinsale. On his own volition he mustered a force of three hundred men and marched south. Under Lord Mountjoy, Tibbot led his men so single-mindedly and courageously that he was lauded by the Crown. Having proven his loyalty beyond any doubt, he returned home to a life of leisure with Maeve and his six children. Miles—for many years a hostage—was released by his English captors and went to live with his family. Like Conyers Clifford before him, Mountjoy befriended Tibbot, took sides with him against a new and unpopular governor of Connaught, and made sure his salary was regularly paid. Tibbot was knighted in the early days of James's reign and elected to the Irish Parliament as a representative of Mayo in 1613. In 1626, by virtue of his valor and faithful service to King Charles I, he was created Viscount Burke of Mayo. He died, age sixty-two, murdered by an O'Connor brother-in-law while the two were on their way to church.

ROBERT DEVEREAUX, EARL OF ESSEX, was taken to the place of execution at Tower Green on February 25, 1601. Standing before the crowd in a scarlet waistcoat, Essex made his last speech—a rather long one—with eloquence and dignity, claiming his sins "more numerous than the hairs on his head." He was still speaking when the executioner struck his first blow. It took two more to sever Devereaux's head. Despite his undisputed treason, Essex was remembered kindly by the English people. Nearly two years after his death, Londoners were still singing a ballad lauding their "great and celebrated noble warrior," called "Essex's Last Good Night." In Ireland he was likewise revered, considered by many rebel chiefs as an ally, and by the common people as the only one of the queen's commanders who had come over to their side.

ELIZABETH I, the queen who many believed waited in vain for Essex to beg a reprieve from his death sentence, suffered agonies after his passing. Despite the victory at Kinsale and achieving her goal of defeating the Irish rebels, she never regained her seemingly inexhaustible zest for life. As the end neared, the queen, despite her obvious weakness, refused to be put to bed and instead stood upright in one place for fourteen hours, sucking on her fingers. She died on March 24, 1603, never having named her successor. She had reigned for more than four decades, and with her died the great Tudor dynasty of a hundred years.

The last days of GRACE O'MALLEY's life are a mystery. There are records of her ships—if not personally captained by her—still patrolling the western Irish coast in mid 1601. She seems to have lived at Rockfleet

Castle near the end, and probably died at the age of seventy-three, in 1603—the same year as Elizabeth's death. Some of her stark, brooding castles and ruined abbeys on the shores and islands of Clew Bay today stand testament to her life, though the whereabouts of her earthly remains are still in dispute. While her ending is shrouded in the mists of time, there's nothing to suggest that Grace O'Malley would have gone gently into that good night. One can imagine that, like Elizabeth, she'd have stood her ground till the Reaper paid his final, insistent call. But thanks to Ireland's balladeers and bards and a handful of Englishmen awed by so remarkable a woman, her last voyage was not into oblivion, but the pages of history and the rich fabric of Irish legend.

# AUTHOR'S NOTE

During the writing of this book, I found myself questioning why the sixteenth-century history of the Irish-English conflict—"the Mother of All the Irish Rebellions"—has been utterly ignored or forgotten. This episode was by far the largest of Elizabeth's wars and the last significant effort of her reign. It was also the most costly in English lives lost, both common and noble. By some estimates, the rebellion resulted in half the population of Ireland dying through battle, famine, and disease, and the countryside—through the burning of forestland—was changed forever. Yet almost no one studies it, writes of it, or discusses it, even as the impact of that revolt continues to make headlines across the world more than four hundred years later.

Likewise, few people outside Ireland have ever heard of Grace O'Malley, surely one of the most outrageous and extraordinary personalities of her century—at least as fascinating a character as her contemporary and sparring partner Elizabeth I. Of course history is written by the victors, and England was, by all accounts, the winner of the Irish Rebellion of the sixteenth century. But the mystery only deepens when we learn that the *only* contemporary knowledge we have of Grace's exploits—other than through Irish tradition and legend—is recorded not in Ireland's histories, but by numerous references and documentation in *England's Calendar of State Papers*, as well as numerous official dispatches sent by English captains and governors such as Lords Sidney, Maltby, and Bingham.

As hard as it is to believe, Grace O'Malley's name never once appears in the most important Irish history of the day, *The Annals of the Four*

*Masters*. Even in the two best modern books on the Irish Rebellion—Cyril Fall's *Elizabeth's Irish Wars* and Richard Berleth's *The Twilight Lords*—there is virtually no mention made of her. Tibbot Burke receives only slightly better treatment. Why is this? Anne Chambers, author of my two "bibles" on the lives of Grace O'Malley (*Granuaile: The Life and Times of Grace O'Malley*) and Tibbot Burke (*Chieftain to Knight*)—the only existing biographies of mother and son—suggests that as for the early historians, they might have had so little regard for women in general that Grace's exclusion would be expected. As for the modern historians, it is troubling that in their otherwise highly detailed books, the authors should ignore such a major player in the history of the period.

It was the mysteries of this period that excited me, spurring me to write this story, to find logical ways to fill those gaping "holes in history." The first and most baffling question is why Elizabeth—already a cranky old woman, deeply troubled by the loss of men and money in Ireland—would allow a known rebel and infamous pirate to march into Greenwich Castle and demand an audience, then grant Grace O'Malley all the rather substantial requests that she made of the queen.

While most students of Elizabethan history know that the Earl of Essex was the queen's last favorite (and perhaps her lover), and was executed for treason, most don't realize that the catalyst for his downfall was his involvement in the Irish Rebellion. I wondered why Elizabeth used and abused him as she did before, during, and after sending him to Ireland. His powers as a commander had already diminished, and she knew she'd be sending a very sickly man into an environment that had already claimed the lives of dozens of her ablest noblemen. She appeared positively bent on Essex's destruction. While she showed leniency to the Earl of Southampton, a man she loathed, for his part in Essex's attempted coup, she denied the same to Essex himself, someone she had once deeply loved.

And finally, what possessed Essex to meet in private with O'Neill at Louth and sign a truce with him when he must have known it was political suicide?

The facts we do have about Grace O'Malley tell a fascinating story. She did have a public meeting with Elizabeth in 1593 at Greenwich Castle, causing a stir with her nose blowing and comments on English hygiene. Previous to this the queen had sent, and Grace had answered, an "interrogatory" of eighteen questions (these are reproduced fully in Chambers's *Granuaile*). We can therefore surmise that Elizabeth was not only aware of Grace's activities, but was particularly interested in her life. History does not record any further meetings between the two women, but to my mind the public meeting might not have fully satisfied Elizabeth's curiosity, and does not explain *why* the queen granted Grace her requests. Thus, the second meeting in Elizabeth's rooms, while clearly fiction, does not seem an impossibility.

There is no documented proof of Essex's making face-to-face contact with Grace and Tibbot. But we do know that Essex, only months before the public meeting of Grace and Elizabeth at Greenwich, had been named Privy Councilor, was constantly at Court, and was enthusiastically involved in the affairs of state. When he learned that the notorious Irish pirate Grace O'Malley was meeting with Elizabeth, there is little doubt he would have insisted on being present. That Robert Devereaux was Grace's deliverer to Elizabeth's rooms, and that he overheard the conversations, is a literary device. But the truth is that Essex did inhabit his stepfather, the Earl of Leicester's old rooms at Greenwich Castle, and there was a secret passageway between them and Elizabeth's bedchamber—one that the young queen and her handsome horsemaster had used in years past to keep their trysts private.

While history does not record any meetings between Essex and Grace in Ireland, we do know that Essex and Tibbot (encouraged by Conyers Clifford) were friendly, and that Essex, knowing Tibbot's worth in the war effort, made every attempt to keep him happy. Essex, once in Ireland, issued orders "to assure him [Tibbot] of my good affection, of my resolution to take to the protection of him and his, to heap upon him as many favors and benefits I can in any way." We also know that Grace and Tibbot, while on opposite sides of the conflict, were still in contact, and it's not inconceivable that while Essex was on his Munster campaign and visit to Limerick, he and Tibbot (and Grace) might have met there.

A central conflict of the story is Tibbot's dilemma. It is representative of the same one faced by virtually every Irish chieftain of the time—and I was fortunate that his struggle was relatively well documented. We know that while Richard Bingham was brutalizing Connaught, he kidnapped the teenage Tibbot and held him hostage. Tibbot was imprisoned by Red Hugh O'Donnell as they battled for control of the MacWilliam title, and he was alternately lured by the English and Red Hugh to take sides in the conflict. Tibbot's firstborn son, Miles, was given as hostage to the English, and at the battle in the Curlew Mountains his friend Conyers Clifford was killed, his severed head presented to Tibbot in a crock. Finally we know that Tibbot Burke chose loyalty to the English over the Irish, and subsequently became an important player in English-Irish politics.

As for Essex's decidedly foolhardy decision to meet and make peace with O'Neill at Louth, few historians have delved deeply into his motivations for such an act. Every one of Essex's biographers record that his health was bad both before and after the meeting, that he'd suffered bouts of fever, dysentery, and was battered—body and mind—by tertiary syphilis. Essex was surely as confused and vulnerable as he had been in the Azores, but with England's very future at stake, the pressure on him had never been so severe. Cyril Falls admits, "It is not easy for the modern mind to measure the enormity of the Lord Lieutenant's folly in conversing with Tyrone without witnesses." Yet all Falls says about the meeting itself is that after saluting the English earl with reverence, Tyrone and Essex "for half an hour talked alone." Lytton Strachey, in *Essex, a Tragic History*, and G. B. Harrison—to whom I am eternally grateful for including in his *Robert Devereaux, Earl of Essex* complete transcripts of all Essex's and Elizabeth's important correspondences to each other during this time—are equally as brief and nonanalytical. Robert Lacey in his brilliant modern biography, *Robert, Earl of Essex*, puts it down to Essex forgetting the political implications of his act, and even forgetting the reality of his outnumbered and diseased army, instead being "seduced" by Tyrone's "simple chivalry . . . the gentle lilt of Tyrone's voice and the moderate logic of the Irish terms." Not much to go on.

So if I've taken liberties in this partnership of imagination and history, it was in the name of clarity and good storytelling—a desire to connect as many dots as possible and make whole one of the most ignored but fascinating sagas of the sixteenth century. It is important to understand this period of Irish rebellion, not least because of the light it throws on events in Ireland ever since. England persists in occupying and claiming dominion over Irish soil, and the Catholics of Ulster continue to resist. It may seem that the policies of Henry VIII and his daughter Elizabeth are quaint echoes of the past, but the spirit of courage and defiance that animated rebels such as Hugh O'Neill and Grace O'Malley still lives in countless Irish hearts today.

# ACKNOWLEDGMENTS

First and foremost, author Anne Chambers must be thanked, for without her singular biographies of Grace O'Malley and her son Tibbot Burke (*Granuaile* and *Chieftain to Knight*), this book could never have been written. Her painstaking research, fashioned into eminently readable history, brought these two otherwise undocumented Irish rebels alive.

During a research trip for an altogether different project, my Irishborn friend and writing partner, Billie Morton, led us straight—if unknowingly—into Grace O'Malley country. There we were besieged by countless western Irishmen and -women who insisted on regaling us with tales of their most famous and beloved heroine. I thank Billie for the serendipitous discovery of my subject, and also for her subsequent support in every phase of the writing of this book.

Lynn Anderson, friend and fellow writer, made enormous contributions in the early days, while this story was first taking form.

As always I am truly appreciative of my indefatigable agents, Kim Witherspoon and Marie Massie, and their wonderful associates who provide unfailingly wise counsel and lift the burden of business from my shoulders.

I am deeply grateful to my editor, Carolyn Marino—the book's champion and cheerleader from the start—whose hard work and impeccable editorial judgment kept me on the straight and narrow. Her tireless assistant, Jennifer Civiletto, perfectly completed the editorial team.

But my most heartfelt thanks are reserved for my husband, Max Thomas, who lives the writing of all my books with me. His honesty, enthusiasm, and support make everything possible.